BLOOD RED WINTER

AN ADDICTIVE MYSTERY THRILLER WITH A SHOCKING TWIST

J.A. CONRAD

ECLIPSE BOOKS LLC

Blood Red Winter
A Trent & Aria Mystery Thriller Book 1

Other books in this series:

Her Unspoken Blood
Blood in Truth
Flesh and Blood
Blood Is Thicker

ISBN: 978-1-7373756-0-9

Eclipse Books LLC

For my grandmother, Helen C. Brown,
who loved mysteries and winter.

TABLE OF CONTENTS

1

JANUARY 5TH

Alone, the footfalls of my work boots scatter the rocks on the rural road's shoulder in Georgetown, Texas, less than half a mile from Tim's unused property. After turning onto County Road 140, it only takes about five minutes until I can see the land. The rusty, barbed-wire fence lies largely disintegrated, and many of the cedar posts are gone, leaving the wire to trail the ground.

I push my feet into the dead grass near the fence and begin stepping carefully through the tangly underbrush. About a hundred feet of overgrown tract spans the distance between me and the house. To my back, the narrow, two-lane country road disappears around a turn, and on the other side, a barren cattle field stretches to the horizon. A bleak, colorless sky fills the space above the empty range, and a sharp wind penetrates my jacket.

There may have been a driveway at one time, but I can't see evidence of one. Dry, untended grass, wiry shrubs, and mesquite trees cover the entire yard. I've never seen a car parked outside. As I continue toward the house, I catch the scent of something vile. The smell irks me like the vague odor of a mostly rotted animal carcass that plumes up from a roadside ditch in a little wisp of misery. It makes me think of a dead deer.

As I approach the house, the faint smell grows slightly less faint. It never becomes strong. Whiffs of rotten air that tell of bloated sewage get into my nostrils and make my stomach writhe. I get another feeling in my stomach, too, an uneasiness, and I glance behind me at the lonely road and vacant cattle pasture. No one there. I keep going toward the house. Whatever I'm picking up has discernible components. Beneath the blanket stench of an open septic tank are human elements. Urine.

I trudge along to the remnants of a rocky path that leads to the covered porch. Its canopy bows in the middle with a defeated sag. Here and there, flakes of peeling white paint fleck the mostly gray, wooden two-story like old skin. The roof appears in the worst shape, but I can't find any holes from where I stand. The shutters might have been lavender once, but those remaining have turned emesis-basin pink.

On the ground near the porch, ashy patches of cactus skeletons lean into the planks, but the wood itself seems stable enough. I test it with my foot, then step up and try the door. I can't open it more than a few inches even though the scuffed Schlage deadbolt isn't locked. The door bangs into something behind it. I put my shoulder against the door, pressing my calloused hands against the old timber, and push, but the dresser or whatever blocks me on the other side isn't going anywhere. I decide to go around back. I can slip in through one of the broken windows, but I don't want to. Not yet.

Maybe a bum has been using this forsaken place as his

regular campground. He isn't here now, nor is his evidence of drained whiskey bottles, but that doesn't mean someone hasn't been here or can't come back. My cynical side knows this idea seems out of place, though, even after Tim's concern about squatters. We don't get much of that in Georgetown, especially not out here. I scan the ground. I search the space near and around the house and head back into the yard. Nothing loiters here but dry grass, scattered rocks, cactus spines, and twigs. Where the hell is that smell coming from?

For the next half hour, I comb the property from one side to the other. If a dead doe or some other unfortunate creature is decomposing beneath the vegetation, I sure can't find it. I'm glad I looked, anyway. The weak winter light is fading rapidly, and I pull out my phone and check the hour. Almost 4:00 p.m. I'll check the house one more time and then call Tim back.

The sky starts to drizzle feebly. I return to the back of the structure and look for another door, finding one after a turn in the wall. It attaches to a small protrusion, like a mudroom. The odor swells strongest here—but still weakly. This door is locked. I breathe in that offensive odor again and wrinkle my nose, snorting to try and rid myself of it. I grab the brass doorknob once more and wiggle it before I press my shoulder against the door. I lean in and shove a little harder. As the wood starts to creak and groan, I let off. No need to split the door in half, especially since I'll be the one fixing it. I back away and go over to the nearest window. The glass is missing between three of the frames.

I squint and try to focus inside the dim space. I can't see much, but as I stick my nose in and take a good whiff, I nearly lose the contents of my stomach. Yeah, that's it —repulsive.

I stagger backward, cursing and trying not to puke. After gathering my shirt collar around my mouth and nose to stifle my coughing, I go back to the window to have a look inside. I pull my phone from my back pocket and turn on the flashlight feature.

My heart pounds so hard it shakes my whole body. I don't know what I expect to find. Before I shine the light inside the window, I try listening for anything. My hands are trembling, and my breath comes out in short puffs of mist in the cold air. There's no reason to think the abominable odor couldn't be from some critter that wandered in and died. A stray dog can make a stench like that, and rats and other vermin may be scuttling around the carcass, which I might be able to hear. I must know I'm lying to myself.

The room inside the window lies silent, still, and stagnant in that impenetrable darkness which my searching gaze can't pierce. The gloomy weather isn't helping. Any noises I do manage to catch are outside noises—the dried leaves in a live oak, the wind between bony cactus shrubs, the grass and gravel under my feet when I shift my weight.

With my adrenaline up, my eyes and ears strain furtively for whatever comes next. I try to rest my hand near the window to angle the light from my phone. A dried-up, cobweb-covered insect falls onto my fingers. I jerk my hand, but the dead bug sticks to my thumb, and I can't fling it off. I smear it onto my jeans and swear under my breath. Enough —I need to quit screwing off and look in that room.

Standing like a soldier, I aim the light into the room, into the black hole beyond the broken window. I watch the phone's glow illuminate the space on the other side of the wall. The beam floods the small room with light, revealing the most horrifying thing I have ever seen.

A shabby, lifeless body lies on the floor in a haphazard position, discarded there like a worn-out rag doll. I can't tell the age or gender, and I can't see the emaciated body's face. Its tattered, soiled clothing is covered in dirt or dried blood. I can't say which. Higher up, against the wall, a vision assaults my senses with painful clarity. A woman dangles from black iron chains, her arms high above her head, the rest of her body drooping in a back-breaking, spiritless position. Filthy, matted hair obscures most of her face, and her white dress is drenched in blood. Dark red blood.

I jump so hard from the shock that my hand slams into the window frame with an audible crack. The single remaining piece of glass bursts out of its frame and shatters on the rocks outside. I almost drop my cell phone inside the room and clutch it with white knuckles. As I stagger backward, my shirt collar slips away from my nose, and the nauseating smell of death violates my senses.

Dead bodies. I've been smelling dead bodies.

With my every muscle shaking, I step forward again and will my hand to steer the beam of light. I force myself to look at the rest of the room. Old, dusty furniture, boxes, a broken lamp, an ancient television set, and other junk fill the corners and lean against the walls. Nothing else is notable except for the filthy floor, which was probably used as a latrine by the captive victims.

I turn away from the house and start to run. I dart through the thick grass and get all the way to the street before stopping to turn off the light from my cell phone. With a clammy hand, I tuck it back in my pocket. I turn around to see the house, which remains silent and crumbling in the diffused winter light. Just the way it appeared when I arrived.

My breathing comes hard and fast. My lungs gratefully devour the fresh air. My eyes relish in the soft, overcast light from the sun. I have no thoughts at all. Nothing. My heart pounds, and the back of my hand throbs from where it smacked the window. My palms and face are wet, and my stomach contracts in little spasms. I glance along the road and at the field, but I remain alone. Detaching from reality in the throes of shock, I jog a little way down the road, just beyond Tim's property. With my eyes on the murder house, I call 911. A few minutes later, I call Tim.

The sense of unreality becomes like my guardian, an unshakable cloak that never leaves me as the authorities begin to arrive at the crime scene. The Williamson County Sheriff's vehicles appear first, four cars, including constables, followed by two ambulances and a firetruck. In a dancing sea of red and blue lights, the vehicles cram themselves into the narrow street in front of the house, and the ordinarily peaceful countryside explodes into life with the activities of the emergency team.

I watch Tim's tan Ford pickup slide behind one of the sheriff's cars on the side of the road. He opens the door, and the truck rocks as he heaves himself out of the driver's seat. His face floats stark white over his red flannel coat. Despite the cold, Tim takes a handkerchief from his back pocket and drags it across his forehead. I wait to see if he notices me standing by the barbed-wire fence, but one of the officers meets him a few feet away from his truck.

On the other side of the street, another officer opens the door of his cruiser, and I raise my hand. I'm the one who made the call, and he'll want to know that. He strides my way across the paving, giving me a visual once-over.

"Trent Lemend?" he asks.

"Yeah."

"Deputy Sheriff Reyes." He extends his large hand, and I shake it. "Thanks for calling us."

"No problem."

I reach for my ID in my back pocket. I try to keep from trembling as I pull my license from my wallet and hand it to him. He gives me no reason to be nervous. I haven't done anything wrong.

While Reyes notes down my info on his clipboard, I put my hands in my pockets and study him. He must be about six foot two because he stands about five inches taller than me. The lines on his face tell me that he's also about twenty years older, which puts him around fifty.

"What's the best number for you?" Reyes asks.

I answer with my mobile number. I also give him my work number for my second job outside the ranch and Tim's cell. Reyes even asks for an emergency contact, so I give him a number for my best friend, Kyle. I have no family in the Georgetown area—my parents moved to Dallas several years ago.

I glance across the flashing police lights to locate Tim's red flannel again. As he continues speaking with the same deputy, he removes his woolen hat and tucks it in his coat pocket. He runs both hands through his brown hair. The officer presses his mouth into a hard, thin line while Tim tells him whatever it is that he's telling him. I can't hear a word of their conversation.

Reyes begins to run through a series of questions, and I do my best with his queries, but other than finding the bodies and the manner in which I discovered them, I don't know much.

"Do you know the property owner?"

"Yes, that's Tim Corbin. He's my boss. I work on his ranch," I say.

Reyes slightly raises his left eyebrow. "How long have you been working for him?"

"Only a couple of months."

"And he asked you to have a look at the property this afternoon?" Reyes asks.

I nod. "He called during my walk. He wanted me to make sure there were no squatters since he doesn't get out here too often."

I bring my brief conversation with Tim to mind. The wind whistled through the space between my cell phone and my ear. Tim mentioned that he'd been neglecting the place and should probably add its maintenance to my list of regular duties. I never asked how he acquired this piece of land, whether by inheritance or as real estate purchased to be converted in the future.

"This is the first time you've been here, Mr. Lemend?"

"The first time I've walked onto the property, yes. But I take walks on this road all the time," I say.

Reyes nods, not taking his eyes off the clipboard. "How many times would you say you've been by here in the last month?"

My stomach cartwheels, my heart rabbiting at a dizzying pace. I swallow, clenching my fists inside my jacket pockets. "Walked by? I don't know. I take a walk almost every day. Probably at least twenty times."

A few passersby slow to a crawl, gawking and craning their necks as they drive by. Several people stop their cars and continue to watch from a short distance away as the authorities break down the house's front door. One of the firemen heaves an ax at whatever piece of furniture is blocking their entry, and with a few more swings and a heavy kick from his boot, the door bursts open. The firemen, officers, and members of the EMT crew file inside. Several officers remain outside by the porch with their guns drawn. Deputy Reyes and I are like actors in a detective movie while the commotion rolls along behind us in the background.

I tell Reyes everything I know without omission, but I don't know much. He not only wants the details of how I found the victims but inquires about the nature of my work for Tim, my private life, and how long I've lived in Georgetown.

"And you said you live near the property?" Reyes asks.

"I live near here, but not on this street. That's my current address on my driver's license."

Reyes nods, scribbling furiously on his paper. "And in all the times you walked by, you never heard anything? Never saw anyone?" He looks up from the clipboard and waits.

I shake my head. "No, never. I've never even seen a car here."

"Okay," he says, his gaze flicking back and forth between my face and his notes. "If you don't mind, please go through the details of what happened today one more time. I just want to make sure I have everything."

What happened today. Like hell if I know what happened, all I know is what I found. I guess he wants to make sure I won't change any part of my story.

"Sure," I say, and I run through my brief inspection of the house and yard again.

Reyes nods and looks at what he's written. "Okay. And how again did you find the bodies?"

I just answered that, but I tell him again. "I looked into the back window. I tried to open the back door, but it was locked. I shined the flashlight from my cell phone into that room."

I sniff, trying to repress the memory of the full force of that awful smell. Even now, I can occasionally detect traces of it, especially since they opened the house.

"I should let you know that I accidentally broke part of that back window. When I saw that—that—those bodies—I jumped, and I knocked a piece of glass loose." As I hold up my right hand, I see a nasty bruise and a one-inch streak of dried blood across the top. In my shaken state, I didn't notice.

Reyes's gaze lingers on my cut. "Okay."

Casting around for Tim, I can barely see him behind two officers. I make out the back of his red flannel coat and the handcuffs around his wrists. The deputy with the hard-set face guides him into the backseat of the sheriff's car. Do they really have grounds to arrest him like that? I blink, plunging further into the surreality that envelopes me in the fading light.

"Deputy Reyes," I say, making an effort to tug my gaze away from Tim's misfortune. "I'd really not like my name released to the media if that's all right."

At least I have the presence of mind to think that far ahead. I don't know if the sheriff's office will even do that, or maybe not this early on, but seeing them take Tim into custody makes me want to protect myself. Who knows what can happen? I must have left fingerprints on the front and back doors, so I'm glad I mentioned that I tried entering both ways. There will be no trace of me on the inside of the house. Reyes doesn't seem to consider me a suspect so far, but I wonder if that's typical. Maybe I said all the right words when he asked.

"That's fine. You can choose to remain anonymous. We'll contact you if we have any further questions," he says. The creases in his forehead deepen. "Probably a good idea to take extra precaution for a while. Make sure to lock your doors. Be aware of your surroundings. Be safe."

"I will."

I expect him to tell me to stand on the opposite side of the street with the small gathering of onlookers, but he doesn't. He nods and turns to join his colleagues near the car where they're holding Tim. After a moment, Reyes slips into his black-and-white cruiser, probably to relay my info to the station. I continue to linger on the grassy area near the old, barbed-wire fence, just beyond the road's shoulder.

Since most of the emergency crew is working inside the house and there's no longer anything happening near the door, I take a deep breath and glance around. The spectators are hanging on with dauntless interest, whispering and talking among themselves. About eight people have gathered—quite a crowd for this area. A middle-aged woman in a black jacket squints at me, looking me up and down. She questions my presence, but I'm not giving her much to see. I'm your run-of-the-mill, average white guy. With brown hair, brown eyes, and a medium build, there's nothing particularly notable about me, good or bad. In this situation, that's probably a good thing.

A little boy next to the woman follows her gaze. He points and asks, "Who's that?" She gives him some answer which I can't hear. Does she tell him I'm a suspicious man the sheriff's deputy was questioning? I know it would be best to leave. There's no further reason to stay here, but something keeps me. I guess I'm no better than the spectators.

The woman's eyes bore tiny, red laser holes into my skull, so I turn to watch the house again. Time passes slowly. Some of the officers are still outside, talking near the cruiser Tim sits cuffed in, but most of the others are inside or somewhere else I can't see.

The temperature drops rapidly as the daylight slips away. Now that it's going on six o'clock, the overcast sky smudges out the sunset with chalky, gray clouds. Finally, the back of a blue EMT jacket emerges from the doorway as they steer the first body out on a stretcher. I can't help noticing it isn't draped in a white sheet.

My stomach twists, and I shiver. The fleeting light gives me just enough visibility. Just enough—I can see. And what I see is a young woman's pale, dirt-streaked face, half-covered by an oxygen mask. Deathly still with closed eyes, her head rolls limply to the side as her carriers jostle her, but she's alive. An odd sensation smolders in the middle of my chest, and I stand here unblinking, watching until they load the woman into the ambulance.

I can't believe it. My mind can't process what just happened or what it means. I stare as the ambulance roars to life with its siren blaring and red lights blinding me. The driver steers it away from the derelict house and pulls past the small gathering, accelerating north along narrow County Road 140 toward the interstate.

The minutes tick by, and I wonder at the whereabouts of the other body. The woman on the stretcher must have been the one chained to the wall. She wore the white dress covered in dark red blood—the most blood I've ever seen.

The other body, which lay on the squalid, wooden floor, looked too wasted away to be living. That being the case, there are forensic procedures to deal with, and it will be hours before they remove the corpse from the crime scene. Agitation still unsettles me, keying me up on adrenaline, and my heart races, but it's over. I've seen everything I need to see.

The sheriff's cruiser holding Tim hasn't budged. I empathize and don't understand why they're arresting him, but there isn't much I can do. Naked beneath the many eyes on me, I turn to head home. I walk away from the flashing lights, the yellow police tape, and the bewildered onlookers. As I trudge along in darkness, I can't keep the question from my mind, even though I tell myself it doesn't really concern me, not ultimately.

Will she live?

2

THAT MORNING

At about 10:30 a.m., I pry open bleary eyes to a pounding headache. I've overslept. It's Sunday, so at least I can justify it a little. I get out of bed and make my rounds to the toilet, the shower, and the sink. When I run my hand over my jawline, the texture reminds me of pumice stone. Five o'clock shadow is one thing, but this is just bad. And as bad as I look, I feel worse.

My bloodshot eyes stare back at me in the mirror as I dab the shaving cream on my face. Still barely able to stay awake, I sloppily drag the razor across my chin and watch as three little dots of blood spring up. I try to concentrate on the motions and ignore the splitting pain across my forehead. My temples are throbbing. Nausea rises from my stomach, but I swallow it back down and finish the task in front of me. I don't give a crap. I don't feel like eating anyway.

I stumble into my tiny living room to find it littered with beer bottles, empty pizza boxes, soda cans, dirty napkins, and various other debris. The place reeks like a garbage can. Straggling odors of alcohol, musty cheese, and old socks make me wrinkle my nose. For the next hour, I pick up my trash and put things away. I throw three full bags into the black plastic bin outside and wipe down the kitchen. I push the vacuum over the carpet and bleach the bathtub and the commode.

By the time I finish taking care of my mess, it's well after noon, and the sun still hasn't shown itself. Outside my window, a muted, gray sky hovers over the barren mesquite trees. I look past the barbed-wire fence, but the sheep haven't appeared in the neighboring pasture yet. They make their rounds to the field behind me several times a day. Since I've never lived near livestock before, I always keep an interested eye out for them. It hasn't been that long since I moved here from Austin.

My stomach continues bubbling, threatening to burst into my esophagus at any moment. I know a beer would help, but I don't want to drink today. It would be better to take a walk and clear my head. I grab my coat and pick up my cell phone, stuffing it in my jacket pocket without checking my messages.

Outside, even the diffused light manages to make me squint. It's chilly out but not cold. The temperature hangs in the lower fifties. A dog barking catches my attention, and I follow the sound to an Australian Shepherd sniffing the grass on my side of the fence. He has large white and gray patches with smaller black and brown spots mixed in. He must be one of Tim's pack. Aussies are good with sheep.

"Hey, boy," I call.

I crouch down and extend my hand. The dog lopes toward me with his ears pricked and tail wagging. When he reaches me, I rub his head and the long, coarse fur on his neck. Beneath the topcoat, my fingers find the softer hairs beneath, a trait common to this breed. Yeah, I know this one —Bandit, I believe. Tim told me the dogs like to chase rabbits and just about anything that moves, so I'll bet that's how he wound up here.

"Let's go home," I say.

I open the passenger's side door of my black Chevy Silverado pickup and Bandit bounds inside. He sits there panting and looking around with his mouth stretched into a canine grin. I've always wanted a dog. Maybe not an Australian Shepherd, but a Jack Russell might be nice.

The engine hums a little louder than usual from the cool air. I start down the long, gravel driveway and pull onto County Road 152 before stopping at the next residence over. Seconds after I park, Tim appears at the door of the farmhouse. He must have heard me drive up. When I reach to let Bandit out, he bursts out of the truck and beelines for Tim.

"It's bobcats," Tim calls from the porch. "Saw one this morning."

So that's what Bandit was chasing. I've never seen a bobcat myself, but I hear of sightings now and then.

"Thanks, Trent," Tim says.

I wave and head back to the road, then turning right to make my way toward Blue Hole Park in town. Technically, I don't live in Georgetown. I live in Williamson County between the cities of Georgetown and Weir. Residents call it Georgetown anyway, and that's how my mail is routed because of the nearest post office location. Back in November of last year, I started renting a small, weathered house out here, which barely consists of four rooms. That was only two months ago.

I love Austin, but I needed to get away, and I managed to change my line of work while I was at it. I went from processing insurance claims at a chiropractic office to working part-time on a ranch and part-time at the gas station near the 130 toll road and Interstate 35. So, I have two jobs, but they're different enough from one another that it's not so bad. The work keeps my mind off things.

I speed down the winding road at nearly fifty miles per hour. This took some getting used to until I realized there's nothing to hit when you live in the middle of nowhere. As I round the bend next to a pasture of Black Angus cattle, my pocket rings. I hastily pull off to the shoulder as far as I can, and with a little swearing, answer the call from my friend Kyle. Unfortunately, my truck isn't new enough for Bluetooth capability.

"Hey," I say. My voice creaks.

"Hey, Trent! You up?" His enthusiasm hurts my head.

"Yeah," I say. "It's one thirty in the afternoon. What's up?"

Kyle laughs. "I'm heading over there. The game is on. You wanna go?"

He doesn't have to explain what "over there" means. We have a favorite bar in Austin named after an infamous Latin American goat sucker that we like to haunt on the weekends. Their drinks are radioactive, and the atmosphere is perfect for forgetting things.

"No, man, I've got a hangover."

That elicits more laughter from him. "Oh, come on. You've gotta get out. You don't need to drink anything."

"I am getting out. I'm in my truck, and I'm driving. I'm going to take a walk. Anyway, I don't want to drive into Austin today. I'm just going to hang around town, go to bed early," I tell him.

"Okay, that's cool. I can come up there. What about that

place we went to last month? What was it, CJ's? I can meet you. Then you won't have to go far."

I sigh and stare numbly out the windshield. One of the Black Angus grazes beside the wooden fence post nearest me. "All right. But I'm not gonna drink anything, and I can't stay long."

"No problem. I'll see you there in about thirty minutes."

"Cool," I say.

OUR PITCHER of beer is nearly empty. I drain the dregs of my mug, and without intending to, almost slam it onto the table. The game drones on overhead, but I barely notice it. I chew the last, salty French fry from our basket and stare at the glossy finish of the wooden tabletop. Condensation drips down the pitcher, making a little puddle of water. The air near the bar is thick with lager and peanuts.

"So?" Kyle asks.

Realizing he spoke to me, I look up. Well, at least my headache is gone. "So what?"

"Have you heard from her?" He raises his eyebrows and adjusts his UT cap over his short, blond hair. Kyle's success as a real estate agent means he doesn't have to work Sundays and usually doesn't.

"Who?" I glare at him, even though I know damn well who he meant.

"Elizabeth."

"Tss. No. Don't care," I say. It's been a while since we broached this subject.

"Oh, come on. You don't know what happened. What do you think? What's your take on it?"

I pour the remaining contents of the pitcher into my mug. So much for not drinking today. "I think people shouldn't lie. That's what I think." My hand loses its grip on the glass handle, and I nearly drop it.

"Well, yeah, but you don't know that she lied," Kyle says.

I don't reply. Honestly, I'm just not in the mood for this topic today. What difference does it make whether she lied or not, really? She's gone, so that's the outcome. If she told the truth, she probably wouldn't be.

"Don't care," I repeat. After setting down my drink, I rest my hand on the table and stare at the creases on my knuckles.

Kyle shakes his head. "Geez."

At twenty-seven, my best friend Kyle is three years younger than me. I know that thirty isn't old, but I can't help feeling jaded and sick of my life already. I don't share his innate sense of optimism.

"Have you thought any more about getting a dog?" Kyle asks.

Elizabeth has an allergy, or at least that's what she told me. Of course, I don't have to worry about that now.

"Not really. It's a big responsibility, and there's no one to let it out while I work," I say.

"I could help you put a fence up, and you could get a doghouse. And we can build a shelter around it so the rain can't get in. Then you could leave him out sometimes when the weather's nice," he says.

I wipe my hands on a napkin. "Thanks, but I can't afford it right now."

He nods slowly and stares at the amber liquid in his

glass. "I get it. No happiness for you." He grins to let me know he's making a joke.

I try to chuckle but only accomplish a grunt.

"You ready to go?" Kyle asks. He pulls a brown leather wallet from his pocket.

"Yeah, I'm ready."

I push back in my chair, and its feet squeal gratingly across the floor. When I stand up, a wave of dizziness hits me. Besides the beer and part of a basket of fries, I've eaten nothing since yesterday.

We pay and walk out to the parking lot. The temperature has dropped slightly, and the wind picks up. It whines weakly through the trees and between cars, tossing up dry, brown leaves at my feet. I inhale the scent of brewing rain. It mingles with the aromas of burgers and fried chicken from the restaurant. A cold, faint drizzle begins to brush against my face.

"You look like hell," Kyle says. "Get some sleep or something."

"Yeah. I will. Thanks."

"Later," he says, and I raise my hand in acknowledgment as he finds his car.

I slide back into the driver's seat of my pickup. The sound of the door closing reverberates harshly inside the cabin. Determined to carry out my original plan of taking a walk to clear my head, I choose the easiest course to go back to my place rather than continue to the park. That way, I can leave the truck in my driveway. Since Kyle was kind enough to meet me in Georgetown, I'm not far away at all.

I weave my way out of the parking lot and pull onto the 35 feeder, knowing that in about fifteen minutes, I'll be home, and after getting some exercise, I won't need to do a thing for the rest of the day.

I wonder what would have happened if I went to Chupacabra in Austin instead of being such a flat wheel and resisting the drive. Maybe I wouldn't have taken that walk down County Road 140. Maybe my life wouldn't have become worse than it was already. Maybe a lot of things. But the universe doesn't care about "maybes."

Three Months Earlier

ELIZABETH PERCHES herself on the couch in our Austin apartment with her feet tucked underneath her like a house cat. She brushes a strand of black hair away from her face, leans over, and starts digging around in her purse, quickly producing a compact and lipstick tube.

"What time will you be ready?" I ask as I peer out at her from the bedroom. We've been planning this dinner for a couple of weeks, on the basis that we don't do enough romantic things. It's almost five o'clock, and our reservation is at six.

"Uh, pretty soon," she mumbles.

I swear her voice shakes. After I finish tying my tie, I grab my dress shoes and head into the living room. Still wearing her faded jeans and cami top, Elizabeth isn't even dressed to go out, which I can't help but notice when she bends down. Her body tends toward the slender side, but I've always liked her figure. She wears her leanness elegantly.

I think about asking if something is wrong, but there isn't any reason to. I sit down on one of the chairs at the kitchen table and slip my right foot into the black leather shoe. I eye Elizabeth as I take the thin laces in my fingers. Although we haven't disagreed about anything today, I do perceive her unusual quietness. Maybe she isn't feeling well.

Elizabeth pulls a brush through her long hair and gathers it back into a ponytail. She swings her feet to the floor and sits with her legs together. She puts her hands on her knees, staring at her fingers awkwardly for a few seconds.

"Trent," she says, not looking up right away. "I was wondering if we could talk about something before we go."

I get a twinge at the top of my stomach. I secure the bow. "Sure."

Instead of speaking, she goes into the bedroom and comes back out with a dark blue top, which she pulls hastily over her head. She crams her arms through the sleeves and pulls down on the shirt, then straightening it out too many times.

"So?" I ask. I finish tying the left shoe and sit up straight. Whatever it is, I need to listen to what she has to say.

"Um." She almost sits back down on the couch, but I think she realizes she's being a coward and comes to sit across from me at the kitchen table. Scents of jasmine and wild orange accompany her. Her eyes are wide and watery. They're the same color as the shirt she just forced onto her body like war gear.

Finally, Elizabeth says, "Well, last weekend when I was at the company picnic, I was talking to a friend. She told me about what happened with Mary, and I realized a few things."

I lean back and look at her, folding my arms. A dark cloud falls over the room, and the attendant silence peals starkly in my ears. "I thought you were at your mom's last weekend. You never told me about a company picnic. And who's Mary? You mean my Mary?"

I blink and run my hand across my chin. That sounded bad. Really bad. I didn't mean to be as defensive as I sounded. Her statement just surprised me. Not only did she never tell me anything about a company picnic—something I should have been invited to—but the way I referred to a girl from my past as "my" could be catastrophic.

"Oh yeah, I did visit my mom, that's true," Elizabeth says. She nods rapidly and straightens her back. I can see the flash of hurt in her eyes over the Mary comment, but she doesn't mention it.

"But I also went to the picnic. We have one every year. And yeah, it was Mary, the same Mary. Anyway, I was talking to a friend, and I just think—I think she's right. I think we're moving way too fast, and maybe this isn't what either of us really wanted."

I frown and wait. I don't see how those sentences even relate to one another. There's something I'm not grasping. "Who told you about Mary?"

She hesitates. "My friend Brittany. She told me what happened."

I don't know Brittany and never heard of her before. "What did she tell you?" My face pulls into a frown.

"She told me about the party and what you did after that. The bad stuff." Elizabeth sits staring at me, and the look in her eyes tells me things are different now. This conversation behind my back has permanently altered our relationship.

"Anyway," she continues. "I was wondering if you'd be

okay with some time apart. You know, just to think things over—get our heads straight."

It isn't my head that needs straightening, that's for sure. I place my folded hands on the table and consider them, carefully gathering my words.

"I'm confused," I say as calmly as I can. "You wanted a proposal, and so, five months ago, I proposed. You wanted us to live together to make sure we can do it, and we've been doing that. Now you have cold feet, but I wasn't the one pushing. I thought I was doing what you wanted to make you happy. Now you're upset when you find out about something from my distant past? I don't even see how that's relevant. And this Brittany person has nothing to do with us."

Elizabeth looks down, narrowing her eyes. She presses her lips together and raises her eyebrows ever so slightly. "She told me what happened. Is it true?"

My stomach tightens into a knot. I want to slam my fist down on the table, but I don't. "She told you what happened?" I repeat, unable to completely keep the sarcasm out of my voice.

"Yeah, she told me all of it. Is it true? Did you really do that? And if so, how come you never told me about it?" Elizabeth asks.

I shake my head and let my breath out in exasperation. "About the stupid mistakes I made when I was a punk kid? Elizabeth, that was twelve years ago! I didn't even know you."

Her eyes flinch with the hurt doe look again, like I'm the one creating the problem and she's the victim. "I know it was twelve years ago, but how could you not tell me about something like that? Don't you think it's pretty important? I mean, after what happened to her. Especially if we're getting married—"

Her voice breaks into a sob, pink blotches blooming across her cheeks. Two little wrinkles spring up between her eyebrows.

So, this Brittany person bad-mouthed me for my adolescent screw-ups, and Elizabeth thinks I might do the same to her. Is that what this is about? "I wasn't trying to keep it from you. It was just so long ago. I was young and stupid then. I'm not that person anymore. I grew up. I didn't think it mattered now."

The tears which fill her blue eyes spill over and roll down her face. One makes it all the way to her shirt and splatters on the fabric. "You didn't think it mattered that you cheated on the girl you were with right before me? And that you didn't go see her when she asked? Is it true?"

"Goddamn it, Elizabeth." I don't like having my inner demons stirred up. She unearths this ancient history and expects me to answer up as though life hasn't punished me enough already.

"Yes. It's true," I say.

She shakes her head, barely looking at me. "How do I know you're not keeping anything else from me?"

Well, she doesn't know. That's what trust is supposed to be. It's when you don't know every little detail of a person's life, but you have faith in them anyway.

"I didn't think it mattered because it was so long ago. And no. I'm not keeping anything from you." And that's true. I'm not.

She nods but keeps shifting her gaze around and won't look at me. She sighs and wipes her face, smearing the black streaks from her eye makeup. "Okay, but I still think we need some time apart. I just need to figure some things out."

I shake my head again. "I really don't understand. But if that's what you want—"

"Yeah. It's for the best." She gets up from the chair and picks up her purse from beside the couch. "I'll call you in a few days."

"Okay," I say.

I blink, watching in numb bewilderment as Elizabeth goes out the door. She doesn't even pause for a backward glance. A hollow sensation swallows me up, and I sit here, wooden and useless, wondering what to make of it.

3

JANUARY 5TH

Arriving home after discovering the atrocity against human life, I unlock the door with quivering fingers and shove it open. I exhale loudly and deeply several times, closing the door behind me and locking it again. I do a quick, visual sweep of the house. Seeing the place so neat and tidy startles me, but then I remember I cleaned the crap out of it before all hell broke loose during my walk. The familiar smells of stale pizza crust and beer residue are gone. Instead, I inhale bleached-clean air and citrus degreaser.

The grim alarm from all my new experiences slowly wanes. I cook some frozen chicken and fries and eat until my stomach hurts. Then, utterly exhausted and weak in the legs, I lie in bed and toss and turn. The cotton sheets feel clingy and heavy where they touch my skin. I can't stop those lurid images from flashing intrusively through my mind—can't get that awful stench out of my nostrils even though it only exists as a memory now. The sight of the girl against the wall affects me the absolute worst—her white dress streaked blood red, her wilted posture as she hung there, defeated and broken. I try to shake it off and sleep.

After two or three hours of unease that threatens never to let go, I finally lapse into a full, dreamless unconsciousness that lasts for about five hours. Then my eyes snap open, and I sit up. I check the clock and read the time as just before 5:00 a.m. Today is Monday, and I have to go to work. With Tim being in custody as a murder suspect, this might present a problem.

I turn on the news and get breakfast going. Listening to the bacon pop in the pan, I place two eggs on the counter. The rich smell of frying meat permeates the kitchen as I watch for the story.

"Williamson County officials are investigating the recovery of two women, one dead and one still alive after being severely beaten and tortured, from an abandoned house on County Road 140. A resident of Williamson County reportedly discovered the women in a back room of the structure at approximately 4:30 p.m. yesterday after smelling a foul odor. The resident has chosen to remain anonymous. Tim Corbin, the owner of the derelict property, has been taken into custody by the Williamson County Sheriff's Office and is undergoing questioning. The identities of the victims have not yet been released to KXAV. However, we have been told that the surviving victim has been taken into care at St. David's Hospital and is in critical condition."

Other than the anchorwoman saying there will be more updates later as the news team becomes apprised, the story ends. But she said the woman is in critical condition—so she's still alive.

I think about Tim. Poor Tim. Maybe later, I'll ask his wife Brenda why he was arrested. Maybe she knows. It seems pretty hard to believe anyone would be stupid enough to hide the victims' bodies in a house that he owns, not to mention driving to the crime scene afterward and speaking to law enforcement. I shake my head. The whole thing is insane.

After removing the bacon and blotting it on a paper towel, I crack the eggs and drop them into the hot pan. A few oil droplets splash my hand, burning a little, but I barely notice. My mind continues playing the torrent of images like a horror movie on repeat. I try to shut them out as much as possible but can't get rid of them completely. Forgetting that scene might take a while. I realize that other than the deputy sheriff I spoke to last night or the bystanders who gaped at us, no one knows about this. None of my friends or acquaintances know me as the "resident" who discovered the crime. Maybe it's best to keep it that way until they catch the guy.

I think of the woman in the black jacket, and I wonder if she, or anyone else, snapped a photo of me. A lot of wary eyes were pointed my way. I now question standing off to the side like that, staying so close to the yard. It would have been better if I joined the spectators. But I wasn't thinking. I blame the morbid part of myself, the side of me that wanted front-row seats to the show. I just *had* to see.

As I wolf down my bacon and eggs, shower, and shave, I think of what to do about work. Brenda should be home, and I can report to her for the time being. The hours for my job on the ranch are Monday through Friday from 6:00 a.m. to noon, and I have shifts at the gas station a few times a week and on some weekends.

Oddly coincident, the small house I rent and my job at the ranch are closely related. The house is on a decent-sized plot of land, which is part of a much larger property of about two thousand acres belonging to Tim Corbin. This is the same Tim I work for, the same Tim they hauled off to the station. He owns quite a bit of property adjacent to this rental, as well as several parcels on County Road 140 that include the murder house. He operates a ranch that raises mostly cattle, sheep, and goats.

My work at Corbin Ranch isn't bad and consists mainly of feeding animals, repairing fences, keeping up the barns, and more recently, bottle-feeding lambs whose mothers rejected them. The pay could be better, but it's steady work, and I found this job right after I moved by virtue of renting the house. One upside is that the ranch is so close I can walk there when I like. It's on the same rural road where I live, but today I'll take my truck.

I drive past the wooden barn where I usually park and continue to Tim's driveway, where I turn and pull up to the light yellow two-story. Tim's truck isn't here, which makes me think it remains parked on County Road 140 or was impounded. I knock on the door, and it flies open a few seconds later.

"Trent," Brenda says. "Come in."

She looks at me with wide, puffy, red eyes. Her brown, shoulder-length hair appears to have been hastily put up with clips.

"How are you, Ms. Brenda?" I ask. The smell of strong coffee greets me as I cross the threshold.

"How dare you ask," she says, sniffing and forcing a laugh. "It's been terrible. It's crazy. I just can't believe it." She motions for me to take a seat.

"I know. Is Tim still being questioned by the sheriff?" I ask. I take a seat in the overstuffed, green plaid chair.

"Yeah. Being held in jail is more like it, but yeah. He had

a warrant out for his arrest for an unpaid speeding ticket—just put it off and forgot. So, they took him. I haven't heard anything else since last night when he called me." She pours a cup of coffee and hands it to me.

So, an unpaid ticket was the grounds for arrest. I take the mug and warm my hands against it. "But do they really think he did it?"

She huffs and takes a seat across from me on the brown sofa. "Well, it sure looks bad. To me, he's a country boy with a heavy foot and a bad memory, but to the police, he's a wanted man with a dead body in his house. And that poor girl!" she says.

"Yeah, but come on. Tim drove out there yesterday to speak with the officers. I saw him. He was a nervous wreck. Why are they continuing to hold him for something disrelated?"

"I know that, but... I don't know." She sips from her mug and stares listlessly at the gray carpet under the mahogany coffee table. "I just don't know."

"I'm sure they'll release him soon."

"Hope so," she says. She leans forward and sets her cup down. "Trent, I know this is a morbid question, but what did you see?" She rubs her nose, and I know she feels guilty for asking.

Well, I can't blame her for wondering.

GETTING on with work as usual feels impossible. With Brenda's curiosity satisfied, and my condolences extended for her difficult time, we establish that I'll continue on my standard schedule. At this point, we don't know much, and with Tim in custody, I'm needed more than ever.

I park my truck near the barn and get ready for the day. It isn't raining, but the weather isn't any warmer or more inviting. I walk through the sheep pasture under a bleak sky that seems devoid of color. Milk thistle and dry weeds make papery rattling sounds in the breeze. Although the wind bites my face, I'm dressed in the right clothing for the job. My ears and hands are covered, I have long johns under my jeans and four shirts on, so for the most part, I stay pretty warm. I make my way to the small pond at the end of the field, not for any particular reason besides I like having a look at it first thing each morning. I'm still trying to clear my head, and this routine might help.

Tall, wilted grasses and reeds dip into the dark water, its still surface rippling in only a few places from three small mallards. Scents of algae and rich, dark earth hang heavy in the air. A dilapidated dock, no longer in use, tumbles gracefully into the water. The center of the pond looms so black, so motionless, that it appears to be a mysterious thing of its own that harbors some deep secret. In actuality, the artificial water hole was dug out for the livestock and goes only about twenty feet down. Tim told me he stocks this little pond every year, and I'm welcome to fish here any time.

Over by the graying outbuildings, the sheep are already milling around, waiting for me. They aren't the white, fluffy ones that I previously thought all sheep were. These are all colors—black, brown, tan, and even spotted. Surprisingly, a few of the ewes have lambs already. I trudge to the feed shed, watching my breath turn into puffs of mist, and then fill a five-gallon bucket with grain. I carry it to the sawed-in-half plastic barrel that Tim made into a trough. Some of the sheep are tame enough to shove their noses into the bucket while I pour. I don't need to put out hay because there's a large roll of it crammed into a wire sectional feeder. Sometimes I've seen one or two of the sheep climb up there and stand on top of the bale. I have no idea why.

I make sure to fill the metal water trough. Next, I go into the old barn and lose myself in the smells of manure and warm animal bodies. After cleaning out the dung as needed, I put new straw down.

My cell phone rings, and I jump. I pull it out of my pocket and look at the caller ID. It only reads "blocked." That isn't Tim. I doubt it's *her*, either. I'm not hopeful anymore, and I don't care. Without answering, I slip the phone back into my pocket.

Irritation clawing at me like a rash, I kick a stray nugget of manure before emerging from the stillness of the barn to tackle my next job. Past the sheep clustering at the feeding area, there's a short string of barbed-wire fence against some trees. It extends near a sharp curve in the road that runs right beside the pond, where the land falls away to a marshy area with a few cattails. There's a break in the middle wire, which needs to be repaired.

I almost turn and get tools from the shed when something catches my eye. A white car idles near the turn in the road. Parked on the side nearest me, it faces my direction. I can barely see it behind a couple of pine trees and a small thicket. From what I can tell, it looks like a late '90s model sedan. Bare chrome shows under the rubbed-off paint on the front fender. I can't see the driver, but exhaust fumes rise in the cold air, so someone is likely inside.

Deputy Sheriff Reyes's words repeat in my mind. *Be*

aware of your surroundings. Be safe. There's no reason to think the car has anything to do with me, but it shouldn't be there.

Not changing the speed of my movements, I pretend to test the strength of a post near the barn. I reach down and pick up a piece of twine from the ground, act like I'm examining it, and casually walk back into the barn. I do own several guns, but my rifle is the only one I bring to work with me. Right now, it's in the cabin of my truck. Tim owns plenty of firearms too, but this fact doesn't help right now.

I want to get a better look, but the barn has no window on the side nearest the road. However, it's open at both ends, so I go to the back and peek around the side to find out if I can see the car from here. With the pond and terrain between the road and the barn, he—or she—won't be able to see me. I crane my neck, but the view isn't good enough.

I decide to fix the fence at a later time and will instead work on another project, one closer to Tim's house. I don't want the unknown person in that car to see me get into my vehicle parked on the other side of the barn. He doesn't need to know what kind of truck I drive. Luckily, he won't be able to see it from his position.

To get to the part of the ranch near Tim's house, I normally take the road, but that will take me right past the car. I need to think about this. Maybe this smacks of paranoia, but I can't help it after yesterday. I rub my forehead with the back of my gloved hand to try and get the image of the girl's blood-covered body out of my head. That filthy, excrement-ridden floor with the corpse on it. The horrible stench of death.

I can drive the back way through Tim's property on the dirt roads that connect the pastures. One place I need to cross might put me within view of County Road 152, but the guy in the car won't be able to see my plates. He probably won't expect to see my vehicle pass by there—he'd have to turn around and drive.

In full view of the person inside the idling car, I head toward the gravel driveway. This is necessary in order to get around the group of mesquite trees concealing my truck on the other side of the barn.

"Hey there," someone calls out.

It's a male voice. Friendly. Probably early forties. An icy wind inches itself up my spine inside my many layers of clothing. I allow myself to get alongside the mesquite trees, and I turn to face him. About a hundred and fifty feet lies between us. I get a good look at him. He has a dark beard, a wide-brimmed, tan Stetson hat, and he's wearing sunglasses on this pallid January morning. The man stands next to the white sedan with the door open in front of him, so I can't see most of his right side, including his hand.

"Yeah," I say. I'm not inviting him up here. If he has something to say, he can say it from the road.

"Are you Trent Lemend?" He maintains his friendly tone.

"Who are you?" I bite his head off. My gaze remains steady, never leaving his face.

The man's fake smile disappears, and he makes a motion with his right arm and shoulder as though he's drawing something out of the car.

You've got to be kidding me.

Instinctively, I pull myself behind the mesquite grove and crouch down. The thorny branches are only inches away from my face, but I prefer getting scratched to leaving myself open. If this guy is actually friendly, he'll explain himself, and if not, I'm not stupid enough to stand out there.

Thud, thud, clang!

The calm herd of sheep explodes into an agitated swarm of bees. Frightened and disoriented, they scatter in several directions, some of the little ones falling all over themselves. What I heard sounded like a gun with a silencer—the "clang" was probably a bullet striking the metal water trough.

I stay glued to my spot, unmoving and unthinking, but that lasts maybe a matter of seconds. It seems like forever. Blood pounds in my ears, and my chest tightens like it will burst. I swear under my breath repeatedly, frozen between the thorns and the rocky ground. Then I spring to my feet and make a mad dash to my truck, get inside, and start the engine. I slam it into gear, and the tires spin on the gravel as I press the accelerator.

Another *thud* follows, coupled with a small crackling. I jerk and duck down, my stomach dropping as the pickup veers wildly to the right. I yank my head back up and narrowly miss a fallen tree limb as the truck rolls off the path. Steering hard to the left, I get back on the dirt road and push the pedal down as far as it will go. I can't stay consistently within the ruts as the truck jolts along the uneven road. The suspension threatens to come apart with each new tire bounce, and the rocks and depressions jerk me every which way. I didn't have time to put on the seat belt. I'm pushing sixty and don't even know where I'm going besides across the field of tall, dried grass and thorny plants. I've never taken this way from field to field.

I glance in the rear-view mirror, and the man, my attacker, grows smaller as I tear across Tim's property. He'll have to go back, get his car, and trespass onto someone else's land to follow me. He may or may not be stupid enough to do that.

Seeing the first gate ahead, I push down hard on the brakes. The truck slides in the mud near the fence, and I almost hit it. My hands shake as I propel myself out of the pickup and start fumbling with the latch. A mechanism with no lock, it's simple to undo, so I yank the gate open within a few seconds. I swing it wide and start to get back into the truck, then check behind me for the man. He's still there, but I can't tell which way he's facing. Looking ahead at the gate, I realize that it's swinging itself closed because of the angle. Panicking, I peer behind me for the man again, but he seems smaller now—he must be going back to his car.

I get out of the truck once more and prop the gate open with a stick. Once I drive to the other side, I slam the gate shut and secure it. I can no longer see my assailant, but that doesn't mean I'm safe. I work the Silverado up to a decent speed on the dirt road as I continue to the field near Tim's house, being more careful now because his Black Angus populate the range on either side of me. If I come to one standing on the path, I'll have to slow down and go around it.

After flinging off my gloves, I fish out my cell to call Brenda. Maybe continuing my job on the ranch isn't such a good idea after all.

4

TWO MONTHS EARLIER

Still wearing yesterday's clothes, I lie on the couch in the apartment Elizabeth and I used to share. The wall clock shows it's nearly eleven as I lethargically change the channels. It's kind of pointless because I don't really look at any of the programs. I see a few images, then switch to the next station with the remote—the remote grasped limply in apathetic fingers, attached to an arm that doesn't want to raise itself.

Over a month has passed since Elizabeth left. She told me she'd call in a few days, but she didn't. Since then, I must have left twenty messages for her, each and every one unreturned. She never sent the engagement ring back either, ridiculous in light of the fact that I don't even know what the hell happened besides her flimsy explanation.

At about noon, I finally shower. I brush my teeth and rid my mouth of the yeasty taste from last night's beer. When I open the closet door to pull out a pair of jeans, the row of Elizabeth's clothes hanging there is like a slap in the face, and I decide that today is the day. I'm getting tired of looking at it.

I get busy. I start taking the clothes off the rod by their hangers and begin laying them on the bed. Despite being laundered, her shirts still manage to smell like her jasmine and wild orange perfume. I'll box them up, along with everything else, and drive to her mother's house later. Since Elizabeth finished the lease at her own apartment before moving in with me, this seems like a sensible location. As I remove items, I spot one of Elizabeth's coats, and on a swinish impulse, I reach into the pockets, feeling around the cool, satin lining to see what I can find. How can she have nothing to hide, leaving so abruptly like that? I pull out a gum wrapper and a paper clip. I snort and throw them into the trash.

After removing everything of hers from the closet, I go through the drawers. Since she lived with me for five months, she has most of her things here, and it remains a mystery to me why she hasn't come back for any of it. I open the bottom drawer, revealing a pile of lacy bras and panties. Reeling like a brick hits me in the chest, I stuff the underthings into a garbage bag, so I won't have to see them again. Then I get a box and toss the bag into it.

Once I return to the drawer, I notice there are still a few things inside. I reach in and grasp two small pieces of paper, which I realize are movie ticket stubs. How much that hurts surprises me—the film might be one we watched together—until I turn the stubs over and read the name of a movie I've never seen. She could have seen it with one of her friends, or at least that's what Kyle would say. I'm not so sure anymore. I wish I could find something more damning. Furtively, I search through the rest of her clothes before boxing them up, but no other evidence appears.

I remove all of Elizabeth's hygiene products from the bathroom and place them in a separate box. The sharp smell of acetone hits me when a bottle of nail polish remover starts leaking onto the cardboard. I take it out, empty it in the sink, and throw away the empty bottle. That crap won't go leaking all over the inside of my truck just because she's too lazy to come and get her stuff.

Other odds and ends belonging to my ex-fiancée are scattered throughout the house, so I carry a bag with me and drop things inside as I make my rounds through each room. At one point, pretty sure I have everything, I go back to the bedroom to tape the boxes shut. My eyes feel drawn to the dresser—maybe I missed something—and I notice Elizabeth's small, brown jewelry box, about the width of a postcard, blending in unobtrusively with the wood beneath it. Annoyed, I grab it roughly and hold it in one hand while debating which box to put it in. Then my suspicion returns, and I set it back down on the dresser, a greedy desire to know its contents mingling with my anger.

The jewelry box can't hold much because of its size. Most of what I find are things I've seen her wear before, among them, a necklace I gave her two Christmas's ago. Disgusted, I clap the wooden lid shut and put the jewelry box with her jeans.

Elizabeth's mom lives in South Austin, not far from Zilker Park. Once, a few months ago, I found a rocky trail off in the woods I didn't know about, and I've been looking forward to exploring it. Maybe after this unpleasant errand, I'll seek it out.

Traffic on 35 isn't too bad since it's Saturday, and I park

outside Ms. Reinhardt's house a little before three o'clock. The small home measures less than a thousand square feet, its exterior painted sage green with brown trim. Sparse in grass, decorative patterns of well-placed rocks, blue agave, cacti, and a group of bushes with blue-gray leaves comprise a yard surrounding a persimmon tree. I look in the driveway and the street but don't see Elizabeth's car.

On the way here, I considered my words but didn't have much. I knock on the door and wait. Ms. Reinhardt appears a moment later, giving me a deer-in-the-headlights look like I didn't choose the best time to arrive.

"Oh, Trent, how are you? It's so nice to see you."

Despite her effort to be cheerful, her face pulls into a frown. She lingers near the door frame, awkwardly placing her hand on it. Ms. Reinhardt, a pretty lady in her fifties, has shoulder-length hair dyed dark auburn. I used to wonder if that's how Elizabeth will look when she's older, but presently the thought makes me sick.

"I'm doing well," I say. I force a smile. "How are you?"

"I'm well also. I'd ask you to come in, but I have some guests today. What can I do for you?"

"I just came to drop off Elizabeth's things. I have a few boxes in the truck."

She tucks a stray lock of hair behind her ear. "Oh. Sure. You can just bring them up to the porch. I'll take them in." She flashes another nervous smile.

"Who is it, Mom?"

My stomach somersaults at Elizabeth's voice.

Ms. Reinhardt turns briefly. "It's Trent."

Elizabeth replies to her mother, but I can't make out the words. Faint laughter echoes them, barely audible, which I swear to be male. I still don't see Elizabeth's car anywhere and wonder if someone brought her. Maybe she got a new apartment and left it there, but it seems weird.

The last conversation I had with my ex-fiancée flashes to mind, the same confusion hitting me now as I stand on her mom's porch like a dope. There were holes in Elizabeth's story. Isn't it only fair that she come out and tell the truth about why she left me? That isn't too much to ask. I swallow hard, the muscles in my jaw tensing.

"Ms. Reinhardt, since Elizabeth is here, do you think you could ask her to please come out for a few minutes? We haven't spoken in months." My voice sounds much calmer than I feel.

Elizabeth's mom shifts her weight to her other sandalled foot and glances behind her into the house. Her hand lingers on the doorknob. "She's busy. As I said, we have guests today."

She cues me to give it up, but I'm not ready just yet. I shove my hands in my pockets. "I understand. Please tell her it'll only take five minutes."

Ms. Reinhardt's frown deepens. "Trent, I don't think she wants to. I'm sorry."

My chest tightens. I exhale and put a hand on the cool, smooth porch railing. "Why? Did she say why?"

She huffs and crosses her arms. "Well, now, I wouldn't know anything about that. Whatever happened is between you and Elizabeth."

I lower my voice, hoping Elizabeth can't hear me from wherever she's hiding. "That's the thing. I don't mean to drag you into this, but I don't know what happened. She just left." I shake my head. "She told me it had something to do with a relationship I had when I was eighteen. I know I was immature then, but... I don't know. I can't believe that was the real reason Elizabeth ended things. Did she mention anything about it to you?" I squeeze the handrail with a death grip.

Ms. Reinhardt gives a few hard blinks. She raises her eyebrows. "She did. She did tell me something about that."

I wait, motionless. Seconds tick by while we stare at each other. "What did she say?" I finally ask.

Ms. Reinhardt pushes her hair away from her forehead by combing it straight back with her fingers. Her scowl goes more worried. She leans a hand on the doorframe again. "I really don't think it's my place to say."

"Just close the door," Elizabeth's muffled voice calls in the background.

The tightness in my chest turns to a dull ache.

"I'll close it," a male voice says.

This time, I know I heard it. I put the guy somewhere around my age, and I know Elizabeth has two sisters but no brothers. My gut clenches, and my heart starts pounding. I take a step forward. Maybe I can get a look at him—her "guest."

"Oh," Ms. Reinhardt says as the door starts swinging closed. She glances at the person I can't see and moves out of the way.

I'm not quick enough. Although I crane my neck, I don't glimpse who stands behind the door. Without a word to me, he slams it in my face. It thuds shut, the sounds of wood against wood and the clang of the brass door knocker reverberating in my ears. I know those sounds. They're real similar to "fuck you." With them comes a draft of indoor air. It carries a masculine scent, like expensive aftershave.

Swearing under my breath, I turn and start down the few porch steps. I get halfway across the walkway when the door creaks open again. Maybe Elizabeth changed her mind.

Maybe she'll indulge me in a five-minute conversation, or maybe her male houseguest wants to have words after all. I turn to see Ms. Reinhardt's auburn hair and fair complexion.

"I'm sorry, Trent. You said you had some of Elizabeth's things?"

Is she sorry about the question or about the door slamming? I don't answer. Despite the need to be polite, I glare at Ms. Reinhardt before turning to go to the truck. Does no one have the decency to tell me anything?

After making several trips to my pickup, I deposit the four boxes on the porch in silence. Ms. Reinhardt stands there with her arms crossed, now tight-lipped and unapologetic. She mostly stares at the greenery or out at the street. She isn't responsible for our problems, but she could tell me something.

"Well, I guess that's it." I wait, giving her one last chance to talk if she wants.

"Okay. Thanks, Trent. Take care." Her expression softens, and she tries a smile again.

"Yep," I say. I turn curtly and leave.

An unwelcome, dull pain swells inside my chest, and my eyes ache, but I smother how much this whole thing hurts. I grit my teeth and wish I could tell Elizabeth to go straight to hell. If Kyle were here, he'd tell me what just happened didn't prove she was cheating—that all I really know from today is that Elizabeth has rude friends. I snort.

As I make my ungraceful exit, a four-inch stone near the blue agave catches my eye. I kick it as hard as I can. I really put my weight into it. My heavy, steel-toed work boot sends the rock sailing across the grass and into the street. It skids, bouncing with a smart *pop-pop-pop* before settling near the opposite curb.

Without looking to see if Ms. Reinhardt saw, I walk away from the perfect little South Austin house, with its perfect little eco-friendly, low maintenance yard. I get into my Silverado. Stuffy air smelling of yesterday's burger wrappers stifles me, but I get going without rolling down the windows. As I pull away from the curb, I realize I neglected one of the most important reasons I came. I forgot to ask for the engagement ring back.

5

JANUARY 6TH

The Silverado bumps erratically along the dirt road to Tim's house as I steer with my left hand and call Brenda with my right.

"Trent, is—"

"Brenda, I need you to call the sheriff. Someone just shot at me. Right now, I'm driving through the cattle field, headed your way. Don't worry—I'm not coming to the house. I just need the driveway to get back on County Road 152. You need to be careful. Lock your doors, keep your gun by you."

She gasps and mutters something I can't hear. "Oh my God, Trent. Are you hurt?"

"No, he missed. I'll call you later to check on you. Call the sheriff right now, okay?"

"Okay," she says, swearing as she takes the phone away from her ear.

The next gated fence looms into view, and I have to stop. Looking back, I don't see the shooter. My stomach plummets as I wonder what I'll do if this guy is waiting for me at the end of Brenda's driveway. I undo the latch like before and pull my truck through, then secure the gate before continuing. As I speed up, I slam on the brakes just as quickly. The cattle in this field are on the move and crossing directly in front of me.

"Son of a—" I swerve to the left off the dirt road, the tires hitting a rock and making me come off the seat. I bounce along as I steer past the herd, finally straightening out and getting back on the path. Pretty soon, I can see Tim's yellow house coming in view at the end of the pasture.

Another gated fence blocks my passage, and my heart pounds harder than ever. My hands feel numb as they grip the steering wheel. He could be there, hiding somewhere, maybe by the house, maybe in the drainage ditch by the county road. I have to be ready but have to get out of here as fast as possible so that Brenda won't get hurt.

I work the latch of the gate, my hands shaking, my breathing loud and irregular as I fumble with the chain. I glance every which way but don't see him. I don't see the white car. When I pull my truck through, Brenda's voice calls above me. I look to see her at the upper story window.

"Just go," she yells. "I'll get the gate."

"No way," I say.

I'm sure that would be the perfect opportunity for this psycho to come over and shoot her just because he can. Watching down the driveway, I latch the gate—gate number three—and get back into the truck. I drive toward the road as fast as I can without inviting an accident. I glance both ways, seeing nothing, and pull onto County Road 152, where I turn right.

I drive in the direction opposite my house. I don't peel out or let the tires squeal, but I do push it to fifty-five in a swift hurry. It will only take about ten minutes to get to the

35 feeder road. I'll drive south on the interstate and find a gas station somewhere. I keep glancing in the rearview, but the man's white car isn't back there.

I drive into Georgetown proper and stop at a Chevron. A convenient free space allows me to park fairly close to the door. I wait several minutes, searching for any sign of the car or the man. Did he honestly give up pursuit? I wipe my hands on my jeans and dig the business card out of my wallet to call Deputy Reyes. Searching my pockets for my phone, I realize I must have dropped it when I hit that rock in the cattle field. I finally find it underneath the passenger's side seat.

By some great stroke of luck, I actually get the deputy sheriff on the phone. He must be between crime scenes or speeders or whatever you call those moments during the day when cops aren't doing anything.

Reyes tells me, "Sit tight. Don't touch anything else in or on the truck. I'll have it photographed, and if we find the bullet, that will be fingerprinted. You'll also need to wait until we're done to clean any broken glass out of the cabin."

"There's not much glass," I say. That isn't relevant. I guess I only say it because I'm stressed.

"Well, good," says Reyes. "Just stay put until I get there. I'm on my way."

Deputy Reyes pulls into the Chevron parking lot in his black-and-white cruiser not fifteen minutes later. The criminal investigations team, two men who arrive in a van, soon joins him. While they run through their checklist on my Silverado, I stand away from my truck and speak to Reyes. I explain what happened, giving him my best description of the man from what little I saw of his face. I have no proof, no evidence either, that the man is in some way connected to what happened at Tim's old house, but I can't help feeling like he is.

"How could this guy know where I work?" I ask.

"I don't know. Did anyone at the crime scene yesterday look suspicious? Or was there anyone there you might know, or you've seen before?" asks the deputy. Apparently, Reyes can't help but think he might have a connection too.

"Suspicious?" I think back and shake my head. "No, not really. A lady in a black jacket kept giving me weird looks, but other than that, no. No one there looked like the guy who shot at me, and there was definitely no one I knew other than Tim. I wondered if anyone would take a photo of me—because they might have overheard, I was the one who reported the crime—but no one did that I saw. People had their phones out, but that was it."

Reyes nods and takes notes.

I think of Brenda and wonder how she made out after I left. "Do you happen to know if Brenda Corbin's okay? She was at the house alone."

Reyes looks up and nods. "She's okay. I heard that call not long before you and I spoke. We sent some officers over there, but it seemed our boy was long gone."

I take a deep breath.

"Do you have any enemies that you know of?" Reyes asks, squinting slightly.

My gut twists. Do I? I consider, shaking my head slowly as I mentally flip through my past and the people I know. "No. I can't think of any."

"You're lucky to be alive. It's good that you reacted the way you did. If you'd have waited a second longer, you'd probably be dead right now," he says.

I nod.

Reyes continues. "Is there anywhere you can go for a while? A friend's house out of town, a family member's house, somewhere like that? Are you able to hide out for a while?"

"Yeah, I guess I could. But I'd rather not. I just moved here from Austin a couple months ago, and if I can't work at the ranch anymore, I'm down to one part-time job, which is close to my house. Do you really think the guy will come after me again?" I ask.

It seems hard to believe anyone would be that bold—or stupid—but if he were criminal enough to shoot at me at work, I suppose it isn't far-fetched to think he might try again tomorrow or another day.

"We should assume he will," Reyes says.

I regret that I wasn't able to see the car's plate number, and I hope the shooter didn't get mine when I drove off. "What do I do if the guy follows me home? He might even know where I live already."

"Well, that's my point, which is why I'd rather you stay somewhere else. If you absolutely must go home, you need to be prepared. If you have a gun, keep it with you. Be extremely careful. If you see anything out of the ordinary, give us a call," Reyes says.

I guess there are only so many ways he can tell me he can't predict the future. We don't know the shooter's game, his motive, or his identity. If he returns, it will be in a way I don't expect, and that's the part I have to somehow prepare for.

I realize that despite my many layers of clothing, my body shivers uncontrollably. I've been doing that since I began talking to Reyes and didn't even notice. Though I'm no gun expert, I own firearms and practice using them sometimes, but I've never been shot at. I can't shake off the shock from fleeing for my life. It jarred my sense of reality, and now I stand here, slammed into the present moment. The sharpness of my vision focuses with a near-painful keenness, while my body feels slightly numb.

I turn to look toward my truck when I overhear one of the investigators say, "Found the bullet." I'd be more curious to inspect it myself were I not spinning. I'd like to know the caliber and get an idea of the type of gun used.

Reyes completes his questioning of me for his report. This is the second one in which I've played a part, occurring less than twenty-four hours after the first.

"I'm glad you're okay. Stay in touch with us," he says. He smiles the kindest smile his hard face will allow, nods, and shakes my hand. If he harbored suspicions of me before, his doubt must have passed.

A shrill wind blasts my face, bringing faint smells of gasoline and burned coffee as I look over the fingerprint dust on my truck's paint. The man didn't touch my pickup that I know of, but I guess the team wanted to be thorough. From the corner of my eye, I watch the cruiser and investigation van pull out of the Chevron parking lot and onto the 35 feeder road. People fill their tanks, walk in or out of the gas station, or get into their cars. Life carries on beneath the ash-gray sky in a world that seems cold and hostile to me. Today is business as usual for everyone else.

The round didn't leave much glass inside the truck's cab, but I remove what I find. I'll need to get the back window replaced, but I duct tape the bullet hole to keep the cold out until then. I call Brenda, and she's rattled, but okay, just like Reyes said. She isn't disappointed that I won't be returning to work, not when a gunman followed me onto her property. I ask her to let me know when they release Tim, and she says she will.

I need to look for another day job but can't think about that yet. I'll do it tomorrow or the next day. Before I go home, I'll take the opportunity to have my broken window replaced.

TRYING to get my mind off what just happened, I flip through a Car and Driver magazine in the lobby of QuickGlass. I can't seem to read a single word. A sweet, chemical adhesive smell mingles with that of the fresh popcorn. It's free for customers, but I'm not hungry. I glance up to watch the technician take an old, beat-up Jeep with mud-encrusted tires into the garage. It's the vehicle ahead of mine. My thoughts wander to Elizabeth and linger there like a bad hangover. She used to have a common gripe about how I'm not going anywhere in life, and unfortunately, this is mostly true.

Before I worked for Tim on his ranch, I lived in Austin, doing insurance billing for a chiropractic office. Though by no means my chosen career, I got the job through a friend of mine, who insisted it was worth it. I did that for years, and the pay wasn't bad at all—definitely better than the pay for feeding goats and mending broken barbed wire. They also provided an insurance plan, which I was allowed to keep when I changed jobs, as long as I paid my monthly premiums. But at my age, although I'm not a slacker, always have steady work, and squirreled away some money in savings, I don't have a real profession like Elizabeth does at the accounting firm. This, I feel, happened mostly because of a series of events after high school, rather than an actual lack of direction on my part, but there's no point in dwelling on that now. Either way, my ex-fiancée wound up being right.

To Elizabeth's credit, she never actually *said* I wasn't going anyplace. She just hinted at it and suggested I should go to school. That would have been brilliant advice were it not for the fact that I couldn't afford it and I worked full time at my going-no-where jobs. It's always convenient to tell someone how easy something is when you're not the one who has to do it.

After flipping through a few more pages in the magazine, I find an article about the best new cars you can still buy with a manual transmission. I read three sentences before I wind up slapping the magazine shut. I dial Kyle's number on my cell and hope he'll pick up.

"Trent! Hey, aren't you at work?" he asks.

I have never known someone to be so happy for no reason at all. I laugh despite day two of my miserable week. "Nope, but I'm supposed to be. Some real bad stuff went down this morning. I'm getting a new back window put on the truck."

"Oh man, what happened? Were you in an accident?"

"Not exactly. Well, I'm not injured. But uh... a lot has happened. You want to get a beer or something?" I ask.

"Yeah, sure," Kyle says. "I've got a showing at eleven, but I could probably meet you at one or one thirty for lunch."

"That would be great," I say.

With no job to go back to, I meet Kyle at Chupacabra on 6th street to have a drink at one o'clock on Monday afternoon. Nothing settles the nerves quite like the aromas of alcohol, lime, and sautéing beef fajitas. Sitting at a high table by the window, I pick at my chips and salsa and tell Kyle everything. It might not be the best idea. Reyes was pretty clear about keeping things to myself if possible. Anyone else with information could become a target themselves.

A Corona dangles limply from Kyle's fingers like he no longer remembers he's holding it. Inertia must be the only thing that keeps it from falling.

"Geez, Trent. Shit." Now he throws back the beer bottle, draining about three-fourths of it. He doesn't much know what to say, an unusual thing for him. "You can probably stay with Laney and me for a while if you want. I could talk to her."

Another thing about Kyle is that he's married. Married and successful with his profession in real estate. Laney is expecting their first child in a few months, and from what I've seen of her, she's Elizabeth's polar opposite. Blonde, bubbly, and happy-go-lucky—well, like Kyle's soul incarnated into a woman's body, that's what Laney is. His perfect mate.

"Thanks, man, but there's no way I can do that to you. There's no sense in bringing you two into this. He had a gun with a silencer. This guy was serious." I pop a tortilla chip into my mouth, but it has no taste today besides salty.

"So why do you think someone would want you dead? You're the one who called the cops, but you don't know anything," Kyle says.

I shake my head. "I don't know why. But we don't even know if the guy who shot at me was the guy who committed that crime—did that to those women." My right hand is wet, so I pick up a napkin and wipe the condensation off my beer bottle.

"And you really think Tim had nothing to do with any of

this? If they arrested him, they had to have evidence. They can't just take him in for no reason, right?" Kyle asks.

"Brenda told me he forgot to pay a ticket and had a warrant out for his arrest, so that's how they got him. But torture and murder? No way. You should have seen him talking to the cops, looking like a scared rabbit. And he was the one who asked me to check on the house," I say.

"I've seen crime shows about something like this. Often, when someone murders someone, like a family member, they get another person involved and pretend to 'discover' the crime together. And that's the way they act, shocked and terrified," Kyle says.

"But what about the guy who shot at me today? Tim is still in custody. You think he prearranged a hitman to come after me? I don't see the point. If I served my purpose, and in addition think he's innocent—which I do—having me killed would only make him look guilty." I stir the salsa with a chip, swirling it mechanically.

Kyle laughs and sets his beer on the table. "Well, thank you, Detective Lemend. That's a suitable argument. Maybe you should tell that to Tim's attorney."

"Eh." I shrug. "I've been dragged into it too much as it is."

"You need to get a concealed handgun license," Kyle says. "Keep your piece on you all the time. Maybe they'll catch the guy, and you won't need to leave town, but if he does come after you, you'll be ready."

Again, a brilliantly simple piece of logic if you're not the one marked for murder. It's easy.

~

THE TRUTH IS, I already applied for a concealed handgun license. I did so right after I decided to move to Georgetown, knowing it takes sixty days or longer to get one. Although I like the quiet out here, I've never lived in such a rustic environment, and I don't like being unprepared. After getting fingerprinted, completing the online class, and the practical portion of the exam nearly two months ago, my license arrived in the mail today—a fact I learned when I returned home after lunch with Kyle. If only it would have come this morning before work, I could have legally had my pistol on me when that guy shot at me. Ironic, maybe, but probably just my terrible luck. Well, at least I have the license now.

Earlier, when I was standing outside Chupacabra, breathing in smog and gasoline fumes from the heavy, downtown Austin traffic, I had to admit that I was afraid to go home. Now it's late afternoon, and I'm in my living room putting my 9mm Browning in its holster under my jacket. Feeling the grip's texture beneath my fingers and the pistol against my body actually bolsters my mood quite a bit. That, and I'm coated in a gunpowder smell from shooting aluminum cans outside. It's invigorating. I don't have anything fancy with a silencer like a sniper, for God's sake, but I have a gun that will do the job in a pinch. It's easy to use and can be fired at close range.

Other than the state-required classes I took, I don't have any formal training in weaponry. Shooting is a hobby for me, something I picked up from friends as a teenager. I enjoy it, and I'm not a terrible shot, but I've never used firearms in a real-life survival situation.

I don't want to sleep here tonight, but I make up my mind that I'm not running either. I head into the bedroom, gather jeans, shirts, boxers, and socks from the dresser and closet, and start laying things out on the bed. I'll give myself a couple of nights in a hotel, and then I'll come back with a fresh perspective, prepared. I pack a suitcase with two days' worth of clothes and necessities, including my other two guns (a .35 caliber Remington rifle and a .22 caliber revolver) and several boxes of ammo. The Remington is a decent gun, the revolver not so much. It's more like a toy for a game of Wild West for adults, but it's small and light.

Driving away from the small house I rent, I check the rearview constantly like a hunted animal. Every white car screams at my subconscious. I hear noises like bullets clanging into water troughs, which are only creaky suspensions on fifth-wheel trailers or someone's squealing breaks.

My cell phone rings, and I hastily answer it before putting Kyle on speaker and setting the phone on my leg.

"Hey," I yell.

"Hey! Did you get your license yet?"

"Yeah," I say. "I'm 'carrying my piece.'"

We both laugh. Humor won't fix this mess, but it sure helps.

"You headed back home?" Kyle can tell I'm driving by all the road noise.

Paranoia grips me like someone bugged my phone. There's no reason to think so, but I'm not taking any chances. I'll make sure not to reveal too much in my mobile conversations until this whole thing blows over.

"No, just left. I'm on 35. I'm just getting some air," I say.

"Good deal," Kyle says. "Keep me posted. And keep your finger on the trigger."

6

TWELVE YEARS EARLIER

The year after high school graduation is arguably one of the worst of my life. I'm eighteen, and so is Mary Durham. In October, she tells me she's pregnant. We've always used protection, but here it is anyway. Now she's about four months along. Our parents are in a state of distress over the whole thing, but no one pushes us in any particular direction. Mary and I have been discussing what to do and haven't formed up any concrete plans either. Life seems surreal. I can't seem to face the shared responsibility of the situation we've created.

Mary stands in my room on a Saturday morning, pulling her thick, blonde hair into a messy bun. She's starting to show a little. We're going to meet some friends at noon for a barbecue, and I hope that no one will notice.

"Have you decided what to do about school?" she asks and sits on the edge of the bed.

Traces of her soft fragrance find me. Whatever she uses always reminds me of honeysuckles. Mary's face looks a little puffier than usual, and I wonder if that's from the pregnancy or due to some other reason.

"No. But I don't think I should quit," I say.

Staring at the floor, I rotate side to side in my swiveling desk chair. I haven't decided. My parents couldn't afford the University of Texas, but they enrolled me at Austin Community College in August, and I'm grateful for it. Besides, I can't say that I'm interested in a four-year degree from a big university. At ACC, I'm working toward an Associate of Applied Science Degree because I want to be an auto mechanic after school. I might work for a local shop for a while, then go freelance. I know a few guys who are self-employed or mobile mechanics, and it isn't unusual for them to make several hundred dollars per day. That won't be bad for doing work I enjoy, and having the degree will be beneficial if I ever want to change jobs or expand on what I'm already doing.

"Would it be better if you were closer to the campus?" Mary asks. She fiddles with the hem of her shirt. "My parents like you more than you realize. They're upset right now, but it'll pass." Her parents live not half a mile from the college.

"They like me?" I frown, halting the rolling, side-to-side motion of the chair. Mary's mom always appears tightly wound, and I can't get past Mr. Durham's stony-faced, unreadable aspect long enough to ever feel comfortable around him.

"They definitely do," she says, flashing me a grin. "If you move in with us, they'll warm up to you in time. It's just their way." Mary grabs one of my mashed pillows and fluffs it before smoothing out the case.

I shudder inside and return to my swiveling. "I don't know. Maybe."

She's fishing around for my full commitment in the matter. She always is, ever since she told me about the pregnancy. She's also insinuating that I need to either start working full-time or get a job outside school. I understand, and I'm aware of those options, but I haven't started looking yet.

"So," Mary says, pushing her lips into a full pout. "What are we going to do? I can only work at Cain and Abel's for a few more months. Then I'll have to take at least a month of maternity leave. I don't know if I can handle living with my parents alone during all this." She smiles weakly.

Neither of us wants to say it. Neither wants to ask the specific questions that need to be asked. Are we going to get married? How are we going to support ourselves and the baby?

"I don't know," I say. My stomach feels sick and empty. I have a sudden desire for elsewhere. "Let's talk about it after the barbecue."

"Okay," Mary says, feigning another smile. She gives the pillow a final end-to-end tug before returning it to the head of the bed.

When Mary stands, I look over her dark denim, boot-cut jeans, and loose-fitting peach top. Her shirt covers the long scar on her left bicep, the one she got during a childhood accident. More importantly, it also conceals her burgeoning womb. No one will notice anything.

~

THE BARBECUE IS a get-together of about fifty people from school and is taking place at Zilker Park. Even in October, here in Central Texas, the temperature rises to almost ninety degrees today. After arriving, it doesn't take long for Mary to begin chatting with girls she knows, and I locate Kyle and a few other familiar faces.

Never mind the fact that I'm not old enough to drink. The alcohol abounds, and I set about getting as much as I can get my hands on. Kyle and I throw back a few beers right off. Someone brings a flask and starts making strong drinks, even in this blazing heat. The smell of flame-grilled beef and sweet, hickory sauce wafting through the air makes it feel even hotter somehow. But we're young, and it seems like nothing. My gaze sweeps the crowd for Mary. I find her sitting with a small group by one of the trucks. She rests cross-legged in the grass, laughing with the other girls, and she seems to be enjoying herself. Being away from her brings me relief.

The bright afternoon sun casts long shadows behind the live oak tree I lean against. The rough bark presses small indentations into my back, but I don't care. From here, I have a decent view of Lady Bird Lake. I don't want to think of anything. I only want to drift off into the alcohol buzz and forget. I watch the sunlight make rows of diamonds on the water. I watch people paddle by in different colored canoes. I look for the half-submerged, rotted logs on which turtles like to line up and sun themselves.

Someone puts another drink in my hand. I look down at a red plastic cup filled with clearish, green liquid and ice. It tastes like lemon-lime soda and something else. Maybe vodka. All I know is that it's strong, and I doubt that alcohol is its only poison. I drink it down way too fast, thinking maybe it will cheer me up.

Those around me start to migrate toward the parking lot slowly. I stand up and know I'm hammered, so I just kind of tag along. I also know I must be forgetting something—someone?—but I can't grasp the thought. I laugh and talk, but I can't remember what I say or what we talk about.

Our group of roughly nine people splits into two vehicles. I cram into the back seat of a red coupe next to a dark-haired girl with black eyeliner and a low-cut, burnt orange tank top. Renee something. I breathe in her strong rose perfume. My leg presses against her shapely thigh, and somehow my arm finds its way around her shoulder.

The driver, a guy I don't know, navigates us out of the park and onto the interstate. By sunset, we're rolling through a different part of town. I make out what looks like hill country in the growing darkness, and I'm pretty sure we just crossed the 360 bridge. The scenery passes by in a blur of dark-hooded mounds covered in trees and wiry bushes. Our driver pulls into a posh neighborhood where every house is a sprawling mansion on a ridiculously expensive piece of Austin acreage. He stops the coupe at the end of someone's winding driveway.

Music trickles out of the house's windows like water from a fountain. I see the notes bubbling down and bursting on the cacti in planter sections near the front door. Landscape lighting in the trees and alongside the path glows in colorful patches of blue, gold, green, and red.

My head becomes heavy and starts throbbing with the beat of the bass from the stereo. Suddenly I realize I feel terrible. I think I might be sick. Crap, did I take drugs? I don't remember doing that. Wait, that drink—what the hell did they put in that drink?

No. No, I feel great—amazing. I've never felt like this. I need to relax and enjoy it. I'll watch the music some more. I'll watch those notes, the colors. I'm floating. I'll go inside to this party and have a good time. Where's that girl I came with? Oh, she's beside me, holding my hand. Right.

I CONFESS my sins to Mary, and my guilt drives me to drop out of ACC like I'm supposed to. I start working full-time at the Arbor Car Wash on Guadalupe. I still can't bring myself to move in with Mary and her parents, even though they offered. They're upset. Mary is upset. My own parents are upset, and it's essentially all my fault, or mostly.

"I'm sorry," I tell Mary. But after I tell her about seven times, I don't want to say it again.

Mary sits at the picnic table in her backyard, sobbing, and I sit opposite her. The smells of orchids and fresh-cut grass mock us. Mary's wearing a knee-length, pink cotton dress with an empire waistline—cute if I wasn't in such a terrible mood. Stiff and bitter, I shift my legs awkwardly on the bench. I know deep down that she hasn't done anything wrong, and she has the right to be hurt. Her life is ruined too.

"How could you do this? You said you loved me," she says.

"It was an accident. I wouldn't have done it if I was in my right mind. It'll never happen again," I say.

"Now what?" she almost screams. "What are we going to do, Trent? Are you just going to abandon me?" A flash of terror enters her eyes and then fades, replaced by anger and betrayal.

"No," I say firmly. "No. I'm working now. I'll make sure you and the baby have everything you need." I place my palms on the table as if this affirms my conviction.

Her eyes widen, softening in fleeting hopefulness. She blinks, a new thought clouding that hope, and she pulls her head back slightly. "So... are we together? Are you going to be helping me, or are we broken up, and you're just going to be giving me money out of obligation? What are we *doing*, Trent?"

"I—I don't know, I just—"

"Okay," she says, trying to compose herself. She sniffs and wipes the tears from her red cheeks. "I guess the question is, do you love me or not? I get that we're young. I totally get that. But if you love me, you'd choose to stick it out with me." She glares at me, unflinching.

I really thought I loved her. When I first told her that two years ago, I believed I meant it. But since she became pregnant, I don't know what happened. I don't feel the same way anymore, and I seem to have no control over these new emotions.

"I'm sorry," I say. And I am. "But I'll help you with the baby, at least financially. I'll take responsibility."

Mary bursts into a new wave of sobs which quickly turn into wild crying. She puts her hands into her hair and pulls them out again. She does this many times, making her hair a tangly mess.

"Oh my God," she says. "You're not taking responsibility for anything! I can't believe you would do this." Her chest heaves as she cries. I feel horrible and helpless, like toxic gas has entered my lungs and is suffocating me.

"I'm sorry," I say. I swore I would stop staying that.

Mary draws a deep breath and says in a broken voice, "If you're serious about leaving me, then at least talk to my parents. They thought we were going to get married."

"I understand, but it's not their decision. It's between you and me," I say. I slide off the bench and stand up.

Mary swings her legs out and leaps to her feet after me. "Then I decide 'no!' Please don't do this. They'll be so upset. I know raising a baby will be hard, but it'll still be easier together. And my parents will help us."

I shake my head, the tiredness, and strain overtaking me. At the same time, what she said irritates me. "Your parents will be upset? Well, they're not too happy now. Mine aren't either."

"They're much happier knowing we're together," Mary says, wrapping her arms around herself. "They don't want me to be a single mother."

"I understand that," I say. "But this isn't about your parents, or mine, and how they feel. They'll just have to deal with it."

Backing up closer to the picnic table, she narrows her eyes. She huffs. "You're heartless. You truly are."

I walk toward her so she can hear me better. "I'm not. I care about you, and I'm going to help. But I'm not going to play-act for your family and pretend to be someone I'm not," I say.

Mary says, "Why can't you just do this one thing for me? You said you loved me, and if you didn't lie, then you'll stay, and we'll work through this together."

I sigh, my posture sagging. "It's not that simple."

"It is, Trent. It literally is." Facing me, she flops back down on the bench with her legs on the outside. Her back hits the tabletop edge, knocking her empty plastic cup to the ground.

"Mary, I can't. Please try to understand that it wouldn't work. It doesn't mean I'm abandoning you. It just means I can't be with you in that way right now," I say.

"I don't understand you at all," Mary says. She leans an elbow on the wooden table and slouches.

"I know," I say. "I don't fully understand myself. I'm just trying to be honest. That's what I would want."

"Oh, for God's sake! You're not the one who's pregnant. You don't know what you would want. You wouldn't want to be a single mom. I'll tell you that."

She has me there. I can't dispute it, and I don't want to. "You're right. Look, I have to go. If you need to call me for anything, you can."

Her mouth drops open, and she sits bolt upright. "How can I call you if you're breaking up with me?"

My patience is stretched to a thin thread, and it finally snaps. "On your phone." I turn to go.

Mary rushes toward me, her flip-flops slapping the bottoms of her feet. She grabs my arm with warm, moist fingers, close enough now that her honeysuckle scent envelopes me. "Don't leave me. How about we just date sometimes? We don't have to live together. Please, Trent." She squeezes my bicep with both hands and pulls me toward her.

My heart starts racing, and I swallow down a sour taste in my mouth. "I can't."

"Can't or *won't*?" she asks.

I don't have an answer. Forcing out a breath, I try to pull

away gently, but Mary digs her nails into my arm. It stings, and I twitch. I jerk my arm away and storm toward the backyard gate.

"I'll never forgive you for this," she says.

I don't turn around. Without another word, I walk around to the front where my beater car is parked, and I drive home.

Five months later, Mary delivers our baby.

7

JANUARY 18TH

Three days after the shooting, I finally spoke to Tim. After paying his speeding ticket plus additional fines and undergoing interrogation, the sheriff's office released him on lack of evidence for the crimes committed on his property. He kept apologizing to me. He was embarrassed by what took place, for my accidental involvement, and now my lack of a job, but at least I wasn't in the slammer for four days. Tim told me that he hopes I'll consider taking my job back when all this blows over. I want to.

That conversation was over a week ago now. Back home, I sit on the couch and follow the story of the victims online from my phone. There aren't nearly as many postings as I expect, especially considering the gruesome nature of the offenses. The most recent article from today, January 18th, yields the most fruitful information yet.

Possible suspect in Williamson County homicide in custody.

Williamson County (KXAV) — A possible suspect in the County Road 140 case, which left one woman dead and another in critical condition, has been taken into custody. Emile Richard Woodard, 43, of Travis County, was arrested on separate charges of attempted murder of a different Williamson County resident two weeks ago. Officials have not determined if the crimes are related. However, Woodard meets an eyewitness description of the shooter.

One of the female victims in the County Road 140 case has been identified. Carol Brandt, 46, of Round Rock, was identified posthumously. Her cause of death was determined to be due to multiple injuries, including head trauma, spinal damage, and starvation. The surviving victim, a still unidentified female in her early twenties, remains in critical condition at St. David's Hospital in Georgetown.

Hospital officials say that the young woman's injuries are still life-threatening. The woman sustained multiple stab wounds and heavy blood loss. Officials responded in the affirmative that this victim was also sexually assaulted.

Sheriff Marcus Gonzales told KXAV that no fingerprints were found in the abandoned house where the two victims were discovered but that DNA samples were taken. Those samples will be compared with Woodard's DNA for a possible match.

Detectives are asking anyone with information on these crimes to call their tip line at...

The top of the article includes a photo of the suspect, presumably the guy who tried to kill me at Tim's ranch. This man grooms his beard a lot shorter, but it's still there, and he doesn't have the sunglasses on. He has thick, black eyebrows and dark eyes. Can I be certain this is the man since I wasn't up close when I first saw him? No. But it might be him. Probably is.

The surviving woman must be in a coma or similar state if they still don't know who she is. It's a given that they wouldn't have found her with ID, but unless she has amnesia, she would have told them her name.

I close my phone's browser and lean back against the cushion. My heart rate has mostly slowed to something like normal. For the first week after my attack, my trigger finger itched to shoot anything that moved. After my two-day reprieve at the Holiday Inn, I bought groceries and readied myself to hole up in the house except for job-hunting days or when I'm scheduled to work at the gas station. So, I've been here, holing up. I figure if I anticipate getting attacked again, it's going to be on my terms. So far, nothing has happened. Maybe the guy they arrested today really is our man.

Since reading the latest news article, I plan to give Tim a call at the end of the weekend. Today is Saturday, and if things are still good tomorrow, there should be no problem returning to work on Monday. With the shooter in custody and no incident in two weeks, there's no longer a need for concern. My life will go back to normal now—my normal, pointless, but safe life.

That night I fall asleep hard with no dreams. At about 1:30 a.m., I wake with a start and sit up in bed. A chill races over my exposed skin. My arms and back are stiff from lying on my side too long. A cloak of quiet blankets the house. I listen for anything outside but hear nothing, not even a breeze. My mind hands me a lovely picture of the young woman's hanging, blood-streaked body, and that horrible stench of feces and decayed flesh seems real again, though it lingers only as a memory now. I can see the matted hair over the girl's grime-covered, sallow face when the EMTs carried her out on the stretcher. And all the blood, the darkness of it, so red and thick. My psyche was unprepared for the stark reality of discovering the broken woman—stabbed, despoiled, and strung up like a voodoo doll.

This is it, my mind says to me. *This is what you're supposed to remember.*

I curse and shove the blankets off in a heap before pushing myself out of bed. I turn on the lights and check to make sure my 9mm still lies next to the pillow, which it does. I turn the light back off and let my eyes adjust to the dark again. I look outside through each window in turn. Nothing. I peer out at my truck which appears undisturbed. The porch light still glows, and my Silverado remains just as I left it. Everything is fine. I just woke up from all the stress. I guess even after two weeks, my body is still running on high alert.

I flip the lights back on, go into the kitchen, and turn those lights on too. I'll just catch some late-night TV until I get sleepy again. I'm wide awake, too mentally active to lie down, and now I realize I'm starving. I retrieve a soft drink from the fridge, but there's nothing ready to eat in the pantry. Well, it's no wonder since I haven't been shopping in two weeks.

Tucking my 9mm in its hiding place beneath my coat, I drive to the gas station by the 130 toll road and buy a few bags of snacks. When I return home, I turn off the truck's engine and sit listening. Still quiet. I lock the pickup, set the alarm, and go inside, and after I lock the door again, I make another sweep of my surroundings. Everything checks out, so I stretch out on the couch and find a sitcom to focus on. I eat an entire bag of sour cream and onion chips.

Somewhere around 3:30 a.m., my eyes get heavy, and I drag myself back to bed. I leave the 9mm in its holster but carry it into the bedroom and set it on the dresser. I collapse back into a heavy sleep. It feels good to sleep again.

Some kind of noise shakes me awake. I can't make it out. A door closing? A window rattling? I don't know, but I rise to full consciousness in about three seconds. When I turn on the lights, I immediately see that my 9mm and holster are gone from the dresser. I bolt out of bed in a heart-pounding panic.

Someone is in the house. Someone is in here.

My Remington rifle is in the truck. The .22 revolver should still be under the bed. Don't know how much good it will do me, but it's better than nothing. I start to reach down but change my mind and back up, looking under the bed first. I lift the duffle bag that hides the gun. The revolver is still there. I whisk it out and turn off the safety. This little gun, one I use to shoot cans on the weekend, against a 9mm. What a sad day.

I check the closet in the bedroom first. Empty. Then I check the living room, behind the couch, and the hall closet. I survey the kitchen, a place with nowhere to hide anyway. I creep up to the bathroom, the door resting half-open. I kick it with my foot, and it bangs hard against the wall, rebounding back at me as I throw my body into the space and aim the gun at the bathtub. It's also empty. There's nowhere else inside the house where someone could hide.

The front and back doors are both still locked. I'll need to inspect all the windows. Still carrying the gun, I go back into the bedroom and get my gloves off the dresser. If there are any fingerprints, I don't want to smear them. In less than a minute, I check all the windows, but every one of them is locked.

I wipe the cold sweat off my face, and the blood pumps loudly in my ears. I go back into the bedroom and recheck the dresser. I swear I left the 9mm there. I know it was there. What if I was so tired that I actually left it in the truck? On the couch? Maybe I took the holster off there instead.

The gun and holster aren't on the couch, and I can't find my truck keys. However the bastard did it, he broke into my house. I need to call the sheriff's office. My mind snaps to the next logical object—my cell phone. I also took it into the bedroom and left it charging the same as I do every night. My stomach plummets as I search my room, but like the 9mm, my mobile is gone. I bring my fist down on the dresser, making a haphazard pile of change scatter. As the pennies and nickels tumble to the floor, I curse the son of a bitch who did this. I scour the whole house but don't find the phone.

Thinking quickly, I open a drawer and pull out my tablet. I don't use it that often, but my devices are synced, and I have an app that can locate my phone. As I turn it on and wait for it to boot up, I think about how I can call the authorities and what I'll say when I do. The early model tablet can't make phone calls, maybe not even to 911—but I might be able to do it via another app since I have Wi-Fi.

With shaking hands, I pull off my gloves and enter my passcode to unlock the tablet. I open the find-my-phone app, and it starts searching, the compass icon swinging back and forth. Maybe I left my mobile in my truck during my late-night snack run. Maybe.

The compass disappears, and the screen shows a map. In the center of the map, a symbol for my cell rotates, putting out a radiant signal that indicates the phone is still turned on. The map isn't accurate to the point of giving addresses, but it clearly shows the street names. I can see the cell phone's location. My breath lodges in my throat, and I cough.

County Road 140.

Whoever did this went through an awful lot of trouble. Not only did this guy break into my house and take my belongings, but he also set this ridiculous trap that I'm supposed to be stupid enough to fall right into. Why am I worth that much hassle? While I slept, he could have fired all fourteen rounds from my pistol and decorated the walls with my brain. Or he could have done something far worse—something not so quick. The thought sends an icy, bone-deep chill through my body. No, he wants to play games instead.

I search again for my truck keys, but now I'm sure those are gone too. At this point, I almost expect it. I left them on the dresser next to my missing 9mm. That key chain also holds my house keys and a couple of keys for outbuildings on Tim's ranch. At least the keys going missing explains why the house doors are still locked. He must have locked them after he left—to dick with me, I assume.

Now, with fear and confusion pinning me down, it starts to sink in. It's a trap, but not necessarily one designed merely to get me killed. It might be to frame me, or for some other purpose I haven't conceived of.

I have to sit down on the edge of the bed, hands on my knees, eyes aimed at the floor, and figure out what to do. I need to think. After a minute, I grab my tablet and open the FaceTime app. I'll try 911.

As the app starts opening, an instant message pops up. The loud *ding* sends a shockwave through my torso and makes my rear shoot right off the bed.

Devices are mirrored. Call and she dies.

I almost drop the tablet. Staring at the words, I keep thinking, "Who?" over and over again. If I call the cops, she'll die. But who is *she*?

The sender shows as 842-251. It means nothing to me.

My heart hammers like a war drum. I close the app. I try to steady my shaking arms and quit hyperventilating. What the hell am I going to do? I don't have a spare phone, and I've never used a landline since I moved out of my parents' house as a teenager.

However, I did place a spare key in a magnetic box on the undercarriage of my Silverado as a precaution if I ever locked myself out. I put it there when I lived in Austin, so unless the guy searched under there with a flashlight—thoroughly—the key should still be there. If that's true, then the intruder didn't tamper with the truck's contents, and my rifle is still inside. Transportation and a decent weapon.

I can drive to Tim's or the gas station and call the sheriff's office from there. I'll have to explain that while I slept, someone broke into my tiny house without me hearing anything and took my 9mm and my truck keys. To cap it, he stole my cell phone from its place next to my pillow and stashed it in the house on County Road 140. Give me a break.

But that isn't even the worst part. This guy won't see me calling the cops from my tablet, but the police will still show up at the murder house in response. Will he then kill "her" anyway?

If I don't call law enforcement, I can drive to the property in some blind, vigilante crusade, walk right into his trap, and suffer the consequences. Then it will be a nearby rancher or passerby calling the cops. When they arrive, I'll probably be named suspect number one in the case—this, of course, is assuming I'll live to be a suspect after visiting a murderer. I wonder if the man taken into custody yesterday was released. I try to guess at the likelihood of him being the same guy who's messing with me tonight. There's no way to know if the cops discharged Woodard unless I ask.

Deputy Reyes is the best person to contact. If I tell him exactly what happened, he'll believe me, maybe. He'll know how to proceed. He came to help me the day of the shooting. However, he didn't actually observe the attack. What he did observe was my busted-up truck window and me as a restless ball of nerves.

To hell with it, I have to call someone. I'll drive to the gas station and call Reyes from the office. I have his number in quick contacts on my smartphone, which doesn't help now, but he also gave me his business card. My stomach gives another short dive as I think of my wallet—I'd bet a two-dollar bill it's missing as well. I dart to the coffee table where I left it, and alarm sweeps through me when I see it still resting there. It's right next to my empty bag of potato chips that still smells like sour cream and onion. He hasn't taken it.

Why? I pick it up and rifle through it. The money remains in the billfold, and my credit card, Visa debit, driver's and concealed handgun licenses, and apparently everything else that should be there, is. Just not the one thing I need at this moment, Reyes's card.

I throw the wallet hard, watching it smack against the wall before it falls. "You son of a bitch! You goddamn son of a bitch!"

I slam my fist down on the coffee table. I don't know who this guy is, but he can't do this. Not to me. I dress for the weather and put on my steel-toed, brown work boots. I take my revolver and its case of ammo, along with my tablet. I turn it off so he can't track me. If the police advise, I'll turn it back on again to confirm my phone's location—that is, as long as the thief allows me to.

I open the front door. The freezing, cedar-scented air hits me as I do a sweep of my surroundings within my field of vision. I do the same thing around back. After giving the space underneath the truck a quick inspection, I drop to my knees. The sharp gravel presses into my gloves. I look for the small, magnetic key case that should still be stuck to the chassis. It's there.

With a sigh of relief, I unlock the door of the Silverado. I put my things inside, noting that the Remington and all my ammo are where I left them. There are other things too, things that are just good to have—extra socks for work, another jacket, a couple of old shirts that I can get extra dirty or use as rags. The undisturbed pickup interior calms me slightly. I should settle down. After I call the police, maybe I can go back to the hotel and give Kyle a ring in the morning. I know his number by heart, and he might have some level-headed advice. Well, I can guarantee that he will.

With my unsteady hand, I put the key in the ignition and turn it. The engine makes no sound, not even a click. The lights won't come on. I grip the steering wheel way too hard, my blood pressure rising and my temples pounding like I might explode. He really went all out. I must really be special. Special, special me.

I take a small, silver flashlight from the glove compartment and pull the hood release. It sounds odd to me like it isn't releasing the latch, or like maybe the hood is already open. Upon inspection outside, I find the hood was forced open with something, leaving the metal badly damaged. When I lift it to have a look at the engine, the empty space which used to contain the battery yawns up at me. "Moron," the empty space seems to say.

Using the bright beam of the flashlight in the surrounding darkness, I check out the rest of the engine the best I can. It doesn't appear that anything else was tampered with, nothing I can see. He must be banking on me not having a spare battery lying around. He banked right.

The hood won't close properly now, but since the truck isn't drivable, I'll deal with it later. I lock the doors and go into the house for more provisions. This is the moment when I know something is really wrong with me, deep down. Scared out of my wits while raging pissed at the same time, I'm crazy enough to do what I do next. And the rush feels good. Really good.

8

TWELVE YEARS EARLIER

In the maternity ward of Seton Medical Center on West 38th Street, colorless hallways, fluorescent lights, and a relentless parade of anxiety keep me company as I shiver on the hard, plastic waiting-room chair. The odors of disinfectant and isopropyl alcohol linger oppressively. I know that on the other side of the wall, the glass doors and windows of the hospital begin revealing the outside world. The soft light of dawn paints a lavender and gold backdrop behind the office buildings of downtown Austin. Pedestrians, cyclists, college students, and steady streams of traffic all appear with the new sunrise of another day. But I can't see any of that. My entire world is gray.

I was right that Mary and I would continue to see each other, even though we aren't together now. My several mistakes and the regret I harbor over each one have pushed me to try harder. I can't make myself feel the way she wants me to feel, but I can still take responsibility within my means.

Five months after I quit ACC, I'm still working full-time,

and I have my own apartment, albeit an affordable one in a not-so-great part of town. I'm locked into a two-year lease, but at least I behave like an adult now. I haven't gone to any parties or done anything stupid since my big screw-up at the barbecue last fall. My steady paychecks from Arbor Car Wash ensure that Mary can buy what she needs for the baby —a little girl, we found out.

Mr. Durham sits beside me in the waiting area, silent and pasty white. He does not look at me. Mary's mother stays in the delivery room with her daughter. Mary doesn't want me there, and I'm fine with that. My parents asked if I would have liked them to be here, but I said no, I'd rather they weren't. There's no need for them to drive down from Dallas, and the fewer accusing stares I have to deal with, however subtle they might be, the better.

Trent Lemend, at the age of eighteen, is going to be a father. I roll it around in my head, trying to grasp its full magnitude, but I can't. I thumb through magazines and set them down. I play a game on my rudimentary, early model cell phone. I try to sleep sitting upright in the chair but only succeed in closing my eyes and listening to my mind race. Soon, Mary will have the baby. It will be the "this is it" moment. We'll have a child to raise, and I'll learn all about parenthood and assume my new role, and have a completely different life, whatever that means.

The maternity doctor, whose name I haven't bothered to remember, comes through the swinging, double doors with a half-masked look of dread on his face. Panic sweeps through me. He motions for Mr. Durham and me to go over there, away from the waiting area. Mr. Durham's face loses even more color than before, which doesn't seem possible.

"Mary's doing fine," Doctor says in answer to Mr.

Durham's unasked question. "The delivery went well. Your daughter did great." He pushes the corners of his mouth into a smile.

Mr. Durham doesn't answer, but he stops holding his breath.

The doctor continues. "I'm sorry, but I do have some bad news. The baby was stillborn. We tried everything we could, but her heart wasn't beating, and she wasn't getting any oxygen in the womb." He waits to see how Mr. Durham will respond.

Blood surges back into the man's drawn face. "How is she —how is my daughter taking it?"

"She's having a hard time right now. But her mom is there with her. She's being a great support. It's usually pretty difficult for a mother to lose a child, even if the pregnancy was unplanned. It's just part of a woman's natural instinct. But Mary seems like a strong young lady. She'll pull through just fine."

"All right. Thank you, Doctor," Mr. Durham says. He looks like he just found out he isn't being called back into active duty after all. "Will you let me know when I can see her?"

"We sure will. You can also have the nurse at the desk check from time to time."

Mr. Durham nods, and he and Doc shake hands. They addressed no part of the conversation to me. They deem my involvement here inconsequential, apparently, and that should bother me.

But as I go back to the waiting area and sit down, some of the stiffness comes out of my back and arms. I stretch my limbs and start to relax. The heavy, burdensome weight upon my shoulders begins to lift, and the waves of relief keep coming and coming. I'm finding solace in my gray-walled prison. I'm glad—glad the child arrived stillborn. I'm a terrible person. I'm happy that I don't have to be a father now.

Several hours later, I straighten in surprise when the nurse tells me Mary has asked to see me. I swallow. I wonder if the bad taste in my mouth stems from more than vending machine garbage. Mr. Durham glares in my direction as I stand up rigidly and follow the nurse into the private room where Mary is resting.

Mary's blonde hair hangs in tangled, sweaty tendrils, and she has dark circles under her puffy, red eyes. A bag of intravenous fluid dangles on a rolling stand next to the bed. The tubing leads down to her arm. She mumbles something to her mother, and the older woman gets up to leave the room. A soft light in Mrs. Durham's eyes portrays an understanding of the situation, as well as her daughter's pain.

"Hi," Mary says. "Thanks for coming in."

"You're welcome. How are you doing?" I offer a weak smile.

She takes a shaky breath, shuddering as though she's about to cry. "I'm okay. I just—" With a wet sniff, tears spill down her cheeks in a stream. "I didn't expect any of this. I didn't think it would be this hard."

"I know," I manage, having no idea what to say. I fumble around for the right words, wanting to be understanding. "It's such a shock. It's awful. I'm sorry you had to go through that."

Mary wipes her face with a tissue from the box. "Thanks. You can sit with me." She motions to the chair where her mother was seated.

I nod and sit down next to her. Her sheets smell faintly of

chlorine, but otherwise, the room doesn't quite smell fresh. I can't pinpoint the odor. We make small talk for a bit to lighten the mood, after which Mary tells me the particulars of her labor and what the doctor said about our stillborn baby. Then with no explanation, she reaches out and laces her fingers between mine.

"Trent," she says. "I know a lot has happened and... I know this is a bad time and everything. And I'm not saying we have to talk about it now. But maybe things happen for a reason. Maybe because this happened—" She shudders with another suppressed sob. "Maybe when things calm down a little, we could start over."

I'm not prepared. Not for this. As soon as the words come out of Mary's mouth, the previous relief that sated me begins to deflate. I'm walking back into the prison cell with a bayonet at my back. What am I going to say? I'm supposed to reject her, here in this hospital room, during her trauma after giving birth to a stillborn baby? Mary's blue eyes beg for succor as I stall for an answer to her question. Her request to start over isn't unreasonable. I remember her parents outside in the waiting room.

"Yes, let's try it," I say. "Let's just take it slow, okay?"

Mary's face breaks into a broad smile, a tear dripping from her eyelashes as she squeezes my hand. "Okay. We can do that."

DESPITE THE INESCAPABLE discomfort that presses me on all sides, I squeeze myself into the self-created mold. Mary and I are in our "clean slate" phase, and she doesn't know how far into my corner I've trapped myself.

About two weeks after Mary's hospital stay, I join her and her parents for dinner. My attendance is mandatory. Mary makes that clear. Her family is holding the dinner in their formal dining room, complete with a cowhide rug and large, lacquered cypress mirrors on both sides of the wall. Despite Mary's periodic bouts of depression due to our stillborn baby, she's doing well and recovering quickly. Getting back together seemed to ignite some sense of hope and fulfillment for her. No one says so, but I guess the dinner is Mary's way of celebrating that the situation isn't a total loss.

Mr. and Mrs. Durham sit on one side of the long, mahogany table, and Mary and I are seated across from them. Their daughter smiles at me from time to time, and I do my best to smile back. The smells of savory mushroom gravy and orange wood cleaner blend as awkwardly as the company.

"So, Trent," Mrs. Durham says. She cuts her meat with a black-handled knife and tries to sound cheerful. "Do you think you might go back to school now?"

It takes me a minute to answer because my immediate reaction is anger. "I don't know. After I dropped out, I signed a two-year lease at my apartment. If I quit my job, I would have to break my lease. That will make it nearly impossible to get an apartment in the future, not to mention that it will damage my credit. But if I don't quit my job, since I'm working full-time during the day, I won't be available for classes." I try not to sound bothered by all this, but I know I don't manage it completely.

Mrs. Durham kind of nods and makes a guttural noise. She pretends to be giving the matter some thought while she chews her steak. It is a decent steak, after all.

"Maybe you could take classes at night," Mr. Durham

says. His eyes tell me that my misfortune is a small price to pay for what I put his daughter through.

"Maybe so," I say. I bite into a piece of well-cooked garlic asparagus.

My parents might not go for the idea of paying for tuition again, especially since they could barely cover it last time. I'll have to cough up every penny in addition to the expenses I already have. Since I make scarcely more than minimum wage, this doesn't seem too likely.

"Mary's going to be starting at UT next fall," he says. He grins smugly and sips his iced tea.

"Dad," Mary chides. Then to me, she says, "I'm still thinking about it, honestly."

"Well, there's nothing to think about," Mr. Durham says. "We have the money, and we don't want you to miss this opportunity."

"Thanks, Dad," Mary says. A little embarrassed, she tucks a stray lock of blonde hair behind her ear. "I admit, I would like to get a degree in nursing."

"What would you like to be, Trent?" Mrs. Durham asks. "I mean, what was it that you were going to school for, again?"

"I wanted to be a mechanic," I say. "I think it would be nice to do it freelance. I was also thinking of expanding on it down the road. Maybe get a Bachelor's in mechanics and work for one of the big auto companies."

"Oh, right, mechanics," Mr. Durham says. "You know, I have a nephew who's a mechanic. He's thinking about going back to school too." He tacks on a sardonic grin, just to be sure I get it.

I stop chewing and look at him. So, he's trying to say that his nephew isn't making enough money in my chosen field, so he needs to further his education to get ahead? What a sad way to insult me.

The woody part of the asparagus spear sticks in my throat. "Good for him," I croak.

"You know, you could always get a student loan. And there's the Pell grant," he continues.

"I'm sure Trent will figure out the right thing to do," Mary says. She twirls her fork in her mashed potatoes. Her smile from earlier has faded.

"I'm sure he will," Mr. Durham says. "Well, now that you and Mary have decided to get back together, what other plans do you have for your life?"

His wife looks up from her plate and frowns, giving her husband a sidelong glance.

"Too much has happened recently," I say. "Once things settle down, I can start planning again."

Mary's father huffs, his fork clattering onto his plate when he releases it too soon. "Things have settled down now, son. She lost the baby. What else is there to settle down?"

"Patrick!" Mrs. Durham says.

"No," he says. He addresses his wife but focuses on me. "I'm tired of dancing around this subject for fear of hurting this young man's feelings. It's time for him to answer up. Now I want to know, what are your intentions for my daughter? Are you planning on getting engaged—are you planning on getting married one day? Or are you just biding your time, stringing her along until you can make your escape?"

A ball drops into my stomach. He knows. I don't know how he knows, but he does. Not only am I not in it one hundred percent with his daughter, but I'm barely in it at all.

Mary gasps and clutches her crumpled cloth napkin. "Dad!"

"Let's talk about this some other time," Mrs. Durham says. "Let's just enjoy our dinner together."

"No. Not some other time. Now," her husband says.

"Patrick!" Mrs. Durham repeats.

"Answer the question," he says. "What are your intentions for my daughter?"

I hold his gaze, knowing that I better answer honestly. Calmly, I say, "I have never had any bad intentions toward your daughter. We were together for two years. I told her that I loved her, and I did."

"Oh, you did?" Mr. Durham snaps.

"We always used protection. We were never irresponsible about it," I say.

"But this was more than you bargained for, wasn't it? What's your excuse now? The baby didn't make it," says Mary's dad.

Mrs. Durham sighs and puts her hands over her face while Mary sits beside me, unable to speak. I can't stand it another minute.

"If you think I'm not good enough, then why do you want me to marry your daughter? That doesn't make any sense. You hate me, you think I'm irresponsible, but you want me to propose to her? I quit school! I got a job. I was giving Mary nearly half my income for the baby. And now I'm a loser because I'm not back in school? But you still want me to marry your daughter?" My hands rest on the dark tabletop as I grip the utensils with white knuckles.

"Life isn't fair, is it?" That's what the old bastard says to me.

Yeah, you're damn right. It isn't fair. Not fair that we used protection every time, and she still got pregnant. Not fair that when she told me, I didn't feel the same way about her, and I had no idea why. Not fair that Mary lost the baby when she seemed to have wanted her. And not fair that I'm being held to some unattainable standard that isn't even being named.

But I don't say any of that. I turn to Mary and put my hand on her shoulder. "I'm really sorry, but I have to go."

"I'm so sorry, Trent," she whispers, as though her dad can't hear her. "He doesn't hate you. He really does like you. He's just angry—"

"I know," I say. "I have to go."

A WEEK LATER, I get a call from Mary's mother while I'm cleaning the spark plugs of my dented, blue Saturn in the parking lot of my apartment complex. I set the wire brush beside the vise-grip pliers on the spread-out newspaper and answer the phone. The voice on the line isn't in Mrs. Durham's usual pleasant and gracious tone. She sounds strained and tired.

"Trent, Mary is very sick. I wanted to let you know. She wanted me to tell you."

Holding my cell between my ear and shoulder, I wipe the black dust from my fingers with a cotton rag. "I'm sorry to hear that. What does she have?"

"She has something you probably haven't heard of before. It isn't common for women in first-world countries. She has something called 'postpartum sepsis.' Sometimes people call this 'blood poisoning.' It's an inflammatory response due to an infection from delivery."

After rising from my makeshift seat on the wheel stop, I lean my backside against the front bumper. The hood is propped up, and an indistinct smell of old engine oil touches my nose. I don't reply because I don't understand. Mary delivered almost a month ago now.

Mrs. Durham continues. "This is a very bad infection that women can get up to six weeks after they have a baby. And I thought you should know. I think it's important that you understand she's extremely ill. It isn't looking good."

I clear my throat and slowly walk over to the bench by the office, where I sit. I haven't seen or spoken to Mary or her parents since the day we had dinner when Mr. Durham gave me a piece of his mind.

"Are you trying to tell me that her life is in danger?" I ask.

"Yes," she says. "Unfortunately, that's what I'm telling you."

My tongue is made of lead, but I need to say something. "What could cause something like this? I thought everything in the hospital was sterile."

"We don't know exactly, but different things can cause it. Contaminated instruments at the hospital, dirty clothing. Even sex can cause it," Mrs. Durham says.

"Oh no," I say. "We never did that after she had the baby. I never touched her—I mean, not like that. We held hands and kissed sometimes."

I don't add that before I ended things—the second time —I wanted to, even though I didn't actually want to be with Mary anymore. I did want to have sex since I was a raging adolescent ball of hormones.

"Well, whatever the reason, the antibiotics aren't working," Mrs. Durham says. "So, if you want to see her, now is the time."

Her words are like a hangman kicking the box out from under my feet while I swing to and fro by the neck, asphyxiating. This is my chance to see Mary before she dies.

"Oh my God. Yeah, of course. Is she at the same hospital? What room is she in?" My forehead starts to bead with sweat, and my stomach knots into a dense ball. I get up and jog to my apartment for a pen and paper.

Mrs. Durham gives me the information I need, which I note down, and I thank her for calling me. The rest of the day is a blur, aside from reading about postpartum sepsis on the internet. I sit at the kitchen island and scroll through articles on my phone. I want to gain an understanding of why this is happening. I don't find it. I decide that I'll go to the hospital first thing in the morning, after a good night's sleep, when I have a clear head.

At night, I lie on my right side for a while. Then I roll over to my left, then back to my right side again, and repeat this pattern endlessly. No sleeping position is comfortable, no matter how I stretch my legs. Mary's face looms in my mind, but I still can't feel much of anything for her—not what I'm supposed to feel. I don't want her to be sick. I don't want her to die, but I can't make myself love her. I get not one hour of sleep, and at 5:30 a.m., I kick the blankets off, get out of bed, and shower.

After getting dressed and eating a quick oatmeal breakfast, I go to work instead of calling in due to the emergency. At Arbor Car Wash on Guadalupe, I drag the long-handled brush across a green coupe's hood and drip bubble-gum scented soap on my trousers. Tired and soaking wet, I find myself completely unwilling to go to the hospital. No matter the actual reason for Mary's illness, I have to accept the fact that her parents blame me for it, at least partially. The hours roll by, and the morning turns into afternoon. Afternoon turns into evening, and I go straight home. I don't leave my apartment.

Three days pass, and I don't go to see Mary. Mrs. Durham doesn't call again. At 6:00 a.m. on day four, when my alarm startles me awake, I finally resolve that I'm not going. I can't, and won't, face them—Mary and her family with their accusing glares and condescending blame. I tell myself it's for the best because Mary won't want to see me anyway after everything that went down this past year. I'm doing the right thing. I might not love her, but I still care for her, and I'll let her have some peace during her illness. Besides, she only has an infection, and infections are treatable. The doctors don't know that she'll die. She'll probably be fine.

9

JANUARY 19TH

I plan on doing something my man won't expect. With a small bag packed, including my switched-off tablet, a few bottles of water, snacks, and my .22 revolver, just in case, I start walking to the gas station where I work. From the back office where the latent odors of burned nacho cheese and cheap hand soap still reach me, I call the non-emergency number for the Williamson County Sheriff's Office. I stand beside the desk with the black landline phone in my hand. After I briefly explain things to the woman who answers, she gives me Reyes's cell number. He picks up after two rings, and I tell him everything. He tries to allay my concerns, explaining that he'll send out a special team of officers who are trained in handling these types of situations. He tells me I haven't endangered anyone by calling him.

"If there is a girl, she has more chance of survival with us knowing. You did the right thing," he says. "But don't go home. Can you go to a friend's house?"

I can. That's what a normal person would do. But I don't

want to wake Kyle at this hour, and Tim has been through enough. And I'm already sick of running and hiding.

"Maybe," I say. "I'm going to the store for a new battery first." I pace as much as the cord will allow.

"Fine," the deputy says. "Leave your tablet off. We'll get deputies out to County Road 140 as soon as we can. If something else happens, you dial 911 first. You can call me too, but I can't always answer right away. Don't wait for me to call back."

My insides squirm as we hang up. The situation feels impossible to me. My call to the police may still mean that she, whoever she is, will die. That's assuming the murderer captured another girl at all. It's painful not knowing.

My hand trembles as I call a cab to take me to the nearest twenty-four-hour retail store. It's ten miles away, and walking is out of the question. I pay the taxi driver to wait for me while I shop. I buy a new battery, beef jerky, trail mix, other snacks, a twelve-pack of bottled water, and a case of Coke. The other thing I buy is a cheap, prepaid phone. The cab pulls into the gravel drive leading to my house as the first rays of golden rose sunlight touch the horizon. Maybe I'll be lucky and get a sunny day for once.

"Can you wait a few minutes before you go?" I ask the driver. "Been having trouble with trespassers lately. I'll be right back to pay."

He sighs, raising an eyebrow before he turns to stare straight ahead at the dashboard again.

Still running on only a few hours of sleep, I set my bags down outside the door and draw out my revolver but keep it in front of me so the driver can't see it. I left the doors unlocked since my keys are gone. I turn on all the lights and scour the house again for an intruder. Finding no one,

I pay the taxi driver and set about the next part of my plan.

Sitting on the edge of the bed to catch my breath, I text Reyes my temporary number from the phone I bought. Part of me wants him to text back that he's already caught the guy. The other, more questionable part hopes he doesn't. I'm reluctant to admit that I'm more than just pissed. I want a chance to look, to see not only what this monster wants me to see but what he's hiding. Why the County Road 140 house again, and why me?

After ten minutes with no response, I put my supplies, snacks, and drinks in the truck, along with a few other odds and ends I might need. I install the new battery, and my Silverado starts right up.

"Moron," I say out loud.

The grim desire to check my cell phone's location once more seizes me, but I don't obey. After setting my switched-off tablet on the passenger seat, I put my truck in gear, roll down the gravel driveway, and pull onto the narrow country road. I have a new surge of adrenaline, a second wind. Within five minutes, I turn onto County Road 140.

The sunny day I wished for has materialized. As I draw closer to my destination, I pass a herd of Texas Longhorn cattle grazing in their bright pasture between islands of brittle prickly pear. I feel better already. My nerve is holding out.

Tim's weathered, old house comes into view, and I put my sunglasses and ball cap on. I drive past the property and regard it from the corner of my eye. I expect to see the yellow police tape flapping above the sagging barbed wire by the roadside, but after two weeks, it's gone. Nothing else looks different, and I don't see a vehicle. It's going on two hours since I talked to Reyes. He or the other deputies that responded to the call have probably already come and gone. If they found anyone, they'd probably still be here, so I wonder at the absence of police cruisers. I'll give it time and make sure.

As I continue, I take stock of the properties after the former crime scene house. I note their terrain, which ones have trees near the road and which ones don't. I drive a good half mile past Tim's property before turning around. I head toward the abandoned house and pass it, but I take my truck off the road and into the grass near the adjoining ranch. A grove of red cedar trees and a few pines cluster to the right, and they'll work fine for cover. The guy probably left a long time ago—unless the police haven't made it out here yet, which seems unlikely. If the man is still waiting inside, he may or may not have seen me drive by. He can't see my truck well here. I, however, can see the house well enough. Who's trapping who now?

I have enough provisions that I can hold my position for a long time. Beef jerky and snacks aren't what I would call a buffet, but they'll sustain me until I decide to quit. Probably the biggest concern is that someone might call the sheriff if my Silverado sits here for days, with me in it. Hopefully, it won't come to days.

Yielding to reason, I call the deputy's cell, but I get his voicemail. I leave a message with my temporary number in case he hasn't seen the earlier text. Hours pass, and it's going on dinner time. The sun has warmed the truck's interior, and it smells like worn vinyl upholstery and jerky wrappers. Nothing has moved at the weathered, gray house. No one comes in or out. I wonder if the guy planted my cell phone and left. Maybe he rigged the place to detonate upon entry. I eat my trail mix and chips while I think about what kind of time limit I should set. The adrenaline rush, which earlier fueled me like a soldier on the warpath, has since abated, and in its place, I find only weariness.

The winter sun fades below the horizon a little before 6:00 p.m. In the field across from me, I can see the silhouettes of cattle against the fiery, red sky. Soon all the color will be gone, and I'll be left in the near pitch black of rural Georgetown. Alone by the murder house. I focus on it as I try to stretch my arms and back. I rub my aching eyes. I need to remain alert, so I open one of the colas I brought. I need the caffeine—anything to stay awake.

Three more hours pass. There isn't anything to do besides watch the house and think. I start to wonder what I'm doing here. I want to try Reyes again and see if he caught the guy. But wouldn't he have let me know? He's not obligated, I guess. Maybe he's too preoccupied with the next emergency to return my call. He did tell me not to wait.

If I drop this stakeout idea and go home, I can email my mobile phone carrier and tell them I lost my cell. I can change my locks and get a home alarm system. But it won't solve the problem of my phone's placement at a recent crime scene and repercussions I can't predict. It won't solve that I don't know what I don't know. It won't allow me to look. Still, I'm beginning to rethink every single aspect of what I'm doing. Nothing makes sense right now. I crack my knuckles and stare out the windshield. I keep my gaze moving back and forth across my line of sight.

At nearly 10:00 p.m., I get the break I'm hoping for. A tiny light twinkles inside one of the windows. It lasts less than a second. This can mean several things. It might be a lighter, an electronic device, or something else—something that a person inside is forced to use from time to time in that hellish darkness. Or it may mean that he's left my cell phone within view of a window, and I've received a text message. I quickly scratch that idea, though, because the screen would have stayed lit longer. There has to be someone inside. If this is true, the absence of vehicles means the only way he—or they—can leave is on foot.

My heart pounds, and a ripple of electricity surges through my limbs, a burst of adrenaline from a backup supply I didn't know I had. I start the engine and take a deep breath, filling my lungs before letting it out. Without turning on my headlights, I quickly pull out onto County Road 140, drive about fifty feet, turn onto the grass again, and shut off the engine. I lean over and partially lie down in the front seat to see through the side window. Positioning my rifle on my right side for easy access seems best. It won't do me a bit of good if I have to fumble for it.

Here I am. Come get me.

I stay in position, watching and waiting, and considering I may not live through this. I expect shooting and window glass shattering in my face, at which point my reflexes will take over, and I'll return fire. Then God knows what will happen, and the world's population might drop by one. Or two. But that isn't what happens at all. What does happen is that headlights, high and bright, flash toward me on the road.

It isn't necessary to sit up entirely. I can see what comes. A semi-truck roars my way, and because of the narrow road, it's a good thing I'm parked off to the side. Unfortunately, the light illuminates my truck very nicely for the creep inside the house. He'll be able to see the Silverado and identify me. I almost take my eyes off the approaching diesel to continue my watch on the abandoned house when I realize the lights are *too* bright—the truck is going to hit me.

Reality slaps me in the face, shocking me into survival mode. My desire to live takes over and commands my actions. I unlock the door, grab the rifle next to me, and dive to the ground. I roll painfully over the rocky shoulder. Woodsy scents invade my nose as I tumble with the dry grass crunching beneath me. Groaning and gritting my teeth, I try to get my footing and run, but my stiff joints won't cooperate. Cold dirt wedges under my fingernails as I claw. When I pull myself upright, I know I have a matter of seconds before I'll be crushed.

In the glaring headlights, I discern the battered down, barbed-wire fence, and I race toward it before sailing over and landing on my feet. I surge into a run and give it everything I have. I get barely ten feet away when the semi-truck collides with my Silverado. A deafening crash and screeching air brakes tell me the diesel is smashing my pickup to pieces. I continue running straight toward the house.

The driver probably fell asleep at the wheel. I bet he's awake now. He'll be fine. There's nothing to hit around here except my parked truck, which his diesel found with no problem. I'd be happy to go back and help him, except now I'm running fifty feet away from the murder house, and someone is shooting at me from its black shadows.

It's tough to hit a moving target. This target—my body—isn't far away, but I sprint like the devil himself chases me. Sometimes I leap over a toe-splitting rock or groin-piercing cactus trunk, beating a fast trail toward the worst place I could possibly go.

I count two shots, and both seem to come from the right,

so I veer left. I tuck myself against the cold, wooden wall around the corner of the house and take a quick glance back at the scene with the semi. The driver has got out of the rig and is looking around. He waves his arms at me and shouts, but I just wave back and give him the thumbs up. He must think I'm crazy.

I catch scuffling noises inside the house, on the same end where I'm hiding. I switch positions to the other side of the corner and cock my rifle. The forestock is smooth and cool in my left hand. The nearest window has glass missing, so I slide the barrel inside and fire a shot. A deafening sound this late at night, it rumbles the country air. My ears ring. I have five shots left—the rest of my ammo is in my pulverized truck, but at least now, this guy knows I mean business.

Soon the authorities will be here for the truck accident. Getting out of this will be a nightmare—a double nightmare. But the murderer is waiting here too. What will he do? Where will he go when the cops show up a second time?

In answer to my question, the back door creaks open, and a pair of feet pound the dry grass. I swing out of my hiding place and dart after him.

At the roadside, the truck driver yells at me at the top of his lungs. "Hey!"

I stick a hand up in his direction but don't answer him. I race after the retreating man. With the brisk wind lashing my face, I can still distinguish him, just barely, in the lights of the Peterbilt, but I won't be able to for long. I skid to a halt and aim toward his legs.

Pow! I fire. I miss.

I stand here in the rifle's echo, thinking him too far away now and the darkness too deep. I shouldn't have stopped—I should have kept chasing him. I know I'm not practiced enough to hit a moving target in the dark. Now I can't see the man at all. I curse under my breath and turn around.

I trudge through the brittlegrass back to the house. I need to see if my phone is in there. The back door yawns open with a cold blackness, and I can still, very faintly, detect that horrible scent of death. That's where I need to go, into the place where only two weeks ago, a young woman drenched in blood hung from the wall. The place where a withered corpse lay on the floor amidst defecation and filth. But I don't have my light. It's in the truck, along with everything else that's ruined now.

The driver waves at me again. I put my hand up and start heading in his direction. I lock my eyes on the mangled pile of wreckage that used to be my Silverado. I was almost part of it. Whether I want to or not, I'll have to be ready to answer the trucker's questions about what he just saw.

More importantly, what am I going to tell Reyes?

10

TWELVE YEARS EARLIER

The local Austin newspaper lies open to the obituaries on my faux granite kitchen island. I hunch over it from my seat on the stool, reading the words again and again.

Mary Loretta Durham, 19, of Austin, Texas, died on April 15, 2004, at Seton Medical Center, due to complications from an illness following childbirth. She was surrounded by her loving family and her best friend Samantha at the time of passing.

A Texas native, Mary was born on February 28, 1985, as the second child of Patrick H. and Rebecca C. Durham. Mary graduated from Austin High School with Honors and a partial scholarship. She planned on enrolling at the University of Texas at Austin in the fall to pursue her dream of becoming a registered nurse.

Mary was an outgoing, energetic, and positive young woman who enriched the lives of all who knew her. Some of her favorite pastimes included aerobics, swimming, studying, and spending time with her friends and family. During the summers of 2001–2004, Mary participated in student volunteer work for the American Red Cross.

Mary is survived by her parents Patrick and Rebecca; her maternal grandparents Harold and Clarissa Masterson; and her paternal grandparents Robert and Betty Durham. She is also survived by her elder sister Stephanie, her best friend of sixteen years Samantha Esquire, and close friends Roberta Jacobs and Brittany Gomez.

Funeral arrangements are being handled by the Cook Walden Funeral Home at 6100 N. Lamar in Austin. Calling hours will be Wednesday from 1 to 4:00 and 7 to 9:00 p.m. A public funeral will be held on Thursday, April 22, at 10:00 a.m., at St. Louis Catholic Church in Austin. Condolences may be sent to the Cook Walden Funeral Home.

Above the text is a photo of Mary that I haven't seen before. She's smiling, and her bright blonde hair falls against her shoulders in waves. Her lips are glossy pink, and her skin glows radiantly. That's how she must have looked before we met. That's how she looked during happier times.

I sip my off-brand coffee that smells like cigarettes and make arrangements with work to take off Thursday morning. When the day arrives, I get in the car and check the rearview because I can't remember if I shaved my peach fuzz or not. I did, but my fingers are dry and cracked against my cheek from the car wash soap. My face is pasty white with dark circles under bloodshot eyes. I barely recognize myself.

The temperature has dropped into the fifties, and an elephant gray, overcast sky swells with rain clouds on the drive to St. Louis Catholic Church. I wear a black shirt and tie and dark sunglasses to blend in as much as possible and pay my respects.

Intentionally arriving after the start of service, I quietly walk up to the massive, white granite church, castle-like in stature, and unobtrusively slip inside. Observing the custom, I dip my finger in the holy water shell near the second door and make the sign of the cross. I hang back near the entrance until I find a place to stand by some older people I don't know. At all costs, I want to avoid anyone who might recognize me. Mary's parents should be in the front row, which means they won't see me.

It's so dark inside the nave that I have to remove the sunglasses. The ceiling and walls of the cathedral are awash in a soft amber. A wooden crucifix hangs front and center, glowing underneath the golden piers of the choir loft. Refracted blue and red light shines weakly through the stained-glass windows. The smell of myrrh incense still lingers from early morning mass.

In the lower space in front of the altar rests Mary's casket, made of rich, burnished copper with silver handles. Surrounding her are stunning floral arrangements comprised of every kind of flower in every color. One is a spray of only lilies with glossy, green leaves. White, pure, and perfectly formed petals gracefully brush the marble floor with delicate fingers. It seems to be a symbol of something above gracing something below.

Because it's an open casket funeral, and I can see Mary's

yellow hair arranged in loose curls around her face. She's been placed in a long, white dress. I can't tell from where I stand, but it might be her mother's wedding gown. It appears costly, strewn as it is with lace and little gleaming points like diamonds.

I take a deep breath and try to ignore how hot and uncomfortable I am in the long-sleeved shirt and tie. For being cold out, the air inside the cathedral stifles me with warmth and sickly-sweet aromas. There are other discomforts too. My facial muscles tighten. My eyes hurt. My torso starts to shake uncontrollably, and something warm and sticky oozes down my cheeks. It rolls onto my lips, leaving a salty taste. I realize I'm crying. I don't dare move and draw attention to myself, not that I can if I want to. My ankles are chained to a half-ton, iron ball of guilt, shame, and irresponsibility. Mary is dead, and it's my fault.

Samantha has taken the lectern and begins a eulogy of her sixteen-year friendship with Mary. Her voice sounds raw as she does her duty, giving a cheery speech for her deceased best friend.

"Mary was always there for me. I always knew if I needed something, she was the one person I could count on. Even though I knew her longer than any other friend, Mary was always the most faithful and trustworthy. In the words of Addison, 'without constancy, there is neither love, friendship, nor virtue in the world.'"

My head hurts, and I become disconnected, almost as though I'm floating above myself. Mentally, I spin. My body seems to turn of its own accord, and I begin a desperate, silent escape of the church. My feet are below me somewhere, but I can't feel them. I pull my sunglasses out of my pocket as I approach the door to the foyer and nearly slam into Mr. Durham headfirst. The recognition is immediate. As my stomach plummets down into the fiery place where one day I, too, will go, I wait for the hatred to materialize in Mr. Durham's eyes.

I start speaking without intending to, my voice choking up. "Mr. Durham, I'm sorry. I'm very sorry that you've lost your daughter."

When he looks back at me, no hatred flashes as I expect, only a face red from crying and sleepless nights. A pair of joyless eyes look into mine to see if there's a soul there, and he probably doesn't find one.

"You're sorry?" His voice is soft, almost insubstantial.

"Yes. I never meant for this to happen."

Mr. Durham shakes his head. "What did you mean to happen?"

A wave of panic sweeps through me as I stare at his ruddy face and watery, blue eyes. A pressurized lump clogs my throat. What did I mean to happen? It's almost unanswerable. Not every teen relationship culminates in marriage —in fact, most of them don't. I respond with the only truth I know with certainty.

"I wanted Mary to be happy."

"You didn't come to see her when she got sick," he says.

My mouth opens. "I—"

"That was my little girl." Mr. Durham shudders. I can't see his face for a few seconds because he covers it, his body racked with sobbing.

When he looks back at me, it's like I'm seeing him for the first time—the real him. Under the hard-edged, callous exterior is a human being like everyone else. He lives, he breathes, he loves. He lost. I guess until this moment, I've never allowed myself to see that.

I say, “I wanted to see her, I just—”

“She was asking about you. She asked about you until the moment she died.” Mr. Durham swallows. “I thought you were a good person, Trent. I always told Mary so. But when you didn’t come see her, didn’t even call...” He glances away and drags the back of his hand through the stream of tears.

“I always thought you hated me.” The words come from nowhere. I shouldn’t make this about me because it isn’t, but I’ve already said it.

“No. I never hated you.” His gaze finds me again. “I saw a lot of myself in you. I was young once—I was hotheaded and immature, just like you. I chased girls. I had my flings. Still, I’m her dad, and I wish things had been different. But I can’t expect a teenage boy to love Mary as much as I did.”

“I did love her.” Every time I open my mouth, it gets worse.

“Did you?” he asks, and surprisingly, his voice isn’t accusatory but skeptical.

I nod slowly. “But I wasn’t prepared—the pregnancy was overwhelming. But I still wanted to help her. I never thought she’d get sick.” A steel trap clenches my stomach. What the hell is wrong with me? I need to offer condolences and leave.

“Why was it overwhelming? The baby died.” His brow furrows.

“I apologize. It was wrong of me to voice that here,” I say. I rub my chin and shift my weight, wishing I could fall through the floor.

“No, I want to know,” he says.

“Mr. Durham, I don’t want to keep you. Don’t you want to get back to the service?”

He doesn't answer but instead replies, "You mean the fear of responsibility?"

A crawling heat races up my neck and into my face. My skin bursts into a hot sweat. "Yes. Forgive me. I shouldn't have been so tactless."

He sighs. "Yeah."

"Dad," a young woman's voice says.

He turns, saying, "There's my girl," and embraces the speaker.

The woman has blonde hair, and blue eyes, a natural pout to her lips, and a slight rose pink in her cheeks. A navy-blue dress hugs her curves, and she's wearing stylish, black pumps. The woman is the same height as the one in the casket. Her figure is nearly the same. I don't know Mary's older sister because they're seven years apart. Stephanie moved out of her parents' house before we met. But this is what Mary would have looked like if she lived to be twenty-five.

Stephanie hugs her dad with a wrinkled tissue dangling from her fingers. When her father releases her from his arms, her eyes find me.

"Thank you for coming," she says and extends her hand. A sweet, warm scent follows her. "I'm Stephanie, Mary's sister."

I already know who she is because Mary told me they could have been twins if not for their age difference.

"Trent Lemend. It's nice to meet you." I give her a firm handshake, realizing her creamy, clove-like fragrance is white lilies—like Mary's casket spray.

Stephanie pulls her head back. She backsteps with one foot and puts her high heel down with a sound like a sword on stone. Her body straightens and stiffens. "You're

Trent? *The* Trent?" She pinches her brows and looks me up and down.

"I'm afraid so," I say.

Stephanie gasps. Her eyes widen. "You fucking bastard! You miserable piece of shit!" Her shrill voice resounds off the walls of the lobby, and without touching me, she thrusts herself right up in my face.

I block with my hands and begin to back away.

"You're not welcome here! Get out! Get out of this church!" Stephanie advances, and I retreat. She lets the crumpled tissue flutter to the brown-tiled floor behind her.

"Steph, that's enough," Mr. Durham says. He puts a hand on her shoulder.

"You piece of human garbage!" Stephanie says.

Her heels clickety-click after me as I backstep. People begin trickling through the doors of the nave—the service must be over. Men, women, and children stop to gawk at us with appalled expressions.

"You killed my sister!" Stephanie half-turns. "Hey!" she calls, waving an arm at the newcomers. "This is the guy. This is Trent Lemend, who knocked up my sister and wouldn't go see her when she was dying in the hospital. This is the guy who killed her."

A gasp. Scattered murmuring. A lady snatches up her daughter, sets her on her hip, and marches back inside the nave. The door eases itself closed behind her.

Stephanie turns back to me, approaching as close as she dares. "Stay away from my family."

"Yes, I'm leaving," I say.

"Oh, you damn well better leave!" she yells.

Mr. Durham's voice booms through the chamber. "Stephanie, that's enough. Stop!"

He takes hold of her arm, and she tries to wrench herself from his grip. Failing, she then pushes, shoving him hard on the chest. Her father stumbles to keep his balance. Flustered, he lets go and attempts to get in front of her. Sure, he could force her to comply if he chooses. He's only in his forties and doesn't look sickly, that I can tell. Mr. Durham could drag Stephanie away or force her to sit on the bench and calm down. But she's his daughter—his only little girl now—and he doesn't want to. As he tries to place his body between hers and mine, Stephanie dances out of the way.

She aims an accusing finger inches from my face. "And if I ever see you again, I'll kill you. Do you understand me?"

After that, Stephanie mostly hurls four-letter words interspersed with insults. My mother should have had an abortion, and I should do the world a favor and go kill myself.

As I flee through the front door, in my peripheral vision, I see Mr. Durham give up. Turning to find his wife, he lets out a deflated sigh. He's a father in pain, and with a bent back, he trudges off, his aspect vastly more like that of a man in his seventies instead of barely forty-five.

I walk to the car under swelling, dark clouds. The wind picks up, but it doesn't rain. The rolling, steel-gray sky withholds its tears, though it might burst at any moment. And like that sky, after that day in the golden cathedral, I never cry about Mary. I lock away those memories in a deeply hidden, thorny place in the back of my mind. Too bad hiding the truth doesn't make it go away.

11

JANUARY 19TH

The round-bellied fellow standing next to the Peterbilt introduces himself as Bradley Premshaw. We make it past the formalities and "are you okays." Both of us are wholly unharmed. The truck driver tells me he hasn't called the cops yet, and although it makes me happy under the circumstances, I realize it's likely due to the accident being his fault. *Really* his fault.

"I've been goin' fifteen hours since Jacksonville," Bradley says. His accent sounds like something from The Green Mile. "I'm over time. I'll probably get fired for this, but my company's insurance will pay for your truck."

Both of us stare at the pile of metal that used to be a Chevy pickup. He swears and clears his throat. "I sure am sorry about this. But glad you're okay."

"Did you get lost?" I ask. I can't imagine what possessed him to bring his rig this way. The semi takes up nearly the entire width of the rural road.

"Nah, not exactly," he says, scratching the back of his head. "I missed my exit and wanted to turn around. I saw on my GPS that I could swing back on these roads and meet up with the overpass again."

Bradley has an interesting habit of rolling something around in his mouth when he speaks. Whether chewing tobacco, gum, or something else, I can't figure out what it is. A licorice scent escapes his pores like he's off-gassing energy drinks.

I nod, and though I'm not sure if the roads circle back or not, I'm in no frame of mind to argue. It has now been nearly forty-eight hours since I've had any real sleep. I hold my rifle upright by the forestock. It's warm now.

"Well, that would be great if the insurance will cover it," I say. I have to figure out what I'll do if the sheriff comes. There has to be some way I can use this.

"Say, what happened over there?" he asks.

He tosses his hand toward the house and glances at the Remington in my hand. His gaze searches my face. If not for the accident, he'd probably be asking if I tried to break in. He wants to look for a way that he, too, can use this.

"No one lives there, but it's my boss's house," I say. "It's been vacant for a really long time. When I was driving by, I saw a flicker of light in one of the windows. I pulled over to see what it was, and when I got out of the truck, someone shot at me." I lift the Remington in my hand. "I always keep a gun in the cabin."

"Hmph." He nods. "You see anybody?"

I doubt Bradley would have been able to see the man zip out and run off. Not from the roadside and not in this dark. "Yeah. I heard him first. Barely saw the backside of him when he went out the back door. I took another shot at him. Missed, though."

Bradley continues rolling whatever it is around in his mouth, digesting what I said and trying to figure out whether he believes me or not. He mustn't know about the County Road 140 case, or he would have called the cops already, accident or no. He takes his flashlight and shines it at the house. The beam reveals the gray, disintegrating wood, the windowpanes containing fragmentary shards, and the untended grounds. Brittle, yellow stalks of winter grass and tangly weeds eat up every inch of the yard that isn't occupied with thorny succulents and rock. There can be no doubt the place isn't inhabited.

A man of few words, Bradley gives another nod, seeming satisfied.

"You mentioned you'd probably get fired," I say. "Why? Is an accident automatic grounds for termination?"

"Naw. Like I said, I'm over time. I shoulda pulled over and slept, but I was already behind. Now it's gonna be tomorrow morning before I can get it there." He turns and spits. Chewing tobacco, then. "And this is my third strike—on being late, I mean. I ain't never had no accident like this before."

"Gotcha," I say. "Well, stuff happens, and I sure don't see any reason for you to get fired." In the lights from the rig, I watch Bradley's thick brows relax. The strain falls away from his posture, a silent thanks for a possible out.

"You want to handle this ourselves? I can get you a tow truck, get you cash, no problem." Then he adds hastily, "But I'm sure fine with callin' the police. That ain't no problem. I want to do it right."

"Well, I thank you for that. I appreciate it," I say. "But there's no reason for you to get fired. If there's a way you can help me with my truck, let's just do that."

"Oh, okay," he says. He brightens like he can't believe his good luck. "What year is the truck?"

My Silverado is ten years old but would have probably sold for around five thousand dollars before the accident, being in decent shape. Bradley and I discuss the particulars and come to an agreement.

"I'll leave you with all my info," he says.

Bradley disappears momentarily into the cabin of the Peterbilt. While he rummages around, I squint at the license plate and try to commit it to memory. He emerges a few seconds later and hands his card to me.

"I'll get you five thousand cash, and once I get back here, we'll get a tow truck, and I'll drive you home. I give you my word."

His belly fat jiggles when he shakes my hand. There's no way to know if he'll do it or not, but I'd rather experience Bradley's no-show than be stopped by the police. The deputies will have questions I won't want to answer. I'll tell Reyes when I'm ready. But carefully.

"All right," I say. "Appreciate it."

The thrumming clack of the diesel engine fades into the blackness on the rural road. I begin to search through the wreckage of my pickup. I get a whiff of antifreeze that reminds me of maple syrup. Underneath that are odors of oil and gasoline. The front end and motor are pulverized, but I hope parts of the cabin might be intact. The force of impact actually pushed the Silverado along for a short distance, but it damaged the truck bed the least since the collision was head-on.

I reach my hand in through the twisted frame of the broken passenger's side window to see if I can open the glove compartment. It's jammed shut. I get my hands around the door the best I can and pull. It comes off at its hinges. After staggering backward, I drop it on the ground and then try the glove compartment again. The dashboard is all smashed in, which is why it isn't budging. Finally, I take the stock of the Remington and pound the small door a few times. The glove compartment snaps open, and I retrieve my prize—the slim, silver flashlight.

A couple about my age in a white SUV pulls over. I set my rifle on the ground by the front tire of my Silverado. The woman rolls down her window and asks if I need any help.

"I'm good," I say. "No one was hurt. Just waiting on the tow truck."

I smile weakly to hide my nervousness. We exchange a few words. The man and woman crane their necks to stare at my misfortunate salvage vehicle before they pull away.

Barely able to see my hand in front of my face, I navigate the best I can all the way to the house. No matter what else happens, I have to make sure my cell phone isn't in there. When I get to the back door, I click on the flashlight and shine it inside. Traces of the sickly-sweet death smell hit my nostrils. I can almost taste it, like moldy pumpkin pulp oozing onto my tongue. Abhorrent. I snort and tuck my shirt collar over my nose.

I step inside and aim the beam at the wall where I found the young woman hanging, nearly dead. Mental images of January 5th come crashing down like a hammer, but it's just a filthy wall now. I inspect the floor below, expecting to see a chalk outline where the corpse lay, but there isn't one. I guess they only do that in the movies.

I swing the flashlight beam to the adjacent wall. The glow illuminates a large, white square with words written in bright red. My already straining heart leaps into overdrive as I read the message.

SHE'S DEAD ANYWAY.

It knocks the wind out of me. I gasp for breath. I step back, my ankles colliding with some garbage on the floor.

She's dead anyway... She's dead anyway. The woman who was hung up to die? Or a new victim—the one he referred to in the instant message? Are these words the killer's reason for luring me here? Why would he want me to know that? Why would I care about a woman I've never met?

He's given me a tiny piece of the puzzle—not that I understand it. I notice how the man affixed a poster board to the wall because otherwise, I wouldn't be able to read the words against the dark wood. It's neatly done, deliberate. Clever, sick bastard. The message adds something to the lingering stench, and my stomach wriggles like a fish. I force the bile down. I need to tough it out and see if my phone is still here.

The rest of the inside of the house is in sad shape, but nothing compared to the back room. In the front, presumably the living area, an old, flimsy table and a couple of metal buckets lie undisturbed. Nearby, a wood-burning stove rests iron feet in the dust, its solid, black metal thirstily drinking up the beam of light. There are still traces of ash on the floor. The kitchen has a more modern gas cooktop and oven, "modern" as in probably from the 1950s. A stainless steel washbasin leans against one wall, between two dust-covered countertops underneath grimy pine cabinets. I explore the rest of the house but don't see my cell phone anywhere.

Going out the way I came, I push the back door closed with my shoulder. For the first time, I notice my left side is sore. It took the brunt of my pre-collision escape dive. I give the yard a cautionary sweep with the flashlight before turning it off again.

Back at the truck, I dig out whatever belongings I can while I wait for Bradley. My tablet has a long, deep crack across its glass face. It won't turn on. However, the duffle bag and its contents are virtually unharmed, which means I have my two boxes of ammo for the rifle, my wallet, and other essential things, like the burner phone. Too bad my tablet wasn't protected inside, too.

What I estimate to be thirty minutes later, the diesel roars down County Road 140. Bradley gets out and waves a wad of cash in the air. I shake my head. Unbelievable.

"Okay, I got your money. Let's go," he says.

Poor guy almost seems happy to be handing me five thousand dollars cash in one-hundred-dollar bills. I thank him and get into the cabin. The licorice aroma is more potent here, as well as a rancid spittoon reek from wherever he spits his juice. That paper cup under the radio, maybe. Crushed Red Bull cans fill the middle console compartment between us. While I buckle up and stuff my Remington in the duffle bag, Bradley calls a tow truck as promised. I request that the Silverado be taken to my house instead of a shop. It's a total loss, and I'll probably sell the salvageable parts.

"Where ya goin' to?" he asks.

It's now 1:34 a.m., but I don't want him to take me home. The place is too trap-like until I can figure out how the house was broken into right under my nose.

"Let's go to a used car dealership," I say.

"Sure thing," Bradley says.

He does a quick search on his dashboard GPS and finds

Buck Shot Motor Company in rural Georgetown, not far from where we are. We take up most of the road as he drives us there in the Peterbilt, hauling the loaded trailer. Bradley drops me off at the driveway leading to the main building. I'll wait by the street until the place opens.

"Thanks," I say.

Ironic to be thanking him for demolishing my truck and nearly killing me. We wave each other off, and I prepare to wait. My tiredness has turned to numbness, and I can no longer feel much of anything. I sit down in the grass, away from the road. I lean against a cedar post. With my duffle bag on my lap, I take out my wallet and put it in my coat pocket. I won't be able to open the bag around people, packing like I am. The car salesmen will think I've come to rob the place.

She's dead anyway, I think. *She's dead anyway.*

As I wonder what the odds are of getting in trouble for being here at this hour, I nod off without realizing it.

"Hey!"

My body jerks and my eyes snap open to piercing daylight. A man calls to me from a red sedan.

"Oh, hey. I was just waiting for the place to open," I say. "I got here early. Must have fallen asleep while I was waiting."

The man frowns but brings me up to speed that it's nearly ten in the morning. I spring to my feet and head up the drive to the main building. Not two hours later, I'm happy in the knowledge that I'm now the owner of a used Dodge Dakota. Unlike the Silverado, it's tan, not black, and it's a truck the killer has never seen.

Finally, it hits me that it's been over twenty-four hours since I spoke to Reyes. I sit inside my new truck in the parking lot and force myself to make the phone call. Stabbing myself in the eye sounds more fun, but I've already put it off too long. Now it's a little before noon.

This time, the deputy sheriff groggily answers. His voice rasps like I've woken him from a sound sleep. "This is Reyes."

"Deputy Reyes, hi. This is Trent Lemend." The stuffy air makes me perspire.

He draws a long breath and stifles a groan. Something rustles. Maybe sheets or something he's grabbing on the nightstand. "Lemend, shit. What happened? Did you call 911 like I told you to?"

12

JANUARY 19TH

Reyes gives me a talking to. That's one way to put it.

"You don't know how stupid that was," Deputy Reyes says when I tell him what I did. He says a lot of other things too, but that's what I remember best. He's wrong about me, though. I do know. I just can't stand hiding while this guy taunts me.

"I thought you guys had already been to the house," I tell him.

"We had. We searched inside and out clean back to the woods and didn't find anyone—and that sign you're telling me about wasn't there either—but that's not the point." He clears his throat and pauses. Gulping and crinkling sounds ensue like he's drinking bottled water.

"I wanted to get my phone," I say.

"Bullshit," Reyes says. "You wanted to get yourself killed. Now, I don't know what you're trying to prove, but you stay out of this. That's not only for your own safety but for that of another possible victim if there is one—and we have to assume there is. I'll be sending the crime scene technicians back out to examine that message and dust for prints again, and I'd better not find yours. Not only would that be contamination, but it raises other questions. So, from now on, stay out."

She's dead anyway, the words repeat in my mind. The truck's warmth and the smell of my sweat compel me to roll down the window.

"Do you hear me?" the deputy barks.

"Yes, I understand, sir." I don't add that if not for me, he wouldn't know about the red-inked sign at all.

Reyes keeps me on the phone while he notes the particulars for his report and then abruptly disconnects. Cell phone hang-ups sure give off a loud silence when someone's pissed at you. Well, the house was no longer yellow-taped in crime scene status when I got there, and it isn't against the law to return fire with my rifle when someone shoots at me. Maybe I do have a death wish, but I also gleaned new information for the sheriff's office.

After my unsuccessful round of cat and mouse with my tormentor, I know I need to get busy. My assumption is the obvious one. This guy, whoever he is, not only wants me dead, but he also wants to make my life a living hell until such time as he becomes ready to dispose of me. That assumption will now direct my actions almost solely so that I can stay alive.

This nutcase successfully broke into my house, stole my

Browning, and baited me into a recent crime scene. The cherry on top was how my truck just "happened" to get totaled in the process, and Bradley nearly killed me—after which the murderer shot at me with my own gun. Call it a run of bad luck, if you will, but it seems to me that this guy is driving the bad karma straight to me with an electric cattle prod.

Once I get home, I waste no time getting things done. I report my phone as stolen and get a new cell. There's no sense in trying to track the old one any longer because the killer will only let me locate it when he wants me to. I'm not going to pay a mobile bill for the privilege. I tuck the burner phone away in the truck's glove compartment in case I need it again.

I also have a basic car alarm installed in the Dodge Dakota, something much better than what came with the Silverado. Now at least if my vehicle is tampered with, I'll know about it. The alarm also has the added benefit that the siren noise might scare him off.

At the pawnshop, I trade in my .22 revolver, paying the difference to buy a 9mm, magazine-loaded Ruger pistol. It's actually a better gun than the stolen Browning.

I practice my aim at the shooting range and read about how to hit a moving target. This won't make me an expert marksman, but it helps. I stockpile food, water, supplies, and ammunition for the rifle and new handgun. These preparations take a chunk out of my savings, but fortunately, selling the salvageable parts from the Silverado replenishes most of what I spend.

Over the weekend, Kyle helps me install a low-end internet security camera system that allows me a view of each side of the house. There are a few blind spots, but all the critical areas are covered—the front and back doors and the windows. It isn't a big place, after all. I haven't figured out what to do in the situation of someone cutting my power. With no electricity, the security system will be useless, so I'll need to come up with something. I can't afford a backup generator.

"You look like a prepper," Kyle says. He grins as he reaches into the fridge and retrieves a Corona. I'm surprised he doesn't fear for his life being in here after everything I've told him.

"Well, I am. I'm preparing," I say. After taking off my coat, I drop it on the couch and follow him into the kitchen.

Kyle frowns. "I still can't believe you tried to handle this guy yourself. I know you said you didn't break any laws, but you did. At least one. You're treading a fine line."

"Part of me wishes I wouldn't have told Reyes anything. I just can't see how I won't wind up getting blamed for that crime." I take a bottle of water from the pantry and proceed to drain it.

"That's why you shouldn't have gone over there in the first place," Kyle says. He leans against the counter to face me. "And the more you involve yourself, the worse it's going to be. The guiltier you'll look. Trust me."

I shake my head. I throw my empty water bottle away and grab a length of unused wire from the table. My eyes go out of focus as I begin coiling it. If other people were as sensible as Kyle, it wouldn't be a problem, but life isn't like that.

"To be honest, I don't even know if Reyes believes me," I say. I stuff the wire in a cardboard box with other spare bits. "Who's going to believe that someone broke into my four-room house while I was sleeping and took my things? And that the person put my cell phone at the crime scene. No one would believe that. Because how the hell could someone do that? But, I played the good citizen and called the deputy and told him."

I grab a Corona of my own and slam the fridge door shut. Smells of ketchup and Chinese food leak out. "And what about my truck? I'm supposed to tell the cops that I was sitting outside the murder house, and an eighteen-wheeler came out of nowhere and totaled my pickup?" I hold my arms out.

The incident with Bradley Premshaw is the only part I omitted in my conversation with Reyes. It served me too well at the time to stay quiet.

"Yeah," Kyle says. "You should have called the sheriff immediately when that happened. That's an accident. You're supposed to report it."

"But I was parked outside a former crime scene—a crime that I discovered! I wasn't supposed to be there." I take a swig. It's good, so I take a few more.

Kyle nods slowly, glaring at me under his eyebrows. "My point exactly. I'm telling you, buddy, this is some bad shit you got yourself into. I wish you wouldn't have gone after him."

"Yeah. Well, it's too late now. I guess all this will blow over if the guy is caught, or you'll be coming to visit me in prison." I pull out a wooden chair and sit.

"You might not get prison," Kyle says. "Or not a very long sentence. You might get a fine. It would depend on how they rule in court when you're convicted for your various crimes. I mean your actual crimes, not if you get blamed for abduction and murder."

I laugh. "That doesn't sound too bad."

We have lots of conversations like this, but it comes down to whether I'll back off completely, or remain involved, at least somewhat. My friend is right that I shouldn't have gone hotheaded vigilante. But to cower at home or be forced to relocate? I don't know if I can do it.

THE FOLLOWING WEEK, I also find two more articles. I read them on my laptop while I drink lemonade at the kitchen table with the overhead light on. I'm alone today. The place is locked up tight with the cameras running.

January 24th
Travis County man no longer a suspect in County Road 140 case.

WILLIAMSON COUNTY (KVUN) — Emile Richard Woodard, 43, of Travis County, was arrested on January 18th on charges of attempted murder of a Williamson County resident. Woodard was also thought to have a connection to what authorities have been calling the "County Road 140 Case," a crime discovered on January 5th in which one woman was found dead and another left in critical condition. While Woodard was detained, DNA analysis revealed that Woodard's DNA did not match that found at the crime scene inside the abandoned home on County Road 140. Additionally, due to insubstantial evidence linking Woodard to the

shooting in Williamson County on January 6th, Woodard was released at the conclusion of questioning and testing.

January 26th
Attempted homicide survivor identified, suspect named.

WILLIAMSON COUNTY (KXAV) — The surviving victim of the County Road 140 case, a twenty-four-year-old female, has now been identified as Aria Owen of Round Rock. After being in a coma for nearly three weeks due to life-threatening injuries sustained during her abduction, St. David's Hospital officials say she regained consciousness on Saturday. Officials also report that Owen is no longer in critical condition but remains under close supervision.

Carol Brandt, 46, who was found dead beside Owen in the abandoned house, has been further identified as Owen's stepmother, with whom the twenty-four-year-old was staying before their abduction. Owen has also provided law officials with the name of the man she says kidnapped and tortured them. Officials say that this information is not being released at this time.

Detective Gerald Menard of the Criminal Investigations Division told KXAV, "This was obviously a crime perpetrated by a very sick individual, and we're grateful that Ms. Owen is still alive. That's something to be thankful for. Because of the nature of this crime and the fact that the perpetrator hasn't been caught, we're taking every precaution to ensure the victim's safety. That includes not

releasing certain information until we can guarantee we're not putting her at risk."

Regarding potential leads in the case, Menard told KXAV that there had been one possible suspect prior to Owen's change in condition. However, current charges for this and another crime, a recent shooting, have been dropped due to insufficient evidence.

This second article comes with a photo, probably obtained from Facebook. It shows the twenty-four-year-old survivor as she looked before the abduction, smiling, with a fair complexion and long, dark hair. Her skin had no dirt on it. Her hair wasn't matted and filthy. Her teeth were straight and white, and she was healthy.

Aria Owen. That is a name I'll never forget. Aria, the girl drenched in her own blood, left for dead. So, she's not only still alive, but she's awake and speaking.

The article on Woodard confuses me. If he's the same person who shot at me on Tim's ranch, it seems strange that his DNA wasn't found in the abandoned house. Unless someone hired him to take care of me. Maybe the guy who planted my phone—the one who lured me—isn't the real man at the top, either. The kidnapper. The murderer. Maybe he hired several people to do his clean-up work and take snoopers like me out of the picture. But why would I be so important?

Aria Owen. Is she the one who's "dead anyway?" With her stepmother gone, I hope she has some other family to stay with. There must be a reason she was living with Carol Brandt. Maybe she left her boyfriend or husband, or perhaps she never left home after college. Who the hell knows. I shake myself out of this pointless mental maundering. I won't figure out any more about a crime victim than what the papers give me.

That evening, I sit down to plan out the following week. I settle into my worn couch. Notebook in hand and a cup of hot chocolate on the coffee table, the taste of those tiny marshmallows lingers on my tongue. It's been a decent day. I haven't been shot at, or threatened, or almost crushed by a semi. Then the phone rings. It's the last person in the world I expect.

"Hello," I say. My voice comes out flat, monotone. I shouldn't have answered, but it mainly was a reflex.

"Hi," says Elizabeth. "I just um, I thought I'd call and see how you're doing."

I sit here with the phone to my ear, confusion coming in on me like a freight train, like the day she left. Anger quickly follows, my face getting hot and red.

"I'm fine." I clear my throat. "Why are you calling?"

"Well, I just thought I would call and see how you're doing," she repeats. "I feel bad about what happened—I mean about getting mad and leaving like that. I'm sorry."

I pause. "Okay."

"So... do you want to talk about it, or maybe get together some time?" she asks.

I don't have an answer. I don't know if I want to or not. "You never gave the ring back."

Silence. "Well, no, I thought... I thought we were just taking a break."

"How in the hell were we taking a break? You wouldn't return my phone calls. I brought all your stuff back to your mom's house, and some guy slammed the door in my face.

Seems to me we're done." Leaning forward, I toss the notebook onto the coffee table.

Elizabeth sighs. "Trent, I told you. I was a little unsettled about what I learned. I needed some time to think it through."

I shake my head. "That doesn't make any sense to me."

It really doesn't. It seems like a flimsy excuse for her to duck out, probably to cover her ass for something she did. There must be a way to get her to admit it.

"So, what did you do?" I ask. I stand up and start pacing the living room.

Silence again. "What?"

"What did you do? What did you do that you're not telling me?" I ask.

She huffs, clearly insulted. "What—what do you mean, what did I do?"

"You expect me to believe you left because I didn't commit to someone when I was eighteen? I don't know exactly what you were told. But I don't buy it. I was young and stupid, and I couldn't commit to Mary. But I didn't kill anyone," I say. I don't really believe my last statement, not entirely. Elizabeth doesn't need to know that, though.

"I'm not that person anymore. I grew up." I exhale but realize I took the bait. She put the focus back on me, and I'm already on the defensive.

"Yes, because it's a really big deal. What if I get pregnant?" she asks.

My insides twist into a squirming pretzel. I halt and grab my stomach. "Elizabeth, are you?"

"No. No! I'm not. But what if it happened? Or what if when we get married, it happens, and then you suddenly don't love me anymore?" she asks.

So, she knows about that part too. "That wouldn't happen. Being married is different. It's not like dating in high school. Marriage is permanent." My feet start burning a track in the carpet again.

"Yeah, it's permanent," she says. "Like if you suddenly decide you don't love me, then we're stuck together forever to raise our children, miserable for life. Can't you understand that I'm afraid? I'm afraid of taking that chance."

She's good. It sounds pretty convincing.

"So, what did *you* do? Were you cheating on me?" I ask. I wander to the window that faces the backyard, turn, and go back to the kitchen.

Elizabeth lets out a rasping, irritated sigh. So quietly as to be almost under her breath, she says, "How dare you."

"When I dropped off your stuff at your mom's, I heard a man's voice. Then he slammed the door on me. Who was it? Is that the guy you were screwing behind my back?" I fire back at her. My socked footsteps thud across the vinyl tile.

"Oh my God! What is wrong with you? You have no right to accuse me of anything. I'm not the one who abandoned my pregnant girlfriend and didn't even visit her when she was dying. She was dying, you asshole."

I stop and lean a hand against the fridge. I deliver the next part slowly. "Were you cheating on me or not? Yes or no?"

"I can't believe this." Her voice shakes. It shivers like a leaf in the wind, dew dropping from its delicate edges, except the dew consists of acid, and it's falling onto a bed of hot coals.

"Yes or no? Answer the question," I say. "It's not a difficult question."

A short click makes me pull the phone away from my ear and look at it.

Call ended.

If that wasn't a confession, I don't know what is. For a moment, I catch a good, cocky high. I slap the counter so hard my hand stings. I'm right! I have to be. Then I sit back down on the couch and rub my face, the burning anger and betrayal creeping up my neck like a spider and turning my skin red. The idea of being right makes me feel worse, not better. And she *still* has the engagement ring.

TODAY IS FRIDAY THE 29TH, which means January is drawing to a close. The week passed without any break-ins or shootings. My shift at the gas station lasts from 10:00 in the morning until 5:00 p.m., and then I'll meet Kyle, Laney, and a couple of their friends at Chupacabra. Laney won't drink alcohol, but she can still eat with us and have a good time. She doesn't go on these outings too often.

The owner of the Texaco station where I work is named Luis Alvarez, but all the employees call him "Louie." He isn't as laid back and likable as Tim Corbin, the rancher, but I find him tolerable. Louie is tall and thin and wears a thick, black mustache. Ordinarily quiet and focused, Louie never says more than necessary, and that's fine by me.

Around 3:30, I'm sweeping up a busted bag of potato chips when the store starts picking up after a slow spell. Louie appears from the stock area where he was doing inventory. He handles some of the waiting customers at the other register while I get my own line caught up.

A lady steps forward with her son of maybe ten years old, and he's crunching on a pickle in one hand and gripping its soggy wrapper in the other. My nose twinges from the sharp dill and vinegar as I watch lime-green juice drip on the floor. Guess I'll be cleaning that up next. I ring the lady up, and they leave. I turn to get a rag.

"Trent, wait," Louie says in his heavy Spanish accent. "I forgot to tell you. Your friend dropped something off for you. There, under the counter."

I rub my chin and peer at the shelves under the register. Skepticism grips me like an ill-fitting shirt. "Did he leave a name?"

"Yes," he says, pausing to think. "He said his name was Kyle."

A white envelope with my name on it lies on the shelf. I pick it up and turn it over. It's sealed. "Thanks. Do you happen to remember what he looked like?"

Louie tugs at the edge of his mustache. "He was a tall, white guy with a hat."

"Young?" I ask.

"About your age," Louie says.

"Did you see his hair color?"

"No, I couldn't tell. He had on a baseball cap. Why? You worried about somebody?"

"No," I say. "I was just making sure it was him. Thanks."

"Sure." He vanishes into the storeroom with his clipboard.

A "white guy about my age wearing a baseball cap" meets Kyle's description, but give me a break. Kyle would never drop off something at my work without telling me. I start to carefully tear open the envelope as my stomach finds its way into its usual knot.

I pull out a blurry picture that was probably printed from a smartphone photo. It shows a man and woman. The pixelation indicates that the photo was taken from a considerable distance, then poorly enlarged. The couple embraces each other, with the woman's back to the camera, and her long, black hair and slim figure make me instantly think of Elizabeth. I can discern a part of the man's face—his right cheek, dark eyebrow, and the corner of his mouth pinched into a smile. Honestly, that guy could be me, but the background makes me uncertain.

A portion of a small, light blue building reminds me of Amy's Ice Creams on Congress. There isn't enough of it visible to be able to tell for sure. I can't recall the two of us ever going there together. I only remember the building because of its distinctive South Austin paint job. My mind struggles to process the image. Is this a photo of Elizabeth cheating on me? Who could have taken this?

"Excuse me, sir."

I look up to find a woman staring at me through her glasses. "I'm sorry, ma'am. I can check you out now."

My hands tremble, and I drop a nickel as I ring up her items. I pick it up, force a smile onto my rattled face, and thank her as I hand her the change. After she goes on her way, I return to staring at the photo.

Louie remains in the back, and the front of the store lies empty again. I shake my head and swear under my breath. I know I should have some bright idea, but I lack the understanding needed to spring it. I've been expecting a death threat, coordinates to my next trap, or poison that will leech into my skin on contact with the paper. This doesn't fit. I turn the photo over.

Who does her sins lament... Then see the sorrow of my heart, ere it be too late.

13

JANUARY 29TH

It's a threat. The shock slams me in the chest like a lead pipe, taking my breath away. I steady myself by gripping the counter with my free hand. I flip the photo over again and study the woman's back. If only I could see her face. The hair seems to be the exact length and color as Elizabeth's, and that's her body shape. It has to be her.

I try Reyes but get his voicemail, so I leave a message. Since I called his cell, I send over screenshots of both sides of the photo, and I text him Elizabeth's contact info. Then I call my ex-fiancée. She doesn't answer either. I don't know what to say, so I hang up. After groaning and walking back and forth, I redial her and leave a lame message. I tell her I'm worried about her, that she should be extra cautious, carry pepper spray, and call me right away so I can explain. But Elizabeth never calls. Five o'clock can't come fast enough.

When I finally get off work, I still haven't heard from either her or the deputy, despite trying both of them again. I even try Elizabeth's office number, but the receptionist says she's with a client. I'll go ahead with the plans I've made with Kyle. There's nothing else I can do, but at least this way, I can get a second opinion.

At Chupacabra, I walk through the door and enter the lively, crowded atmosphere filled with aromas of cilantro and honey jalapeño chicken. Laney introduces me to another couple, her friends Shauna and Alex. Shauna is late twenties with short, dark red hair, and Alex is probably my age. They seem nice enough.

I put on my best face and try to relax and enjoy my Friday, at least for a short while. The salsa is extra citrusy, even better than usual. Two beers later, however, I can't contain myself another minute, and I follow Kyle into the men's restroom. That's a first for me. As soon as we get through the door, I grab his arm.

"Hey," I say. "I have to tell you something. I think the guy is after Elizabeth."

Kyle's face turns to stone. "What? The same guy? Are you sure?"

"I can't be exactly sure, but it has to be. Look at this." I pull out the envelope from my back pocket. I folded it once to make it fit. I withdraw the photo and hand it to Kyle.

His eyes devouring it, he walks over to the sinks in the slightly better lighting. He shakes his head. "I don't know. Are you sure that's Elizabeth? We can't see her face."

"I don't know."

"Does she have a shirt like that? That blue one she's wearing?" Kyle asks.

"Oh man, I don't know. She's got like a million shirts, and lots of them are blue. That looks like her hair and her figure. Turn it over," I say.

He turns it over. “What the hell does that mean?”

“Tss, I don’t know. I mean, I guess it’s some kind of threat. What if he’s going to kill her? Goddamn it, I don’t get it,” I say.

Kyle turns the picture over again. “Who’s this guy in the photo? Is that you?”

“I don’t think so,” I say. “I thought it was too, but the background doesn’t fit. This must be the guy she was cheating on me with.”

“But we don’t know that this is Elizabeth,” Kyle says. “And we don’t know that she cheated.”

“I know, but… goddamn it!” I say, unable to find better words. I pace back and forth like a restless horse, my hand covering my mouth.

“Okay. Okay,” Kyle says. “You’re freaking out, and I completely understand that. First of all, you can’t see enough in this picture to really know anything. But I think this guy is messing with you. I don’t think he’d hurt her, but this probably isn’t even her. He could have photoshopped something he found on Facebook. You just don’t know.”

“That’s the thing. I don’t know. What the hell am I going to do?” I say, facing him.

Kyle shakes his head again. “Did you make up?”

“What?”

“Did you and Elizabeth make up?” he asks.

“No. God, she called, and we had this fight. It was bad. I don’t know what to do.”

“Okay. Here’s what you’re going to do,” Kyle says. “You’re going to call the sheriff’s office and show them this. You don’t have to call 911. You call Reyes, and you give him Elizabeth’s description and address. You let the police protect her, you understand? You don’t try to be some vigilante going after this guy. You nearly got yourself killed doing that."

I bite my lip, blankly staring at the wall.

Kyle grabs my shoulder and shakes me with one hand. "Okay? You understand?"

"Yeah, I already did that. I called Reyes. I tried Elizabeth too. Neither one of them answered. I sent screenshots to Reyes, but I can't just sit here. I can't do *nothing.*"

Kyle pulls his head back and stares at me hard. "Trent, she will be absolutely fine. The police will keep surveillance on her if they think she's in danger."

"I guess," I say.

"It's going to be fine. You did the right thing." Kyle slaps me on the back, and I twitch. He doesn't have any more idea about what to do than I do. Well, he tried.

"I need to get some air. I'll meet you back at the table in a few," I tell him.

As I leave the restroom, the next man coming in nearly smacks me in the face with the door. I dodge and put a hand on the cold, textured wall to let him by. I tromp off to my vehicle's unideal location about a block and a half away. This trendy area of Austin isn't known for its great parking. Inside the quiet cabin of my pickup, I try Elizabeth again with no luck. I check to see if I have any messages. I don't. Reyes hasn't returned my texts either.

After standing outside for a while to let the cool wind fan my face, I head back to the bar. I walk along the sidewalk, threading through groups of college students. Under a flickering, yellow lamp post, several hippies pass around a sweet-smelling herb. They seem to have no attention on whether or not anyone sees. I step over an indiscernible food item on the concrete and round the corner. That brings me back to the entrance of Chupacabra. I weave between more night-goers on the way to join my party at the table. As I come up to them, tossing around vague thoughts that if I switch to whiskey tonight, I can always call a cab, I notice an additional body at the table—a woman with long, black hair.

"Elizabeth!" I say. I can't believe the sound of my voice. It divulges my relief, maybe even happiness, at seeing her.

"Hi, Trent," she says. "I hope you don't mind that I tagged along."

Over the tall bar table, she peers at me under her dark eyelashes. The eyelashes flutter over her round, white, terrified-to-see-me eyes.

I glance at Kyle, and the blankness of his face tells me he doesn't know a thing. Well, she's here and alive where I can see her, much preferable to her being missing or dead.

"I don't mind," I say. "Glad you decided to come. Did you get my message?"

"No, I forgot my phone today when I went to work. What a disaster," she says and flashes me a nervous smile.

Fair enough. I'll tell her everything once we have some privacy. Elizabeth knows this as my usual haunt, so it was easy for her to find me on a Friday night. Laney grins at us and squeezes Kyle's arm. The other couple, Shauna and the guy whose name I already forgot are picking at their chips and salsa and deciding which drinks to order next. Someone has already placed an empty stool next to Elizabeth so that I can sit beside her.

Through the corner of my eye, I find myself taking in every little detail of Elizabeth's appearance. I listen to her comments and watch her facial expressions while she speaks. Her jasmine and wild orange fragrance drifts over to me, and I take it in. What transpiration provoked her to show up like this to make an effort? For sure, something changed, and despite how guarded and angry I still feel toward her—sometimes downright bitter—this change couldn't have come at a better time. I actually start to relax. I begin to enjoy my Friday night, despite all the reasons I shouldn't.

Eleven o'clock rears its head, and since we aren't the party-till-3:00-a.m. crowd, we say our farewells and make our separate ways. Elizabeth trots after me in her tight jeans and long, fleece coat with a fur neckline. Her loud, pointed-toe, brown leather heels can probably be heard from Neches Street every time she puts a foot down. She has this "going out" thing down pretty well. I let her come up beside me.

"Trent," she says, glancing at an empty bench. "Would it be okay if we just sat and talked for a minute? I don't know when we'll get a chance again."

Her words sound eerily correct. "Sure. We can talk."

I sit down with her on the stone-cold metal. Elizabeth sniffs nervously and tosses the hair away from the front of her coat, where it stuck to the fleece. She crosses her legs and turns to face me. There are people here and there along 6th Street, but for the most part, we're alone.

"I need to tell you something." She takes a deep breath. "It's not easy, but I need to tell you that... You were right."

I stiffen. I wonder what game she's playing. Before I can respond, she spills the rest.

"Now, before you get mad, let me tell you this. I didn't sleep with anyone. But you were right. I started seeing someone, kind of casually as friends at first, and then it started to go further. We started to get more personal. No physical stuff, but too personal—it was like we were dating."

I remember the movie ticket stubs I found in the drawer.

"It wasn't appropriate," Elizabeth continues. "I started thinking about what you said. I realized that when I found out about Mary, it really scared me, but it also gave me a reason to leave."

I rub my chin, considering what she's telling me. "What do you mean, no physical stuff? You mean you just hung out with this guy?"

Elizabeth nods ruefully. "Right. But we hung out way too much. And we texted and called each other. It was more than friendship. There was flirting... Exchanging feelings. Stuff like that. It was cheating."

"But no physical stuff at all? Nothing?" It really grates my pride to think of Elizabeth with another man. It stings like a nail in an infected wound, and the pain makes me grit my teeth.

"No, no physical stuff," she says. "But there probably would have been if I hadn't ended it."

I realize I've been holding my breath, and I let it out. My pulse still rabbits with apprehension, but at least she stopped the affair before the point of no return. I nod, letting her words soak in. A measure of disbelief at the timing of her confession gives me pause as well. I don't believe in divine intervention, but it will be much easier to protect Elizabeth if we're together or are at least speaking on a regular basis. For once, the universe has handed me a lucky break. I guess there's a first time for everything.

"I have to say that I'm stunned," I say.

"I know," she says, her gaze dropping shamefully. "I'm really sorry, Trent. You didn't deserve it, and honestly, I don't even know why I did it."

"No, I mean, I'm shocked that you came to tell me this. Impressed? I don't know. It's just not what I expected."

"Are you mad?" she asks.

"Well, hell yeah, I'm mad. I'd have to be dead inside not to be. But more than what you just told me, it's the things that happened earlier. How you left me, and I had no idea why. You wouldn't return my phone calls, and our relationship was just over. After years! With no explanation. I'd be crazy not to be mad. I mean, don't get me wrong, I'm not thrilled about the cheating thing—but I'm glad you told me. I wish you would have told me sooner."

She nods and laces her fingers together in her lap. "I know. I completely understand. I'm really sorry. About all of it."

And I can tell she means it. "Okay," I say. "I believe you."

"So," she says, her voice timider this time. "I also wanted to know if you'd like the ring back?"

"No," I say. "Why don't you hang onto it? We can talk about it more on another day when it's not so late."

She blinks a few times with her heavy, black lashes. "Oh. Oh! Yeah, that would be great."

It seems to hit home that I might be willing to give her a chance. That her telling the truth might not be the worst decision she's ever made. She adds, "I have a new apartment that's closer to work. I'd like you to see it sometime. I think you'll like it."

"Sure. I'd like to," I say.

Elizabeth's face flushes with relief, even in this cold.

I succeed in giving her a brief smile. It quickly fades, my mind riveting to the threat I received. "Elizabeth, about the message I left for you earlier—the one you didn't get."

"Yeah?"

I reach around and slide the white envelope from my back pocket. Her gaze locks onto it. In the last few hours, our relationship has gone from utterly finished to something with an eggshell-like fragility. Some unnamed state more in the realm of possibilities than anything. I don't know how Elizabeth will react or if she'll even believe me. I have to try.

I swallow. "There's something I need you to see."

14

JANUARY 30TH

Deputy Reyes calls me back after midnight on Saturday. He tells me to submit the photo to the sheriff's office as evidence the following morning. Reyes also says that since Elizabeth lives in Travis County, he'll notify the Austin police department. They would enter her home and work locations into their regular patrol route. An officer would also stop by and meet Elizabeth and brief her on what to do.

Before we hang up from our late-night conversation, Deputy Reyes tells me one more thing. From now on, anytime I acquire information or something odd occurs but isn't an emergency, I'm to get in touch with Detective Gerald Menard. The name sounds familiar, and it strikes me that I saw it in one of the news articles. Menard has taken up the County Road 140 case, and as I have a connection to it, I now fall within his scope.

Saturday dawns mockingly sunny with a biting, cold wind. The temperature has dropped into the thirties. I'm glad to be off work. I check the *Statesman*, but it yields no more information on Aria Owen or the case in general. Elizabeth is my priority now, no matter how messed up things have been between us or what she's done. She owned up to her mistakes, and she needs my help.

I've been up since a little after six and have already been to the sheriff's office and back. I haven't eaten anything yet, so I microwave a breakfast burrito. When I smell the ham and cheese, I realize I'm starving. No sooner have I taken a seat on the couch with my plate than my cell rings. It's now 8:30 in the morning.

"Trent!" Elizabeth says. Her voice trembles and I get the idea that she's pacing the floor, clutching her phone with a death grip. "A Deputy Reyes from the Williamson County Sheriff's Office just called me—just like you said. About the threat you showed me. He said a police officer from Austin's going to meet with me soon."

So, maybe she didn't entirely believe me when I told her last night. Or maybe it's finally beginning to seem real. I wasn't able to fill her in on everything that's happened, so she's far from having a complete picture.

"Good, I'm glad you spoke to Reyes," I say, sitting on the edge of the sofa. I set the plate on the coffee table. "Elizabeth, a lot has happened since you left. Why don't I come over there, and I'll tell you everything?"

Her apartment seems a wiser meeting place than my house in the middle of nowhere. I get up and grab my sneakers by the door.

"What do you mean, everything?" she asks. "There's more to this? Why didn't you tell me last night? What's going on?"

"This threat against your life just happened. I just got that yesterday, hours before I told you. As for 'everything,' it's too much to explain over the phone," I say. I return to the couch with my shoes.

"What the hell did you do?" she asks.

I take a deep breath. Cradling my cell between my neck and shoulder, I shove my right foot in my shoe. The laces are tangled, so I bend to undo them.

"Okay, just listen. Like I already told you, I notified the sheriff's office right away when I got that photo. I also turned it in to the evidence department this morning. A lot has happened since you left, and it has nothing to do with anything I did—nothing I did on purpose, anyway. Let me come over, and I'll fill you in."

"Oh geez, Trent! Do you have people after you?"

I lag for an answer. Will she refuse to speak with me again if I say yes? I wish she'd stay calm and talk to me instead of reacting. I tie the laces on my right sneaker.

"Elizabeth, the thing is—"

"Yes or no, Trent. People after you or not?"

I shove my left foot in the other shoe and grab the laces. The phone almost slides out from under my ear, but I catch it.

"Yes. I discovered a crime and reported it. That really pissed this guy off, and he's after me, and I guess threatening you is part of it now. Go online and look up the County Road 140 case. I'll be there in forty-five minutes."

"Oh my God," she says. She sniffs wetly, following it with a long, shaky breath. "Okay. Please hurry."

"I will. Stay inside until I get there."

I tie the laces of the left sneaker into a tight bow and grab my keys and wallet off the coffee table. This is my chance to protect Elizabeth and not screw it up. There isn't a moment to waste. I fire up my Dodge Dakota and, without letting it warm up first, pull out onto County Road 152.

Elizabeth's apartment is in an older Austin neighborhood known as Tarrytown, three miles from downtown Austin. I might call it a high-rent district, though she would probably disagree. Being a good CPA, she can afford it. Tarrytown is just east of the MoPac Expressway, our loop highway so named because its constructors built it along the right-of-way of the Missouri Pacific Railroad in the 60s. On the west side of Tarrytown, you can find Lake Austin, which is actually a water reservoir on the Colorado River.

On the way to Elizabeth's complex, I pass a couple of brick homes built about fifty years ago with ornamental, wrought iron porch columns painted white. They remind me of my grandmother's house in Dallas. I half-expect to see an old Chevelle parked in one of the driveways. Next to the houses stands a newer, generous, estate-style home modeled after a quaint, stone cottage. It has two brick chimney stacks, a sharply peaked roof, and an arched front door made of heavy, dark brown timber attached by medieval, black hinges. Turning my head to keep the landscaping in view as I roll by, I admire that the trees and bushes are professionally manicured, and there doesn't seem to be a blade of grass out of place. Following the suburban mansion, a clean and well-kept but modest bungalow with gray siding huddles beside azalea bushes lining a gravel walkway. There's something for everyone.

Elizabeth's apartment building isn't nearly so posh as the mansion. One of several complexes built in the mid-twentieth century, it's been upgraded and remodeled inside but is nothing to drool over on the exterior. This is a different complex than where she lived before we moved in together, but she's been renting for about seven years while saving for a house. She plans to buy a home in cash, or mostly, in a few years. Unlike me, Elizabeth used the days of her youth wisely, setting herself up very well.

Grabbing the railing with its rough, peeling paint, I propel myself up the steps to Elizabeth's unit. She opens the door before I can ring the bell. Once I'm inside, she turns and hastily locks us in, and secures the deadbolt with unsteady fingers. Elizabeth has pulled her black hair into a messy bun, and she's wearing a faded t-shirt and jeans. She doesn't smell like jasmine and wild orange today, but something more subtle, like lavender deodorant. The faint scent of pancakes clings to the air.

"I read the news articles. Trent, tell me everything." Her eyes portray a token of disbelief and something else. Intrigue, maybe. She hugs herself and gives me room to pass.

I take off my shoes and leave them by the door. We sit next to each other on the plush, dark blue sofa, and I start from day one, the dreary afternoon when Tim called me to check on his neglected house on County Road 140. In the middle of our conversation, someone knocks on the door, and Elizabeth jumps, cursing under her breath. She runs her hands over her face and gets up to answer the door.

"I'm Officer Jeffery Spade," the visitor says.

He has dark brown skin and stands well over six feet tall, with a build like he pumps iron on a daily basis. The police uniform barely contains his nearly three hundred pounds of lean muscle.

"Nice to meet you, Officer Spade," Elizabeth replies. She extends her hand, and they shake. "I'm Elizabeth Reinhardt. This is my fiancé, Trent Lemend. Thank you for coming."

Spade and I nod. He already knows my name from Reyes in Williamson County, as his report transferred this part of the case to Austin.

I stand by while Officer Spade and Elizabeth exchange information, keeping my mouth shut since my input isn't necessary right now. Spade briefs Elizabeth on how police watch works. He confirms her employer's contact information and her mother's as well.

"All right, ma'am," Spade says, putting Elizabeth's card inside the compartment of a metal clipboard. "Do you have any questions?" His face relaxes into a smile.

"Yes," Elizabeth says. "What do I do if I can't get a hold of you?"

"You should always call 911 first," Officer Spade says. "Then call me. The dispatcher will send whoever's closest to your location."

"Okay. Always 911 first, then you."

"That's right. I'll be patrolling the key areas throughout the day, but if I get other calls, I may not be able to respond. But I can follow up as soon as I'm able." His forehead draws into a frown as he confronts Elizabeth, making sure his next words sink in.

"Keep something on you at all times for self-defense—a can of pepper spray, a Kuboton, something you're comfortable using. Always keep your doors and windows locked. That includes your car doors—at all times. Don't speak to strangers, don't go into unfamiliar places. If anything seems fishy, stay away. If something seems fine, but you just have a bad feeling about it, don't do it. I can't tell you how many people wouldn't have become victims if they'd just trusted their gut instincts. So, trust your gut instinct."

"Okay," she says. "I will. Not a problem."

"Any other questions?"

"How close are you to catching this guy?" Elizabeth asks. She holds a hair tie in her right hand, which she works in and out of her fingers nervously.

"Unfortunately, I don't have that information, ma'am," Spade says. "But as soon as we get him, I promise that you and Mr. Lemend will be the first to know."

Elizabeth exhales and thanks him. I like this Spade guy. He can probably break someone's neck with one hand while maintaining a professional demeanor. The officer hands Elizabeth a second card for me so that I can call him when I visit Austin if needed.

After Officer Spade leaves, Elizabeth leans her back against the door, closes her eyes for a moment, and takes a deep breath. I've been hanging a few feet away, and now her gaze finds me.

"Do you want some coffee? I think I need some more," she says.

"Please," I say. Although I'm ravenous, I don't think I can eat now.

As she slips behind the pony wall into the kitchen, I sink to the couch. I lean over and rub my face. The callouses on my fingers are already softer due to my sojourn from ranch work. A few minutes later, Elizabeth pads across the light gray carpet with a hot mug.

"Thank you," I say as I take it. She added creamer, and it smells syrupy. I take a sip to find overly sweet hazelnut. Not my favorite, but I'll live.

After Elizabeth settles in beside me on the couch, I get back to recounting things. She listens until I finish.

"I want to see the photo again, the one you showed me

last night," she says. "It was creepy at the time, but it's worse now. I want to look with a new pair of eyes."

I open up the camera roll on my cell phone. Though Reyes made me hand over the original as evidence, I snapped a picture of each side. I hand my mobile to Elizabeth. Her expression morphs from strained panic to muddied confusion.

"Where could someone have got this?" she asks. Her gaze flicks up to me, searching my face.

"Like I said, I don't know. Is that you and the guy you were—"

"Jared has blond hair," Elizabeth says. She raises her cup to her lips.

Jared, then. Nice.

"Is that you?" she asks.

"No," I say. "Kyle asked me the same thing. But honestly, I'm not a hundred percent certain. Is that you? Have we ever gone to Amy's on Congress? Look at the background." I thought showing Elizabeth the photo would help resolve things, but her reaction is a lot like mine was.

"I can't tell," Elizabeth says. She squints at the pixelated image. "That looks like me from the back, but without seeing the face, there's no way to know for sure."

"Who else could it be?" I ask. I set my half-full mug down on the glass coffee table, shift my legs, and turn toward her.

"Maybe he has the wrong people," Elizabeth says. "The girl you found—the survivor. I saw her picture in the news article. How do we know this isn't her?"

I thought of that, too, like anyone would have. Mistaken identity, something I thought occurs mostly in crime novels and rarely in real life. It's just a little hard to believe that someone could be that off base when it comes to tormenting someone as thoroughly as he's been tormenting me. Wouldn't this jackass have done his research? Marking someone for murder isn't a decision you make over breakfast.

"Well, we don't know it isn't Aria Owen," I say. "I guess it's the hair that makes me doubt it. This woman in the photo has black hair, the same length as yours."

Elizabeth hands the phone back to me. I close out of the camera roll and open another app, where I saved all the news articles I've found to date. I scroll to the one revealing the survivor of the County Road 140 case.

"Here's Aria," I say. "Her hair is dark, but I guess I can't say it's black. And we can't see how long it is."

Elizabeth tilts the phone and frowns. "You're right."

Outside, the wind begins howling in a painful whine which skirts the apartment complex. The morning has slipped away, and it's almost noon, but with all the blinds closed, the living room is dim, even with the side lamp on. Maybe we'll get a winter storm.

"Do you know anyone else besides me who looks like this guy?" I ask, bringing the strange photo back onto the screen.

Elizabeth puts a finger to her chin, biting her lip. She shakes her head. "I don't know. It's such a bad image it could be almost anyone your age with dark hair."

"You mean any average white guy my age with dark hair," I crack. It wins a faint smile from her.

"I'll think on it," she says. "But like you, I don't think we've ever been to Amy's on Congress together. That's the tell, in my opinion. Either that, or he took this photo of us and changed the background." She wrings her hands and tries to shake off the cold that stems from more than the weather.

"The thing is," she continues, "he can do anything. He could have taken other people's bodies and put our heads on them or taken pictures of us separately and put them together. Or these people aren't us, but he's trying to get us to think they are. We don't know." Elizabeth pulls her legs up and bends her knees. She scoots closer to me.

"Agreed," I say. "Let me show you the back again." I open the image I took of the other side of the photo.

Who does her sins lament... Then see the sorrow of my heart, ere it be too late.

"What does that even mean?" Elizabeth asks. "Why not just kill me and be done with it?"

"Geez, Elizabeth," I say.

"No, I mean, why the weird bit of poetry? To scare us more? To make us try and figure it out while we wait?"

"No idea. You don't understand how sick this guy is. What I saw in that room—" I'm not going to give her a graphic description. Aria's body, violated, bloodied, and hanging limp, coupled with the smell of her rotting stepmother, will defile my memory forever. I pick up my cup and drink, letting the strong hazelnut taste and aroma fill my senses.

"I know," she says. The strain in her blue eyes softens in a desire to understand. "I'm just saying, for the sake of our safety, we need to think with the clues we're given. *Think.*"

The idea of Elizabeth as a guileful detective makes me smile. "When did you become a crime solver?"

Elizabeth tries to keep the tremor from her voice as she

manages a crooked grin. "Tax deductions. I can find *everything*."

I laugh, believing that she can.

For the rest of the day, I stay with her. We make a trip to the store and buy pepper spray and a Defender Ring with a concealed spike she can wear for self-defense. Talking things through and preparing together seems to help Elizabeth's state of mind.

Our relationship has definitely entered reboot mode. While neither of us pushes the other away, a certain cautiousness prevails. We hold one another in a long hug toward the end, but that's the most that happens. It seems fitting under the circumstances. Around 8:00 p.m., I get ready to leave since I have work in the morning.

"I'll see you soon," I say.

Elizabeth stands at the door and watches me descend the stairs. Her knowing stare tells me not to make promises I can't keep.

15

FEBRUARY 5TH

New suspect named in County Road 140 case.

WILLIAMSON COUNTY (KXAV) — The Criminal Investigations Division has now released the name of the prime suspect in the County Road 140 case. According to survivor Aria Owen, she and her stepmother were abducted by Owen's ex-boyfriend, Korey Nemeth, of Round Rock.

Nemeth is described as twenty-eight years old, 5' 10," brown hair and brown eyes, 160 pounds. He was last seen driving a white GMC Suburban with the Texas license plate number DL7–xxxx. Nemeth's last known place of business was the City of Austin's Developmental Assistance Center on Barton Springs Road. A City of Austin representative tells us that Nemeth ended his employment with the city in early December, stating that he was taking a higher paying job at the Georgetown Municipal Court. Georgetown municipal sources say that

Nemeth did apply for a position. However, the job was awarded to a better-qualified applicant. It is unknown whether Nemeth is currently employed.

Aria Owen, the twenty-four-year-old survivor of the brutal abduction, is in stable condition and recovering at St. David's Hospital. Hospital officials report that Owen will be released as soon as her health allows. Per Owen, she and Nemeth had ended their four-year relationship in early December due to a pattern of jealous behavior that concerned her. Owen said that Nemeth had never been violent. She told KXAV that on the day she and her stepmother, Carol Brandt, were kidnapped, she was walking to her car, where her stepmother was waiting. Someone tapped Owen on the shoulder, and when she turned around, someone sprayed something in her face. She lost consciousness, and when she woke up, she and her stepmother were lying on the floor in the abandoned home on County Road 140. Newspaper had been stuffed into their mouths, and they were tied in a way that they could barely move. Owen has declined to give KXAV a full account of what happened at this time.

"Once he's caught, and we get a DNA sample, we'll have enough to keep him off the street, and we can prosecute," said Williamson County Sheriff Marcus Gonzales.

Nemeth is considered armed and extremely dangerous. We ask that if you see Nemeth, call your local law enforcement right away. Do not approach him. You can also contact KXAV's hotline at...

I lean over my laptop at the kitchen table, barely tasting the bacon-and-egg bagel I chew as I read. The article features a crystal-clear photo of the killer. He doesn't really look like a psycho. The only "tell" is a faint trace of crazy in his eyes, like a school shooter who loaded himself up on psychotropics. But it isn't that obvious, not really. He has brown eyes and dark hair, but he shaved his head almost to the skin. No beard and no other facial hair. Long, thin nose, and yellowish complexion. Kind of a sallow color, except still young enough not to look ill. We all know that isn't true, of course. This is the face of the sickest man I've ever seen.

As I wipe my hands on a napkin, I can't help but wonder why the article would let all of Central Texas know that Aria Owen will be released from the hospital soon. It reeks of carelessness. Then again, I'm not a reporter or a police officer, so what would I know? I'm just a guy who works at a gas station. After tearing my gaze away from the screen, I get up and begin washing my plate.

Our situation might be grounds for Elizabeth to insist that I come to stay with her—if she wants that. We're still engaged. It makes sense, and I've been expecting her to ask, but she hasn't. That seems admirable under the circumstances and reinforces my decision to give her another chance. I keep close tabs on her and swing by her apartment as often as I can. Elizabeth knows she's forbidden from my place. It's absolutely off-limits.

So far, we've made it through the week in one piece. Officer Spade has checked on Elizabeth several times by phone, in addition to keeping an eye on her apartment as he makes his rounds. Even the weather has cooperated. It hasn't stormed after all, and the temperature has risen into the upper forties with mostly sunny days. By the 5th of February, slate gray clouds roll back in, but there still isn't any rain.

Today is Friday, and as I'm tying the trash bag to take it out before I leave for work, Kyle calls. He invites Elizabeth and me to a party hosted by Kyle's real estate firm. It surprises me that a company would have any kind of get-together only a month after Christmas, but Kyle explains that the company just acquired a new location in San Antonio. The boss is the celebratory type.

"The Salt Lick in Driftwood?" I ask as I go out the front door. Driftwood is about an hour south of Georgetown. Since Kyle's broker is in Austin, that's the closest location.

"I'm afraid so," Kyle says. "Come on. It's better for you and Elizabeth to be out of the house anyway. You're back under one roof, right?"

"No," I say. "We're not living together. And I told her she can't come here until the guy is caught." I throw off the lid of the black, rolling trash can by the side of the house, letting out odors of onions and spoiled fruit.

Kyle hesitates like he finds my answer odd. "Do you think that's best?"

"Well, I think she shouldn't be anywhere near this death trap, yeah," I say, dropping the full bag in. "Anyway, she didn't ask. And I can't live with her in Austin. I need to be closer to work."

"You need to get a different job," Kyle says. "How long are you going to be able to hold out at Texaco?"

"I don't know," I say.

I haven't even been looking much. All I can think about is surveilling my place and keeping Elizabeth safe. With my free hand, I swing the lid over to cover the trash bin. The draft of fishy air makes me snort.

I add, "If things stay calm, I'll probably get some applications next week."

"Good," says Kyle. "What time are you going to show up tonight?"

"Damn, Driftwood? Really? You're killing me," I say. "I don't get off work until seven."

Kyle laughs. "It's not a problem. It's not unusual for these parties to last until ten thirty or eleven. I went to one last year after we opened the San Marcos branch."

"Please tell me your boss didn't make you go to San Marcos," I say.

I grumble under my breath, and he finally gets me to agree. I concede on the basis that it's only half an hour farther than Chupacabra. I call Elizabeth and confirm her interest. She'll be leaving from Austin and will arrive at The Salt Lick around 6:30.

When my shift ends at seven, I already feel tired. I decide to do the sensible thing and take the 130 toll. I'd rather pay and use a longer route than risk getting stuck in the madness of Austin's rush hour traffic. I fly along in my newly acquired Dakota at eighty. At times my foot gets heavy, and it's more like ninety. The winter night doesn't give me much to look at besides dark fields, and soon my mind wanders to the latest news article.

What will happen when Aria Owen gets well enough and leaves the hospital? I assume she has family, not that I know of any reason to think that. Will her release mean that this Nemeth bastard will forget about Elizabeth and go after his prize? Or will it mean nothing at all in terms of Elizabeth and me? I'll have to call Detective Menard. With no new incident in weeks, I need to know how things stand. I need to know how close he thinks they are to catching this guy.

At around 8:20 p.m., I roll up to The Salt Lick. Customers have packed the parking lot full, and I'm forced to find a place way in the back. A welcoming aroma of barbecue draws me through the rows of cars to the front door. The building reminds me of a Texas ranch house with the warm, orange glow of the lights against the stones.

When I step inside, meat roasts in a giant pit to my right, and a fragrant cloud of mesquite smoke hovers above it. The beef sizzles as I walk by, and I crane my neck to locate Kyle and Elizabeth. My stomach rumbles with emptiness. I haven't eaten anything since noon.

I weave my way toward the back of the restaurant, where the waitstaff has joined a few tables together. Laney and Kyle have their backs to me. Across from them sits Elizabeth and people from Kyle's firm I don't know. On Elizabeth's left, a man about my age sticks his chin out to have a look at me as I approach the table. There isn't a seat available next to Elizabeth, so I take one by Kyle. He turns.

"Hey, you made it," he says. He whacks me on the back with the palm of his hand. I say hello to him and Laney and wink at Elizabeth.

"Yeah," I say. "Famished."

A tray piled with beef brisket, chicken, and sausage links has been placed near this end of the table. A similar tray is positioned on the other side. I take an empty plate from a stack and start loading it with meat from the tray.

"Beer?" Kyle asks. He nods toward the six-pack someone brought. The restaurant has a bring-your-own-beer policy.

"No thanks," I say. "I'm getting sick of drinking."

Kyle raises an eyebrow, and I sit back and stare blankly at the carnal feast in front of me. I've said something strange.

"Huh," I say. Utensils in hand, I start tearing into the beef brisket. It's tender, smoky, and well-spiced with cayenne and garlic.

"Trent," Elizabeth says. She has that round-eyed look like the night she showed up at Chupacabra. "I didn't um—I didn't know that—I'd like you to meet my friend Jared."

I almost drop my fork as my gaze swings over to the guy with the blond hair next to her. That same guy who was eyeing me when I walked up.

"Well," I say. "Hi, Jared."

My words come out with utter sarcasm. I extend my hand, and Jared shakes it, barely looking at me, barely smiling. What a pathetic coward. But what unbelievable nerve for him to show up here. I shoot Elizabeth a look, and she can tell I want to know if she invited him.

"Jared was here with some family when I arrived," she says.

Did she ask him to sit with her? I stare at her for a second longer, then start slowly cutting my sausage with the steak knife. Kyle's gaze hones in on me, and I know he's starting to pick up on things.

"So, you guys know each other?" he asks.

"No," I say. I manage to keep the snide out of my voice this time. "This is Elizabeth's friend."

"Oh yeah?" Kyle says, directing his attention toward Elizabeth. "You guys know each other from work or something?"

"Yes, from work," Elizabeth says. "Jared works at Hollis with me."

She never told me that. How sweet.

"Cool," Kyle says. "What do you do there?"

"He fucks with other people's fiancées. That's what he does there," I say to my food. I jerk my head up and glare at the man next to Elizabeth.

In his blue striped, button-up shirt, Jared replies, "Whoa, damn, I think you got the wrong guy here." He holds up his hands in offense.

"Do I, Elizabeth? Do I 'got the wrong guy?'" Snide is back. I glare at her.

She remains femininely mute. Actually, the whole table has quieted down within the last few seconds.

Kyle says, "Trent, you need to eat. I bet you haven't eaten since noon."

Laney gives us all a warm smile and reaches for the meat tray. "Trent, have you tried the chicken? It's amazing. There's some sauce over here—I can pass it down to you."

My hands, which are still busy slicing the sausage link into neat, little coins, shake as I look back to Elizabeth. "Wrong guy or not?"

Elizabeth's bottom lip hangs limp like she's going to throw up.

"I think we should go outside and talk about this like adults," Jared says.

His eyes meet mine for a brief instant. When he stands up from the bench seat, he gives Elizabeth a wave and a weak, little frown. Like, "sorry your fiancé had to show up and call me out, and life just isn't fair."

"Yeah, I think we should," I say.

I set my knife and fork down carefully so as not to slam

them. I can communicate just fine. No need for both of us to act like victims. I stand up and step away from the bench, where I wait for Jared to go around and start walking.

"Jared," Elizabeth says.

"Trent," says Kyle. "Come on, man, let it go."

"There's nothing to let go," I say. "He wants to talk outside. We'll talk outside."

I glare at Jared as he passes around the table and heads out. I proceed to follow him.

"Trent!" Elizabeth says.

Her voice calls from somewhere in the background, but I barely hear it. Kyle grabs my arm and tries to pull me back to the table, but I've already moved too far away for him to get a good grip.

I'm only five-nine, not a six-foot-five bruiser like Officer Spade, but that doesn't mean I'm afraid of a little confrontation. Jared sneaks a quick look back as he gets to the door and gives it a shove, letting himself out in a draft of icy wind. A flurry of conglomerated ruckus explodes in the background from Kyle and the others. No one rushes after us, but a few people get to their feet. There probably isn't any need for them to be concerned. We'll have our words, Jared will leave, and I'll go back to the table.

I catch up to Jared and slip out the door after him. On the front patio, I glare at him beneath the orange lighting that washes over the stone building. He's a few inches taller than me but about the same weight.

"Okay. Let's talk," I say.

Jared snorts. "Yeah. The thing is..."

He runs his hand through his hair and glances at the entrance of The Salt Lick. With no warning, he turns and punches me in the face.

16

FEBRUARY 6TH

I stagger back a few steps, unprepared for a guy with product in his hair to hit me out of nowhere like that. I swing at him, and he ducks. As he comes back up, I hit him with an undercut to the jaw. It murders my fist. But his teeth slam together in a gratifying *clack,* and that makes it worth it.

Jared's face goes rigid. He wobbles sideways and catches his balance on the stone wall of the building. His eyes stare at nothing like he's utterly flummoxed that I popped him one after he sucker-punched me. He takes a couple more steps on his unsteady legs and refocuses his gaze—right at me.

Good. I'm ready.

But Jared takes off. He pushes himself to a breakneck run in several smooth, springing motions, and he gets almost to the parking lot before I can even react. The guy is like a gazelle. Oh yes, he's quite the runner.

My muscles twitch, and I surge into action. I race after him onto the asphalt, past the rows of parked cars. I snatch a glimpse of a few people in my right-side peripheral vision, but otherwise, the coast is clear. No one blocks Jared, and no one blocks me. Our feet pound the blacktop in a fevered cadence, and a few more pumping strides bring me right up behind him. He readies himself to flit around the left side of a gray sedan.

I grit my teeth—maybe even growl like an animal, but I'm not sure—and I jump. For a second, I'm airborne. Then I make contact. Grabbing for the shoulders, I get hold of him right before hurling myself onto his back.

Jared grunts from the impact. In the next instant, when I mash him against the vehicle's hood with my body weight, he can't make any sound at all. We collide against the steel car body in a union of arms and legs, bone and muscle, and my side smashes against the side-view mirror. It jabs into my ribs with splitting pain. But because we've hit so hard and fast, that part is already over. Now we're sliding from the enameled surface—or more like bouncing off. I wrap an arm around Jared's torso and hold on as we hit the pavement. Jared lands underneath me on his side.

Uhhh, he says as the jolt knocks the wind out of him.

I try to catch my breath. My ribs continue to throb from the blow, but I barely notice. Jared wriggles like a fish. He thrashes wildly and gets in a few good pops to my face. With the reek of expensive aftershave in my nostrils, I roll off him and spring to my feet. A brief wave of dizziness passes through me as I straighten.

Jared puts his palms on the asphalt and tries pushing himself up. He half stumbles, half crawls before getting his footing and standing. He backs into the gray sedan. Then he jumps in shock as though he didn't realize the car was there.

He glares at me and starts to open his mouth. Clenching

both fists, he holds them away from his body with his elbows bent, like he's about to spring and start pounding me—or try. He rushes at me. And I lunge at him. He swipes at my head, and I duck. But he swings with so much force he nearly falls over. Jared teeters on one leg and skips a few paces. At that moment, during his vulnerability, I see an opportunity. I seize it.

With everything in me, I throw my body at his and grab him around the waist. The force of my weight launches him backward, and I toss him onto the car hood. He grabs my neck, and I loose a solid punch to his stomach. Letting go of my throat—which he barely has hold of anyway—he doubles over. I stand up straight and shove his forehead with both hands.

Jared's head whips straight back and smacks into the hood, where it hits with a dull, metallic thud. He cries out and throws forth his hand, then grabbing at the wipers in frantic, involuntary motions. He slaps the glass windshield a few times and finally grasps one of the blades. Jared pulls, and it vaults upward. Then he gives it an exaggerated yank—whether intentionally or by accident, I can't tell—and the blade snaps off with a loud *crack*.

Concurrently, in his panic to get away from me, Jared pushes with his feet and propels himself across the slick surface. As he slides over the car's hood, he whips the wiper blade at me and lets go. It slashes my cheek.

I swear and grab my face, putting a hand up in case he throws the other blade. But Jared is mid slide. He slips from view, disappearing on the other side of the sedan. His body hits the blacktop in a soft flapping of designer clothes and high-end leather shoes.

I swing around the front end of the car to meet him, but

Jared has already got to his feet. He takes off toward the fence line. It's darker that way. I've always wondered what was back there, thinking it's probably agricultural land. Maybe vineyards.

"Hey! Hey!" a man yells from somewhere behind us. "Stop! We're calling the police!"

I don't recognize the voice. I don't try to get a look at the speaker or take a headcount of how many people are coming to break up our fight. Never taking my eyes off Jared, I surge after him. He races across the parking lot toward the shadowy farmland. My breaths are coming in big, deep gulps, and my whole body trembles from the adrenaline and exertion. I can quit now. I can. But I don't want to.

When Jared gets about twenty feet ahead, he nears the fence and slows. The Salt Lick's parking lot lights give me enough visibility to make out shiny, new barbed wire and pinkish-brown cedar posts. The fence stands a good five feet high. With a hand on a post, Jared puts a foot on the bottom wire and bobs there for a second. Then he thinks better of it. He steps down and takes off running toward the restaurant at a forty-five-degree angle from me.

I change direction to pursue him. My lungs ache, and my sides are splitting in two, especially my right ribs, but I still have enough fight left in me to finish this. I pant as I run, pushing myself harder. He's a better runner than me, and he darts behind a row of vehicles. I wonder where he thinks he's going—probably back to his car.

"Hey!" the same stranger calls again.

I glance toward the building and find several people standing near the grassy area at the front. A small crowd has also gathered by the doors. Ignoring them, I scan for Jared. I drive my body to work harder, to run faster, and by digging deep within myself, I manage to increase my speed. After taking a slight turn to get on the other side of the row of cars, I find Jared.

He has stopped. Semi-hidden between a black SUV and a blue truck with dualies, Jared leans over with his hands on his knees, panting. His head shoots up when he sees me. A little string of blood runs from his lip to the bottom of his chin.

"Stop!" he says. He puts out his left hand.

I slow my pace and jog up to the rear of the two vehicles.

"Stop? You want me to stop? Then I want an apology. But not here. Inside, in front of Elizabeth. And you tell her that you acted like you wanted to talk and then punched me in the face!" My arms tremble. Intermingled with the burn in my quads, hamstrings, and shins flows an overall buttery sensation that runs through both legs.

Jared doesn't answer. He sidles away from me into the open. I follow.

"Hey," I say. "An apology, or not?"

This time he holds up both hands. That isn't an answer. I make a fist and rush toward him while the onlookers yell. They're background noise. I pay no attention and don't catch a single word. Jared bursts into a sprint but stumbles. He's wearing himself out, too, with all the rabbiting he's been doing. I catch up to him, and he whirls before lunging and shoving me on the breastbone. I break stride but don't fall this time.

"Back off!" he says. His voice breaks.

"Yeah, back off!" a man by the grass echoes.

As Jared trots backward to keep his eyes on me, I clench my fist. I take a few long strides to close the distance between us, and I hit him with a clean right hook to the cheek. Jared grunts and returns with a well-placed throw to my left eye.

Sweet mother of God that hurts. Pain explodes in my nose, eye socket, and eyeball, and for an instant, my vision on that side blurs in a glittery cloud. I've never "seen stars" before, but I guess this fits the bill. I let out a moan of pain and stagger toward him, but he takes off again.

I expect him to go to his car, wherever it is, but he doesn't. The realization occurs that he might not have arrived with family but may have ridden with Elizabeth after work. Maybe she lied. I feel sick.

Jared runs past the gawkers and onto the walkway toward the entrance door. By some miracle, I still have enough strength left to catch up to him. Drawing a deep breath, I grab Jared on the patio.

Voices protest in the background. "Hey! Knock it off! Stop!" they say. They say other useless things too, but I don't have time to listen. Kyle's voice is in there somewhere. So is Elizabeth's.

Jared turns and flails his arms, but I swing myself around behind him, ignoring the stinging pain in my face from his desperate slapping. We dance around erratically, and the crowd parts. Someone—Kyle, I think—lunges at us and misses. As we see-saw back and forth and almost collide with some woman, I get my arm around Jared's neck and squeeze with my bicep, then letting my full weight fall on his back.

Struggling and thrashing at my head with his left arm and grasping at his constricted neck with his right, Jared slams me, back first, into the heavy, metal doors. They resound with a clanging thud, and one swings open. The hinges squeal, and the metal push bar shudders. Then Jared falls on his knees, and I let go of him. I take him by the back of the head and slam his forehead against the door.

Jared's body wavers at the shock of this. He quivers in a moment of disorientation, then he springs forward and swings at my face. I duck and punch him square in the jaw. My fist cracks into it nicely, and his breath comes out in a grunt. He says something inaudible, and I start unloading on him, pounding him in the face again and again. Sometimes he successfully blocks me with his hands and arms. He gets in a good swing and smashes his fist into my left ear, which hurts like hell. Then he gets in another one under my right eye.

I shove his head into one of the doors again, and he gets his hands around my neck in a death grip. I poke my thumb into his eye. He screams bloody murder, swings his foot out, and kicks my legs out from under me. I sail onto the pavement, landing right on my tailbone—so hard I don't know if I'll be able to get up again. God, it hurts so bad I think I've broken my spine.

With his face contorted in a dry sob, Jared throws himself on top of me. He starts whaling away on my face with everything he has. He gets in maybe a dozen really good, solid licks to my left cheek. I take a cheap shot and jab him hard in the groin with my knee. Well, no cheaper than what he's been doing with Elizabeth.

At first, he freezes, and he stops assailing me. Finally, he manages to get a few gasps of air. He falls forward and catches himself by his hand on the cement, with his chest against mine.

"Ahhhh, you piece of shit," he says into my ear.

It was cruel, after all, that I fought back after he hit me with no warning. I wrench my knee up to my chest, get my foot against his stomach, and push hard, with enough force to get him off me and dump him on the concrete. He lies there on his side, immobilized. He protectively cradles his package while blood dribbles out of his busted mouth. Tears run down his swollen face.

The crowd swarms us. Seconds later, another flood of about twenty people comes bursting through the doors. They're all set to grab Jared and me and stop the fight, but it's already over. Three big men get between us even though we lie on the pavement, unmoving.

"Okay," the guy hovering over me says. "You guys are done." He has a goatee and a wife-beater t-shirt. And those motorcycle boots that bikers wear.

"Obviously," I say.

I want to laugh. Something about this strikes me as funny, although nothing can compare to earlier when Jared pulled off that wiper blade. Yanked it clean off. Threw it right at my face, the nutjob did. But I can't laugh or even grin. I'm hurting too bad, afraid to move. I wonder if I shattered my pelvis.

Elizabeth rushes out from the crowd and looks back and forth between Jared and me, her face twisting into various expressions of horror. "Trent. Oh my God."

Looking at both of us, it isn't difficult to see that Jared has sustained most of the damage—at least most of the plainly visible damage.

"Can you get up?" the guy with the goatee asks.

"I don't know," I say.

When I swallow, I taste blood. I try to raise my back, and a sharp, splitting pain shoots through my tailbone. I grit my teeth, groaning and laying myself down again on my right side. The smoky mesquite aroma from the firepit irritates me now.

Elizabeth stares at me, but she crouches down next to Jared. She puts her hand on his shoulder. I cover my face and look away. I don't want to see any more. My stomach starts a free fall like I'm trapped in a sinking elevator bound straight for hell. I feel a real good dose of reality coming on. I stare up at the dark sky. Unlike in rural Georgetown, here, the city lights obscure the stars.

Kyle comes to stand beside me and looks me over. I know that only because I move my hand long enough to glimpse part of his shoe. He doesn't say anything.

It seems like a long time passes, a period in which I listen to all the people around me talking. Some speak in hushed voices, and occasionally some woman laughs. I pick up things like "idiot" and exclamations about what's wrong with us. Most of the guests have no idea who started the fight or what happened. Only those from Kyle's table saw me follow Jared out the door, but not one of them witnessed Jared sucker-punch me.

After a moment, Kyle squats. "Can you get up?"

"No," I say.

"Okay. I'll call an ambulance," he says.

"Wait, I'll try again," I say.

I manage to get my elbow out and grind it into the concrete. I push against it and try to lift myself. The incredible, bone-deep pain races up my tailbone and into my lower back in electric waves.

Someone yells. That someone might be me, but I'm not sure. My head rolls back, my body goes slack, and my arms fall limp on the ground.

17

FEBRUARY 6TH

I come around slowly. A rhythmic beeping sound pings from somewhere to my right. That must be my alarm going off. I pry open my eyes just long enough for the blindingly bright room to make me shut them again. Did I oversleep? I must have got pretty hammered last night. Grogginess I can't shake off persists like someone slipped me a drug.

Trying to stretch, I drag something along, which pinches me in the crook of my arm. I fully open my eyes to find an unfamiliar, paneled ceiling. When I try to sit up, I learn that I can't. I lift my left arm to see an IV tube inserted and secured with medical tape. I turn my head and look around the room at the heart monitor, the bag of fluid, the white walls, and the sink. A closed, white curtain segregates my space. Smells of antiseptic spray and rubbing alcohol pervade the atmosphere. I'm in the hospital.

Kyle told me he was going to call an ambulance. I swear and close my eyes again. I really did it. The fight with Jared —that was real.

I need to find my cell phone, but as I search for a likely table, the swinging door comes open. A nurse with short, blonde hair bustles in.

"You're awake," she says. She smiles and begins fiddling with my IV. "I was just coming to check on you. How are you feeling?"

I don't know how I feel. "Can't feel much of anything."

The nurse laughs. "Well, good. The meds are working then."

"What happened? Did I break something?"

"You fractured your coccyx. That's the bone on the end of your tailbone. It looks like you landed on it pretty good. You're lucky there wasn't enough damage to require surgery, but it'll be uncomfortable for a while until it heals," she says.

"Mmph," I say after not finding the words. "What about my back? Did I do anything to my spine?"

"No, your back looks okay. You probably just strained it. But let us know if you have any pain," she says.

"So, my tailbone is fractured? What does that mean, exactly?"

"If you mean as far as getting around and living a normal life, you'll be fine. I mean, not right away. You're going to need some rest, and then you might use a cane for a while. But once you heal, you'll be just fine," she says. "That was quite a nasty fall you had."

I finally look at her name tag: Alice.

"Yeah," I say. I feel like a fraud—like I somehow manipulated my way into the hospital and shouldn't be here. If the pleasant nurse knew what happened, she might not be so pleasant then.

"Is anyone in the waiting room to see me?" I ask. I grope for the blanket.

"No, not that I know of. No one's come to the emergency desk. But I'd be happy to check. I can even page someone if you like."

A medicine ball drops into the bottom of my gut. Logic dictates that Elizabeth should be out there, waiting to come see me and make sure I'm okay. The memory of her crouching down by Jared as I blacked out doesn't help. Maybe she's in another part of this same hospital, holding his hand and speaking soothing words to his pretty face, which he probably moisturizes daily with Tom Ford aftershave. I want to throw up.

"That would be great. Could you page Elizabeth Reinhardt? Just in case she's on this floor," I say.

"I sure can," Alice says. She slips out the same swinging door through which she entered, and the request with my fiancée's name sounds through the speakers. Alice promptly reappears.

"I'll let you know if she turns up," she says.

In my fog of numbness from the anesthetic, I question Alice enough to orient myself. She tells me the ambulance brought me to Seton Southwest in Austin, about fifteen minutes from The Salt Lick. Alice estimates I'll be staying only a few days and explains what my recovery will be like. I'll be taking prescription painkillers. I'll be taking stool softeners so that using the can won't be painful. For right now, though, I'll use the bedpan. I'll need to buy a special donut cushion so that I won't put pressure on my tailbone when I sit down. Then there are payment arrangements that need to be made. I was admitted and treated for Pete's sake, and that isn't cheap. I'm grateful to have my health insurance, but there will still be a copay.

Alice hands me a plastic bag which contains yesterday's

clothing and the rest of my things—belt, wallet, phone, keys, and shoes. I check my cell to see who called. Not so much as a text from Kyle.

Elizabeth left a dispassionate message. "It's me... I'm just calling to see if you're okay. Call me back... Or text me."

I can't blame her for being disgusted with me. I'm pretty disgusted with myself too. The no-communication-whatsoever from Kyle, though, is an outright slap in the face, which lets me know how bad I messed up. I type out a text, apologizing, then delete it. I pull up his icon and press "call." He answers within one ring.

"Yeah," he says.

I wonder if I misdialed. "Kyle. Hey, man, I just want to say I am *really* sorry about—"

"You just want to say you're really sorry about starting a fight at The Salt Lick in front of my boss? And most of my co-workers? Is that what you're sorry for?"

I lie here holding the phone to my ear, numb from the meds but frozen by his reaction. In over twenty years of friendship, I'd be hard-pressed to recall a time Kyle was angry with me. Usually, even my worst behavior seems to roll off him like water off a duck's back.

"I didn't exactly start it," I say. I stare stupidly at the white wall. "He hit me out of nowhere, and—"

"And you're *really* sorry? You're really sorry for almost blinding someone that you don't even know? You're really sorry for committing a crime? Do you understand that? You committed a crime. Assault and battery—and you damaged someone's car. That is the reality of what you did, and what you did was illegal. And you want to know what the fucked-up part is? This isn't the first time! It's what you do. And I'm no longer going to be a part of it."

I pull my free hand across the length of my face. Stubble is already forming around my mouth and chin. "I understand."

"Do you? Do you understand?"

I try to clear my throat. My eyes get tight. "Yeah, I do."

"I really hope so. For Elizabeth's sake, especially. Goodbye, Trent."

He may as well have slammed the phone in my ear. The silence shreds my eardrums like a mallet to a bronze gong. I watch the words "call ended" disappear, leaving my Dallas Cowboys star.

Alice pops in and leans her head in my direction, her stethoscope swinging at her chest. "Did you get a chance to call who I paged?"

I clear my throat again. Kyle didn't even ask if I was okay. "Not yet. I was just talking to—I just called someone real quick."

Alice squints at me. "No problem. You're still doing okay, right? Unless you need something, I'm going to go ahead and move you now."

"I'm fine." No need to be a chump in front of a complete stranger. "Move me?"

"Uh-huh. This is Emergency, but since you're stable and responding well, Doctor Linneman wants me to move you to the second floor."

"Oh. Sure, yeah." If it were up to me, I'd be moving myself right out the front door. I push the heels of my hands into the bed, again attempting to push myself up. It isn't happening.

"No, no, just stay like you are," Alice says. She smiles and firmly presses a sanitizer-scented hand on my arm. "I'm going to wheel you there."

She unlocks the wheels of the bed, grabs the IV pole, and we're away. White coats whisk by us as Alice adeptly and efficiently wheels her bed-bound patient toward the elevators. Sometimes a doctor or nurse politely nods as we pass. Sometimes they even smile. With a slight bit of jostling and wheels thumping over ridges, the bed slides into the elevator compartment, and we make our ascent.

On Floor 2, Alice thrusts the bed through the door and says a few words to a dark-haired woman with glasses at the desk. The walls in this ward are painted in a watered-down hue of kidney brown. We turn into a hallway. The spaces between the curtained rooms are decorated with abstracts of floral arrangements. A blue and yellow helium balloon has migrated to the extruded aluminum ceiling, where it tilts and flaps in the draft from the vent.

Alice parks my bed in the new room. An older man connected to oxygen snores softly on the other side of the open curtain. Alice smiles and quietly draws it closed.

"Are you hungry?" she asks.

"No. Actually, I feel kind of sick." I haven't brushed, and my mouth tastes like stale bread. "Can you prop up this bed?"

"Sure," she says, raising me to a sitting position. "Nausea isn't unusual. The anesthetic sometimes does that. Just push this button to let the nurses know if you want anything. If not, you'll get lunch at noon."

"Thanks," I say.

"Sure. I have to go back to my floor but take care. I hope everything works out okay. You'll be just fine."

Soon Alice disappears, and a different nurse comes and introduces herself. Vicky, I think, a mid-thirties lady in pink scrubs with a long ponytail. I think of Elizabeth again.

Maybe she responded to the page, but I was relocated too quickly for her to find me. I set my small bag of possessions on the bedside table and lift my cell phone from its place on my lap.

I dial up Elizabeth. It rings for a long time and goes to her voicemail. Maybe she's on the other line. I leave a message.

"Elizabeth, it's Trent. I'm at Seton Southwest on the second floor. I'm doing okay. It turns out I fractured my tailbone, but they say it's not too bad, and I won't need surgery." I manage a shaky laugh. "Yeah, so I should be out in two or three days. I'm really—"

I don't know what to say anymore, especially after the conversation with Kyle. I sigh, struggling for something, anything, that won't make me sound like a jerk.

"Look, I know it probably doesn't matter, but I didn't start that fight with Jared, and I'm really—"

A long beep tells me that her mailbox is full and can't record a message beyond that length. I throw the phone onto my lap, resisting the urge to smash it into tiny pieces against the wall.

In a whisper, I repeat my words sarcastically to the empty space in front of me. "I'm really sorry. I'm really sorry."

I snort and lay my head back down on the pillow. Within a few minutes, my phone lights up, and I know I've received a text. Elizabeth responded to my chopped-off message.

Trent, I'm glad you're okay. I want to come see you, but I have mixed feelings about it. I love you, but I have to say that after last night I'm a little afraid of you. Please try to understand. I'm working through it. I really want everything to be okay. I can't call right now, but I'll try to call and check on you later. xo

"Why can't you call me now?" I ask no one.

I swallow down the jealous thoughts of Elizabeth sitting beside Jared—if, in fact, that idea isn't pure fiction. It's time to get real. It's my fault she isn't calling.

A nurse's voice somewhere outside my room attracts my attention. "Ms. Owen, you're all set. I've called him, and I'll let you know when he gets here."

"Thank you," a young woman answers. "I'm just going to stretch my legs."

The name "Owen" stands out to me, but I know this hospital is in south Austin, and the Owen I'm thinking of should be in St. David's Hospital in Georgetown. Still, curiosity seizes me. I watch out the open door of my room, and I wait in hopes that she'll walk by.

After a moment, a human shape emerges. A pale female slowly makes her way down the hall. She appears more adolescent than woman, her frame emaciated like that of an anorexic teenager. The jeans and gray t-shirt she's wearing seem too big for her. Her elbows are too sharp, her waxy cheekbones too prominent under the enlarged, dark eyes. Is it her?

"Aria?" I call. Crap. I don't know where that came from—I didn't mean to speak.

The girl gasps, halting in mid-step and turns in my direction. She takes one look at me and starts backing toward the wall on the other side of the hallway.

"No, it's okay," I say, speaking barely above a whisper. What the hell am I doing? "I don't know if it's you—if you're who I think you are, but if you are... I'm the one who found you."

The young woman shakes her head, glaring at me with

her watery, brown eyes. Her pointed jawline juts out in defiance. She must be her. She *looks* like her, the woman in the photo.

"It's okay, it's okay," I say, softening my voice even more. "I just wanted to say, um, glad you're okay. I'm Trent. I'm the one who found you in the house in Georgetown."

I try to smile. The young woman continues glaring at me, her chest rising and falling in stricken panic as she attempts to calm herself. She looks both ways down the hall and begins to walk into my room.

My lungs strain as I watch her approach. She seems like an apparition, a spirit visiting from beyond the grave, and yet here she stands in the flesh. This must be what it feels like to see a ghost.

Aria doesn't speak but sits down in the chair inside the room by the door and continues to stare at me. She narrows her almond-shaped eyes, setting her hands in her lap and looking me over. I notice Aria doesn't have a clear plastic bag with clothes and such like I do. Then I realize she brought nothing with her but her body—she barely brought that. A chill crawls over my shoulders and settles in my heart.

"How do I know you're the one?" Aria asks, her voice shaking. It sounds papery and thin, much like the rest of her looks.

"I—I saw you and your—your stepmother," I say. Stammering is unusual for me. "I found you. Chained to the wall. You were wearing a white dress, covered in blood."

The papers didn't provide those details. I wonder if she knows, if she's been following the articles, or if she avoids them like the plague.

"My name is Trent. Trent Lemend."

Aria's eyes flash. She blinks as terror and recognition

consume her countenance. Her memories invade her. She nods and sits there, letting her gaze fall to her lap. "I'm going into protective police custody today."

"I'm glad to hear that," I say.

She looks up at me, and I wonder why she hasn't gained more weight during her hospitalization.

As if she hears my thoughts, she says, "I have trouble eating. Korey had a dog." She chuckles faintly, rubbing her forehead with her hand and shifting her gaze to the wall at my right. "I hate dogs."

I don't see the connection between those statements. I remain silent, unable to stop staring at the thinness of her.

She searches me with her overly large eyes. "Trent, do you believe in God?"

I blink. Well, I have no idea whether I do or don't believe in God, but all signs point to "no." "I don't know. Not really. I'm not the religious type, I guess." I try a small smile that I don't feel.

"I do," she says. She nods and glances at her lap again. "I do. I prayed. When there was no hope at all, I prayed. And God sent you to me. And when I woke up in here, I wondered if I'd ever meet the person who God sent—"

Her voice breaks, and her face contorts with a sob. Tears spill down her cheeks. Aria smiles, almost laughs. "But now I am. I'm meeting you. He sent you here, so I could meet you and know."

Aria covers her face with her hands and cries quietly, her bony frame quivering, her chest heaving now and then for a good breath of air.

"I'm glad. I'm glad it worked out, and you're okay," I say. That isn't quite what I want to say, but the words elude me. I fold my hands in my lap and wait respectfully.

She nods and starts wiping her face.

"So, they moved you here from St. David's?" I ask.

Aria says, "Yeah. From what I was told, the sheriff's department didn't think it was safe for me to stay there, so they moved me weeks ago. But they just kept telling the press I was at St. David's."

"That was smart," I say.

She takes a deep breath, shuddering from all the crying. She looks me right in the eyes again, which gives me the uncomfortable tightness in my chest like my windpipe is starting to close. "Tell me about yourself, Trent. I want to know about you. I want to know something about the man who saved my life."

I rub the five o'clock shadow on my chin. What is there to tell? I feel like a worthless sack of nothing. "I'm not sure you want to know."

"I do. I truly do," she says, the tension leaving her face a little.

"Well, I work on a ranch—*used to* work on a ranch." Lame.

"Oh, with horses?" she asks. Straightening in the chair, she pushes her hands against her legs.

"No, with cattle, sheep, and goats. But I had to quit that job because—" I don't want to tell her why. "—because of some scheduling conflicts, so now I'm working at Texaco and looking for something else full-time." Double lame. The woven pattern of the cotton blanket itches my fingers as I smooth the fabric to distract myself.

"That doesn't sound so bad," Aria says. "What are your parents like?"

That's a better subject. "They're nice folks. I miss them since they moved to Dallas, but we still talk and see each other on holidays. My dad sells insurance, and my mom has a house cleaning business."

"What are their names?" she asks.

"Walter and Penelope," I say. "Everyone calls my mom 'Penny,' as I'm sure you can guess."

Aria smiles subtly, mostly with her eyes. "They sound nice."

"Aria?" a woman's voice calls from the hallway.

Twisting in her chair, Aria glances out the doorway.

"Oh," the same nurse says when she finds her patient. A large woman with short, brown hair strides into view and observes us. "Is everything all right?" She glances between Aria and me, scowling.

"Yes," Aria says. "Is my ride here?"

"No. I just wanted to make sure you were okay," Nurse says.

Aria nods rapidly, almost frantically. "Oh yes, yes. I'm fine. I was just talking to Trent. We know each other."

Nurse scowls some more. Her thick brows pull into one. "Okay. I'll be right outside if you need me."

Aria nods. The nurse is guarding her until her escort arrives, and that's a good thing. Knowing the staff are protecting her, I don't mind the dirty looks. The attentive healthcare worker slides beyond sight past the door frame.

Aria turns back to me. "And what about you? What are you like? What do you like to do for fun?"

"Well, I like football. Not to the point of obsession, but I like it. And I like dogs," I say. My face burns and I want to kick myself. "I mean, I like *some* dogs, not all of them. But I've never had any kind of dog... I'm sorry."

Aria fiddles with her hospital bracelet. "It's okay." She studies her long, near-skeletal fingers, holding them out and stroking them. "What kind of work do you like to do? I mean, besides ranching."

I sigh and let my vision go out of focus. "Well, when I was younger, I wanted to be an auto mechanic."

Her gaze flits up to mine. "Oh, that's nice. I've always admired people who know how to do that." Her comment seems so sincere, almost innocent.

I grin. "Thanks. What about you? I mean, what is it that you do?"

"I'm a real estate assistant—*was* a real estate assistant. Before... well, before." Somehow, she grins back at me, a genuine smile complete with teeth.

"That sounds nice too," I say.

Nurse pops back in. "Aria, he's here." She eyes me like I'm suspect number one, I guess because the odds of Aria and me knowing each other seems slight.

Aria jerks and rises slowly from the chair. "Okay. Just one minute." To me, she says, "Well, now what?"

I shake my head. I have no idea. Sticking my nose into her life, in any way at all, can't possibly be a good thing. I frown and stumble over the words. "I don't know. I guess—"

"This is goodbye?" she asks. She gives a little snort, and her mouth pulls into a sad smile. "Of course. Of course, it is." Her huge, brown eyes fill with tears again.

"I just don't want to intrude," I say. "It's not my place."

Aria laughs. It starts strong and dies quickly like the exertion pains her. "If you wouldn't have intruded, I would be *dead* right now." She cocks her head as a tear slides down her waxy cheekbone. "So."

"When you put it like that," I say, forcing a chuckle. "Well, what would you like?"

I'm out of my element. Drowning. Kyle would know what to do, but he hates me now.

"I want to stay in touch," Aria says. "Can I have your number? I don't have a phone now, but when I get another one, I'll call you."

That ball drops into my stomach again. Shit. This is bad. Something about this is really, really bad.

"Sure," I say.

A pen and pad rest on the bedside table. I write my number down, tear off the page, and hold it out. Aria smiles as she walks over. When she takes it from my hand, I get a whiff of her shampoo, a blend like strawberry and mint. That isn't hospital issue. One of the kind nurses probably bought it for her. Aria stands beside my bed for a moment, some of the color coming back into her face.

"Thanks. I never asked you why you're in here," she says.

I laugh. "I fell on my, um, backside and fractured my tailbone."

The hint of a smile touches Aria's lips. "Are you telling me that you literally busted your ass to come see me?"

18

FEBRUARY 9TH

Since returning home from the hospital last night, I don't feel safe sleeping in the bedroom. Instead, I lie sideways on the couch. I put my computer close by on the coffee table so that I can access it if needed. The rifle rests above me on top of the back cushion, and my pistol is within arm's reach beside the computer. This way, besides my alarm system warning me, I'll instantly know if anyone comes through the front door and will be ready to say hello.

The doctor explained that it might be as long as six weeks before I can sit long enough to drive a car. Going to work at the gas station, at least right now, isn't happening. I'm loaded up on a strong painkiller, and there's no way in hell I can walk there. It's only a few miles, but it's mostly country roads with no sidewalk and then highway with no shoulder. I let Louie know I injured myself. He'll take me back in a few weeks, or he won't. That's life, I guess.

Elizabeth hasn't sent me any more texts or called since several days ago. I have no way of knowing whether she's okay or not. Doesn't she understand that? As badly as I messed up, doesn't she realize that it's in her best interest to have me around? There's no sense in leaving lots of messages, so I only sent one text last night to check in. I apologized yet again, told her I wondered how she was doing and that I loved her. Not only did she not reply, but the text still shows as "delivered," not "read," as the other texts do.

If it weren't for the pain relievers, I'd probably be drinking again. Instead, I have a case of bottled water nearby. I'm not terribly hungry, but the aroma of cheese and tomato sauce remnants inside last night's empty pizza box reminds me I should eat. I'll be ordering in for a while or having microwave meals. Slipping into apathy and forgetting about my wretched, miserable failure of a life would bring welcome comfort, but I don't have that luxury. I need to heal as soon as possible. I don't want to be crippled if something happens.

Staying on my side, I search "County Road 140 case" and "Korey Nemeth" online to see the latest developments. It turns out that as far as forensics is concerned, there are two types of DNA—incriminating and non-incriminating. This Nemeth wasn't dumb enough to leave the incriminating kind at the crime scene, but with Aria's eyewitness account, he'll still be arrested and held until they can convict him.

After flipping through channels aimlessly, I can't bear Elizabeth's silence any longer. It isn't about me. It's about her safety, and she has to understand that. I call her mom's number, and it goes to voicemail.

"Hi, Ms. Reinhardt, it's Trent. I'm just calling to make sure Elizabeth is okay. I haven't heard from her. Thanks." I hang up.

The medicine has me so groggy and leaves a dry, metallic

taste in my mouth, but besides that, I just don't feel right. Who else can I call? My stomach dives as I dial up Kyle.

He answers almost instantly, just like when I called from the hospital. "Yeah."

"Kyle, hey," I say. My voice creaks from being unused for so long. "If it's not too much trouble, could you check on Elizabeth? She's not returning my texts. I tried her mom, and she's not answering either. I just want to make sure she's okay."

Silence. "Yeah. Sure. I'll check on her." More silence.

"Thanks, man. I appreciate it," I say.

"Yep. Anything else?" asks Kyle.

"No. Thanks."

Kyle hangs up, and blood rushes into my face, making it all hot and sweaty. I guess he'll let me know if he gets a hold of her. On a whim, I dial Elizabeth just to see if she'll answer. Like the call to her mom, it goes straight to voicemail. I leave a brief message asking her to text me that she's okay.

I receive a text back from Elizabeth's mobile number. *She's not okay. :)*

My stomach plunges like I've been dropped off the side of a building. I push myself to a sitting position, gritting my teeth and yelling as the pain shoots through my tailbone in an electric ribbon of agony. I curse and lie back down on my side, waiting for it to subside.

How can I possibly find her? I rub my hand across my sandpaper chin and squeeze my eyes closed hard, trying to think. I speak out loud to try and get my wits together.

"You've got to be kidding me. You've got to be—" As I open the friend-finder app, I only manage expletives.

He's doing it again. It's really happening, this time not with my cell phone, but with my fiancée's. My stomach does another dive as I wait for the app to locate Elizabeth's cell phone. I half-expect to find it at the murder house. Why wouldn't it be? That will make everything oh-so-perfect. But her cell isn't there. Elizabeth's icon shows in the middle of nowhere in rural Georgetown, in an even more out-of-the-way area, if that's possible. The image makes it appear that she's out in a field somewhere between County Road 152, Berry Springs Park, and County Road 140. Close. Real close. Close enough that an injured guy could walk there, probably.

I let my hands fall slack. The cell phone drops out of my limp fingers and bangs against the coffee table before it lands on the carpet. I groan and slide my body to the edge of the couch, then I dangle my legs off the side and heave myself to my feet. Standing isn't too bad. Walking isn't either, but this won't be an ordinary walk. I reach down and pick up my Ruger. It's loaded and ready to go. I shake my head and again try to think. What the hell am I going to do?

I have a soft holster that can slip inside my jeans, so I clip this on and tuck the pistol inside. I take my keys, twenty dollars cash, my concealed handgun license, and my ID. They'll need to know who I am when they take me to jail later, won't they? When they find this bastard dead and me standing over him, it won't leave much room for doubt.

The walls around me start to sway, and a wave of nausea makes my mouth water. I'm not used to taking painkillers. I can't get my head straight. Isn't there something else I'm supposed to do?

Call the sheriff. I dial 911. I provide the operator with as many details as I can, giving her the approximate location. I don't think it will be easy for law enforcement to find. I put on my work boots and long trench coat. I grab my cane and head out the door. Maybe I'll meet them there before it's too late.

I carefully make my way along the shoulder of County Road 152, heading toward Berry Springs Park. It's late afternoon, and the air is tinged with scents of a far-off fireplace. For once, the sun is shining. I squint my eyes, shoving my left hand deeper into the pocket of my trench coat. My right hand guides the cane. The cold wind already makes my face hurt, and I do my best to ignore the throbbing pain in my tailbone. At least walking doesn't hurt as much as driving does. To keep my mind from racing with terrifying thoughts for Elizabeth's safety, I focus on the thorny mesquite trees beyond the barbed-wire fence to my right, and next, the pasture containing one of Tim's barns and several sheep. I have to remain aware of my surroundings. Letting my mind run wild won't help matters.

My coat pocket rings, and I visibly jerk mid-step and stumble, then groaning as my reaction costs me another wave of pain from my backside. I nearly drop the cane. My heart hammering, I yank the glove off my right hand. I hope it's Elizabeth calling to tell me that she's fine and that the text message earlier was actually from her—that she was just really pissed at me. But it isn't Elizabeth. It's Deputy Reyes.

"Trent, I'm headed your way now. Is Ms. Reinhardt's phone still showing at the location you gave us?"

With my hand shaking, I say, "Hold on. Let me check."

I open the app, and yes, Elizabeth's phone is apparently still in the same place.

"Still there." My voice sounds thin as it's carried away by the cold air.

"Okay," Reyes says. "Trent, I hear that you're outside. You

need to go home immediately. Do you understand? We'll be there shortly and will do a thorough investigation. I can assure you of that."

That's about all he can assure me of. I want to punch something. There's no telling what happened or what will occur. I hold the phone to my ear and plod along, not really knowing how to answer him.

"Trent?" Reyes says. The edge to his voice tells me that he means business. He doesn't want me doing anything stupid again.

"I can't go home. I can't just sit by and do nothing," I say. "What should I do?"

"Trent, you're doing exactly what he wants you to do. You're walking right into a trap, and you know it. You won't find Elizabeth this way."

My stomach plunges. He's right. Being loaded up on medication, I'm not thinking straight. I'm only playing the fool out of anger, desperation, or both, just like the day I went to stake out the murder house and wound up not only getting shot at but getting my truck smashed in by a semi. There is zero chance of finding Elizabeth like this.

"Can I wait at the park entrance for you?" I want to be there when they complete their investigation and retrieve her cell phone.

"No," Reyes says. "I need you to go home. Now."

I stand on the pebbly shoulder and sigh. I turn to put the wind at my back. In front of me, a tangly thicket of shrubs and cacti rustles in the wind, the tall, brown grass making a papery, rustling sound. I can't disobey the deputy sheriff's order.

"All right," I say.

Relief floods through me for a second, even though I'm a

ball of nerves, pain, and fear for Elizabeth's life. The relief won't last but a minute or two, I know, but it still feels nice. For once, I'll make myself listen to reason like I should have done so many times before. Did he still care, Kyle would be proud.

"Will you call me if you find her?" I ask.

"I guarantee it," Reyes says.

I wait for him to say more, but he doesn't. He doesn't know any more than I do. I thank him, and we hang up, and I begin the short walk back to the house. I drag my feet, realizing how awful I feel.

I reach my gravel driveway. Somewhere in the distance, a dog barks. Silence ensues for a few seconds, and I strain to pick up any birdsong. I study the sunlit yard, the grass, the truck, the house—*the house.*

Something lies on the porch by the front door. It actually looks like a person lies there, but I can't be sure. This might be trap number two. I'm not choosing to avoid one disaster, only to walk right into another, so I hesitate. I slide my gun out of its holster, ducking behind my pickup to get a better look before approaching. Bending down like that hurts, and I grit my teeth to keep from groaning. The wind picks up, and the person's hair flutters. It's black—black like Elizabeth's hair.

A panic attack makes me nearly fall over, slamming the breath out of me. My heart races so hard it's dizzying. Oh my God, this can't be real.

With another grimace, I push myself to my feet, dropping the cane. I run around to the other side of the house, with mind-splitting pain radiating into my pelvic bone. I slide to a halt when I find no one there. I continue around the backside of my place and turn to come around to the front again, this time heading straight for whoever lies on the porch. I walk up slowly, holding my pistol. The person lies face down, wearing a light blue hoodie, with a few tendrils of dark hair spilling out the sides. The left arm extends from the body, and the soft, delicate hand definitely belongs to a woman. An engagement ring encircles her finger. Elizabeth's engagement ring, the one I bought for her.

I drop to my knees, barely noticing the pain this time. I put my hand on Elizabeth's shoulder and try to see her face. Maybe she just got drunk, came looking for me, and passed out on my porch. Like that would ever happen. But no, that's me thinking crazy, and her car isn't here.

"Elizabeth," I say, my voice thick. "Hey."

I use both hands to lift her slightly and turn her over. When her head rolls around, her blue eyes stare up at me, blank and lifeless. Her lips are halfway parted, a cruel, red gash extending from the corner of her mouth and through her cheek. Blood has dried over most of the left side of her face, thick and caked where it bled into her hair.

I try to speak, but no words come. I hold together just long enough to look at the rest of Elizabeth's body—the part below her sliced face. My gaze follows her graceful neck to the collar of the sweatshirt and down her torso. There, at the navel, the hoody's light blue fabric and the shirt underneath are torn away—no, cut. Below her belly button, he stabbed her to hamburger meat.

My throat tightens. My stomach contracts and I lean over to empty it off the side of the porch. I cough, catching my breath as waves of anguish crash against my being. The world around me spins, and I whirl somewhere within it, a helpless speck tossed on the wind. I pick up Elizabeth's ruined body and rock her in my arms. I can smell the blood. Sweet and metallic, it accompanies me now. It saturates my thoughts of her last moments. The pain she endured. Her unspeakable terror, with no one to help her. I wasn't there.

Squeezing my eyes closed, I curse and beg some higher power to make this reality not true, but my pleas are impotent. They evaporate into the empty yard. They drift like vapor into the surrounding trees, where the birds keep singing as though nothing unusual has happened.

My cell phone rings, and I can't do anything about it for several seconds. From somewhere deep in my mind, a voice tells me that it might be Reyes, and I need to answer. I continue to sob, unable to stop looking at my fiancée's butchered face as I cradle her under the prying afternoon sun. The sun, which shows all and sees all, but does nothing as the February wind makes frigid tears roll down my cheeks.

The ringing continues. With one hand still around Elizabeth, my fingers are limp as I drag my mobile out of my pocket. I answer the call from Reyes.

"We found the phone," Reyes says. "There was no sign of—"

I interrupt him with stilted speech, choking on my tears like a child. I barely understand myself when I answer.

"She's here. Oh God, she's here, and she's dead. She's dead. She's dead."

19

FEBRUARY 9TH

I numbly sit across from Detective Menard, my body placed in the metal chair in an impossible sideways sitting position. I balance mostly on my hip. No one heeded my argument that I couldn't sit down because I fractured my tailbone. Maybe Reyes believed me, but nobody else did. In the end, I gave in when some officer whose name I didn't know gave the old line that I needed to sit down, or he'd make me, so I sat down. Sort of.

They put me in one of those cop questioning rooms like I've only seen on television. It actually doesn't look quite as grungy or dark as that but certainly feels as small and intimidating. The space holds an odd smell like sweaty sauna wood. Now it's only Menard and me. Reyes was here earlier as my most ardent defender, but he's since left the room. The detective feels there have been many shady occurrences with my name attached to them, and it's high time for this mess to get sorted out. I need to answer up, and I won't be getting off the hook so easily. No, I'm not going to be treated like some poor, dumb chap who just "stumbled into it" *this* time. Menard makes sure I understand that.

By this point, it's well into the evening. I glare down at the metal table with my arms folded on top of it. The medication has worn off, and my pain is immense, though, in a way, the pain is what keeps me tied to the present moment. I keep slipping off into images of Elizabeth's beautiful face. Beautiful and utterly ruined. And dead. Then my mind becomes wholly consumed by a deep, black void of loss, after which I see Aria's body strung up against the wall, her white dress covered in dark red blood. And Korey had a dog...

Menard clears his throat, and his Rolex clicks against the tabletop as he repositions his arm. I realize I've been staring at the gray wall again. My eyes are probably glazed over. I need another one of those pink tablets the doctor gave me at the hospital. I dare not move my legs or back at all, knowing my injury will punish me for it.

"Tell me again," Menard says. He's Reyes's age, but instead of Latino, he's an overweight, white guy with thinning hair.

I sigh. "Which part?"

We aren't only talking about Elizabeth's murder now. Oh no, there are other things we need to discuss, which are apparently equally important. The detective flips back one page in his notebook.

"You said you went to the house on County Road 140 and were shot at. You returned fire, and the shooter escaped out the back. Then you went inside and saw 'she's dead anyway' posted on the wall. You searched the house for your phone but didn't find it. After investigating to your satisfaction, you called Deputy Reyes and told him what you did." He glares at me, raising his eyebrows.

I nod. "Yes, like I told you, this guy stole my cell phone and put it in the house. I did let the deputy know that as well. But part of me wondered if he or anyone else would believe me, and I thought I'd get framed for the whole thing, so I went there myself to try and get it. Also, I was... irritated that I was being targeted in my own home. It was hard to sit idle and wait."

"That's the most ridiculous piece of bullshit I've ever heard," Menard says. "You're telling me you took a nap, and this guy breaks into your house and takes your phone and your gun while you're asleep? And then plants them at a former crime scene?"

I rub my sharp beard growth. "Yes. That's exactly why I almost didn't call Reyes at all. It's hard to believe and makes me look guilty."

"And do you think you look any less guilty now? You called us with a dead woman on your porch today. Things aren't looking good for you, boy, so if you're hiding something, I suggest you come clean," Menard says.

"And what would be the outcome if my phone turned up in the murder house anyway? Exactly the same," I say.

He jabs a finger at me. "The outcome is that I want the truth. You're not telling all. I want to know exactly what you did. I want to know *exactly* what part you played in all this."

I shake my head. My gaze wanders up to the ceiling before finding the umbilical-cord gray wall again.

"I didn't play any part. I've told you everything. The only thing I can figure is this Korey Nemeth guy got pissed off that I discovered Aria Owen, and she lived, which means now he's been found out and is wanted for kidnapping and murder. Why he's spent so much time on me, I don't know. But he wants to ruin me. And he has." I clench my jaw, putting my hands over my face. My skin feels grimy.

Menard taps his pen on the table. The door whooshes open behind him, and I uncover my eyes. Reyes steps into the room with his brow pinched into a stern frown.

"I think you should tell him," Reyes says, looking at the detective. He crosses his arms.

The detective gives a little huff, letting his gaze flick up to Reyes before locking it on me again. "It's inconsequential."

"I think he needs to know," Reyes says.

I lift my head a little higher. Is he about to tell me that if found guilty of crimes I didn't commit, I can go to jail for life? I guess technically speaking, that is pretty "inconsequential" next to my fiancée's murder and the killer leaving her body at my house for me to find. I've been shot at, hunted, stolen from, baited, and now framed for murder—maybe two murders. What else can anyone possibly do to me besides dealing the final stroke of killing me, of course? Not sure I even care about that now.

Menard peers up at Reyes, his eyes appearing small above his ample jowls. "You can tell him if you want. I'm done here. For now."

He pushes himself out of his chair and swipes the notebook from the table with his massive paw. His accusing gaze settles on me until he departs the room.

Reyes seats himself across from me. I force myself to meet his eyes, and he searches my face before speaking. "Trent, Korey Nemeth was taken into custody last night."

I blink a few times at Reyes, then stare at the table again. I sniff. I swallow a tacky, bitter taste, frown, and begin squinting because this new train of thought hurts my brain. I look back to Reyes.

"When was Elizabeth murdered? Has the coroner been able to estimate the time of death?" In my mind, I see the gash across her soft cheek, remembering the caked blood that was already beginning to dry. But her body hadn't grown stiff. Her limbs were still supple as I turned her over.

"The time of death was approximately 1:30 p.m.," Reyes says. "About two hours before she was found."

I shake my head. So, whoever carried this out did so even after the fact of Nemeth's apprehension. "What about Emile Woodard, the guy who we think shot at me on Tim's ranch? And someone shot at me from the house on County Road 140. That could have been him too. Do you think that's the person who murdered Elizabeth for Nemeth?"

My side and hip are screaming from the awkward sitting position, and I try to swivel my pelvis slightly. I grit my teeth, groaning as pain shoots into my tailbone again. Putting my left hand on the edge of the chair helps support my weight.

"There's always that possibility," Reyes says. "What else can you tell us? You said you were home all morning. Is that still your recollection?"

My alibi isn't very good. I stayed at my house all day, the same house where my fiancée turned up dead. "I was home all morning. I can't go back to work right now, and I'm not even supposed to be sitting in a chair like this. Like I said, I can show you my discharge papers from the hospital. I'm supposed to sit on a donut cushion."

"From the fight you were in," Reyes says, nodding and leaning back.

"Yeah, but I didn't start it."

Defending myself for brawling outside The Salt Lick

sounds juvenile, but at least what I said is true. Of course, it's also true that I chased the bastard across the parking lot and tossed him onto a car. I suppose if others had their way, I would have walked off after Jared clocked me with no warning.

Reyes turns up the corners of his mouth ever so slightly in the hint of a smile. His dark stare probes mine, but I don't know for what. From earlier, I know that he doesn't think I murdered anyone. He defended me with a sort of nonchalant ambivalence when Menard jumped down my throat and demanded answers I didn't have. Or was that just the old "good cop, bad cop" routine?

"Trent, I like you. I don't know why, but I do. And I think you're actually a good guy, despite the fact that you manage to get yourself into some really stupid situations. But I need you to understand that you are now a prime suspect in these cases," he says, folding his hands on the table. His forehead starts to shine from being in the close, stuffy room.

"These *cases*?" I ask.

It all seems like one big case to me—County Road 140, the shooter by Tim's ranch, Elizabeth's murder. If I didn't find the victims, I wouldn't be a target, and Elizabeth wouldn't be dead.

Deputy Reyes says, "Yes. It probably seems like there's a lot of bad things happening and that those things are all part of more or less the same scene. Sometimes that turns out to be true, but not always. These different incidents are usually recorded as separate cases, each with its own files of information. As we investigate, individual cases often link to other cases, and we can see a bigger picture. Regarding what happened today, we don't yet have enough information to establish what Elizabeth's murder links back to.

"The fact is, she was murdered this afternoon and was found dead at your home a couple of hours later. You previously presented us with several threats you said you received. However, you've also entered premises against police orders, displayed violence of a jealous nature regarding Elizabeth, and even admitted to shooting at someone on former crime scene property, whom you hadn't identified. There are a lot of pieces to this puzzle, Trent. And none of them are fitting together yet."

A bead of sweat starts to drizzle down Reyes's forehead slowly, but he keeps his gaze steady on me. Is he trying to tell me it looks like I'm using the County Road 140 case to cover up Elizabeth's murder?

I shake my head again. He isn't going to like this. "There is one thing I haven't told you."

"Yeah?" he says.

"Yeah. But it's pretty unbelievable, even more than what I told you about my cell phone being stolen and planted in the abandoned house." My fingertips brush something sticky underneath the chair. I lift them but keep my hand in place for balance.

"I'm listening," Reyes says. He tilts his head and waits.

"Well, that same night I went to Tim's old property to try and retrieve my phone and 9mm, my pickup got smashed by a semi-truck."

Reyes's face blurs in front of me as I call up the image. The headlights way too bright and high, the diesel truck hauling a loaded trailer down a tiny country road in the middle of the night. The driver being so accommodating for the damage he caused me.

Reyes stays silent, narrowing his eyes. He waits for me to explain.

"It happened right outside the house on County Road 140. When I was parked, a diesel truck smashed into my pickup and totaled it. I barely got out in time. The driver's name was Bradley Premshaw. He said he was 'over time' and he'd be happy to pay for my truck rather than report to the insurance and possibly lose his job because that was his third strike on being late. He went and got me five thousand in cash, then drove me to a used car lot. I didn't think much about it besides what a fluke accident it was—just one more crazy thing on top of everything else, but—"

Reyes starts writing on the paper on his clipboard. He looks up at me. "Bradley Premshaw? What company did he drive for?"

"Uh, Pall Transport, I think," I say, trying to stretch the ache out of my back.

"Did you get a phone number for him, his license plate number, anything like that?" Reyes asks.

"He gave me his card with his cell phone number," I say. "And yeah, I got the license plate number off the Peterbilt."

Reyes shakes his head and sighs. "Well, that's something. Write down the number for me. Were you hurt in the accident?"

"No, like I said, I got out in time, and I ran straight for the house. That's when someone started shooting at me," I say.

"Why didn't you tell this to Detective Menard?" Reyes asks. His frown grows deeper than before. His eyes widen.

"Number one, I didn't think it was relevant, and number two, I didn't think you'd believe me," I say, thinking of all the other things they didn't believe. "But even more than that was..."

"Was what?" asks Reyes.

"When it happened, I was afraid that if I called the police, I wouldn't have been able to have a look inside the house myself because I'd be caught up in talking to the officers."

Reyes says, "I get that. But you didn't think it was relevant that you got nailed by a diesel when you were staking out a thief at a former crime scene?"

"No, not really. It happened, but as far as being relevant? I shouldn't have found Aria and her stepmother in the house in the first place. But that doesn't mean finding them means something. It happened. Sometimes awful things just happen and discovering that crime was the worst thing that ever happened to me," I say.

I stare at Reyes, not managing to keep the anger out of my eyes. With Elizabeth's murder, though, I know it's different. I was supposed to protect her, and I didn't do it. I couldn't help her because I chose to fight with her friend from work and landed myself in the hospital. I guess, ultimately, there's no excuse for it. But as for the rest of it, I could only try and figure out so much.

"You said you shouldn't have found Ms. Owen," Reyes says. "Do you know her or something?"

"No, I don't know her. I just met her at the hospital." My stomach falls through the floor, along with my tailbone, which screams for another pink tablet. There it is. I'm walking right into it yet again, right here and now, with Deputy Reyes. I can't keep the chaos of my life contained for one minute.

"You met Aria Owen at the hospital?"

"Yes," I say.

"You met the victim of a violent crime at the hospital, but you're saying you don't know her?" Reyes's eyes are huge and glaring. A vein on his forehead bulges as another drop of sweat runs down his face.

"Yes. Right. Yes," I say. I formulate my next statements carefully. What I say has to be correct, but I can't mess up anything else. "This was just a few days ago when I was admitted for my tailbone. They moved me to another room. I was resting in bed, and Aria walked by my room. She saw me and sat in the chair by the door, and we spoke for a few minutes. She said she was glad to meet the person who saved her."

Reyes sits up straighter. "Okay. What hospital was this?"

"Seton Southwest," I say, and Reyes frowns, furiously scribbling on his paper. I continue. "She told me she'd been relocated from St. David's."

"Okay. Did you have any physical contact with the victim?" Reyes asks.

I glare at him, my mouth falling open. "What?"

"Physical contact. You touch her, give her a hug, anything like that?"

"What? No, of course not. Are you kidding me?" I ask. My upper lip twitches in disgust.

"Just checking. Did you exchange information at all?"

My stomach does another dive. "She asked me for my phone number, so I gave it to her. I didn't want to, but she was crying and seemed upset."

He lifts his head and almost rolls his eyes. "She *asked* you for your phone number?"

I huff. "Yes. She was crying, and she said a few things that didn't make sense, at least not to me. She also said she has trouble eating..."

Korey had a dog. I hate dogs.

Reyes shakes his head and scrawls on his clipboard.

"Okay, Trent, so what you're telling me is that this young woman who was kidnapped, raped, tortured, and starved asks a man she doesn't know for his phone number. That's what you're telling me?"

In exasperation, I groan and lift both hands at Reyes. "Yes! That's what happened!"

This gesture naturally includes my left hand, which is helping support my body in the awkward, sideways position. My backside slams down on the plastic chair, putting the full weight of my torso directly on my fractured tailbone. The ribbon of agony that sweeps up my spine makes me scream in pain. I cry out, steady myself with the table, and push myself to a standing position.

Cursing and wincing as Reyes stares at me, I say, "I'm not sitting down again."

Reyes ignores my comment. "Did she call you?"

"No," I say.

"Did you try to call her?"

"No," I say. "Aria said she didn't have a phone, but I don't want her to call me—and I *didn't* ask her for her number. The only reason I gave her mine is that she was crying, and I thought if I didn't give it to her, it would make her more upset."

Reyes snorts and keeps writing. He writes for a while as I alternate between glaring at his face and the wall. Hinges squeak, and the heavy door swings open. Still standing, I watch as Detective Menard walks in.

"Were you listening to any of this?" Reyes asks.

"Yeah," Menard says.

He and Reyes exchange glances. So, are they both "bad cop" now? I've lost track.

Deputy Reyes stands up, grabbing his clipboard. "Okay,

Trent. You're free to go. I'll escort you to the front desk, and we'll have someone drive you home."

I stare at him, narrowing my eyes. He has to tell me more than that.

Reyes says, "Yes, you are still a suspect. So, prepare to get called back in for questioning and possibly even detained if we have enough evidence. As of right now, we don't have enough to hold you. The biggest favor you could do yourself is to stop putting yourself in bad situations and start reporting anything—I mean anything—out of the ordinary that happens to you. It doesn't matter if it doesn't sound believable or not. That's not the point. If you report suspicious activity to us, then there's a record of that. When you don't report it, it looks doubly suspicious, and it can even make it appear that you're the perpetrator."

I nod. "I understand. I'll report everything from now on."

Menard glares at me while Reyes lifts his right palm in the direction of the door. I slowly walk out into the fresher air of cubicles and offices that smell of coffee and someone's bakery run. Grinding my teeth against the stabs of pain, I hobble along while the deputy sheriff and detective follow. Menard breaks off into one of the adjacent hallways, and Reyes takes me to the lobby.

Reyes brings me to the front desk. An officer about my age tells me he'll be driving me home. Before we go, the deputy puts his face close to mine.

"I'm counting on you, Trent. Don't make me have to do this again."

20

FEBRUARY 16TH

"Thanks again for offering to drive me to the funeral," I say.

Laney sits in the passenger seat next to her husband, so pregnant I wonder if the seat belt pinches her stomach. I'm seated behind Kyle, and Laney turns her head slightly to look at me. She smiles brightly under her blonde hair, which today she wears curled and pulled together in the back.

"Of course, Trent." Laney's smile fades, and her eyelids droop a little, her eyebrows pinching slightly in the middle. "We just can't imagine what you're going through, and we're so sorry. We're happy to help in any way we can."

"That's very kind of you both," I say.

Kyle nods but remains silent.

From the back of Kyle's silver Audi sedan, I stare out the window as we head down County Road 152 toward the Interstate 35 access road, where we can board the freeway. An overcast and drizzling sky canopies our passage, and the cattle in the field on the left huddle together in a black clump between prickly pear and tall, brown grass. I put my fingers under the blue tie around my neck, loosening it slightly. Sitting isn't as painful as last week, but then again, I'm still taking the meds. On the seat underneath me rests a small donut cushion. My hands lie slack in my lap.

Laney and I make small talk on the drive into Austin. We pull up to the white cathedral on Burnet Road, the church appearing towering, white, and immense, holding its fortress-like position under the wintry, gray sky. Kyle lets Laney and me out at the door. I carry the cushion under my arm. I never thought I would return to St. Louis Catholic Church again, and definitely not like this.

Laney frowns as we wait for Kyle to park and come to meet us. "Did you choose not to be a part of the funeral procession?"

"No, I wanted to be. But Ms. Reinhardt didn't seem to want that," I say.

Laney sighs. She puts her hand on my shoulder and shakes her head. "That's not right. We know it wasn't your fault. You should have been allowed to be there for Elizabeth. I'm so sorry, Trent."

I try to smile. "Thanks, Laney. I appreciate it." I can't say that Kyle wholly shares her viewpoint, but that's all right.

"How's your injury?" she asks.

"It's better. I brought this so that I can tolerate the wooden pews," I say. I indicate the cushion.

"Good," she says. "I'm glad to hear it."

Kyle joins us, and we make our way to the front of the church, where Elizabeth's closed casket rests on the warm yellow marble tiles at the foot of the altar. We're some of the first people to arrive, even ahead of the funeral procession. Kyle and Laney take their seats in the third row on the right side. I set my cushion in the front row at the end to save my seat. Ms. Reinhardt and the rest of Elizabeth's family haven't arrived yet, but as Elizabeth's fiancé, I'll be damned if anyone is going to tell me I can't sit in the first row. Anyone who dissents will have to remove me themselves.

I walk up to the casket, noticing the arrangement of red roses and white delphinium off to the left. I'm glad the flowers I sent arrived properly. They're pretty but don't do Elizabeth justice. I offered to pay for the casket spray, but as with the funeral procession, Ms. Reinhardt didn't seem to want that either.

My vision starts to blur as I see the top of the polished, caramel-colored, rustic oak casket spilling over with blue orchids and other blue flora. Their light, floral scents mingle with Damascus rose incense. Blue was Elizabeth's favorite color, hence my blue tie. Hence, the blue flowers I would have happily paid for—and should have been allowed to pay for.

I put my hand over my mouth to stifle a sob that threatens to consume the mostly empty church. Nothing can repair this black hole in my heart, this immeasurable well of never-ending grief. Just because we had our rough spots doesn't mean this hurts any less. It doesn't mean I love her any less. She's gone, and there's nothing I can do about it. Elizabeth was taken from me.

I tug a tissue out of my black suit jacket pocket and wipe my eyes before taking a seat on my cushion at the end of the first pew. I cry quietly as the church slowly fills up with Elizabeth's mourners. I pick out Ms. Reinhardt's voice among the crowd and know she's taken a seat at the other end of the pew, near the aisle. An older woman with short, gray hair and glasses pushes past the others to come to sit beside me. I look up and recognize my fiancée's grandmother—Ms. Reinhardt's mother. I stand to greet her.

"There you are," Mrs. Bouchard says. "It's so nice to see you. It's a shame that it's under these circumstances, but I'm so happy to see your face."

She wraps her arms around me in a warm hug and softly sobs as she tightly holds on to me. Her musky perfume and baby powder scent are oddly consoling. Mrs. Bouchard doesn't think I'm a murderer. She doesn't think I murdered my Elizabeth.

"It's nice to see you too," I manage and sit back down. I listen as the priest performs the service. I listen to the eulogies, one given by Elizabeth's sister and one by her father, who I don't know well since my fiancée's parents were divorced for some time and she and her dad weren't that close. I half-expect one of them to glare at me accusingly when things like "her life was cut short" or "she was taken from us" are mentioned, but nobody does. It wouldn't matter if they do, I guess. At the end of the service, I stand up to exit at the right side to avoid Ms. Reinhardt's eyes.

Mrs. Bouchard grabs my arm. "Trent, she knows."

I blink, a vise grip constricting my stomach. I ready myself to turn my back on her if needed. "What?"

"She knows. Tiffany knows you didn't do it," Mrs. Bouchard says. "She's in a lot of pain right now, and this is her way of dealing with losing Elizabeth so suddenly. I just wanted to tell you." She dabs at her cheeks with a handkerchief and peers up at me.

I let out the breath I'm holding. "I'm glad of that. Thank you."

Mrs. Bouchard squeezes my hand, and we say our goodbyes.

I leave the pew, turning to meet up with Kyle and Laney two rows back. Laney's eyes are red and puffy. Kyle looks rather peaked, his eyes dry and his lips drawn together tightly.

"That was a really beautiful service," Laney says as I approach. "I'm so glad you sat in the front row. Elizabeth would have wanted you there."

I nod. "I agree. It was a nice service."

Kyle's hard glare alights on me. He looks at the floor, then looks back at me and forces a purse-lipped smile. He grabs my arm and pulls me into a hug, patting me hard on the back a few times. For the first time since they picked me up at my house this morning, he speaks to me for real. "Do you want to go up one last time before we go? We don't mind waiting a few minutes."

I pause and think about it. "No. I've said everything to her silently during the service. Thanks, though."

"Okay." Kyle nods, studying my face before we begin weaving our way down the aisle to the exit.

We walk through the first set of doors, shaking the Father's hand and thanking him for the ceremony honoring Elizabeth. I dip my fingers in holy water and make the sign of the cross as we enter the foyer. As we head to the wide, glass doors that open to the outside, I notice a man standing alone, almost off in the corner, watching me. More funeral attendees stream into the entrance hall, obscuring my view as the man briskly turns his back. I don't get a good look at him beyond seeing a dark hair color. He must be another of Elizabeth's relatives, and it's only natural that he'd look at me.

I hold the door open for Laney and Kyle while the

whistling wind bites into our faces. An odd discomfort follows me out into the cold, misty morning.

February 20th

ON THE FIRST sunny day since Elizabeth's funeral, I decide to drive into town. On 7th street, there's a coffee shop called Cianfrani, and it's right across from the historic Williamson County Courthouse. I've been there only once before. Kyle is speaking to me again, and we've been texting some, but I don't think he'll want to come along. Maybe in time.

I go inside with the donut cushion under my arm, glancing around at the burnt orange walls and little, round tables. Although festive aromas of cinnamon and mocha greet me, reality doesn't feel very real since this is the first time I've left the house in four days. It's also the first time I've shaved or taken a shower. There are a few other people in the shop, but for the most part, it looks like a slow business day.

I shuffle to the counter and order a strong coffee drink. I gather up a few sugar packets and look around for a good place to sit. It might be nice to sit up front where I can see the courthouse. The dark brown leather couch faces the front of the store, and I choose it as my vantage point when I notice that someone is already occupying the space.

I halt and stand frozen, uncertain of what to do. I court the idea of turning and walking out the door before she looks up. I no sooner lift my right foot than the young woman sitting there speaks.

"Trent?" She begins to stand as she waits for me to acknowledge her.

I hesitate, every nerve in my body telling me to bolt. There's no way my luck can be this bad. There's no way that *anybody's* luck can be this bad. Slowly, like a kid getting called back into school from recess, I turn my head and look at her.

"Yes?" I ask.

I wish I could play it off. I wish for some way out, some way to say I don't recognize her or can't talk to her, or that I could throw out some lame excuse that will work.

"Trent, it's me, Aria. Don't you recognize me?" she says, her huge, brown eyes drinking up my entire face.

I sniff awkwardly, shifting my weight since I practically stopped mid-step. I cock my head. "Oh. Aria. Oh, hi. Yeah, you look..." What the hell am I supposed to say? "...a little different than when we met. How are you?"

God, what the hell is wrong with me?

Aria smiles. "Yeah, I know. I'm okay." She gestures for me to sit down.

I tentatively inch forward as though I'm uncertain of the surface beneath my feet. I guess I don't feel certain of anything anymore.

"Aria," I say as I walk over to the couch. I keep my voice low. "This isn't easy for me to say, but I don't think the sheriff's office wants me to associate with you."

As soon as the words are out of my mouth, her face falls, her mouth hanging open as though she's highly insulted. But I can't be careless anymore. I have to think my way through everything. I have to think about results and consequences. If I had done that sooner in my life, Elizabeth would still be alive.

21

FEBRUARY 16TH

"No, I didn't mean that *I* don't want to associate with you," I say to Aria, still keeping my voice barely above a whisper. I drop my donut cushion on the couch and sit down beside her—but not too close.

I add, "Deputy Sheriff Reyes seemed to find it odd that we met in the hospital. I think he just wants to make sure that you're safe. I mean, since you don't know me."

I look around for somewhere to set my drink. There's a small table, but it's on the side opposite Aria. I hold my cardboard coffee cup and sugar packets, having no free hands to mix them.

Aria's face softens, and she smiles, shaking her head. She still smells faintly of strawberry mint shampoo. "Oh, that's ridiculous. He's worried about the man who found me and saved my life? Geez. Well, I guess cops have to think of everything, right?"

I force a laugh. "I guess they do."

For the first time, I allow myself to look at her—*really* look at her. Recognizing her and actually seeing her are not the same things. She does indeed look different than the emaciated girl with hollows under her eyes. Her straight, dark hair is parted on the side, neatly brushed, and flowing down her shoulders. Her large, brown eyes aren't so stricken. Her skin is still fair, but not sickly, and her face has filled out more. I can't see her cheekbones now.

I think back to the news article, which mentioned that Aria was twenty-four, but in studying this woman, her age would be difficult to place if I didn't know that. I suppose the living nightmare she survived bestowed upon her visage some indiscernible, unnamable quality that may never go away.

Aria turns her body to face mine and rests her clasped hands in her lap. "So, how have you been?"

I open my mouth and shut it again. I can't tell her what happened. That would probably be violating some rule or endangering her or something else I can't imagine. I don't even want to talk to her, not because of anything against her, but because my involvement in the County Road 140 case has already completely ruined my life. Not her fault, just the way things are. I stare blankly at the floor, shaking my head.

"That good, huh?" she asks, trying to laugh.

"Yeah," I say. "How about you?"

Aria's gaze flicks to the front of the shop, though currently, no one sits in that area. "Did you know? Korey got arrested."

"Yeah, Reyes told me. I'm glad—really glad." I force another closed-mouth smile. I am genuinely glad, but it's still hard to smile.

"I've been able to sleep ever since I found out. Eating is harder, but I've been eating too." She blinks and looks briefly at her cup before picking it up and taking a sip of coffee.

"That's great," I say. *Korey had a dog. I hate dogs.*

Aria regards me again, this time tilting her head slightly to the other side. "Trent, I'm sorry, but you don't look well. Are you not recovering quickly from that fall you had?"

I sniff. I'm still holding the coffee and sugar packets in my lap. I finally resolve just to drink it black. Taking a sip, I find it harshly bitter. "I—I lost my fiancée. It was pretty sudden. We just had the funeral a few days ago."

I probably wasn't supposed to tell her that for some reason. Then again, I wasn't supposed to meet her at the hospital, and I'm not supposed to be sitting here next to her now.

Aria puts her hand on her heart. "Oh my God! That's awful. I'm so sorry."

For the first time, I notice her faint Texas accent. Somehow, I've never developed one myself, although both my parents have it.

"May I ask what happened? Was she sick?" Aria asks.

I swallow and clench my jaw. "We—we don't know exactly what happened. She… it was unexpected."

Aria's eyes never leave mine. "I see. Well, if you ever need someone to talk to, you can talk to me about it."

"Thank you. That's very kind," I say.

Her gaze keeps probing mine, and it irks me. She's looking for something there, and whatever it is, I hope she doesn't find it.

"I feel like I'm bothering you," she says. "I don't want to keep you."

"No, you're not bothering me. I just don't want to say the wrong thing or put you in danger somehow. Just thinking of my talk with Reyes a week ago," I say. I force another drink of black coffee.

Aria sniffs. "Well, Korey's in custody now, so I'm no longer in danger. There's nothing he can do. They put him in the slammer, and he'll probably get life. Maybe even the death penalty. What is Reyes afraid of? Did he actually say you're not supposed to talk to me because he can't do that—" Her eyes start to tear up, and she glances down at her mug. She takes a sip to steady herself.

"He didn't specifically tell me not to talk to you, but that's the impression he gave me," I say.

"Well, it's strange," she says. She fails in bringing herself under composure the way she wants, and her left cheek is wet.

"I'm sorry, I didn't mean to upset you," I say. "I should probably get going."

I start to rise, and Aria grabs my arm.

"No," she says, her big eyes blinking up at me. "I'm the one who's sorry. Trent, I have no one. I don't have anyone in the world. The only reason I came here today is that I thought I might run into you, this being Georgetown. Please." Her arm shakes as she grips mine, the knuckles of her small hand turning white. "Please, just sit down and talk to me. I have no one."

I relinquish, and she lets go. She turns and places her coffee cup on the table next to her, putting her hand over her face so she can cry into it soundlessly. I suppose the correct protocol in this situation is to place a comforting hand on her shoulder or extend some similar gesture. Instead, I sit here mutely, unwilling to touch her after what Reyes said during my interrogation. I don't move and wait until Aria finishes. She gives a loud, wet sniff and wipes her face with her napkin.

"Do you know how I lived?" she asks. "Besides you finding me. Do you know how I lived as long as I did?"

I shake my head.

Aria keeps her voice so low I can barely hear. "Korey had a dog."

My stomach hits the floor and writhes with sickness. A kind of sickness I can't describe, like being dropped into a barrel of grub worms. My left hand relaxes involuntarily. The three sugar packets fall, dropping quietly onto the beige tile.

"Korey hadn't been feeding us, not really. Maybe a scrap of something here and there. We were tied up in that back room, and we were starving to death. But Korey had a dog, and he kept the bag of dog food in that same room. That room where we were. I would scoot over to the bag of dog food and get some. Then I'd take it to my stepmom. She'd have to eat it out of my mouth. I mean, I had to feed her like that, like a bird feeds her young because our hands were tied behind our backs. I'd do this a few times, scooting back and forth across that nasty floor. Then I'd drag myself over to the bag again and feed myself," she says.

I shudder, letting out a sigh of relief in a long, shaky breath. My extremities suddenly grow cold. I didn't notice the temperature in here, but now it feels like a meat locker. I wrap both hands around my coffee cup to warm them.

Aria continues. "This whole thing was hard to do, not just because our hands were tied behind our backs, but because the bag was only open partway. I had to shove my face into it. Not my whole face, it wouldn't fit, but I had to press my face onto the bag and push it down so that I could get my mouth to the food. But it kept us alive.

"Then, one day, Korey caught me feeding my stepmom. And he beat us. Beat us bad. After that, he raped me—not the first time—and then he beat my stepmom so bad that she went unconscious. She was still breathing. I know since I checked later because, for some reason, he never separated us. But she never woke up again, even though she kept breathing for several days. And Korey took the dog food out of the room. So that was the last time I ate before I was found." She looks up from her coffee cup. "Before you found me."

I let out another audible breath. "That's why you have trouble eating."

She nods, saying softly, "Yeah. And shortly after my stepmom died, Korey stabbed me and chained me to the wall. So, I wouldn't have been able to get to the food even if he'd left it there."

I sit here in silent horror. There's nothing I can say. Finally, I ask, "I don't want to pry, but you said you have no one. You have no friends or family?"

"Please, pry," Aria says, forcing a smile on a face that has taken on a wan aspect it didn't have earlier. "No. I mean, I do have friends up north in Dallas, but no family. No close friends anymore. It's a long story. My stepmom was the last person I really had, besides..."

So, she has no friends and no family. Where is she staying? Maybe she's still in protective custody, living with whoever the police arranged. That probably won't be needed much longer.

"I see. Dallas? Are you originally from there?" I ask.

"No, I was born in Waco, actually, but my mom moved to Dallas when I was young, and I pretty much grew up there. Then when I was seventeen, she died, and I moved here to live with my stepmom, Carol."

"Your dad?" I ask.

"He died too, died of cancer when I was eight. Of course, my parents were already divorced by then," Aria says.

I never thought I'd meet anyone whose life is worse than mine. Not knowing what else to say, I just tell her I'm sorry.

"It's all right. What can I say? I'm cursed." She smiles weakly, meeting my eyes again.

I nod and stare off in the direction of the window. I can just see the tan bricks of the historic courthouse building from where we are. Aria stares out the window too, but what she's actually looking at, I'll never know.

Aria turns back to me. "How's your injury?"

"It's better," I say. "At least I can sit down now."

We laugh, and I consider it a much-needed reprieve from the taut conversation. I stand up and stretch my arms, forcing my expression to appear more relaxed than I really feel. The barista's mixer whirs in the background and releases an aroma of fresh whipped cream and something else. Chocolate, maybe. Remembering the sugar packets, I reach down and pick them up. I tuck them between my fingers and the warm, cardboard coffee cup. The donut cushion practically leaps into my hand.

"It was good to see you," I say. "I think I'm going to head out."

Aria blinks, and she rises from the couch. Her wide, umber eyes flash with some emotion. "Oh. All right. You know, I have a phone now, if you ever want to call me. I mean, you can. If you ever want to."

Without really meaning to, I frown at her. Where does she think this is possibly going to go? I don't mean to be heartless, and I'm not. Not really. It isn't that I don't care or don't want to help her, even if my help would only consist of lending an ear from time to time. But it isn't my responsibility to care for a violent crime victim, especially at present when I'm not working and have a dead fiancée. When is it callousness, and when is it reason?

"Thank you," I say. "And you still have my phone number too."

Aria forces a tearful smile. She pulls in her lips and glances at her lap. She knows I don't want to get involved with her.

I add quickly, "It was really nice seeing you. I'm glad we got to talk."

She keeps her gaze downcast, and I know I've blown it, whatever "it" is. Chivalry? Social convention? Common decency? Because I guess that's what I'm supposed to think. It's "common decency" for me to offer her a place to live, keep her safe, and take care of her, probably. Just finding her in the abandoned house made me a target and got my fiancée murdered. *Murdered.* And if I don't want to end this chain reaction of destruction, I'm a cold-hearted, unfeeling bastard.

"Take care," I say.

Without waiting for her response, I turn and walk out the door. I never allow Aria to tell me her phone number.

22

FEBRUARY 21ST

Kyle says over his newspaper, "Well, it is your responsibility, at least somewhat."

The story of the County Road 140 case is turning up a lot now, and we read an article of Nemeth's apprehension. Korey Nemeth confessed to the abduction of the two women and is planning on pleading guilty to Carol Brandt's murder. A trial is scheduled for March 19th. It seems doubtful Aria will have to worry about that monster again.

I shake my head and peer out the window of the grill house in Pflugerville, where we're immersed in smells of seared steak and butter-sautéed onions and garlic. We met here for lunch on the interstate frontage road, about halfway between Austin and Georgetown. The restaurant isn't packed at noon on Tuesday, but we sure don't shout in discussing something like this. Considering Kyle's comment, I munch down several French fries. They're spicy from a dusting of Tony Chachere's.

I say, "I disagree. First of all, I'm living off my savings

money until I can go back to work. And secondly, what am I supposed to do? I'm supposed to offer her a place to stay and take care of her?"

Kyle snorts. He sets the paper down on the table. "Of course not. But you can be concerned and try to help in other ways."

"Like what?" I ask. "All I can think about is..."

Elizabeth. I see her face when I try to sleep at night. I see her vacant eyes staring up at the clear sky, her torn cheek yawning open in defeated submission. The indescribable horror of her mutilated abdomen. Elizabeth was my responsibility, and I failed her.

Kyle nods and picks at his onion rings. "I know, man. It's going to take some time. But with Aria, I don't know. You're certainly under no obligation, but you might be able to assist in some respect you never thought of. For example, if you know of an arrangement where she could be a live-in housekeeper or nanny, you could show her the ad."

"She can find ads herself," I say. "She doesn't need me for that. She feels emotional toward me because I found her, but that isn't a healthy association. It's a reaction."

Kyle chews his burger thoughtfully, swallows it, and takes a swig of his soft drink. "Sure. But she's in a pretty rough state right now. She's probably still getting used to the idea that she's safe now and is trying to adjust her mind to how she can start over and live again."

"Yeah," I say. "Well, if I have some brilliant idea that won't involve the complete upheaval of my life, okay. Otherwise, I'm steering clear." I bite into my own burger. Mushroom and Swiss was a good choice.

Kyle looks up from his food, raising his eyebrows slightly. "You said you called the sheriff's office. You reported your conversation with Aria to Detective Menard like Reyes asked you to?"

I nod. "I did. And I made sure to tell him that I didn't accept her phone number. Talking to her wasn't my idea."

Kyle laughs. "No kidding."

I laugh back, but my smile evaporates. "Reyes doesn't like the idea of us speaking, but I didn't break any laws or do anything wrong. And I plan to keep my distance as much as possible. To tell you the truth, I'm surprised you're in favor of the idea of me talking with Aria at all."

"Trent, Reyes probably wants to make sure you're not going to take advantage of her," Kyle says. "That's why he jumped on your case at the station."

I shake my head, contorting my face in disgust. "Are you kidding me? I would never."

"I know that, but the authorities don't. And some people would," he says. He shoves an onion ring into his mouth.

I stare at my plate. "Not someone with any sense of decency. And not someone who just lost his fiancée."

We sit in silence for a few seconds.

Kyle asks, "Have there been any new leads?"

"No," I say. "That's the biggest part of why I'm a suspect. As you already know, the time of Elizabeth's death was after Nemeth was arrested."

"You're also a suspect because of your vigilante escapades, for lack of a better term," Kyle says, hardening his brows slightly. "But at least you're still talking to Reyes about it."

I nod.

"Did you find out anything else about that truck driver? The one who totaled your Silverado?" Kyle asks. He takes a few drinks of Coke.

"No. I gave Reyes his info at the sheriff's office when he and Menard questioned me, but I haven't checked otherwise. Why do you ask?"

"It was just such an odd thing," he says.

I shrug and pick up my mug. This coffee contains amounts of cream and sugar to my liking. "Yeah."

"You're not drinking anymore?" Kyle asks, noticing that neither of us has a beer, or a pitcher, on the table.

Well, I guess I'm not. The painkillers they gave me at the hospital forced me to stop, and after that, I just forgot about alcohol. "Nah. I don't need the expense."

Kyle nods slowly, turning down the corners of his mouth like he might be having some great, new revelation about me, but I don't ask.

"Okay, buddy, I gotta run," Kyle says, removing the napkin from his lap.

Earlier, I offered to pay for lunch. This is the first time we've got together as friends since my fight with Jared at The Salt Lick.

"Later," I say. I reach to get the bill.

I have to get going too because this is also the first day I return to work at the gas station. My shift will be from 2:00 to 8:00 p.m. for a few weeks, and then I'll eventually go back to evenings and some weekend days like before.

Before lunch, I also checked in with Tim. We established that I could return to work in a month. By then, I'll be healed enough for ranch work, and there's no reason I can't resume, discounting any more shooters turning up. Tim knows they put Nemeth behind bars, but he doesn't know about Elizabeth.

As I drive north on I-35 to Texaco, I listen to the roadway noise and think about her killer. Whoever my tormentor, he made a point of murdering my fiancée after Aria's abductor was captured. He may not have realized that Nemeth was in the slammer while he carried out his boss's dirty work. Or, like Reyes pointed out, the killer may have no connection to Nemeth at all. But I don't have any other enemies and only draw a blank.

At eight o'clock at Texaco, I turn my register over to Matt, a new guy who started since my absence. As I walk outside to my pickup, a familiar face watches me under the lights in the parking lot, and I almost turn back around. This scenario keeps repeating itself like a recurring bad dream.

Aria stands not far away from a white sedan, smiling bleakly and giving me a passing wave. Gasoline odors drift on the breeze as I stop short by the pumps. I stare at the car. No, it doesn't look like the one the shooter used. That one was older, probably a late '90s model. This one appears far newer. I wonder if it's hers.

Sighing under my breath, I walk across the stained asphalt to Aria. She has her dark hair down, and the wind blows it back.

"I'm stalking you," she says, laughing weakly. "Just kidding. I filled my tank a minute ago and went in to use the restroom. I saw you inside."

I pretend to laugh back. I didn't see her come in, and I definitely would have noticed unless she came during one of the few times I went to the storage area. I wonder if this meeting mimics the one before it in which she predetermined to run into me, one way or another.

"Oh yeah? Have you been job hunting in Georgetown? Any luck?" I ask.

"No luck with jobs yet. I was out applying today, though. Got this far and decided to turn around and head back," Aria says.

"Good call," I say. "This isn't really Georgetown here, it's unincorporated Williamson County, and if you keep heading north, you'll wind up in Jarrell. That would be a long commute." I assume she's still staying somewhere between Austin and Round Rock.

She nods. "For sure. Well, I don't want to keep you. It's funny how we keep bumping into each other like this, but I'm sure you have somewhere you need to be."

Relief sweeps over me in a tidal wave, and I grin too readily, but then I remember what Kyle said. Kyle is usually right, and if I listened to him more in the past, my life might be very different than it is now. I don't have to get emotionally involved with Aria, give her money, or do anything ridiculous, but I can at least not be indifferent.

"I'm just getting off work, actually," I say. "I don't have anywhere to be."

Aria blinks and cocks her head a little, looking up at me. "Oh. Well—well, great. Do you want to—do you want to grab a bite somewhere? I can buy."

I laugh. "You don't have to buy. I'll pay for myself. But sure, we can grab a bite."

~

We take our separate vehicles and meet up at an Applebee's on the Interstate 35 access road in Georgetown. While I park and curse under my breath, my stomach dropping the more I think about this, I remind myself that I don't have bad intentions and I'm not doing anything wrong. I only intend to visit with her because it seems more logical than being cold and distant, even though that's what I want.

"Thanks for agreeing to meet with me," Aria says as we take our seats across from each other in a booth.

"Sure, no problem," I say. I rest my elbows on the smooth, wood tabletop.

I keep my expression even, hoping she can see this doesn't commit me to anything, nor does it have some special meaning. Better to launch into conversation. We chat until our server takes our order. I get steak and shrimp, and Aria chooses a chicken and pasta dish.

"Aria, if I might ask, where were you working before? Is there any chance you could get your old job back?" I unroll my utensils from their napkin.

Aria's eyes grow wider for a moment, and she rubs her hands as though she's cold. "Um, no, I worked for my stepmom. She was a real estate agent."

Bells and whistles. Now I remember Aria telling me she was a real estate assistant, but I was so edgy at the hospital, it didn't register. Kyle is a real estate agent, and also the person who suggested I try to help out if I could. Making a mental note to ask him if he needs someone, I decide not to mention this to Aria yet.

"I'm sorry," I say gently. "I'll keep an eye out for something in your field."

We try to make small talk until our food comes, but I

know our banal chatter will eventually solidify into something more substantial. Our waitress arrives and sets our plates down. The grilled vegetables smell like garlic and butter and sizzle invitingly next to my steak.

"I hope you don't mind my asking, but how have you been coping with your loss?" Aria asks. "I know it must be hard because it's hard for me losing Carol. Are you getting support from friends?" She picks up her utensils.

I swallow a large bite of sirloin and clear my throat, hesitating before answering. Well, I can't sleep. Waves of pain sweep over me like a freight train throughout the day, giving no sign of letting up. When I'm alone, I cry, and that helps sometimes, but nothing stops those unabating currents. I guess I could always go back to drinking, but I'm afraid to. The guy who killed Elizabeth is still at large, and I don't need to be drunk if—or when—he comes for me too.

"I've been doing okay. My friends are being supportive," I say. I look back down at my plate and spear a shrimp. It's garlicky, and the outside is seared to a pleasant crisp.

"That's good," she says, cutting her pasta with the side of her fork.

She stares at me and pushes a strand of dark hair out of her face. I watch her gaze flick back and forth between me and her food. It dawns on me that we share something in common—the fact that we both recently lost someone we were close to, and that's part of why she's interested. What she doesn't know is that we both lost those people in the same manner.

"Aria... I didn't tell you this before because, well, we don't know each other well, and I didn't want to say anything I wasn't supposed to. Especially after what you've been through," I begin, still formulating the rest of it.

Aria's focus locks onto me and holds.

I drop my voice down. "But my fiancée Elizabeth was murdered."

The color drains out of Aria's face, and she leans back in her seat, never taking her eyes off me. She starts shaking her head. "Trent, that's horrible. I'd tell you I understand, but you already know I do. But I also know that one person can never truly understand another person's pain."

I exhale, a deep ache welling up in my chest. "That's true."

Aria's soft tone matching mine, she asks, "Do you know who did this? And has he been caught?"

"No, we don't know, and he hasn't been," I say.

The waitress drops by with the bill, and I nod and thank her absent-mindedly.

"When did this happen?" Aria asks. She grips her fork more tightly, and her posture stiffens.

"It happened the day after Nemeth was arrested," I say. "That's part of why I didn't want to tell you. And that's part of why Reyes thinks it might be dangerous for you to associate with me. He thinks there's a possibility it could be connected."

Aria's chest heaves as she stares at me, and I wait for the culmination of the disaster I caused. After a moment, she shakes her head. Her words are calm. "I don't see how. Korey didn't have many friends. And even if he did, why would he send someone after you?"

I think it's the most straightforward reason in the world. "Because I found you and your stepmother. You lived, and he got caught. Like you said, he'll probably get life, if not the death penalty."

"Korey doesn't think like that. I doubt he even knows

who you are," Aria says. She lifts her glass of sweet tea and takes a drink.

"He doesn't want revenge against the person who found him out? What psychopath doesn't want revenge?" I ask.

"He is a psychopath, but not all psychopaths are the same, and they're not all smart. Sometimes people are just crazy, Trent. But really, I highly doubt Korey had anything to do with it."

I sit back, letting her words sink in. It almost sounds like she's defending him, but that notion seems far-fetched. Stockholm syndrome does exist, but I can't bring myself to believe this is a shade of it.

"Why?" I ask, leaning forward. "Why don't you think he had anything to do with it?"

"Because I know him, Trent. I was with him for years, and I was in that house with him for three weeks. I know what he does. He doesn't have that mob boss mentality of hiring somebody to kill someone else. His motives with me were always about possession—of showing me who was in charge, that he owned me. But if he really did want to kill you, he would have killed *you*, not your fiancée. And he would have done it himself," she says. She lowers her head slightly, her brown eyes narrow and dark. "That's just the way he is."

Well, if anyone knows what that sicko's like, it's this girl. What amazes me is how she composes herself while speaking of him—much more than the last time I saw her.

"Okay," I say. I sigh. "But I don't understand. If what's been happening to me doesn't have anything to do with County Road 140, then..." I shake my head.

"What's been happening to you? Did other things

happen?" Aria asks. She lifts her fork and takes a bite of chicken. I can smell the parmesan.

"Yeah. I got shot at, at the same house where Korey held you. I also got shot at on the ranch where I worked. I got threats."

She's dead anyway, read the words in red on the wall of that filthy back room in the murder house. I always thought they referred to Aria. And the text, *Devices are mirrored. Call and she dies.* Could those messages really have been about Elizabeth?

"The same house? What, you went back there?" Aria's mouth hangs half-open, and she shuts it. She frowns.

Now I'm back doing the same dance I did with Deputy Reyes. "Yeah, in a way, I felt like I had to. The guy stole my cell phone, and he put it there. I think he wanted to frame me." I snort, disgusted with this whole thing. "Look, a lot of really bad shit has happened to me, and it's not going to make any sense." I knew it was a mistake to tell her about Elizabeth in the first place.

"Someone stole your cell phone and put it in that abandoned house? How did he do that?" Aria asks.

"I don't know."

"Did you call the police?" she asks.

"I did. And I've talked to them about it since then, but they never found my phone or the guy who stole it. I think the deputy sheriff believes me, but I'm not sure about the detective," I say. I don't mention that my pistol was stolen as well. I still entertain the idea that it might turn up somewhere, making me look guilty of something else.

Aria stares down at her plate and pokes at her pasta silently.

"Now you see why I wondered if it might not be a good idea for you to associate with me. I've had a lot going on," I say. "And if you don't believe me, I understand." I can't help but think that she, like Menard, also feels I'm lying or is suspicious of me now. I cut another piece of steak with my knife.

The young woman shakes her head. "No, it's not that. I mean, it's unusual, but after what I experienced, I'd believe just about anything." A faint smile flees her face. "Do you have any enemies?"

"No, absolutely no one," I say. "That's what has always led me to believe it was related to what happened to you. He has a motive—I found him out. But enemies otherwise? I don't have any."

"Everyone has enemies, Trent. You just don't always know who they are."

23

FEBRUARY 23RD

In the morning, I catch a brief news story on one of the local channels about the day someone shot at me on Tim's ranch.

"The investigation continues as Williamson County officials have a new lead in the January 6th shooting on County Road 152, in rural Williamson County near Georgetown. Though no one was injured in the shooting, thirty-year-old Trent Lemend was the intended recipient of the shots fired. Previously, Emile Richard Woodard of Travis County was brought in under suspicion for this crime, but his name was cleared. Authorities are now reporting that upon obtaining new evidence and a warrant for Woodard's arrest, Woodard has been taken into custody and has confessed to the shooting. Detective Menard of the Criminal Investigations Division told KVUN that Woodard claims he doesn't know Lemend, the intended victim, personally. Officials have yet to determine Woodard's motive for the shooting."

At the mention of my name, I sit bolt upright on the

couch, set my coffee down, and grit my teeth. I wish they would have left me out of it.

The image on the screen changes to a clip featuring Detective Menard and the reporting journalist, Mia Fernandez. It looks like they're on scene at Tim's ranch. Behind the two of them are a rusty, barbed-wire fence and the empty sheep pasture. Tangly, brown grass, scattered rocks, and pale green cacti plants stretch behind them, ending where the terrain turns to mostly packed dirt at the feeding area. Part of the weathered, gray barn is visible in the background.

Menard stands board-straight with his hands locked together, his great bulk towering over the female reporter as he politely answers her questions. Besides his stiffened posture, like he has a post strapped to his back, he keeps his brows relaxed, and he smiles slightly while listening.

"Detective Menard," Ms. Fernandez begins. "It was previously believed that the shooting incident which occurred here on January 6th might have a connection to the County Road 140 case. Since then, the evidence seemed to indicate the two weren't related. Is that still the belief of the Criminal Investigations Division at this time?"

"At this time, yes, that is still our belief, based on the evidence we have," Menard says.

"You've told us that analysis of two bullets found here at this Georgetown ranch indicates that the shooter used a .22 caliber rifle and that the locations of the recovered bullets show that this gunman was experienced in long-range shooting. Have you and your team come to a hypothesis on why Woodard would have tried to kill a ranch worker?"

"With something like this, we have reason to believe Woodard was likely paid by someone. For someone to be able to aim this well from the distance of the road behind those trees..." Menard turns slightly, pointing to the wiry bushes near the pine trees by the pond. "...this was probably someone hired as an assassin. The weapon used, the accuracy, and now Woodard's confession are all strong supporting evidence. What's needed now is full disclosure from Woodard."

"You mention the accuracy. However, the victim wasn't actually injured during the shooting, is that correct?" Fernandez asks. The wind pushes a lock of black hair into her face, producing modest background noise into the microphones.

"That is correct," Menard says. "However, the shooter was able to penetrate the victim's vehicle while that vehicle was in motion. And the previous shots, which were fired into that area over there, were very close to the target despite the shooter being so far away with obstacles between himself and the target. We have reason to believe there's more to this case than meets the eye, which is why it's receiving particular attention from myself and our investigations unit."

The screen changes back to the newsroom, the anchorwoman then thanking Mia Fernandez before launching into her next story.

I lean back on the couch, rub my chin, and wonder what else Menard knows that I don't. Even Aria, who was stolen away from the world and tortured for weeks, seems to know more about my life than I do. Regardless of that fact, I can't understand why law enforcement thinks County Road 140 and the shooting on Corbin Ranch aren't related. It's as obvious to me as the fact that Woodard is an experienced gunman, and it should be obvious to the authorities that he was either hired by Nemeth or someone else involved in the County Road 140 case who hasn't come to light yet.

Yes, Nemeth had his jealous motives for what he did to Aria and her stepmother, but that doesn't mean he didn't have someone else helping him. Someone to watch the house. Someone to throw the police off the trail. Someone to off me after I went and blundered into the murder house and discovered his crimes. I still don't know how that factors into Elizabeth's murder happening after Nemeth was jailed, but Nemeth's man probably didn't know the cops apprehended his boss until later. That's the only thing that makes sense.

I stretch and stand up, realizing I feel better than I have in a while. For once, I got enough sleep, and I'm not hurting too much. Unfortunately, my relief soon ends. A memory of a day Elizabeth and I took a picnic at Zilker Park flashes up at me, and for a moment, her face materializes as clearly as if she's sitting in front of me. Her blue eyes dance as she laughs and dodges a bee. Our visitor had come to pilfer from our small buffet of offerings set out on the blanket. The bright image of Elizabeth and the lake behind her bathed in shimmery sunlight lingers in my mind.

I can't keep that remembrance out of my head as I have breakfast. The taste of bacon lingers on my tongue, and the kitchen smells like maple and hickory, but I'm eating alone. With the television switched off, dismal silence floods the house as I shave. Finally, I take the memory and stuff it away, squeezing my eyes together to stem the flow before it starts. Elizabeth is gone, and these episodes of daily pining won't bring her back.

I'm still shocked that Aria doesn't think I'm making something up. Detective Menard wasn't shy about expressing his doubts during my interrogation. Since that dinner at the restaurant with Aria, however, I've toyed with the idea of doing a little detective work of my own.

Sitting on the couch with a notebook, I call the mobile number Bradley Premshaw gave me, and he answers right away. The rumble of the diesel engine and the noise of the freeway roll along in the background.

"'Lo?" Bradley says.

"Hi, Bradley, this is Trent Lemend." I wait. "Is now a good time to talk?"

Bradley coughs and gives a loud sniff. "Yeah, Trent. What can I do for you?"

"Well, I got hauled in for questioning by the sheriff about the accident we had," I say. I wait again.

"I gotcha. Is there anything you need from me?" he asks.

I hope he'll offer something about being questioned by the sheriff's office also—about Detective Menard contacting him. But Menard has his plate full and may not have done so yet. I doubt it, though.

"Could you tell me anything else about that night? The night we had our accident." I word it carefully as though the wreck was mutual and not entirely his fault.

"What's this about?" Bradley asks. He spits, probably into his tobacco juice cup.

I get a better grip on my cell phone and stand up from the couch. I pace because it helps me think better. "Bradley, I need your help. Like I said, I got called in for questioning by the sheriff about the night of our accident. Is there anything else you can tell me? I'm trying to think of both of us. It was really decent of you to pay for my truck. I'm grateful."

Bradley clears his throat. "I don't know anything. I was so tired I could barely keep my hands on the wheel. Then I wake up to your truck sliding off my grill. It was so dark down that damn road it just came up on me. I'd a liked to had a heart attack."

I don't know anything. He does know something, or he would have worded it differently.

"I understand," I say. "Do you remember that guy who shot at me from the house?"

"I didn't see *nothin.*' All I saw was you shootin' and you runnin.' I don't know anything about what was going on there."

"Okay," I say, pretending to chuckle. "Well, I figured it was too dark for you to see anything but couldn't help but ask. I'm curious, though. That night you told me you came down County Road 140 to turn around because you missed your exit. Why didn't you use one of the overpasses on Interstate 35? There was one not far from where we were."

"I told you, I was so damned tired I couldn't see straight. Couldn't think straight neither. I was just gonna follow the roads around and get back on 35 South that way. It was late enough that there wouldn't be any traffic way out there. If I woulda been more awake, never would have happened. And that's the truth." Bradley clears his throat again. This grain-fed country boy is a terrible liar.

"Fair enough," I say. "Does your insurance company know that you paid for my truck yourself? When you're working for someone—" I pause. "—like Pall Transport, for example, it's customary for the company's insurance to pay. I would think it not unreasonable that your boss assumes some of the liability. After all, driving a big rig like that, you put yourself in danger doing his work. Don't you agree?"

"Now look here, I don't know what you're getting at, but I've done my part. I paid for your truck. If you want to report it to my company, I can't stop you. I already gave you all the info," he says. His voice wavers.

He knows that I know. He just doesn't know how much I know. I assume the only reason he doesn't hang up is that doing so would admit I'm right. So, he's thinking this through, only not as much as he should be.

"No problem, Bradley," I say. "I told you, I'm grateful. I just hope you got reimbursed. Did your boss reimburse you?"

I again expect him to hang up. He doesn't.

"No, sir," he says. "That came out of my pocket. I was glad to make things right. I'm just happy I didn't get busted for being over time. I'd been goin' fifteen hours since Jackson."

Jackson. The night he hit me, he told me he came from Jacksonville. Mississippi and Florida are two different states, and an over-the-road trucker would never say Jackson in place of Jacksonville, whether in recollection of a traumatic night or not.

My silence must be like a siren in Bradley's ears because he says, "Tell you what. I'll have my lawyer phone you tonight. We'll get this sorted out."

"That sounds great. I'll be expecting his call," I say.

I manage to keep the surprise from my voice but frown as we hang up. Hiring a lawyer would likely make his position worse, not better. I sit down and see-saw the pen in my fingers before jotting down notes of our conversation. For the rest of the day, I wait for the phone to ring, but it never does.

After letting Detective Menard know the specifics of my chat with the trucker, I run into a brick wall. The conversation with Bradley was insightful, but since then, he won't return my calls. His attorney, if, in fact, he has one, never contacts me. My conclusion is that Bradley was paid by someone, the same as Woodard. When he failed to end me with his rig, my guess is that the southern truck driver chose to try and make things good with me, so I'd stay quiet. I certainly prefer that to the alternative of him finishing the job. Premshaw doesn't seem the murdering type, so he must have been desperate to work for blood money in the first place. But I can't see how to locate the man who hired Bradley without his help.

I LEAVE work at Texaco at 8:00 p.m. as usual and drive home. I pull into my long, gravel driveway, the headlights of the pickup illuminating the small, white house. The place is dark. I wonder why the porch lights haven't come on. Since Kyle helped me install the security system, the lights in the front and back are on timers. The bulbs might need replacing—but both of them? It's dark around back too. There may be a power outage, but I saw lights at Tim's house, and we're likely on the same grid section.

After ensuring my truck doors are locked, I call Reyes right away and leave a message. Then I call 911, explaining to the operator that this isn't about busted porch lights but the several attempts on my life.

"I understand, Mr. Lemend. We'll send somebody out," the nice lady says. Either I've spoken to her before, or she's well up to speed on my story by now.

With my hands on the steering wheel, I sit for a moment with the truck idling. I shouldn't remain here, but at the same time, I don't want to be far when the cops show up. If the guy is here somewhere, my presence will keep him. We'll have a chance at catching him. But staying also puts me in danger. And if I leave, he'll just try again on another day—or night.

I can't see much, but I observe what I can. The headlights reveal the white exterior of the shotgun house, the empty yard, a few prickly pear cacti, and a strip of little bluestem. The light washes over the bare patches of dirt and pebbles until it fades into the darkness by County Road 152. From the corner of my eye, I catch some motion by the house.

My heart pounds, and I grip the warm steering wheel. Something stirs in the grass by the front porch. Stalks rustle. A raccoon's yellow eyes gleam at me before he skitters off to the barbed-wire fence and disappears into the mesquite prairie.

I exhale. I put the truck in drive, turn around, head up the driveway, and park on the shoulder a little way from my place. I can just see it from my new position on the other side of the road. From here, I'll be a hard target to hit if someone's hiding by the house.

Keeping the windows rolled up, I sit still and listen. Nothing much reaches me. Faint sounds of wind, the distant wheels of a moving car, and a dog barking—probably Tim's—meet my ears. I strain to discern any movement nearby but don't perceive any.

I text Reyes to confirm that he received my message. He doesn't reply. He told me before not to wait, and I've already called 911, so I'm not bothered. I'll just have to be patient until he or one of the other sheriff's deputies show up. I know I might end up waiting a while since burned-out porchlights aren't exactly a reason to call the SWAT team.

The gasoline gauge reads the tank as one-eighth full. I'll need the fuel if I wind up leaving for the night. If I shut off the truck, though, I'll need to distance myself from the house even more. I decide to drive to the curve in the road near Tim's pond. From there, I'll also be able to listen better without engine noise, and I can watch for the sheriff's vehicles. I put my foot on the brake to shift into drive.

Something ignites in a deafening explosion under the hood. It shakes the truck, jarring me rigid as I jerk from the shock. Black smoke pours out of the seams. Orange flames lick the air like snake's tongues, with nothing but the windshield and dash panels between them and me. I fling open the driver's side door and thrust myself out into the heat. With a few long strides, I sprint away from the pickup just in time. Smells of burned oil and rubber make me cough as the thick smoke climbs higher. Beads of sweat gather on my forehead and upper lip. My clothing stifles me.

Turning to keep the house in sight, I stand here, useless, and watch the Dakota burn. The fire gleams painfully bright against the shadowy countryside. Angry, gold flames grow in intensity, overtaking the vehicle's front end and cabin as they reach for the night sky. They're too real. Too threatening.

Lightheaded with my heart hammering, I try to catch my breath. My gut sinks as this new reality registers. My truck exploded while I was in it. The fact that the blast discharged under the hood and not in the cabin is likely the only reason I'm not injured or dead—that, and as explosions go, it wasn't that big. Strange. I swear and wipe the sweat from my eyes.

The fire's doing a bang-up job of lighting things up, so I don't need my flashlight yet. I whirl and look all around me, but I'm still alone. I need to call the fire department. With an unsteady hand, I reach for my cell phone but can't find it. I pat the outside of my coat in a pulse-racing panic. Did I leave the mobile in the Dakota?

No. Here it is, in the bottom pocket. Gripping it with damp fingers, I dial 911 and start running down the road. The operator answers, and I explain as I jog. It doesn't take long. I shove the phone back in my pocket and continue along the shoulder to wait for the authorities. It's probably been ten minutes since my first call, so the police should be here any time.

I follow the downward slope of County Road 152 toward the turn, aware that I can hear the blaze crackling all the way from here. The house is hidden from view now, but firelight still races across the pavement. I cough again. The smoke irritates my nose. Bitter carbon clings subtly to my tongue. As I get hold of myself, I watch shadows from the flickering, orange flames stretch slender fingers through the brittlegrass.

He set explosives. That's the only logical explanation, so he must have. Woodard failed him. Premshaw failed too. His late-night baiting attempt at the murder house didn't quite work out, so now he's trying to blow me to bits. This guy is as lousy at explosives as he is at everything else because I don't have a scratch on me.

Tim's pond lurks like a puddle of ink on the other side of the fence when I finally stop running. I'm a good one hundred feet from my place now. With my flashlight on, I check my surroundings. No one's here. Readying myself for another attack, I reach for my Ruger. My fingers close around the grip when something crashes down on my skull like iron.

24

FEBRUARY 26TH

I stagger, sensing my thrown-off equilibrium as I stumble forward. I grab out at nothing. The bone-deep pain throbs in a sharp, piercing wave all the way to my teeth. Dropping the flashlight and pistol, I gasp and try to break my fall with my hands. I can't gain control of my body but manage to roll on my back to protect my head from another blow. Rocks and twigs press into me as I slide. Blocking with my arms, I push with my legs and try to scoot away from whoever struck me.

The ground moves beneath me like a tilt-a-whirl. Smoky carbon residue taunts my nose. I'm going to throw up. A man stands over me, but I can barely see him. He has something in his hands. A flashlight? A large, metal flashlight that he plans on knocking me out with.

I slide myself backward on the ground a few more inches, and my stomach dives like I'm falling out of a plane. The vague silhouette of the man blurs into two, then four. His image won't stay still. He lifts his workaday weapon and heaves, bringing it down full force with another bone-splitting blow. A brief burst of violent pain shatters my vision.

~

If only the ground would stop moving. I moan, squinting as the worst headache of my life assaults me. Something sticky and wet trickles down my face. I try to open my eyes. The surface on which I lie is unsteady, jostling me. It won't remain static, like the image of the man before he knocked me unconscious. I can remember that, barely.

The melodic hum of a running car engine vibrates my body as I stretch out my hand. My fingers find a short, coarse carpet over the shape of a wheel well. I can move my legs, only can't stretch out all the way. My tailbone screams, but it isn't that bad compared to my head. For some reason, my hands and feet aren't tied. I smell gasoline and leather, the terror of the tight space consuming me—the terror of being a prisoner.

Oh, God. God, no.

I grope the pockets of my coat and rifle through each one, scooping my hands inside and tearing around madly. I search every crevice of every pocket. Furtively, I pat the pockets of my jeans, but my phone is gone.

I groan and turn on my side before lifting my torso slightly as I discharge the meager contents of my stomach. When nothing else will come up, I shudder and collapse onto my side again. The smell of fresh vomit envelopes the trunk of the car, and in a couple of seconds, I'm dry heaving. It isn't hot in here, but my body breaks out in a cold sweat, leaving me shaking. Putting my palms down on the carpet, I try to think of it as something that isn't moving, something to be a stable point. The dizziness won't let up for me to get my bearings.

The car engine drones on, the bobbing from the tires over the road magnifying the sick, warm, stuffy feeling. I force myself onto my back and push up on the hatch with my hands. The cords in my neck bulge as I strain. With my heart pounding and my mind racing, I want to scream. I want to beat the inside with my fists, to yell for help, but a voice in the back of my head tells me that no one will hear me.

I squeeze my eyes closed, grit my teeth, and stifle the cry in my throat. I have to focus. I have to think. Thrashing around in here will let him know I'm awake, and I don't want that. Better for him to think I still lie unconscious. Better to lie quietly in the smell of my puke.

The car will eventually stop, which is the worst thing that can possibly happen, but also a chance for escape. A deluded chance, but it's all there is. The vehicle makes a right turn. It slows, jerking me slightly as he applies the brakes. But when the car finally pulls to a complete halt, and the driver kills the engine, I can't keep my thoughts straight to come up with a plan. My heart hammers in a wild rabbit panic, knowing that the trunk is going to open. The hatch will come up, and he'll be there. I have a concussion, a half-healed, fractured tailbone, and no weapon.

The driver's side door swings open and slams shut. Booted feet amble across gravel and stop behind the rear bumper. A few noises I can't place, then a zipper. A coat zipping closed? A duffle bag opening? The man sniffs and clears his throat, and then he lapses into a fit of coughing.

This flicker of hope adds a little fuel to the flame of my adrenaline—something to ignite the fight instead of flight. He sounds sick or like he has some kind of breathing problem.

Stabs of pain ripple through my pelvis as I twist my body around to wriggle out of my coat. I lie on my right side and wad the jacket into a loose ball, gripping it with my shaking hands. The trunk opens, and the man stands there in a black ski mask, the flashlight in his right hand. When he sees me awake, he raises the weapon, and I throw the balled-up jacket in his face.

It's enough—just enough to make him miss my skull, grazing my ear instead, before the heavy housing thuds onto the trunk bed. A searing, burning pain consumes the left side of my head. It feels like he's torn off my ear.

My terror and racing pulse silence my scream. I shoot out of the trunk like I'm possessed by the devil and throw myself on top of the man, getting my arm around his neck and squeezing. He pounds my back with the flashlight. I gasp as he knocks the wind out of me, but I hold on. He wheezes. He hammers the right side of my back over and over, and a sharp pain in my ribs makes me nearly let go. So, I make myself constrict him harder, calling up every last bit of strength my body possesses.

The ground beneath us dips and wheels, and I see double again. The man's legs wobble. He stumbles and slumps to the ground, releasing the flashlight and dropping to his knees on the gravel driveway. He's ceased pounding mercilessly against my back, but he thrashes around and struggles wildly, pushing forward against me.

My legs come out from under me, and I fall backward onto my tailbone, crying out as he forces me to let go. Seeing his chance, my attacker lights into my face with his fists. He hits my jaw and whips my head to the right. Then he hits my eye straight on, making a knife-like pain shoot into my head, and for a second, I can't see at all.

I put up my hands and roll out of the way, kicking him in the face with my work boot. His teeth crack together, and he grunts. As I stagger to my feet, the man pulls something from his pocket—something small—and blasts me with an eyeful of chemical spray.

I yell and reflexively throw my hands up, lashing out at thin air. I can't see anything through the fiery pain of the mace. Tears gush down my cheeks, and I blink and squint, trying to see him. I *have* to see. My double vision turns to a blur of watery gray.

The murderer looms over me, locks his hands around my throat, and constricts my windpipe with his shaking fingers. My lungs ache, and my eyes bulge in their sockets as I flounder and thrash out with my legs at nothing. I can't breathe, and the pain in my chest becomes worse. He's crushing my windpipe. I start trembling, the cloudy silhouette of the man beginning to fade away as my vision dims even more. If I don't find a way through this, I'll pass out, and he'll strangle me until I die.

Finally, forcing my weak, quivering arms to obey, I reach up and push my thumbs into his eyes. They slide in with a warm squish, and the man howls. He releases my neck before screaming and falling sideways over me. Gulping in deep breaths, I shudder and cough. I'm finally able to breathe again.

I shove hard against the man's chest, and he topples back, his head landing in the gravel. I roll away from him and grope my way along the driveway for the heavy flashlight. I can't find it. I grasp dry grass and know I've gone too far, so I crawl to the left, finding the rocky path again. The car stops me when I bang into it with my shoulder. After turning again but staying on my hands and knees, I run my fingers along the rocks, and at last, I make contact with the metal shaft.

Grabbing it tightly, I lurch forward to the blur on the ground that is the man. His body bent in the fetal position, he coughs and moans softly with his hands over his face. My arms falter, and I'm barely able to raise my weapon and aim. I swing, making the bulb housing collide with the skull under the ski mask in a satisfying crack. With a slight roll of his head, the man stops moving. He lies there in silence. He's maybe even dead if I hit him just right.

Still straining for breath and gripping the flashlight, I start to run for the road but hesitate. Teetering in an unsteady directional change, I realize I can't not know. I have to know, and the police have to know, and I have to be able to tell them what they need to know.

I stagger back to where my unconscious attacker lies, and I kneel down. The rocks grind into my knees, but I barely feel them. My vision starts to clear a little, though it still makes double images, and the ground rolls unsteadily beneath me. I grab the top of the ski mask and yank it off.

The man's head hangs sideways, so I turn it upright. Blinking, I stare hard at the person in front of me. I concentrate, trying to make my eyes bring his image into focus. He's maybe in his late fifties, with dark hair, possibly brown or gray, starting to thin on top. He has a narrow nose and sunken eyes with dark circles underneath. I lift one lid to see his eye color, but his irises are rolled back inside their bloody sockets, and even with the flashlight, I can't discern their hue. It was worth a try. I study his features again, the pinched face that looks drawn and sickly. He's older now, but I know that face. I know it.

I search the man's clothing for my cell phone, or his, but don't find either. I don't find a wallet or anything else with ID. Next, I search the entire car and still come up empty-handed. A pack of zip ties lies on the passenger's seat, but besides that, the whole vehicle, including the trunk, comes up pretty clean and empty. It seems like a miracle that he didn't bind my hands and feet.

After confirming that my abductor remains unconscious, I follow the driveway to the rural road and try to run. Because of my injuries, I can't tear off at full speed in a stricken panic, and I find it nearly impossible to keep my footing with this degree of vertigo. The ground is a swing, and it's swinging me, to and fro, left and right.

A tree trunk up ahead turns into two, then four, and I stumble. I curse, pant for breath, and look behind me, seeing nothing. I dread to see headlights, yet at the same time want to see them if they belong to someone besides the person I've just walked away from. I pick up the pace again, forcing one foot in front of the other, setting my jaw against the pain in my tailbone, my head, and my back. I concentrate on the sound of my feet on the shoulder of the narrow road. I smell pine and cedar trees, and there are woods and fields on both sides.

There are no lights or houses here, nothing to tell me where I am. I only know I have to keep going. I'll eventually run into the main thoroughfare and find a gas station, but my stamina is already fading after jogging the short distance. The throbbing in my head threatens to make me blackout, and the weakness worms its way into my limbs, making me stumble again.

My bootlace catches on something, and I trip. Falling flat on my stomach on the hard asphalt, I groan as the agony threatens to tear me apart. I swallow acidic bile caught in my inflamed throat. I can't figure out why my back and ribs hurt so much, but it must have something to do with how many times he hit me. My arms tremble as I curse and thrust myself up. My hands are raw and stinging from trying to break my fall. I retie my left bootlace, check the right one, and then push myself into a dragging run again.

A white sign comes into view up ahead, and I lean forward as I run, trying to make my legs go faster. Concentrating on focusing despite my distorted vision in the darkness of the country, I make out that the sign reads 219, but I have no idea where that is. If it's a Georgetown road, I don't know about it. Maybe a mile ahead, I can faintly detect some light. I think I hear sounds from a busier street. Just a little bit farther. I have to keep going.

Taking rasping breaths and clutching the stitch in my side, I make it to the intersection. I glance around for the street sign but only find another one indicating 219. This new, unmarked road has four lanes, and a lamp post stands not far away. Not a busy thoroughfare as I hoped, but busier than where I came from. This is probably a ranch-to-market road.

A few cars pass as I trudge out into the weak light. With my legs going buttery and shuddering beneath me, I start waving my arms, coughing as I try to call for help. I don't think I can walk anymore. I won't last until I find a gas station or a store.

None of the cars slow down. I shout at the broken white

line in the asphalt, begging the universe to make someone hear me and stop. Then the ground rolls around me like a blanket, my vision dances in double, and an invisible force spins me on a wheel. My eyes flutter back. My head weighs a thousand pounds and rolls to the side. I grasp at empty air as my body goes slack and crumples to the pebbly shoulder by the cedar trees.

25

TWELVE YEARS EARLIER

Months after Mary's funeral, and eons after I hid her memory away deep beneath the cellar floor of my mind, I receive a postcard. I remove it from the mail slot outside the main building of my modest Austin apartment complex. There's no name or address indicating the sender. The card is postmarked from Illinois and isn't addressed to me specifically, but only to my apartment building and unit number.

It's a beautiful day, sunny and warm, and I take the rest of my mail and go to sit on the bench in front of the office. The gardenia bushes beside the brick wall are loaded with thick, milky blossoms. Their warmly exotic scent touches me like a lover's perfume. I turn the postcard over to find a strange poem handwritten in ink.

When rising from the bed of death,
O'erwhelmed with guilt and fear,
I see my Maker face to face,

O how shall I appear?

If yet, while pardon may be found,
And mercy may be sought,
My heart with inward horror shrinks,
And trembles at the thought.

I read it many times, trying to understand what it means. The haunting words in their flowing script dazzle my vision on this bright day, but I can't understand what they have to do with me. There must be some mistake, especially since the card isn't made out to me. I frown, checking again for an address or a sender's name, but there are none.

I've never understood religious things. Maybe someone intended for the poem to inspire a friend to go to church. Besides, I don't know anyone from Illinois. But with a tightness in my chest and a cold finger stroking my soul, something about it forces me to drag Mary out of the cellar one last time.

Probably a year and a half ago, when we were sixteen, Mary and I went canoeing at Lady Bird Lake. It was a glorious summer day, bright and full of promise. Mary sat before me in the canoe, and we pushed off from the bank, laughing and digging our oars into the water. We spent three hours counting turtles on their island logs, paddling under the Congress Avenue bridge and back again, slipping through occasional water plants, and letting the wind caress our faces.

As we neared the landing sight, I could smell the salt and sunscreen on Mary's skin. She turned to me, heaved out a long sigh, and smiled. "I'm exhausted, Trent. But this was so much fun. I'm glad you talked me into it."

"I thought you'd like it," I said.

I had a good time too. Mary sat right in front of me the whole time, and her hair in the sunlight and her backside in those shorts were killing me. They really were.

"What do you want to do when we get back?" she asked.

We had left my house that afternoon and planned on going back before dinner.

"I don't know. Eat. Maybe take a nap," I said, laughing.

She agreed. "Great idea."

We were burning hot but weren't perspiring much and stopped for sugary drinks at a small building just uphill from the launch. My car at the time was an ugly, blue, two-door Saturn with two hundred and fifty thousand miles on it. Dad had bought it for five hundred bucks as a reward for keeping my grades up and passing my driving examination.

Mary didn't seem to mind me driving her back to my folks' house in my beater car. She sat in the passenger seat with her legs crossed, sometimes looking out the window and sometimes mentioning something or other to me. The car had no A/C, and being out of the direct wind, we were sweating now. Mary took a hairband from her pocket and pulled her blonde mane back, working her fingers to tie up the hair. It didn't seem possible that anyone who was sweaty, sunburned, and windblown, with her hair in a messy bun, could look so damned *good.* I only kept my eyes off her because I had to watch the road.

Back at my parents' house around four o'clock, we had a quick snack and retreated to my room, where we didn't nap at all. We made out for an hour. We hadn't "done the deed" yet, and I was sure I would certainly die if she didn't let me soon. Patience was a virtue, I told myself, and there was no way I was going to mess this up.

However, nothing stopped us from kissing and pawing each other like the world was going to end tomorrow. Mary's warm mouth tasted like strawberry slushy, and she was flushed, her soft skin glowing. After our fun of barely keeping our clothes on, Mary pulled away and sat up to face me on the bed. She folded her legs crosswise. She was still wearing her tight, pink tank top and black shorts, and her bare feet were just as tan as her legs, with her toenails painted red. Mary looked across at me with her tousled blonde hair now coming loose from the bun and half in her face.

I had told her something. It slipped out unintentionally, but it was the truth. There was nothing wrong with telling the truth.

"Do you mean it, Trent?" she asked, then giving me a crooked smile and narrowing her eyes. She placed her palms on the mattress and leaned forward.

I lay on my back with my head on the pillow. I laughed and pushed myself up on my elbows. "Of course, I mean it. Do you think I'd say it if I didn't?"

Mary shrugged and smiled. "Some people would."

She crawled forward, coming to lie next to me. "You can't take it back, you know. If you say it and you really mean it, you can't take it back."

She looked over at me with her eyebrows raised, still giving me that quirky smile and blushing. Her blue eyes consumed me. She knew I meant it.

I grinned back at her, pushing her hair out of her face. "I mean it."

She wriggled closer to me, and I wrapped my arms

around her heated body. Mary said quietly, "Then say it again. Tell me again."

"I love you," I said softly into her ear.

"Trent, I love you too."

She put her hand on my heart and rested her head against my chest. We lay there like that for a long time, and I knew I was happy. Happy to be with my beautiful girl, who was also smart, funny, and kind—and she was mine.

Slowly, I come back to myself in the present moment of sitting on the bench in the swelling Austin heat, holding the postcard. The brilliant morning mocks me. The velvety gardenias tease me with their feminine scent as they nod in the wind. The piece of misrouted mail, bearing a poem I don't understand, comes as a harbinger of death. A herald from an inquisitor sent to torture me until only God is left to judge me.

You can't take it back.

And she was right. I can't. I can't take back loving her. I can't take back not loving her, breaking her heart, ruining her life. Killing her. I can't take it back.

March 1st

A VOICE SAYS, "MR. LEMEND."

The voice stretches across a great distance, calling out to me from a desolate road between the cedar trees. I think it belongs to a man. Or maybe it belongs to a woman.

"Can you hear me?"

The light blinds me. It must be from the passing cars. Maybe someone is finally pulling over.

"Mr. Lemend," the voice insists.

I moan and put my hand in front of my face, trying to shield my eyes from the brilliance. A sharp, stabbing pain ribbons around from my back to the front of my ribs, where it digs in like a knife blade.

"Ah God, what the—"

I try to turn my head but can't. I open my eyes slowly, blinking in case the headlights are too close. My vision is white, blurry, and unstable.

"It's all right. Try not to move too much. You've been unconscious for three days," the same voice says.

It's a woman speaking, after all. I squint and try to focus on her. She has dark skin, round glasses, and black hair put up in skinny braids.

A beeping sound in the background increases its tempo as I again try to turn my head but can't for some reason. None of the images in the current scene make any sense. This reminds me a lot of being in the hospital when I fractured my tailbone, but I know I'm still on that unfamiliar street trying to flag down a car. What was the name of that road I just came from? County Road something. I've never seen it before.

I grab handfuls of what feels like stiff sheets, and I ball up the fabric in my fists. The smell of rubbing alcohol makes my stomach turn. As I bend one of my knees, my tailbone, back, and ribs scream in agony. I scream back.

"Okay, okay," the woman says, putting her hands on my shoulders and pushing down firmly. "Mr. Lemend, I need you to calm down. You're in shock. You've been unconscious for three days, and you have some injuries. You are in shock," she repeats. "Do you understand? Blink twice if you do."

I pant, glancing around furtively at the bright, unfocused, white room. I don't want to throw up again. My throat aches as I mumble, "No."

"All right. It's all right," the nurse says. "Just stay calm. Can you tell me your name?"

"Yeah." My voice sounds raw, and it hurts to talk. I try to put my hand to my throat, but my fingers hit something soft, and I can't touch my neck. "My name is Trent Lemend. I live in Georgetown."

"Good," she says. After nodding and patting my shoulder, she removes her hands. "My name is Bella. I'm your nurse. Do you remember what happened?"

Nausea rises up in my stomach, and I put my hand over my mouth. I swallow down the bile and something else. It's bitter, like the time I bit into a Tylenol as a kid.

"Are you gonna be sick?" she asks.

"No. I'm good," I say, though I don't believe myself. I try to think back so I can answer her first question. "He tried to kill me. I was in the trunk. I got—I got away, and it was County Road, um, something. I didn't know where I was. I tried to get help. Elizabeth? Is Elizabeth okay?"

I squeeze my eyes closed tightly. Smothering the grief just makes my chest hurt worse. Elizabeth is dead.

"Someone else was with you?" Bella asks.

"No, sorry. I'm not thinking straight. No, I was alone when I—I know who did this. I need to talk to someone at the sheriff's office. The detective. I need to talk to Gerald Menard in Williamson County."

"Yes, I'll help you call him right away. I want you to know that you were found on the side of FM 2657 in Florence. You have a grade three concussion and two bruised ribs. Fortunately, there were no serious internal injuries. You're lucky someone saw you and called an ambulance, especially with those scalp wounds."

I gingerly raise my right hand, feeling at my throat again, and realize I'm touching a neck brace.

"You have a neck injury as well. The brace will help it to heal," she says.

I swallow once more. "The guy who did this took my phone again. I don't want him putting it anywhere." That sounds mental.

My face contorts into a grimace, and I stare up at the ceiling tiles. I can just make out the square edges around each one. The rims of my eyes are wet, and my chest heaves up and down, but I keep my mouth shut and grit my teeth. I'm not okay with being constrained and helpless. I want to do something effective.

Nurse Bella asks, "Are you hungry?"

"No," I say.

"We just removed the feeding tube a few hours ago. You're okay to start eating light foods when you're ready."

"Oh God," I say, still glaring up. My voice comes out in a scratchy croak. "How long will I be in here?"

"At least a couple more days," she says. "Do you have any pain right now?"

"Only when I move or talk," I say.

Bella gives a little chuckle. "I know, you're going to be sore for a while. We can see about increasing your meds. How's your vision?"

"Horrible."

"Any dizziness?"

"Yeah," I say.

"Okay. That's from the concussion and your neck injury. It should improve with time," she says. Noticing how my gaze refuses to stop darting around, she says, "We'll make that phone call for you now."

I no longer have the detective's card. Since, for the moment, I'm not in danger, the nurse dials the sheriff's non-emergency number, and I explain what happened to the best of my ability. I let the woman know my memory is spotty in places but that I'm safe in the hospital and don't know where my attacker is. I do, however, give his name and description, as well as the name of the farm-to-market road the nurse told me. Afterward, the woman gives me Menard's cell phone number. I repeat it out loud, and Bella writes it down. Once she reaches him, I repeat everything for the detective in my raspy voice.

Nurse Bella and I exchange a few more words, and I give her the name of my insurance carrier. When she leaves the room, I slowly lift my hands to my skull. The coarse gauze bandages winding all the way around are bumpy under my fingers. I can't recall exactly where on my head I was struck, although I know he hit me more than once. I wonder how bad the scalp wounds are.

I run my fingers down the sides of my head and find a bandage covering my ear as well. So, the bastard didn't rip it off. Below that, I press my palms against the neck brace. Struggling awkwardly, I tug off the thin bedsheet and lift my hospital gown. The doctors wrapped a thick bandage snugly around my torso. I don't even want to think about my tailbone.

My eyelids are heavy, and I can barely stay awake. I try to collect my thoughts so when I speak with Menard again, I'll be able to fill in any gaps. Maybe I'll even get to talk to Reyes. I like Reyes.

There are still too many holes in my memory. I doze off

and on, succumbing to the mind-numbing fuzziness of the morphine and whatever else they're giving me. After falling into dark dreams, I reach out my hand in my sleep. My fingers touch something coarse, and I drag my hand over a rounded surface. A wheel well.

I jerk awake in a cold sweat, accidentally knocking a cup of water off the side table. The splashing sound as it hits the tiled floor makes me jump. I swear and wipe my face as the heart monitor's rhythm mirrors my rabbiting pulse. Nausea taunts me again.

A hand pushes open the white curtain at the edge of my room, and the nurse from earlier—Bella, I remember—comes in with a chart in her hand. She smiles as she walks over and sits in the chair next to the bed.

"Mr. Lemend, I have some good news. Doctor Pennington gave the okay to increase your pain meds, so that should help keep you more comfortable."

"Thanks, but I feel sick. Are the meds going to make it worse?" I ask.

"No, these shouldn't make that any worse. The upset stomach is likely from the concussion and the neck injury. But I can get you something for the nausea, too, if you'd like."

"That's all right," I say. "It's fine as long as it doesn't get worse."

The nurse opens the chart and takes a pen from the pocket of her top. She makes a few notes and says, "You also have a visitor. There's a Ms. Owen here to see you. Are you feeling up to it?"

"Yes, definitely," I say.

My chest gets all fluttery. The idea of seeing Aria—the idea that she somehow found out I've been hospitalized and has come to see me—is oddly comforting. It means something else too. Something I can't name.

"Okay, I'll let her know," Bella says. "Glad you're feeling a bit better." She pats my hand, turns, and her braids disappear through the curtain.

Several minutes tick by, and I frown. Did Aria change her mind? I close my eyes against a pang I don't understand. Maybe she deemed it best not to see me in this condition. I have no idea what my face looks like, but it must be bad.

When I finally resign myself to try and go back to sleep, the curtain rustles, and Aria appears. She isn't entirely in focus, but I can make out her dark hair. As she slowly walks over to me, I try to stop the double vision and shaking camera effect.

Aria forces her mouth closed and blinks, staring at me with an emotion between terror and relief. She takes the seat next to me. "Trent."

Now that she's this close, I notice her red eyes and their puffy lids. Her face has filled out all the way.

"I'm really glad you're alive," she says. She starts to reach out her hand but withdraws it.

Somehow, I crack a smile. "I'm really glad to see you. God, you have no idea."

Kyle doesn't even know about this. No one does, except Aria, and I have no idea how she found out. She smiles and gives in to the urge to reach up and put her hand over mine after all. A welcome reprieve from isopropyl alcohol and bleach, her skin moisturizer smells like mango aloe.

"You wouldn't return my calls or texts," she says. "So, I started checking around at the hospitals." When I don't reply, she adds, "I knew something was wrong. It was either this or..."

"Dead. Yeah, I was on my way," I say. "But you were right."

"Right?" she asks.

I swallow. "It wasn't Nemeth. It had nothing to do with him."

Aria blinks. "Oh, yeah. I knew it couldn't be. Did you see who did this? I mean, did you see his face?"

"I saw him. I know who he is. I know his name. I want to tell you what happened, but I can't remember all of it, only bits and pieces."

"You have a head injury," she says. "I'm sure your memory will come back as it heals."

Forgetting about the neck brace, I attempt to nod but can't.

"Want to tell me the parts you can remember?" Aria asks. "It helps." She squeezes my hand.

At that moment, I fully realize Aria's strength. The woman who first appeared to me like a starving, adolescent girl, with her gaunt cheekbones and too-large eyes, sobbing and talking nonsense at Seton Southwest. After surviving something ten times worse than what I experienced, Aria has recovered physically and is trying to live again. Now she's here, trying to help me through my own trauma, which doesn't seem that bad in comparison.

"He hit me over the head with a metal flashlight," I say. The heart monitor's rhythm follows right along as I evoke the grim terror of falling to the ground on the roadside.

"I woke up in the trunk of a car. For some reason, he didn't tie my hands and feet. I don't know why." I have to stop. I don't remember what comes next. "Then, I don't know. There's a gap. But later, we must have fought. I must have knocked him out because he was on the ground, and I pulled his ski mask off. Then I ran down the road in the dark. And that's it. That's all I can remember."

Aria's brows knit, and she gives a faint, sad smile. "That's a lot, Trent. I'd say you remember very well."

"I wish I could remember the name of that county road where he stopped the car. It was somewhere I've never been before. The nurse said they found me in, uh," I strain, trying to penetrate the fog of medication. "Florence, I think. That's northwest of Georgetown. I'll get the nurse to tell me the intersection. I think I can find the place he took me once I wake up more."

Aria nods. "I can help too. We can look it up on a map together."

I laugh, and my ribs protest. "Are you being my guardian angel now?"

"Yep. God wants me to return the favor. That's the way the universe works. Or at least, that's the way it's supposed to." She grins. If she's telling me that karma is real, it's no wonder my life is a living hell.

"Karma," I say, fighting to keep my eyes open. The increased meds are working. "I wish it always worked in the good way."

"Trust me, Trent, everyone wishes that," Aria says. She drags her silky hand across mine, and her voice fades into the background. "I'll see you tomorrow."

26

MARCH 7TH

The next day, both Detective Menard and Deputy Reyes pay me a visit in my room. Aria and I have just finished eating lunch together, and the space still smells like the basil pesto pasta from the cafeteria.

"Good morning, Mr. Lemend," Reyes says. The clipboard slips in his hand when he sees Aria beside me in her chair. He furrows his brow at me, clears his throat, and looks back to the young woman. "Good to see you, Ms. Owen."

"It's nice to see you too," says Aria, reining in a smirk.

She insisted on being here while I give all the gritty details so that she can "remind me" if I leave anything out. I like her sense of humor.

"Mr. Lemend," Detective Menard says, nodding at me. A solid frown covers his face as he gets his recording device ready.

Aria gives up her seat to him, and he plops down, making the plastic chair creak at the screws. The detective glares at me with his hard, little eyes, giving me an I-told-you-so look—as though from what we discussed in our last meeting, he isn't surprised to find me wrapped in bandages.

Reyes drags another chair in from an adjoining room. "Trent, you have got to be the unluckiest—and luckiest—person I have ever met. I'm sorry to see you under these circumstances, but I'm glad to see you."

Alive.

Reyes gently claps me on the shoulder before sitting down. "What else can you tell us about what happened?"

My memory has returned, and I recall the County Road 219 sign, along with all the other grim aspects of my escape. I lie in my bed and tell Reyes and Menard everything about the attack. Most importantly, I give the man's name and where he lives—at least, where he lived when I last knew him. I impart what I understand of his motive, at last grasping how all the scattered pieces form a whole.

I tell them something else, too. "The time I went into Tim's old house, looking for my phone, the message on the wall said, 'She's dead anyway.' First, I thought it was referring to Aria. Then I thought it must be about Elizabeth. Now I know it wasn't about either of them. It was about Mary. That was Mr. Durham's way of telling me that no matter what my intentions were or what I actually did or didn't do, the result was the same. Mary is dead."

"And it was twelve years ago when his daughter died of postpartum sepsis?" Menard asks.

"Yes," I say. "But as far as he's concerned, it probably wouldn't make a difference if it were a hundred." My neck itches and I try to scratch it, but the cumbersome brace prevents me.

"I don't know if she has anything to do with what happened," I continue, "but Mary's older sister, Stephanie, threatened me at the funeral back then. She screamed at me in the lobby and told me if she ever saw me again, she'd kill me." It's been a long time since I've thought of that incident, but I do my best to recount what I recall.

Reyes nods and takes everything down. "We'll look into it. What else can you tell us?"

I draw a breath. "When Mr. Durham stole my cell phone and put it in the murder house, he texted me, 'Devices are mirrored. Call and she dies.' *That* was about Elizabeth. He thought I knew or would suspect, but I didn't. He was counting on it drawing me to the house." I shake my head. "And I went anyway, even though I didn't know."

When I can't think of any more to convey, Reyes stands up and shakes my hand. "Thank you, Trent. Looks like we have enough to proceed. We'll contact you if we have anything further."

Menard rises as well. He checks the time on his Rolex and wishes me a speedy recovery.

After the detective leaves the room, Reyes stops and turns to us with his eyebrow slightly raised. "And Trent, you might consider moving back to the city. It's safer."

With a wink so brief I almost miss it, the deputy sheriff disappears through the curtain.

THE HIGHLIGHTS of my days are Aria's visits, and she usually stays for hours. There are still things I can't figure out, and it's nice to have an outside viewpoint. Sitting up in bed, I give her the particulars of the night Durham broke into my house.

Aria says, "He must have got in while you were out. I know it seems incredible, but he could have used locksmith tools to open the door. Then he hid somewhere, and while you were asleep, he came out, took your things, and left through the front door."

"Impossible. I checked everywhere when I got back. I know I did," I say. I hold the small, paper cup of water the nurse brought.

"I believe you," says Aria. "But even if you were thorough, there was probably someplace you didn't think of. Like under the sink. Did you check there?"

I shake my head. "No, but a grown man can't fit under there."

"Yes, he can. It's tight, but in a lot of kitchens, you can squeeze your body in. Uncomfortable, but doable." She turns her body in the chair, so she faces me better.

"Not at my house. You should see how small it is. It's like a crusty, little shotgun shack out of a Western movie." I laugh. Aria's thinking in the right direction, but it can't be that simple.

"Do you keep your trash can under there?" she asks. She props her arm on the chair's back.

I frown and tilt my head. It's freeing having the next brace off. "No. Why?"

"Because if you did, that would be a place you might have looked when you got home. You know, to throw something away."

I nod slowly. "The trash can is in the corner by the cabinets and the wall. But I keep other stuff under the sink."

"Like what?" Aria says. She raises an eyebrow, proud of her logic as she anticipates my frank answer.

"Uh, a couple of bottles of cleaner and some bug traps. I guess he could have moved them." I sip the water. It smells like chlorine, is way too cold, and hurts my teeth.

Aria grins. "I guarantee it." Her smile fades, and she folds her hands, falling into contemplation before speaking again. "Ever since what happened, I think about everything. I try to reason situations out. I never used to do that. I remember finding it strange when people dissected things too much. But it's good to think about the little details—the long shots or the possible but unlikely. Those are sometimes the most important."

That makes me think of something else. "Why didn't he tie my hands and feet? If he had done that, I wouldn't be here right now."

"Trent, he knocked you out cold," Aria says. She glances back at the curtain, and though we can't see anyone nearby, she says more quietly, "I listen to the doctors and nurses when I can. The nurses in this wing see a lot of trauma patients. I heard one of them say you're lucky to be alive. When he hit you over the head like that, he didn't expect you to wake up, or at least not so soon. Sometimes, people are unconscious for hours, and when they wake up, they can't do much. You're alive because you woke up. I don't know how you woke up. I don't know how you were able to fight and escape, but you did. It's... well, it's a miracle, like the nurse said. I guess it's yet another sign that the universe is paying you back for rescuing me." Aria smiles slightly.

"But how could he see how bad my head injury was in the dark?" I ask, setting the water cup on the side table.

"He probably didn't need to see it because he knew how

hard he struck you. But he had the flashlight, and he would have seen blood everywhere when he loaded you in the trunk. Head wounds bleed a lot," she says.

I nod, meeting her eyes which are so dark they're almost black. "What you said earlier, about the little details being the most important. You're right. If I would have learned that sooner..."

I don't know what. What would I have done? I would have committed to Mary. I would have got married, I wouldn't have met Elizabeth, and she wouldn't have left me. I wouldn't have moved to Georgetown. I would never have looked into that back room of the house on County Road 140, and I wouldn't have saved Aria's life. Seems like she isn't the only one who thinks about the long shots these days.

Then it all comes out. Blame it on the morphine, but somehow, I spill the entire story of Mary and the sins of my youth. I shed my secrets like a broken man talking about a bad breakup with a bartender, and they flow out of me into a bottomless shot glass. But I'm not drunk. I can't recall the last time I had a beer.

Aria sits motionless at the bedside, barely blinking. Sometimes she nods. And after probably an hour, when I've milked so many pathetic details from my shameful past, it dawns on me that the reservoir is nearly empty. I'm draining the dregs of the whisky bottle.

"There was something else," I say. "A few months later, I got this postcard with a poem. I think it was mailed to me by mistake. There was just something about it that stuck with me."

"Can you remember any of it?" she asks.

"Actually, yes." Having mulled it over as an addled

teenager, I know most of the lines fairly well. I repeat them to the best of my recollection.

Aria twirls a strand of hair in her fingers, frowns, and pushes out her bottom lip. She leans back in her chair. "That sounds like Addison. Yeah, those are lines from 'When Rising From the Bed of Death.'"

I grunt, pushing myself back to sit up straighter. "Addison. That sounds familiar. How do you know the name of the poem?"

"I like to read," Aria says. "And he's a pretty famous poet. You heard of him?"

Addison. *Addison.* I know the name somehow. Where do I know it from? And then I remember. I slowly rub my arms to stem the chill as I call back the smoky, snapshot memory of the golden cathedral and white lilies gracing the altar.

"Mary's best friend quoted Addison in her eulogy. What is the poem about?"

"I haven't read that one in a long time," Aria says. "But from what I remember, it's about asking for forgiveness and having a clean conscience when you die. And about the terror of being judged by God for your sins."

Looking down at my hands in my lap, I take a deep breath. Well, it seems I have indeed been judged, but not by my maker. Seems it's the other deity who calls for me. I've long since abandoned any quest for redemption and have cast myself into the abyss.

"Trent?" Aria says.

Barely hearing her, I study my knuckles. They still bear the dark scrapes and discoloration from the struggle.

"Trent," she repeats. She places her smooth, pale hand over my mottled one.

I lift my gaze to hers and constrain the urge to turn on

my side and stare at the wall. Retreating into my soft cloud of narcotic pain relievers would be so nice.

Aria tells me, “You're free to feel about it however you want to feel about it, but it is *not* your fault that she died.”

Her dark eyes remain so still, so motionless as she silently compels me to understand. I know somehow that she believes what she said. As Aria leans against my hospital bed with that compassionate look on her face, I think it's only fair I tell her the rest of Mary's story—the part I omitted.

So, I do.

THE UNEXPECTED JOY which permeates my soul after Mary lost the baby is a package tied with a neat little bow of guilt. I shouldn't feel so good about what happened. Mary is crying her eyes out while I float on my lofty cloud of irresponsibility. Mostly anyway, besides the newly enforced relationship part. I've just agreed to give it another try. To start over.

Mary's room in the maternity ward has a peculiar smell. Really, it's more of an echo smell. It's a hint of things past that abate only reluctantly, traces of afterbirth and blood and mucus and amniotic fluid. Those things aren't here anymore, but whispers of them are, and they make certain I know. I hold Mary's hand and try to listen to what she says between sobs and soggy tissue blows.

“It's just so hard, the fact that one minute I had a daughter and the next I didn't. How can a life be snuffed out so quickly? She never had a chance to live, not even for one day. I didn't get to hold her even one time." Mary wipes roughly at the tears gathering in her dark circles. She sniffs. Her eyes vaguely focus on me before she continues.

"I was so angry at you, Trent. Do you remember a few months ago when you asked what I would name the baby if it were a girl? And I told you I didn't know?" She dabs her cheeks with a crumpled tissue.

I swallow. "Yeah. I remember."

"Well, I had name ideas almost as soon as I learned I was pregnant, but I really wanted us to discuss them together. But when you broke up with me, I felt like you had no interest, and I was on my own. So, I went ahead and decided on names myself. Patrick, for a boy, after my dad. And Norah, for a girl, after my favorite aunt." Her face pinches into another pained grimace, her skin reddening.

"That's part of what makes this so painful, I think. Not just that a fetus died, like if I had miscarried a child very early on, but that *Norah* died. She was my daughter, a real person," Mary says. Tears stream down her cheeks, and she stares at nothing, her eyes glazing over in a salty haze.

Hearing the baby's name for the first time sends a wave of emotion through my body. The room becomes brighter. Sharper.

My chest tightens, and I squeeze Mary's hand. I'm young and full of piss and vinegar, but even now, I know I can't possibly understand her pain. I haven't just carried another human being to term, built castles in my mind, labored for hours, and then lost everything in one shattering moment.

"I'm sorry," I say. "If I had the power to bring Norah back, of course I would." I'm not lying. Yes, the outcome relieves me, but I'm sorry for Mary's sake. She's done nothing to deserve this.

"Do you mean that?" Mary asks. She blots her pink cheeks.

I nod. "Of course, I do. Raising a baby at our age would be hard, but like you said, she was still our daughter."

Our daughter. The words roll through my mind like a clap of thunder. They fill all the empty spaces in my head, the intermittent gaps that should be consumed by grief but are taken up with liberation instead.

I shove the thought away. I put my other hand over the top of Mary's, enveloping it. Her warm skin bonds to mine. She takes a deep, shuddering breath and her face relaxes slightly. Her lips press together as she attempts a smile.

"Thank you, Trent. It means so much to me that you feel that way." Mary squirms, easing herself sideways. She rolls to face me on the narrow bed. After blinking a few times, she shakes her head before continuing.

"You know, there's been so much I blamed you for. I was so hurt. But this isn't your fault. And even when I was blaming you for everything—even if I blamed you for this—it wouldn't make the pain any less. So, it's silly, really, to place that much blame on someone, especially someone I lo—"

I guess she can't bring herself to say it.

"—anyway, the nurse said she's going to give me some literature on how to cope with losing a child. And I can also get counseling if I need additional help. I think my family's insurance covers it, like for postpartum care..."

But somewhere in there, I've stopped listening. Something strikes me as odd, and I can't put my finger on it. Why did she blame me for "everything," as she put it? Mary and I are at least equally responsible for her pregnancy. We never had unprotected sex, not even once. I never even asked to try it. We never knew a broken condom. I know because I always checked every single time afterward without fail—though, to be honest, we only had sex a handful of times. Sometimes we only fooled around. Then there's the fact that we always used a backup method of spermicidal cream, something I knew about thanks to my sex-ed class at school. Not everything I do is stupid.

As she talks, Mary stops crying. "I guess I can return the stuff from the baby shower. There's such a lot of it, but at least people would get their money back. I'd hate just to give it all away..."

I sit up straighter, withdrawing my hands from hers. Her skin adheres to mine briefly, like a toddler's fingers coated in hard candy residue and drool.

"Mary."

"...although my cousin Sophia just had a baby. Maybe she could use a few things."

"Mary," I repeat gently.

Mary's eyelids flutter, her gaze snapping up to me. "What?"

"How did you get pregnant?" I ask.

"What?" Her face falls.

I gulp down the lump gathering in my throat. "We used condoms and spermicide, and there were no accidents. And we only had sex, what, maybe ten times?" I force out air. "It just doesn't make sense to me. How is it possible that you got pregnant under those conditions?"

She pulls her head back and props herself up on an elbow. "How could I possibly know that, Trent? I was as shocked as you. It can happen. My mom's sister got pregnant after getting her tubes tied, so I guess I shouldn't be surprised that I got pregnant using condoms."

"And spermicide," I say.

Mary huffs. "Yes, and spermicide."

She pushes herself to a sitting position and fiddles with the IV in her arm. "Ugh, I feel like I've cried every drop of water from my body. Do you think you could get me some lemonade from the cafeteria?"

"Sure," I say. "I'll get some for you."

I will because I want to be compassionate. I want to help her. I want to try to understand what she's going through. Unfortunately, at the same time, the most devilish thought is forming inside me. It grows like a tumor, tiny at first but engorging itself on forbidden nectar until it devours me. And this thought seems even more relieving than getting out of fatherhood at eighteen. It's also infuriating. It's delicious, and it's disturbing.

Our daughter. But what if little Norah, whose life ended prematurely for reasons unknown, wasn't our daughter? That is, what if she wasn't Mary's and mine? What if she was Mary's... and someone else's?

Mary asks, "Is there something you want to say?"

I've been staring vacantly. Now I bring the image of Mary's fatigued expression, weary eyes, and tangled hair into focus. I force myself to say the words. There's no point in hiding anything.

"I'm going to get your drink. And while I'm out, I'm also going to ask for a paternity test."

27

TWELVE YEARS EARLIER

Six days later, Mary is crying again. "This doesn't prove anything."

She glares at me hot-eyed from her seat on my couch, her right hand still gripping the purse strap around her shoulder. Her other hand clutches a paper from LabCorp.

"I'm afraid it does," I say. "It means I'm not the father because the baby didn't have my DNA."

Since we're a couple again in some fashion, I invited Mary over to my apartment after work. Maybe it was cold of me, but I wasted no time getting right to the point. Once I handed her the paternity test results, there wasn't much she could say. Of course, that doesn't mean she didn't try.

Mary's torso shakes. She pushes the purse strap off her shoulder and crosses her arms. "What kind of monster are you? You had to get a DNA test on a stillborn baby so you could feel better? So that you could be right? Those tests can be *wrong*, Trent. It's not even that uncommon. It happens all the time—up to thirty percent of the time."

I sit on the barstool by the kitchen island that smells faintly of off-brand cleaning products. My efficiency isn't big enough for a dining room table and chairs. My arms are crossed too, and I clench my jaw so hard it begins to hurt.

I ask, "How the hell do you know that paternity tests are wrong thirty percent of the time?"

She blinks. "I looked it up after you said you were having one done."

"Right. Because you knew it was going to be negative," I say.

"You're sick! Who would do this?" Her face and ears flush crimson. She puts her face in her hands, her loud sobbing echoing throughout my scantily furnished place.

"Who would have a paternity test done on a stillborn baby? Someone who doesn't understand how you got pregnant by immaculate conception." I uncross my arms and lean an elbow on the counter. "So, who was he? Someone I know?"

"You're horrible, Trent. You're absolutely horrible. I wish I didn't love you," Mary says. She digs around inside her purse and pulls out a small pack of tissues. She won't look at me.

"And you're a cheater, just like me. Except that you cheated first. Didn't you?" I ask.

"No, I fucking didn't!"

Wow. Very uncharacteristic of her to use that word. But at least she's looking at me now.

"Then how did you get pregnant?" Shifting on the stool, I raise my eyebrows and rest my palms on my quads. I lean forward.

"What do you want from me, Trent? You want me to tell you that a piece of paper proves I did something? Well, it doesn't. It doesn't change the fact that our daughter died, and it definitely doesn't change the fact that you cheated."

Now my own face starts to burn flame red. I shake my head and slap the faux granite countertop, unable to believe she's pulling this. Then again, what did I expect? If she didn't tell me that she was unfaithful before, why would she tell me now? At least I came clean about my mistake.

I say, "I want you to admit that you cheated on me. I want you to admit that you led me to believe Norah was my baby and that you were perfectly fine with me shelling out every penny I made for her care. Damn it, Mary, I dropped out of college for you. I've got this apartment and a full-time job. I'm so strapped I can barely pay my rent and buy food. And you can't even be honest with me?"

"I never cheated on you," she says. She stares at my Dallas Cowboys poster, one of the few decorations on the textured, off-white walls.

"You didn't? The test is 'just wrong?' Sperm can materialize through latex and survive chemicals?" I hold out my hands. They're shaking. In fact, so is my whole body. I was upset when I got the results, but I didn't really plan on her disputing them. Now I'm just plain pissed.

"Can't you just accept that something bad happened to us?" Mary asks. "Like I said, I was blaming you, but I'm not anymore. As much as it hurts, this is our chance to start over. We're young. We still have our whole lives ahead of us, and you can go back to school now."

"No, I'm locked into a lease now, just like I was telling your dad," I say. I sigh.

Mary stops dabbing at her eyes. She lets the damp tissue fall onto her lap, her bottom lip quivering like something frightened her. "You don't—you don't want to break up with me again, do you?"

I huff. "Well, yeah, I kind of do. I barely have my own life together, and after all this, you won't even tell me the truth. I guess there's nothing else to talk about." I get up and head toward the door to let her out.

Mary leaps to her feet, her brows pinching in wild desperation. "No, Trent. Please wait."

She races ahead of me across my tiny living room, her sneakers skittering over the carpet like a frantic cat. After shoving her body between me and the door, Mary grabs the doorknob to block my hand. She looks up at me. "I don't want it to end like this. Not again."

I exhale and take a step back. "Mary, even if the baby was mine, I don't know if I can take any more of this. But I don't think she was. Unless you can admit that, just go."

"I can't admit something that isn't true. And I'm not leaving. You told me you loved me, Trent. If that's true, then I want to work this out," Mary says. Another tear rolls down her cheek, and she turns down the corners of her mouth. She swallows hard to suppress a whimper.

I stand here watching her. Mary Durham, the picture of innocence and tragedy. Am I truly the monster she says I am? I just can't shake the sinking sensation in my gut. And the evidence.

I put my hands on my hips. "Fine. Then we're going to set a few things straight first. Since you're so sure paternity test results don't mean anything, I'm going to show this to your father. Then at least I won't keep being blamed for something I didn't do!"

Mary's arms, which are outstretched across my apartment door, go limp. They slide toward her body as gravity takes over, her posture sagging along with them. The color drains from her skin. She manages a weak nod. "Okay."

"'Okay,' I can show it to him?" I ask.

"No, no. Okay, I'll tell you the truth," Mary says.

She drags her feet across the floor toward the couch. Her back slouches, and her eyelids are heavy with apathy. The air whooshes from the worn cushions when she plunks herself down. Mary stares at her open hands, palms upturned on her lap.

I don't take a seat right away. For a moment, I just stand here by the door, letting my newfound realization of power fully sink in. Mary doesn't want Mr. Durham to know the baby wasn't mine. The thought petrifies her. Why? I can't figure what difference it makes since the man hates me so much. Maybe he'll be glad to know she got pregnant by someone else.

I shove my hands in my pockets and saunter back to the barstool. "And you'll be honest? I want the guy's name. I want the whole story."

She nods. Her face isn't red now but chalk white. "I'll be honest if you promise not to tell my dad. Do you promise?"

Well then. I draw a long, deep breath and sit up straight. If I want any sort of revenge, now is my chance. Nothing prevents me from going to Mr. Durham anyway, just to hurt Mary the way she hurt me. But I don't want revenge.

I want the truth.

"I DID CHEAT ON YOU," Mary says. "His name was Gabriel Ward. I'm sorry. I just... back then, I felt like you were getting distant, and I was always worried you were going to dump me. Gabriel is related to a guy who used to date my sister. I met him at the park one time when everyone was hanging out."

A blunt force hits me in the chest. Even though I already suspect her, even though the paternity test came back negative, hearing her say it still hurts. The shock surges through my core, dropping a stone in my belly.

"So... how many times?" I ask. Maybe she only screwed up the one time like I did. We all make mistakes.

Mary bites her lip. She tucks a lock of blonde hair behind her ear. "Um, I didn't keep track." She casts a furtive glance at me before lowering her gaze again. "But I—" Her shoulders tremble, and she begins to cry once more. "Gabriel and I saw each other off and on the whole time you and I were together."

My mouth drops open. "And when did you finally stop seeing him? Or did you?"

"I haven't seen Gabriel since I found out I was pregnant. Once I broke the news, he wouldn't talk to me. He wouldn't return my calls or texts," she says. She sniffs.

Her words punch me in the face and stab me in the back at the same time. My eyes go wide, and I grab the sides of my head with both hands. I lean over, reeling and trying to breathe. "Did you know it was his baby when you told me you were pregnant?"

"No. I didn't know for a fact, I... suspected, because we..." Her gaze falls to her lap.

"You what?" I ask.

"We never used protection. Gabriel wouldn't." Mary rubs her arm and stares at the floor.

Waves of pain sweep through me and keep on coming. I can hardly move. "Mary, this whole time, you let me believe I was a piece of shit. Now I find out you've been playing me. How could you do this? Why couldn't you have just broken up with me when you first met that guy?"

She looks up, the wounded crease of her blows pleading with me. "I'm sorry, Trent, I was so lonely when I met Gabe, but I still didn't want to lose you. And after I got pregnant... I didn't know what else to do."

I've been a complete fool. Before the whole pregnancy scare, I thought we were happy together—two teenagers in love. Even worse is what I've agreed to since I just promised Mary I wouldn't tell Mr. Durham. I committed to this, thinking I don't want revenge, only the truth. But now, I'll get no justice either. Not even a little.

"Why shouldn't I tell your father? You're allowed to lie and manipulate me, and I can't even clear my name? I don't deserve that," I say.

Mary leaps to her feet. "Trent, you promised! Please don't tell him. Please."

"Give me one good reason why I shouldn't." I glare at her and stand up as well. Then I pick up my cell phone and start scrolling for Mary's landline number—her parents' phone.

"Trent, no! Please!" A primal emotion dances in her eyes. Dread. Or maybe terror.

Before I can reply, Mary surges across the room to me. She erupts into hysterical weeping and throws herself on the floor at my feet.

"No! Please, please, no. I'll do anything!" She wraps her arms around my legs, squeezing and pulling like she's trying to make me lose my balance. She wriggles into a sitting position and yanks.

"Please, no! Don't tell him!" And then just, "No, no, no," her words getting lost in an ocean of sobs.

I sigh. To stabilize myself against Mary's jostling, I place both hands on the countertop. The crumbs on the not-immaculate surface grind into my palms. I get a whiff of Mary's perfume. It always reminds me of honeysuckles. My gaze finds the Dallas Cowboys poster on the wall next to the sofa, and I let my vision go out of focus. Is Mary genuinely terrified, or is this just another dramatic play?

"Mary," I say, my voice flaccid and barely audible over her cries. "Come on. Let go."

"Trent, please! It hurt him so much when I messed up before. Please! I can't go through that again," she says. She blinks her wide, blue eyes at me.

I let another exasperated breath escape. "What do you mean, before?"

"Please, Trent, please!"

I reach down and grab her arms, getting a firm hold so I can try and pry her off me. "Mary, just stop. What about messing up before?"

She wrenches her face into such a red, distorted grimace it reminds me of a gargoyle. "When he caught Gabe and me together. We—we first started dating when I was fifteen."

I readjust my grip on her arms and tug upward, forcing her to release her fingers. Then I step aside. My calves collide with the second-hand coffee table under my flat screen. The picture of my parents falls, its gold frame hitting the wood with a loud slap. I hop away, putting several feet between Mary and me.

"But you said you met Gabe recently at the park," I say. My chest heaves, and my heart pounds a hole in my chest.

Mary sits up straighter and pulls herself into a cross-legged sitting position. "I did. It had been years since I'd seen him. But we really met earlier."

She quivers as she draws a breath. At least she isn't screaming now.

"Look," she says, pulling up the left sleeve of her purple t-shirt. "That's how I got this scar. I've never told anyone. I guess… I've always felt ashamed."

She reveals the shiny, white streak, like something left behind from a deep scratch. I recall asking her about it in the past, and she told me it was from a childhood accident. The scar is about three inches long. I can't help but notice its perfect straightness.

I sink into the lumpy softness of the frayed couch. At some time during the screaming and crying and leg grabbing, my anger dissipated. Now I just feel tired.

"I don't understand," I say. "You and this Gabriel guy got hurt together? Like in a car wreck or something?"

"No." Mary stands. She pushes her hair from her face. Her unsteady hands straighten her wrinkled shirt. "Gabe and I lost our virginity together."

With that last utterance, she gives me a right hook straight to the groin. I've always thought I was her first—she was definitely mine. Silly me. My eyelids sag as I wait for her to explain.

"Gabe and I were together in my room. My dad caught us, and he was so upset. I've never seen him so angry. And then I missed my period." She rubs her face. "I don't really understand it, and I talked with my mom to try to get it to make sense, but my dad got upset all over again. It was like something flipped inside him. He was furious and shouting and telling me what a huge disappointment I was. We all thought I was pregnant—we thought that for weeks. So…" She shakes her head and begins pacing.

"So?" I ask.

"So, I cut myself." Her throat flashes as she swallows. "My dad had a pocketknife that he always kept in his back pocket. I grabbed it and dragged it down my arm. I did it as hard as I could stand, and I made sure it hurt. I cut so deep the blood ran down to my fingers." She wipes her nose on her bare arm.

"I was just so ashamed of myself. I wanted him to see that —then he'd know I was really sorry. He finally apologized for losing his temper, but he asked that I stop seeing Gabe for good. My dad said he never liked him." Mary's blue eyes are dewy and far away. Her footsteps swish across the carpet in her distant pacing as she hugs herself against the traumatic memory.

Through my exhaustion, I try to grasp her incongruous statements. "But you weren't sorry, right? Because you did the same thing again, with the same guy, and got pregnant for real this time."

She stops and looks at me. "You don't understand. You don't know what it's like."

I frown. "I don't know what *what* is like?"

Mary huffs. "To have someone expect you to be perfect all the time. To have to get straight As, and volunteer for charity work, and score high enough on standardized testing to get a partial scholarship to UT. And just... I don't know, be a perfect daughter. Because if I don't do all that—" She shudders. "He won't love me."

"Did he say he wouldn't love you?" I ask.

"No, of course not." She slides her hands in the back pockets of her jeans and slouches.

"What did he say?" I ask.

"I pretty much already told you," Mary says.

"Not really." I lean forward and rest my elbows on my legs.

She rolls her eyes and tilts her head back. "Ugh. He said he couldn't believe I'd been so irresponsible, and my behavior really upset him, and he couldn't—" Her annoyance evaporates, and she gulps down a sob. "He couldn't believe his own daughter would do such a thing. And that didn't I think about how my actions would affect my future and our family?" She takes the bottom of her shirt and wipes her eyes.

"I see," I say. I don't really, but my mouth is so dry my tongue sticks to the roof. I get up, pull a glass from the kitchen cabinet, and fill it with water from the tap. "Thirsty?"

Mary nods.

I hand her the glass, and before sitting down again, get another one for myself. While I drain it, I puzzle over the disturbing story. "Mary, correct me if I'm wrong, but what you told me sounds like what a lot of parents might say if they thought their kid got pregnant at fifteen. I'm not saying your dad's reaction was right, but it's not uncommon for people to freak out about stuff like that."

Mary sniffs and swallows. Her bottom lip droops before she answers. "You don't understand. Your parents don't expect anything of you."

"Hey!" I gape at her.

"Well, it must be nice. It must be nice to be able to do whatever you want. To have your parents love and accept you, and you never have to do a thing for it," she says.

I slam my empty glass down and stand. "What are you talking about?"

She hides her hands from me, shoving them behind her

back somewhere, maybe into her pockets again. With a flick of her wrist, she whips out a small pocketknife and clicks it open. She sets it against the inside of her arm and presses. A dot of blood springs up.

"Mary, stop!" I rush forward, but she only pushes the blade in deeper.

"Okay," I say. I put my hands up and back away. "Just please stop. You don't need to do that."

"You don't get it, and I knew you wouldn't," she says.

"I'm trying."

"You're not. You're really not. Just swear not to tell my dad about the results of the paternity test," Mary says. She starts dragging the knife along her inner forearm.

"Okay. Yes!" I heave out a breath, my mouth hanging open.

"Yes?" She turns so I can see the knife better. The trickle of blood flows in a thin line toward her wrist.

I exhale, and the last bit of strength leaves my body. There's something terribly wrong with Mary. How have I never seen this before? Well, I guess I never looked. I've always seen a beautiful girl, carefree and kind, and never this —whatever it is.

"Trent?"

"Yes, I swear, Mary. I won't tell him. Not ever. I'll let him think the baby was mine."

"And we can stay together? I know you think my dad hates you, but he likes you a lot more than—" She winces, whether from embarrassment or pain, I can't tell.

"Put the knife away. I said I swear." I motion toward her trembling hand that clutches the small weapon. "Put it away."

Mary exhales and removes the blade from her skin. She

holds it out for a moment and stares at me. I nod. With one hand, she flips the pocketknife closed and returns it to her back pocket.

"I'll get you a bandage," I say. Although I've been working all day and haven't eaten dinner yet, my stomach churns. My tongue retains a sulfur-chlorine taste from the tap water here in the low-rent district. I turn to head for the medicine cabinet.

"Did you lie when you said you loved me?" Mary asks.

I stop. "Did *you*?"

"No. Please, Trent. My dad likes you so much he wanted us to get married. Just be my boyfriend until I start school. Then I'll be gone, and you can do what you want," she says.

Without answering, I retrieve a Band-Aid. "Come on, let's go wash that."

Mary drags herself to the kitchen sink, turns on the water, and lets the stream run across her cut. I sit down on the sofa again and lean back. My eyes find their way to the ceiling fan. If I concentrate, I can bring a single blade into focus and follow it around and around and around.

She dries her arm and affixes the bandage to it. "So, will you? Be my boyfriend until school starts? You don't know what a big deal it is that my dad likes you."

"I think you're confused. Nothing would make your dad happier than never to see me again." I cover my eyes with my hands. Now I can just barely see the whirling blades through the slits between my fingers.

"You're wrong, Trent. Please, I'm begging you. Just try," she says.

I don't want to try. I want this to be over.

"Please," she repeats when I don't answer. "I'll do whatever you want. We can have sex again as soon as my stitches heal, but until then, we can still fool around. I can do stuff to you."

My chest constricts, and I sit bolt upright. I cover my mouth, unable to speak as I study her. The rose pink of her cheeks. The pout of her full lips and the curve of her breasts beneath the fitted, purple tee. She just offered me sex as barter, and I feel ill.

But I also realize something. I finally understand what it is that Mary really wants, whether she gets it from her father or me or some other man. Approval. Whether this approval is real or imaginary is another matter, but I have no control over that.

"You don't want me?" Mary asks when I say nothing.

I'm eighteen and full of hormones. She'd probably have to be covered in boils or grow a third eye for me not to want her—and I'm not sure a third eye would deter me, to be honest. I rub my eyes. This whole thing is beyond sad.

"I do, but not like that," I say. "No more sex. If we can omit that, I'll be your boyfriend until you start school. I'll try."

"You promise?" she asks.

I groan. "Yes, I promise."

"Oh, Trent, thank you!" Mary hops down from the barstool and comes to sit beside me. "It'll be fun, like old times. You'll see."

Her lips press into a soft smile, and she reaches to touch my cheek. She strokes downward with her warm fingers, and beneath them, my skin heats. I cringe.

28

PRESENT DAY

"I broke my promise and left Mary again," I tell Aria from my hospital bed. "I just couldn't deal with Mr. Durham criticizing me on top of everything else—on top of what I knew. But I've always wondered what would have happened if I'd toughed it out and stayed with Mary until school started. Maybe then she wouldn't have got postpartum sepsis. She was so miserable inside. A lot of illnesses are precipitated by stress."

"Trent, you don't have that kind of power," Aria says. "No one does. Mary's life was in jeopardy before she even met you." She offers me her bottled water.

I shake my head and pull the freshly bleached sheets closer to my neck. I swallow, which hurts.

"I'd like to think you're right," I say. "She just seemed so confused, and she really had no one—not even her mom since she was another parent to please. In the end, I feel like the only thing I did for Mary was keep her secret. It's the one thing I did right."

Aria sets the water on the table in case I change my mind. "Your silence nearly got you killed."

It nearly did. To this day, Mr. Durham doesn't know the baby wasn't mine. I reach my hand down to the side of the bed, pressing the button to raise my back more.

"Yeah," I say. "And even after all this, I still feel guilty."

"That's because you're a good person. Some of the best people don't know that they are," Aria says.

"If you say so."

I look away, pretending to be mildly annoyed, but I can't maintain it, and pretty soon, I start grinning. Being complimented or admired isn't something I'm used to. Maybe in time, I can come around to the idea. Maybe someday, when the pain relievers wear off, and I can walk straight again.

"But there's something I still don't understand about Mary's father," I say. "Why did he want revenge for her death after all these years? Why not punish me back then?"

Aria tilts her head thoughtfully as she untangles my IV line. Her slender fingers patiently work through the loops.

"It has to do with the way someone like that thinks. In his mind, everything he did was for Mary's own good. We don't know exactly how he raised her, but it sounds like he held her to an impossible standard and wanted her to live up to his idealistic expectations. When she died, he probably felt immense guilt over that, even if he'd never admit it. Blaming you for Mary's death probably relieved some of that pain. But as for why he waited so long, people like Durham obsess, and he had over a decade to build things up in his mind."

A chill from more than the air conditioning bites straight to my bones. I push my feet under the blanket, wondering how it is that Aria understands people so well. Maybe she'll rub off on me.

Aria drinks the rest of her water, tosses the empty plastic bottle in the trash can, and gets up. Grabbing her purse from the arm of the chair, she awaits my response.

"I think you're right," I say. "I don't think anyone could have explained it better."

A smile flickers on Aria's face. "You're not responsible for what other people do, Trent. And all the regret in the world won't change the bad decisions of others."

I exhale, a great heaviness leaving through my lungs as I glance up at her. Aria leans over and hugs me. Closing my eyes, I bury myself in the strawberry mint of her hair. We say goodbye for the day, and she turns to go. I fiddle with my ID bracelet as I watch her walk to the end of the small hospital room.

"Aria," I say. The irritating ache behind my eyes needles me.

"Yeah?"

"Thank you. I mean it. Thanks for everything."

"You bet." With a swish of her dark hair, she vanishes through the doorway.

THE DAYS PASS, and the hospital releases me. Reyes's joke about moving back to the city where it's safer unfortunately rings true, and the thought of going home launches a cannonball into my stomach. But as it turns out, the ghost from my past is a lot better at playing sick games and ruining my life than he is at hiding from the police. On the morning of March 20th, I sit on the couch in my shotgun house and read the following news article on my laptop.

Austin man arrested on murder charges.

AUSTIN — (KXAV) Patrick H. Durham of central Austin has been in custody since Wednesday after the alleged abduction and battery of Trent Lemend, a resident of unincorporated Williamson County. Since Durham's arrest at his second residence in Florence, the partially blind 57-year-old man confessed to the first-degree murder of Elizabeth Reinhardt of Austin and several accounts of attempted first-degree murder, including hiring others to assassinate Lemend, before deciding to take matters into his own hands.

Emile R. Woodard of Travis County, who was already in custody and undergoing interrogation by police at the time of Durham's arrest, admitted to being hired by Durham as a hitman. Bradley Premshaw of Fairhope, Alabama, was also named by Durham as someone he paid to dispose of Lemend. Premshaw, a truck driver for Pall Transport, Inc., has not yet been located by police for questioning.

Lemend, who was rendered unconscious with a flashlight and later woke up a captive in the trunk of Durham's car, has declined interview at this time. However, Williamson County Deputy Sheriff Alberto Reyes stated that the victim knew Patrick Durham from approximately twelve

years ago when Lemend was in his teens. Durham was born in Champaign, Illinois, and in 1982 he and his wife moved to Austin for work reasons.

Reyes, who has been an officer with the Investigations Division for fourteen years, told KXAV, "We're glad to see the particulars of this case extricated from County Road 140, which we previously thought may have a connection. With these developments and Durham awaiting prosecution, we're able to put things into the correct perspective. The Williamson County Sheriff's Office is grateful that Mr. Lemend, whose call to 911 in January saved a woman's life on County Road 140, lived through this crime and helped us get Durham into custody. While Ms. Reinhardt's murder is a terrible tragedy, and we mourn her family's loss, putting Durham behind bars will ensure he can't do this to anyone else."

Forensics matched the DNA taken from blood in Durham's vehicle to Lemend's DNA, another piece of evidence that will be used in prosecution. Durham is currently being held in Travis County...

I take a sip of coffee and let it sink in. For the first time, I make the connection regarding Illinois. It's the state from which someone mailed the postcard I received in my youth. Since Mr. Durham originally lived there, he was probably visiting family when he sent that strange message to me—an omen "in the words of Addison."

A few minutes after digesting the news, I try reaching Bradley Premshaw again, though I know he's about as likely to answer as a steer is to volunteer for branding. His number gives me the "disconnected" message. Without talking to him, I can only expand upon my original hypothesis. Given the details in the article and the little I know of Bradley's nature, I think Durham indeed paid him to wreck my pickup, but Bradley probably thought it was empty. He needed money, and when Durham offered him a reasonable sum to crash into an abandoned Silverado parked out in the middle of nowhere, he took it. It was just an old truck, anyhow. But realizing what he'd almost done—killed someone—he'd rather make it right than have that on his conscience. So, he paid me in cash and gave me a lift. I guess I shouldn't feel sorry for that good old boy, but I almost do.

After finishing my coffee, I set the mug in the sink and open the living room blinds to let the light stream inside. While I wash my breakfast dishes, I allow my mind to run and make the last few connections. I have to hand it to Mr. Durham because for all his mistakes, he did a pretty thorough job of things. Even Jared played his part. He delivered the photo with the obscure threat on the back—more lines from the poem by Addison. Jared looked enough like Kyle to pass when Louie described him to me. Mr. Durham even saw to it that Elizabeth cheated on me, just like I did to Mary. But Elizabeth was a better person than he gave her credit for. She stopped the affair early before it went too far.

I dry my hands and wipe the edge of the sink with a towel. Kyle is coming over shortly, so I pick up a few things—although my housekeeping skills have greatly improved in the last few months. Not an empty beer can to be found.

As I step outside to sit on the porch and wait, my sore body courses with energy. I can't wait to tell Kyle about Korey Nemeth. His trial concluded yesterday, and he got life without parole. Not only is Aria strong, but she was right about so many things, and she deserves the peace of mind his sentence brought her. A few days ago, I put her in touch with Kyle, ironically based on his suggestion, but apt under the circumstances. Aria was grateful to take the job working at the real estate agency, an area in which she's already trained and experienced. Now she's able to rent a room in a nice home in central Round Rock, something she prefers to living alone in an apartment.

I sit down on the faded, white porch and turn toward the pasture. Masses of small, pink wildflowers skirting the fence give off a sweet fragrance. Someone told me they're called "brownfoot." Looking beyond them, I watch two tan sheep and a dappled white ewe I recognize nibble the brush. I kind of miss feeding them. Tim gave me the green light to return to the ranch as soon as I'm able, and I'm counting the days since I've almost depleted my savings. With no further threat of my presence attracting snipers, I'll resume when my body allows. My Ruger will accompany me, just in case.

After setting my phone beside me, I reach for the soft holster under my jeans. My weapon is there, safe and sound. At least I don't need to replace yet another pistol after being attacked. When I returned from the hospital, my 9mm lay on the ground exactly where I dropped it before I got knocked out. I didn't get as lucky with the cell phone. I'm now on phone number three in as many months.

A coating of light green oak pollen dusts my new truck. It's a used, silver Chevy Colorado with an extended cab. After my first truck got totaled, I upgraded to full coverage, so my insurance company replaced my Dakota when Durham blew it up. Detective Menard called me the other day and explained what happened. The investigation revealed that a small, crude IED had been attached underneath the pickup's front end and was detonated remotely. Its purpose wasn't to kill me but to keep me near the house.

Menard also told me his team investigated Stephanie Durham, who's now married and goes by "Marshall," and she came up clean. She lives in San Angelo and hasn't spoken with her father in seven years. Per the detective, Stephanie grew apart from her dad after what she called "years of him obsessing over Mary's death." She knew nothing of his plans for vengeance. Once again, I'm stunned at how spot-on Aria's assessment was.

Deciding I need more back support, I change positions so I can lean against the house. I stretch out my legs in front of me. The cool air fans me, and I inhale the earthy smell of dewy grass. This has been the pace of things lately while I recover. I guess I'll have to get used to it because time will pass more slowly from now on.

Nothing can entirely halt the image of Elizabeth's face or the sharp pains that tear at my soul. No amount of guilt or sorrow can ever bring her back. However, in the wake of my life's wreckage, there's a tiny comfort. That part of my life has finally ended. My troubled past has concluded, and Aria and I are safe now, free to make our lives into whatever we can make of them, in whatever way we find.

I glance across the yard, toward the back where my roughly mown lawn merges with the woods beyond. My thoughts turn to Aria. We have each other as we recover from our trauma, and that trauma hasn't broken us. And while Aria proves one of the strongest people I've ever met, she has her own demons. She fights them, but they're relentless. During conversations, her eyes will sometimes glaze over. I never know what she's looking at. Is it the filthy back room of the house on County Road 140? Is it Carol's withered corpse lying on the floor while Aria was chained to the wall? Or is it something else she sees, some grim memory of things Korey did to her so painful she peers only into a black chasm of terror? I don't ask.

Already, my relationship with Aria has become complicated. She never directly asks, but she wants something from me—something more than friendship—but I don't know what it is. After what we've gone through, any kind of romantic relationship is off the table. It doesn't even need to be said. However, with Nemeth and Durham behind bars, my place in the country is safe again. Aria is free to come over, and she does. She comes several times during the week and usually both weekend days. Sometimes she stays the night. Sometimes she even sleeps beside me, which seems to help her feel safer.

"I like waking up next to the man who saved my life," Aria said one morning. "When we're together, I feel like nothing can hurt me."

When she wakes up screaming in the middle of the night, I try to comfort her. Usually, I put my arms around her and let her cry, but she doesn't always shed tears. Sometimes she only trembles. Her body breaks out in a cold sweat, and her hands feel like ice. These spells last anywhere from minutes to hours, and there's nothing I can do besides offering a shoulder. Or an ear if she wants to talk about it.

Aria is my confidante as well. When I need to unburden about Elizabeth, she doesn't mind listening. She's sharp, intuitive, and always seems to know the right things to say. And she's patient when I'm not in a conversive mood and want to go off and deal with things alone.

Overall, Aria's presence in my life came as an unexpected

gift. Yet, in my gratitude, I'm also careful. Even with all I know about Aria's recent past, much about her remains a mystery. What if she doesn't fully recover from her experience? Can a person recover from such a thing? A part of me fears that the earlier pattern of my life will repeat itself or that I'm being cast into an impossible situation of trying to help a woman who can't fully be helped. But Aria isn't Mary, and I hope she'll prove me wrong. In fact, I'm counting on it.

The tires of Kyle's silver Audi crunch over the gravel of the long driveway. He parks in the grass to let a red service truck rattle in behind him, its bed filled with lumber and spools of wire. It pulls a trailer carrying a yellow, riding post hole digging machine.

I get to my feet, stifling a groan as my body protests.

Kyle comes up to me with a grin on his face. "Today's the day. Are you excited?"

I grin back. It feels good to smile again. "I am."

"You're going to love having this fence," Kyle says. "Especially when you finally get a dog. You *are* getting one, right?" He takes a swig of his bottled water, eyeing me.

"Maybe someday," I say.

"What's that old saying? There's no time like the present?" He turns as the doors of the red truck swing open, and two men get out. Kyle calls to them, "We've got it marked already."

He jogs over to the fence guys, so I won't have to walk much. They exchange a few words. Kyle points to the orange flags we've placed at the perimeter of the yard. A few green ones indicate the septic tank and pipes, so the workers will know to steer clear.

Since Tim was kind enough to pay for this as the property owner, all Kyle and I need to do is sit back and watch. I have to admit it's pretty exciting. The final product isn't going to be a barbed-wire fence but cedar posts and steel mesh—a real nice build.

Kyle's sneakers thump up the few porch steps, and he takes a seat beside me with his knees bent. We have a view of the entire backyard and most of the driveway and neighboring fields from here. I open my mouth to share the outcome of Korey Nemeth's trial, but Kyle is already speaking.

"Aria said you picked up a brochure from the Austin Police Academy," he says.

I laugh. He must think I've lost my mind. "I did."

Kyle swishes a buzzing insect away from his face and raises an eyebrow. "Care to tell me anything about that?"

"Well, I thought it was worth looking into."

One of the men turns on the digger. The engine quietly hums as he backs it down the trailer ramp. The other guy begins unloading bags of concrete mix from the pickup bed.

"You're considering it for yourself?" Kyle asks. He drinks the last of the water and crushes the empty bottle against his leg.

"Yeah, possibly. It's something to think about for the future," I say.

Kyle turns down the corners of his mouth and nods. "Well, if that's what you want, then I'm behind you one hundred percent. Just one question. Why?"

I chuckle. I shift my weight and wonder if I should have brought my donut cushion. Although my tailbone is so much better, I hardly need it now.

"It's hard to explain. The last few months were the worst of my life. There are things I'm trying hard to forget. But there were also times, just brief moments here and there, that I actually liked. I know it probably doesn't make much sense," I say.

"No, I think it does," says Kyle. "I get it."

"And I don't know," I say. "I felt so directionless for so long. Suddenly, I don't anymore. But you know, moving forward, moving on with your life, that's a direction. I never understood that until now."

Kyle claps me hard on the shoulder. "Man, that gave me chills. I'm happy for you."

We both laugh. Our gaze follows the fence man as he drives the yellow digging machine near the road, where he positions the auger for the first post hole. The spiral blade whirls, descending slowly and rhythmically through the hard ground. It's going to be a good day, with many more to come.

Mary's story has finally ended. If I could write one last chapter, it would be written to her father, though I doubt he'd comprehend a line of it. If I could bring Mary back from the dead by murdering the man who wronged her, I probably would have tried it too. But just as the universe doesn't care about maybes, it doesn't make things right again through desperate acts of revenge.

The news article about Durham appeared today, coincidentally on the first day of spring like a good omen, and Kyle and I immerse ourselves in the bright, warm morning. Scents of wildflowers, grass, and newly milled cedar posts combine in a woodsy fusion. The mesquite trees in the sheep pasture are starting to green, and soon I won't be able to see between them. Bluebonnets are bursting up in the yard, in patches in the fields, and along the shoulder of the rural road. Winter has drawn to a close, without letting so much as one snowflake fall. I've always known that winter in Central Texas is seldom white. Sometimes it's blood red.

Thank you for reading! I hope you enjoyed Blood Red Winter. Trent and Aria's story continues with the following books of the series, in order:

Her Unspoken Blood
Blood in Truth
Flesh and Blood
Blood Is Thicker

Connect with the author:
https://jaconrad.com

DRAGONFLY NIGHTMARE

Erin Richards

.Y NIGHTMARE

ls

›y:
Ииuse Publishing
yette St., #5812
ıra, CA 95056

Print ISBN: 978-1943800056
Digital ISBN: 978-1943800049

Cover Designer: Sarah Hansen @ Okay Creations
Cover Image: Mandy Hollis @ MH Photography
Editor: Laurie Larsen

Books by Erin Richards

Psychic Justice Series
Chasing Shadows, Book 1
Twilight Rising, Novella
Stealing Twilight, Book 2

Wicked Paradise

Young Adult
Vigilante Nights
Dragonfly Nightmare

DRAGONFLY NIGHTMARE

CHAPTER 1

My life turned a corner today to a kickass summer. A glorious day sliding past GO and collecting $200 on the highway to my freedom, two days after the ultimate Independence Day. I wanted to shout my bliss to the world, but I refrained from killing my mother's eardrums any further. *Nerd, much*?

For the first time in my short sixteen years, I was headed to summer camp. How stupid exciting was that? For others it was no big deal, or even lame. For me, camp meant paradise, considering I'd begged my parents to let me go for the last four summers and got the big, fat no every flipping time. It wasn't even about money. Just major overprotectiveness due to The Incident That Shall Not Be Cloned.

Although I was joining the Teen Leadership Program as a Cabin Leader, I was coming apart at the seams to revel in the whole camp experience. Not all would be work, though. My best friend slash partner in crime, Laurel Montgomery, and I had dibs on fun. Escaping the house for two weeks was a major step toward more freedom in my life. I just wished my parents held my same excitement. The thought deflated my insane joy.

My gaze bounced to Mom's white-knuckled grip on the steering wheel. I brushed my fingers over her thigh. "It'll be okay. You have to let me go sometime." The four black beads rolled on my leather cuff as I withdrew my hand from her leg. I spun the beads around the band, ignoring their significance for a change.

"I know, Allie. I'm just—"

I curbed the urge to pull more of my hair out before baldness set in. "We've hashed this out. You've checked out the camp a zillion times. Carla Amadori's family has owned the joint forever. Laurel and Logan love her, and you spoke to *all* the other parents." *Overkill if you ask me.* "And you know Laurel and Logan will kill anyone who even looks at me wrong." Even though I kidded, I mentally kicked myself for dredging up that bit of paranoia.

Four years ago on my twelfth birthday, a psycho abducted me and held me at gunpoint for twenty-four hours. My father's investment brokerage had fired the freak and he flipped. I knew the man from attending various company events. I was lucky he didn't lay his grubby paws on me or *physically* harm me. The mental damage was bad enough. Now everyone looked suspicious, and I couldn't go anywhere without spying one person who looked like a deranged kidnapper. After counseling, I'd learned ways to cope with the trauma, but I still watched my back whenever I left the house. Seriously, I had developed eyes in the back of my head.

The Incident shaped my teenage existence in so many ways. Worst of all, it royally curtailed my freedom. Four smothering years later, because Laurel and her seventeen-year-old brother, Logan, my appointed watchdogs, talked my parents into letting me go, promising they'd stay with me 24/7, I was on my way. Without Laurel's nagging, I'd be stuck at home this summer with the swimming pool, my cat, and the housekeeper eagle-eyeing my every move.

For the most part, I had buried the memories of the abduction. When I dwelled on them, I made myself believe The Incident was a fictional movie about a girl named Alex. Now, I just wanted to appease my mother before she changed her mind and locked me up at *Casa* Bailey for the summer. The gates to my prison had opened. By the skin of my dead body, I wasn't going back inside.

"Happened a long time ago, Mom." I fingered the bangles on her right wrist. "You have to let it go." *You have to let me go.* "Everything will be fine."

"I know. I know." Mom's fingers loosened on the steering wheel. "You have your phone?"

Groaning, I knocked my head on the headrest. "For the millionth time, you know we aren't allowed to bring them." The camp was electronic-free, back to nature, home to crappy cell reception. I had no problems living off the grid for two weeks. I wasn't big on social media or texting anyone except Laurel anyway. The parentals also forbade me to engage on social media, so my phone was simply a phone.

"Right." Eyes on the road ahead, Mom dug through her purse and withdrew a new smartphone. "Take this." She stuck it in my hand. "Keep it with you at all times." A charger landed on my lap.

"Are you kidding me? Mom!" I held the phone as if dog crap coated it. My nose wrinkled. "Paranoid, much?"

"No, I'm not kidding. Don't tell anyone you have it. Not even Laurel or Logan."

"You planning to call me every flipping day?" I stuffed the phone in my hobo purse and clutched the bag to my chest, my irritation fading as we neared the school.

"Watch your tongue." She wheeled the car into the parking lot.

We passed through the familiar scrolled wrought-iron gates of my private school. The campground had a deal with the San Francisco school to use their bus to cart local kids to the camp. Otherwise, you wouldn't catch me dead or *alive* on school grounds during the summer.

Vehicles jammed the small parking lot, ignoring the white parking lines. Logan stood by the Montgomery's silver van. He'd morphed into a taller, sinewy geek with pale skin sorely needing a tan. Maybe he'd buy one at camp, far, far away from me.

Ugh. Why'd he agree to come this summer? Seeing him set off a tumble of thoughts inside my head and an odd crick in my heart I wanted to avoid. I'd once had a tiny crush on the gangly, too-tall-for-his-body loner. Into mixed martial arts, he had a black belt which made him king of the geek squad. Laurel, Logan, and I used to hang like birds on a wire at their home when my parents worked, which was all the time. Then the abduction happened. Next thing, I had the plague as far as he was concerned. He'd disappeared without a word to boarding school in Arizona, and then abruptly returned home this past December for his final semester of junior year. My crush evaporated along with many emotions and feelings that year. We'd avoided one another since his return, both of us burying our heads in the sand. Logan had much ado about the kidnapping, and neither of us had confronted each other about that gruesome event. Talk about lame times ten. Blame, resentment, guilt, sorrow, it all boiled up into a mixed stew when I thought about him. Confusion skewered me most of all. *I repeat, UGH.*

"There's Logan." Animation elevated Mom's voice, perking up her spirits. She parked the car next to Mrs.

Montgomery's van.

Logan slung suitcases, duffels, and sleeping bags out the van's rear cargo. The morning sun highlighted blond strands in his golden brown hair. The sun-dappled strands mimicked the highlights in my darker brown hair. I swallowed and wheeled away, disgusted at myself for looking. After all, he'd abandoned me twice when I needed him the most, further ignoring my every note, plea, and text during my mental recuperation. He'd ignored my every "why." So *why* should I give him the time of day?

Oh, right, he'd struck a deal with my parents to play babysitter, bodyguard, whatever.

"Hi, Logan." Mom climbed out of the car. "Can you grab Allie's bags?" She didn't wait for my pissy retort and strode off to gab with Mrs. Montgomery and a group of parents.

Logan sauntered over, a tentative smile casting a flush across his dead pale face. "Hey, Allie." His voice shook as he reached inside the trunk.

"Hey. Where's Laurel?" I nudged my sunglasses up on my nose.

"What? I'm not good enough to talk to?" He hid his face behind the trunk lid as he hefted out my bags.

I blinked in surprise. "Sure. I guess." I paused, gave in. "You never want to talk anymore. I thought *I* wasn't good enough." May as well lay my cards on the stupid table or my summer was doomed.

He slammed the cargo door, jangling the license plate in its frame. Locks of windswept hair fell over half his face. "What happened to the three musket-rats?"

"You tell me." Reeling at his use of our nickname for the three musketeers-slash-mall-rats, my pointed stare shot his glare to his sneakers. "So how will you handle two weeks without video games?" The words hemorrhaged out of my mouth before I realized what I'd said. I wiped my brow, wishing to retract the words and sink them in my brain. The boy rattled me in every way possible. Him *and* his stupid video games. I couldn't even look at a video game console without thinking about the abduction, which then brought up that mixed bag of emotions. *Wash. Rinse. Repeat.*

"Allie! Allie!" Laurel screeched and dashed across the parking lot. "Move it, karate dork." Logan turned to lug suitcases to the bus and she pushed past him.

Laurel clasped my hands and tried to twirl me in her excited dance, but the pavement claimed my feet. "What's with the frown, missy?"

"Logan."

She rubbed the side of her nose, her joy fading. "We'll have fun this summer like we used to. The three of us."

The *three* of us? Whoa, what? I squinted. "And?" Before the parental bribe, Logan hadn't planned to attend camp. I assumed Laurel had talked him into helping me escape Bailey Prison. I guess I technically owed him one. It's not like I hadn't known Logan was coming...I'd just chosen to bury it deep. Okay...sand was my friend. *Sigh.*

"And what?" She did her avoidance nose rub again.

I yanked her hand from her face. "Spill."

"Logan wants you to have a fun summer, your first time at camp. We both do."

Surprise threaded through me. Why did he care? Now of all times. "That's all?"

Laurel play-slapped my arm. "What did you think? Jeez, your mom's paranoia is dripping out *your* pores."

"You don't know the half." I tugged the phone up to the top of my bag. "Don't tell anyone. She gave me this to hide for emergencies."

"*Oy vey.*" Laurel swiped her forehead, using her fake Jewish accent. "Does she think we're heading to East L.A.

or the wilds of the Amazon?" She rifled through my purse. "Where's the gun? Did she give you a gun too?"

Mom and Mrs. Montgomery snuck up behind us. Do or die time. If I survived the goodbyes and made it on the bus, I was home free and camp bound. Mom would have to pry my butt off the bus seat with a crowbar.

Mom wiped tears from her cheeks. I wobbled my head until whiplash set in. The bus loomed, open doors beckoning. I wrapped my arms around her and she kissed me, almost tightening her arms rather than let me go.

"Have the best summer of your life," she said and finally dropped her arms, a release of great magnitude. "I love you."

"Thank you *so* much. Love you too," I whispered in her ear before turning and escaping her protective bubble.

I bounded up the steps behind Logan. He waved to his mother and gave a thumbs-up to my mom. *Wonderful.* Their collusion better not ground me at camp. I parked it in an aisle seat next to Laurel.

Logan sat across from me, head dipped, already engrossed in a martial arts magazine covering a graphic book about zombies. I cringed. Nothing had changed. His comic book geekiness had merely grown into half-assed novels. I flipped my eyes and mind off him, in essence burying him in that dark cesspool of quicksand.

A boy my age sat in front of Logan and shifted to scope Laurel and me out. Long black hair framed a tan face and vivid blue eyes. *Hello, gorgeous.* He wore an oversized T-shirt and board shorts hung off his ass. I bet his underwear did more than peek out the top of his waistband. The world was done with his fashion statement, but I didn't care if he wore bell bottoms and a long-sleeve polyester dance shirt from the seventies. He winked, and I fell into the refreshing blue pools of his eyes.

His full, kissable lips stretched into a big smile. “Hello there. Nick Constantine is glad to meet you lovelies.”

Evidently, hotness could forgive cheesy pickup lines too. He *was* all that.

“Laurel Montgomery.” I waved at Laurel. “Allie Bailey.”

Laurel nearly pushed me off the seat to shake his extended hand. I grasped the back of Logan’s seat to catch my fall into the aisle. Shy wasn’t a word I’d ever use to describe Laurel. Her over-eagerness and outgoing personality helped me escape my own anti-social prison caused by my parents’ overprotectiveness.

I gave Nick a tremulous smile. Welcome to summer camp, host to fun, freedom, and freaking hot guys. It was all I wanted for summer.

CHAPTER 2

We passed through California gold country and climbed into the Sierras. In preparation for camp, I'd read that the Dragonfly Meadows Campground's property extended into the lower foothills down to an old gold mine. Miners used to pan for gold in the river flowing through the canyon near the campground. I was dying to go on a gold expedition, one of the camp activities.

Four endless hours after leaving the schoolyard in San Francisco, our bus rolled to a stop in the campground's tree-shaded parking lot. Anticipation fired my pulse onto the NASCAR racetrack as I absorbed my new home for the next two weeks. Laurel and Logan had attended camp for the last five summers and could describe it in their sleep. Sweeping my gaze around the buildings in front brought the camp to life after seeing tons of photos over the years.

Kids chattered and laughed, a few moped. In the moping group, the youngest kids looked anxious, the older ones bored or sullen. Another group of twelve- and thirteen-year-old boys stood off to the far left under an arbor, probably planning their pranks for the summer. Older girls, wearing tight skimpy tees and shorts, primped into their hand mirrors and checked out every boy over thirteen. The older campers, Cabin Leaders, nicknamed CLs, gathered near the front of the office building. Two college-aged female Camp Counselors rounded up the stragglers and grouped the kids by age.

Laurel and I bounced on our toes at the top of the steps inside the bus, awaiting our breakout to freedom until a rowdy trio of boys behind bowled us down the steps.

The bus driver yelled, "Slow down."

Too late. I tripped, falling against Logan. Laurel fell onto me as Nick tried to grab her. We all tumbled to the ground, Logan taking the force of our weight. My breasts smashed against his chest, and his arms locked around me to save me from rolling into the gravel. Laurel and Nick rolled off us, arms and legs entwined, laughing up a riot.

Logan's cheekbones had sharpened over the years, but his full lips had stayed soft. My face flushed, a bare fraction of an inch from kissing him.

"Sorry," I mumbled, pushing against his arms still coiled around me. He was surprisingly solid. I guess that made sense, for a black belt.

Despite the scarlet patches on his cheeks, he chuckled, the skin at the corners of his green-hazel eyes crinkling. At twelve, I used to press my finger into the tiny dimple on his chin when we were the three musket-rats. At sixteen, mortification burned my flesh as my mouth landed perilously close to that dimple, and perilously close to confronting a hateful truth within him, within what used to be *us*.

Laurel snorted. "You gonna spoon with my brother all day and put on a show for the campers? This camp is PG, ya know?"

The heat of embarrassment burned me to the depths of my soul. Logan released me, and I leaped up, grabbing Laurel's hand for support, nearly cringing at the contact with *him*. Graceful as a lion, Logan flowed up off the ground, exhibiting suave movements he must've learned from his martial arts training. He shook off leaves and plant bits stuck in his hair. In dismay, my gaze followed a trail of ants we'd scattered, hoping the buggers would cart off my dumb luck and renewed annoyance. A slow crawl of ants seemed to truck up my spine.

Reluctantly and feeling guilty for barreling him to the ground, I swatted the remaining debris and ants off Logan's shoulders.

He scooted away as if I carried the plague. "Let's go. CLs are meeting," he growled out.

Nick glided off in the opposite direction, which meant he wasn't a CL. My attention drifted to his lean back and slid lower. His nice round ass filled a pair of board shorts better than any butt I'd ever seen. *Jeez. Not a full day out of prison and I'm totally boy crazy.*

Logan joined the gathering Cabin Leaders in front of the office, wheeling the biggest pieces of our luggage. Believe me, Laurel and I brought *big* luggage. Logan had always been a nice boy, the kind who'd help his mom carry in groceries without being asked, or held the door open for women. I was impressed he hadn't changed in that regard. Even happier that he managed to tote all the crap I brought. Laurel and I grabbed the remaining smaller bags and slogged behind him.

I tripped on a stick in the gravel, throwing myself against Laurel to catch my balance.

"Jeez, Allie. Get a grip." Laurel pushed me off her,

holding my arm steady. "You freaked about being away from home or what?"

"I guess. I don't know." My tone grew shrill. "Why is Logan really here?" I whispered under my breath.

"Is that what's spun you out? He won't bother us much. He'll do his job." She did air quotes.

I scuffed my sneakers in the gravel, scattering my thoughts with the rocks. "Yeah. I keep thinking he'll bag our fun. I mean, I came here to party, not be smothered by bodyguards all summer."

"Screw him. We'll have a blast no matter what." Laurel knocked her shoulder against mine.

We dumped our bags in a pile of mismatched suitcases and duffels, then joined the five other teenage CLs, which consisted of three guys and two girls. This was Laurel's first year as a Cabin Leader. Since I was CL age, they allowed me to come as her assistant instead of a regular camper. One "assistant" CL existed, as if they'd made a slot just for me. It gave me a sense of belonging and importance. The oldest, a tall eighteen-year-old guy named Marco Lorenzo, an Italian with a big nose and dark bushy eyebrows, had spent the last eight summers at the camp. He knew it like the back of his stumpy-fingered, dark-skinned hand, handing out our group and cabin assignments.

"Hey, Laurel. Who's your friend?" His chocolate eyes lingered on Laurel and then me, sweeping his gaze up our pre-tanned legs to our straightened hair.

We'd spent the last month by the pool to jumpstart our tans and put natural highlights in my mousy brown locks. Laurel's blonde hair looked like gold and copper with the sun glinting off it. *Bitch.* It might've all paid off, according to the glances numerous boys were casting on us. Laurel pushed out her boobs, and I smoothed down my shiny straight hair.

"Allie, Marco. Marco, Allie." She gave him a loud smacking smooch on his cheek. "Don't let him faze you. He likes *everyone*, if you know what I mean." She winked at him.

No, I don't know what you mean. I haven't been here for a million summers like you two have. Part of me felt left out of the festivities like a wallflower at a dance.

Marco's attention bounced to a shorter, muscular boy named Jesse Martinez before clasping Logan's hand, doing bromance bonding slaps on their backs. I swear Marco cupped Logan's right butt cheek too. It didn't faze Logan a bit. *Oh…kay. Whatever floats your man boats.*

They assigned Laurel and me to the youngest group, the ten- and eleven-year-old girls. A boy and girl CL were each assigned to the respective boy and girl groups of twelve- and thirteen- year-olds and fourteen- through sixteen-year-olds. In my excitement, I lost track of names, relying upon Laurel's absurd memory.

Everyone sat or chatted, awaiting our next steps. Heat climbed as the afternoon deepened, leaving me standing in a patch of blazing sunlight. I backstepped under the shade of a towering pine, hauling Laurel alongside me.

"What're we waiting for now?" I asked.

"Mrs. Amadori will greet us and go over the CL rules and expectations." Laurel sat on a large suitcase.

I took a moment to check out the camp and get my bearings. Ferns and multi-colored flowerbeds edged the log buildings built to blend with the natural habitat. I spotted a few cabins to the left on the closest hill, but hills and evergreen trees hid the other structures, giving the cabins privacy. Mom thought the campers' cabins were spread too far apart, lending to a lack of security. Not me. I loved the woodsy privacy. Sunlight tapped a small lake off to the right between two hills, luring my eye to a sparkling blue wedge. *Dying here.* I couldn't wait to explore!

A tall, lanky man in his late twenties or early thirties stomped onto the porch, holding a tablet device. "Hey, Cabin Leaders." His excitement spilled out in the grin plastered on his swarthy face. "Come inside to the breakroom."

"Who's that?" I whispered as I plucked Laurel off the suitcase.

"Beats me. Never seen him before." She cocked her head to the side, studying the man. "Could be family. Other than the light brown eyes, he doesn't resemble Mrs. A much. She prefers having family and friends work here. Ya know, like her niece, Martina." She let the other CLs go ahead of us. "This is weird. She *always* welcomes the CLs on the patio before giving a tour of the grounds." She swished her arm toward three umbrella-covered tables and chairs on a wood deck. "It's ritual."

Logan waited for us on the steps, ever watchful, making sure I never left his sight. *Babysitters 'R Us. Not.* I suppressed a shudder at the sight of him.

"No lollygagging." He swatted Laurel's arm, stepping aside to avoid touching me.

I stumbled up the stairs behind Laurel, pushing her from behind. "Let's not be late on our first day." The words gushed out to hide my new disease, a disease called *Loganitis.* It caused acute annoyance, extreme embarrassment, constant stumbling, and a red rash to eat your entire body.

Thank God, Laurel didn't rat out my balancing act, or lack thereof. She must've thought I'd gone off the deep end already. I followed her to the rear of the large house converted into homey office space. A couch, several comfy chairs and end tables, a dinette set, and a large flat screen TV jam-packed a family room/kitchen combo. We were elbow to elbow in the remaining space.

"You're in the breakroom for CLs and camp staff," the man said. "The only time you'll venture through the hallway is if you have a meeting with camp management. Otherwise, you'll use the French doors to enter and exit this room." He pointed to the doors along the rear wall leading to the common area of the campground. "By the way, I'm Dante Amadori, and I'll be running the show this year." He grinned, displaying slightly uneven teeth. His beard scruff on a square jaw, black shaggy hair flopping underneath a University of Nevada, Las Vegas baseball cap, and a long, wide-flared nose fit a guy used to roughing it. He wore worn jeans and the green campground polo shirt. A logo sewn on the polo's left breast illustrated a blue dragonfly fluttering over a meadow in front of the Sierra Mountains above the campground name.

The squirming noise of surprise arose from the CLs. Eagerness danced in Dante's bright eyes. I resisted the sudden urge to hide behind karate dork. As though Dante's summer promised more than babysitting a bunch of kids, his overly zealous gaze lit on me. I swore they lingered much longer than on anyone else. His smile widened in recognition, or I might go so far as to say, in my limited experience, longing, before his attention bounced onward. *Eww. Halfway handsome old dudes didn't do it for me.*

My palms dampened. I focused on the silver-blue sliver of sunlit lake visible through the French doors. Paranoia had taken extra spins in my head, or my mom had rubbed off on me in the worst way possible.

"Where's Mrs. Amadori?" Logan asked, a strange hesitancy in his smooth voice. He'd lost his squeak and crackle from four years ago.

"Good question," Dante replied, studying his tablet,

"Logan Montgomery?" He caught Logan's nod. "I'm Mrs. Amadori's nephew." He addressed all the CLs, "My sister, Martina, whom most of you know, and I will be filling in for her this summer. Aunt Carla experienced an unfortunate accident a few weeks ago and broke her leg in three places. She'll be okay, but she's taking it easy in her private cabin. Her doctors won't allow her to join in camp activities. She'll record periodic messages for you and the campers. In fact, I have a welcome message from her that we recorded yesterday." He picked up a remote from a knotty wood coffee table.

My suspicion heightened my senses. Dante exuded weird vibes of the mistrust sort. I squeezed between Laurel and Logan as they faced the flat screen. Logan grunted and made the barest hint of room for me. Laurel gripped my arm in her excitement. She took her CL duties to heart and was dying to boss around a gang of mini me's.

The video flickered on, and red-headed Mrs. Amadori filled the screen before the shot panned back and placed her in a wheelchair in a cozy living room in her private cabin. A cast encased her right leg from ankle to thigh.

"Hello, Cabin Leaders, welcome to Dragonfly Meadows." Carla Amadori's low, smoky voice entered the room, quieting the CLs. "We hope you'll enjoy your camp leadership training and might one day become a Camp Counselor."

The local news show on the flat screen to Mrs. Amadori's right drew my attention. The date on the Sierra newscast read June 12 below the temperature and time. That was over three weeks ago. Who recorded newscasts on a DVR? I studied her TV setup and the simple satellite box. No DVR. A chill chased over my flesh.

I elbowed Laurel in the side and whispered, "Did

Dante say he recorded this yesterday?"

"Yes. Shhh." Laurel honed in on the TV as Mrs. Amadori recited camp rules.

I tuned voices and the TV out and peeked around Logan. Dante Amadori's dark gaze was latched onto me, his eagerness a palpable presence of evil in the air.

Chapter 3

After the mysterious video, Dante gave us our handbooks containing rules and schedules, our polo shirts, and then led us toward our assigned cabins. Despite Laurel casting sly glimpses at me, I remained glued to Logan's side, deriving a bizarre degree of strength from his nearness, despite our awkwardness and the deeply-ingrained anger I harbored.

Laurel couldn't hold back any longer. "You're acting weird, Al."

Logan scowled at her. "Camp's all new for her."

"Not new enough for her to act like a head case."

Needles of shock scored my back. *Logan, defending me? Will wonders never cease*? "Better a head case than a no case." I gave Laurel our trademarked crooked half smile, half sneer, trying to regain my excitement. Dante gave me the creeps, and my alarm over his lie created an ache in the rear of my throat. I didn't want to go home. Or have her think I was lame.

We reached a *T* in the trail, each side leading to

deeper woods where the living quarters melded into trees. Girls' quarters resided to the right. Logan veered to the left. As he gave me his back, something inside me fragmented, and I suddenly didn't mind adopting a bodyguard.

"Logan, hold on a sec." I snagged Laurel's suitcase strap looped over her shoulder, catching her off guard on the fir-strewn pathway. Logan stopped, glanced over his shoulder.

"Oww, Al." She stumbled and banged her arm into a humongous tree trunk.

"Get a move on," Dante called. "Time to meet your kids. You can talk later during free time after dinner." The other CLs took off toward their assigned quarters.

"I need to talk to you," I murmured to Logan.

Dante approached, resting his hand on my shoulder. I flinched, trying to prevent my neck from locking in place.

"Is there a problem?" He squeezed my shoulder. I wanted to melt to the ground and slither into the forest, or inject a dose of venom in his ankles.

"No. No problems," I squeaked out and jerked from under his slimy paw.

Logan eased between me and Dante, a darkness engulfing his sunburned skin. "Allie's new. Laurel and I'll teach her the ropes."

"No need. Allie will be my special project this year." Dante's grin stretched wide, crinkling the skin bracketing his eyes. "It's why we gave her the CL rate as an assistant rather than a regular camper."

"What do you mean special project?" Stunned, I stared at him, unable to keep my mouth shut. Something definitely smelled rotten in Dodge.

Dante's easy smile slipped. "You'll assist Laurel and help me with special assignments."

"She didn't sign up for that," Logan blurted out.

"What the hell are *special assignments?*"

Exactly what I was thinking. Logan coming to camp might not have been such a bad thing, after all. As long as we had a come to Jesus meeting soon, one way or another.

"Watch your language or I'll send you packing," Dante ground out between gnashed teeth. "As for any CL, you'll go where I assign you. Got that?"

No way in hell was Dante sending me home. Not after the Acts of God it took to get to camp. Maybe my head was on the bonehead train or Mom was rubbing her paranoia cooties on me. "It's fine," the words tumbled out. Nope. No going home for me. *Special Assignments 'R Me.* I touched Logan's wrist, wiped my fingers off on my shorts. "I'm game." I forced a tight smile for Dante's sake and turned to Laurel. "Let's go."

Logan headed down the left fork toward the three-sider cabins for the middle boys. Dante stomped off back toward the offices.

"Are the Mothers of the Paranoid Police getting to you?" Laurel asked, slow and deliberate.

We began a slight incline on the trail to the right. "Dante gives me the willies. He said they filmed Mrs. Amadori's video yesterday. But the TV behind her displayed the news from June 12, and she didn't have a DVR."

Laurel cast a thoughtful expression. "Sounds fishy. I don't know."

"Dante Amadori shows up out of the blue after Mrs. Amadori supposedly broke her leg. What about me being his special project? I don't like it. I think something's wrong with Mrs. Amadori, something he's hiding."

"Come on, that's cracked, even for you."

"Anything else off here from what you remember?"

"Not really." Laurel swatted at a fir bough in our path. "Too early to tell."

"Do you know where Mrs. Amadori's cabin is?"

"Sure. She took me and Logan up there to help her with her computer last year."

I grew thoughtful, unwinding my thoughts. Laurel and I trudged the last twenty yards up a small hill to a level area of four-sided cabins assigned to the youngest girls. Beyond our cabins, the three-sided cabins for the twelve- and thirteen-year-olds sat, and the oldest girls got to party in the super chill tree houses.

"Bathroom and showers are over there." Laurel pointed to the long, narrow building. "It's for all girls, except one of our cabins has a full bathroom for our girls. There's another bathroom without showers between the tree houses and three-siders."

Breathing heavy, we stopped in front of the first cabin. This high elevation hiking might kill me. I inhaled the fresh mountain air, and my lungs nearly took a hike for the lower foothills. A squirrel darted off into the brush, and a blue jay squawked at it, competing and losing to the animated chatter of the girls in the cabins. Their excitement was infectious, and I grinned to their tune. Laurel dumped her over-sized bag on the steps to the cabin.

Two girls charged through the door and crashed into her. "Hold on there, little missies." Laurel held out her arm to block them from escaping the porch. "Hey, Serena, Michelle. Glad you're back! You get me and Allie here as your CLs this year. Two for the price of one!"

Serena, a short, chubby girl, batted adoring lashes at Laurel. "Oh, awesome. We were hoping to get you as our CL." The three hugged and squealed so loud I expected to see buried treasure in their hands. Laurel drew me into the group hug, and I met my first camp charges.

A wonky smile contorted her face and shifted my mind to the fun and sun at Dragonfly Meadows. I buried my curiosity in a shallow box to dig up later with...Logan. Something I never thought would happen here. Yet part of me didn't want to tell Laurel. She'd blurt her mind at inappropriate moments that might land me in more trouble than I wanted. Über excited voices decimated my thoughts.

Laurel and I were in charge of fourteen screaming and caterwauling girls. It didn't take long for me to join in unpacking, organizing, and learning about *our girls*, as Laurel called them.

The two larger cabins had adjoining doors with a living area between them, and the third cabin was set off separate from the others. My bed was in the smaller third cabin while Laurel captained the other two with the bathroom. I lugged in my duffle bag and tossed it on my bed. My alcove held a double bed on a platform of drawers, a small closet, and nightstand. Old and well-kept, the cabins had recently received a fresh scrub by the hint of pine cleanser in the air. A bear holding a clock on the wall across from my bed ticked precious minutes away.

"This bed's usually for a camp counselor, but I guess they're changing the rules this year. I didn't see many counselors." Exhausted, Laurel lolled against the doorway. "That's one thing different this year."

"How fun will that be?" I arched my eyebrows and grinned. "Less watchdogs."

Laurel perked up and pointed at me. "Good thinking." She toed my small pile of shoes, searching for a particular pair, then shouted, "Hey, we're voting on a group name. Everyone go to Dragonfly Lily now." Indicating her cabin, her voice vaulted over the noise of my four girls. My cabin was dubbed Dragonfly Lily Two.

I shoved her black flip-flops behind my suitcase to hide them from her. I checked to make sure everyone had skedaddled and dropped my voice to continue our previous conversation. "I want to check on Mrs. Amadori tonight. You in?"

She rummaged through my T-shirts and snagged a purple one that belonged to her. "Owner and staff cabins are off limits. Besides, we won't have time to go up there before dark."

"Then we sneak out after dark." I dug my fingers into the soft flesh of her forearm and tried to ease the T-shirt from her clutches. No dice. I was hoping she wouldn't remember the shirt belonged to her. Maybe I had a little kleptomania in me.

Tension tightened the skin around her mouth. "Not a good idea." She randomly plucked and smoothed the hem of her shirt over the top of her shorts.

"You afraid?" I chided. "Laurel Montgomery's afraid of the big, bad, dark woods?"

She gnawed on her bottom lip. "So what if I am? Besides, we can't leave the girls alone."

An idea hit me, sending warm and cold spikes in my veins. I was stuck with him for two weeks. I may as well get to the root of our evils and boot the awkward phase behind us. "I'll ask Logan to go with me," I suggested. "It's really bugging me."

"Oh, Allie." She shook her head. "Okay. I know you'll never rest until you find out."

I tweaked her hair. "Thanks. Give me a minute and I'll be over to vote."

Alone, I unpacked my small Pigeon Point lighthouse snow globe. Logan had given me the globe after we'd visited the lighthouse the year I'd had my tonsils taken out. I was scared to stay in the hospital, and he'd told me the lighthouse would always light my world and chase away my fear. The world inside the globe became my escape when my anxiety tripped me up. Most often, I lived outside it since my older practical mind didn't equate living inside a dome to freedom, especially after The Incident. At other times, the inside of the globe became my haven. "Nose pressed to glass looking in, looking out," I whispered and hid the globe in a drawer.

I joined the girls in the small sitting room of Laurel's double cabins, a house without a kitchen. The girls tossed out group names while Serena jotted them on a whiteboard.

"I dig Laurel's Lilies." Laurel double-starred the name on the board.

"As opposed to Dragonfly Divas?" I grimaced at the generic name Laurel's pen hovered over.

"How about DragonLily Flyers?" said Caitlin, a pale eleven-year-old first-timer from my cabin. She blushed down to her toes.

I slung my arm across her tense shoulders. "Smart. I love it."

She softened under my arm. The girls cooed over the name. We voted unanimously for DragonLily Flyers.

Ironically, the camp theme that year was based on the TV reality show *Survivor*. I sure hoped we survived the summer and didn't wither into the husks of dragonflies at the end of their summer life cycle. *Okay, sue me for researching dragonflies last week.* And for having freaky feelings and a killer curiosity.

Amid the roar of a million excited kids in the multi-purpose dining hall, Laurel and I joined the Cabin Leaders at a long table in the rear corner. I slid my food tray onto the table alongside Logan's. Silent, he checked me out and scooted to the end of the bench. Instead of his polo shirt, he wore a red T-shirt with the word "bacon" spelled out on a chemistry periodic table. *Geek rebel, lover of all foods pig.*

Burnt macaroni tickled my nose. "Seriously? Sliced hotdogs in boxed mac and cheese?" My throat clogged up, already objecting to the meal. "What happened to the gourmet food you told me they served here?"

"Beats me." Laurel prodded her pile of wrinkly peas, nudging a few onto the table, and picked up her thin slice of sandwich bread between thumb and index finger. "The bread's stale." The feistiness in her tossed the bread onto Logan's tray. "You can have it, if you can stand it."

"I'm not that hard up." Logan chewed on a mouthful of macaroni. "Maybe they hired a new cook."

"One who recently graduated middle school." I frowned at the Sahara dry macaroni on my fork.

"Mom complains how much money camp costs every year. We tell her how good they feed us and how great all the activities and excursions are," Laurel complained. "This sucks green eggs and rancid ham."

Nick Constantine sat down across the table from Laurel. He brushed his tousled black hair out of his eyes and cracked his knuckles. He shoved half the discarded bread in his mouth. "Not bad," he mumbled through the bread. "Thanks, babe." He winked at Laurel. Bad manners and all, he managed to enthrall her with his to-die-for model looks. I lost her. Laurel was clearly gaga over him. She had first dibs. We had rules.

I nibbled the bland processed food. We hadn't eaten since lunch in the last small town off the highway before ascending deeper into the Sierras. The food tasted as bad as it looked, and I washed it down with watery fruit juice. Most campers enjoyed their dinners, or at least they weren't complaining. Making a gagging sound, Laurel slid her plate to the side of the table.

"I told you things are off." I jabbed my elbow into her side.

Prickles scraped my spine, and I felt eyes on me from the other side of the room. I glanced up and found Dante staring at our table before his attention bounced to the young woman sitting next to him. Thin to the point of anorexic and vampire pale, she had long dark hair and appeared twenty-five or so.

"Who's sitting next to Dante?" I asked.

"Oh. My. God," Laurel whispered. "That's Martina Amadori. Talk about death warmed over."

"I take it she's not a Goth reject?" I set my plate on Laurel's plate and swept the bread crumbs into a pile.

"No way. She used to be on the pudgy side with a healthy glow, you know, like she was *alive*." Laurel stared at Martina.

"Speaking of," I whispered, head leaning close to Logan, "I need to talk to you. This camp's tripping me out." Despite our long separation, I had no problems spilling my guts to Logan. *Okay, maybe just some guts. I still needed to vent a spleen to him.* Nothing or no one would stand between my freedom and me. I'd even ally with a mean girl to maintain it, or in this case, Logan.

"Sure." Since I'd apparently invaded his air space, he slid a few inches away. Did I carry mountain ticks? "You and Laurel meet me behind the girls' main bathroom after campfire."

"Just me. Laurel needs to stay with the girls." I placed my hand on his thigh, surprised at the steely strength beneath. He jumped at my touch, and my cheeks burned as I wrenched my hand away.

Dante's voice echoed through a speaker from the stage at the front of the hall, saving me from acute embarrassment and advanced Loganitis. "Campers, Martina Amadori and I welcome you to Dragonfly

Meadows. I hope you're enjoying your meal." Cheers and applause drowned the fake retching and boos stemming from a few older girls.

Martina stood next to him, her hollow gaze darting every which way like she wanted to dig herself six feet under. She took the microphone. "There won't be a campfire tonight, but you'll have an hour of music and free time." The hall erupted into jeers and moans. She held up her hand. "Don't worry, we'll have plenty of campfires this summer. We want everyone to get a good night's sleep for tomorrow."

Dante leaned into the microphone. "The games begin tomorrow," he yelled. "Dragonfly Island style!"

The clapping and cheering deafened the hall. Once the room quieted, Dante and Martina explained tomorrow's activities. I tuned them out and soaked up the activity surrounding me, my head in the clouds of liberty. Laurel and Nick flirted with each other, not paying me an iota of attention. I turned my back on Logan and let the atmosphere sweep me up.

"Allie," Dante said behind me.

I startled, jerking against Logan's shoulder. "Yes, Mr. Amadori?" I stuttered.

"Can I borrow you?"

"For what?" I asked, surprised he'd singled me out.

Dante held out a placating hand. "I wanted to apologize, to both of you." He nodded at Logan, forcing a tight smile. His left eye twitched as if a bug flew into it. "I came on too strong earlier, you know, first day jitters." He forced a stilted chuckle. "I want Allie to announce the games, you know like Jeff Probst, if you want. I read on your application that you're a big *Survivor* fan. No hard feelings, okay?"

I sucked in my stomach, released. "I'd love to."

"Martina has the scripts in the office. Come by after

breakfast tomorrow." Dante sauntered off. Soft rock music blared through speakers on the walls, and Laurel joined Nick on the stage to dance. Adrenaline tingled beneath my skin, despite the sparks of interest my trust meter spat out.

Logan took my hand and hauled me off the bench. "Let's talk now."

We disappeared into the milling kids, and exited a side door into an enclosed patio with a decorative lattice cover. Yellow light streaming from the wall-to-wall windows on the long side of the cafeteria didn't penetrate the patio, leaving us in darkening twilight. Logan dropped my hand and scoped out the patio for open ears. I shivered from the evening chill.

"You cold?" He rubbed my bare arms, his hands warm, feeding my nervous anticipation.

"It's okay." I stepped away, his touch creating a weird pang in my chest. Too familiar, too fast, and I regretted initiating the touchy-feely business at the table.

"Tell me what's freaking you out. I trust your instincts better than anyone I know."

Shock froze me. "You do?"

"Why does it surprise you? After all these years?" His voice cracked, as though admitting a thorny truth.

"You used to make fun of my hunches and curiosity," I chided, a little miffed. I digested his uncomfortable truth, glad he wasn't afraid to open up. "That's what I wanted to talk about." I unloaded my suspicions.

His spine stiffened. "You think Dante's lying about Mrs. Amadori?"

I sniffed, the emotions overwhelming me. "I do, Logan. Seriously. I want to check on her, to go to her cabin."

"Then let's go. Everything's off in this place. The crapass food, corpse-like Martina. Did you read the activity list? They cancelled and replaced a slew of offsite excursions for river rafting, rock climbing, boating, stuff that doesn't cost much. My mom paid for the expensive excursions."

"Mine too." Hearing him agree spun my suspicions out of control.

A dull ache of unease radiated from my tailbone up my spine. "This is gonna sound batshit crazy, but I think Mrs. Amadori…might be…dead."

CHAPTER 4

Logan stiffened. "Dead? That's kind of radical, even for you." He moved his thumb and index finger on a mystical game controller. A movement so familiar to me, my breath caught.

I gripped my wristband, spun a couple of beads. "Prove me wrong then. That Dante dude is giving me weird vibes. Doesn't he look like he could be a psycho ax murderer?"

"I don't know. I guess." He paced the patio. "Hell, all the counselors resemble criminals. None of the ones who worked here the last few years are here."

"See what I mean?" A prickly silence rained down until I cut through the tension. "I won't feel right until I find out one way or another."

"I know. Okay." He blew out a breath. "We can't go now. Management cabins are on the other side of the offices. We need to wait until everyone settles down for the night."

We snagged Laurel and gathered our kids. We had an

hour before ten o'clock lights out. The entire way to the fork in the road to our cabins, Laurel was on one side of me, babbling about Nick Constantine, and Logan glued himself to my other side. Nick volunteered for kitchen cleanup and remained behind, scoring points to dodge scheduled chore duty later.

Millions of glittering stars blanketed the dark sky, darker than I'd ever seen in the city. I lost myself in the foreign world of space, not a normal view at home in the reflection of the San Francisco city lights or through the seemingly perpetual veil of fog.

"Allie! You're running me into the trees." Laurel skidded on tree needles carpeting the path borders and shouldered me to right herself. "You're such an airhead today."

"Sorry." I resembled that remark.

"Did you two talk?"

"Yeah. You'll need to cover for Allie tonight," Logan replied.

We reached the fork in the path. The kids marched ahead to their cabins, droopy from a long and exhausting day, excitement for tomorrow the only fuel to their steps.

"Who's covering for you?" I faced him, the landscape lights reaching our knees, leaving his face in deep shadows.

"The boys will think I'm checking on the other cabins, bathrooms, and perimeter, part of my job."

We agreed to meet in two hours outside my cabin. Lights pooled small yellow circles on the trail to guide our way. Laurel and I rounded the last stand of tall trees before the small clearing where our cabins sat nestled in long grasses and ferns waving gently in a breeze. They beckoned us into their safe midst.

"You're really doing this?" Laurel halted me in my tracks. "With Logan?" Better than anyone, she knew our history. It was as much a mystery to her as to me since her parents were as tight-lipped as Logan.

"Why not?" I shrugged.

"Just be careful." She sucked in her bottom lip. "Don't get caught."

"Don't fret. I'm not tripping off the reservation." I guided her onto the path to her porch.

I made my way to my own cabin. The girls were heading in the opposite direction to the bathrooms. "Don't take long. We have a big day tomorrow."

The second I stepped inside my alcove, a strange unease skittered up my spine. My travel clock sat farther to the left from where I'd left it. The lampshade I'd straightened after unpacking was slightly off kilter. The top drawer beneath my bed was pulled out half an inch, my clothes stacked neat the way I'd left them. Had one of the girls been snooping around? Nothing was missing from the room, even my snow globe was tucked in my drawer between my jeans and sweats.

A bang on the wall outside my open window startled me. I dashed out and around the rear of the cabin. Heavy footsteps tore to the right, toward the three-sided cabins. The darkness surrounding the unfamiliar land pressed on me, and I hugged my arms to my chest.

I walked to the front of the cabin, and met my girls dragging up the path. "Hey, Michelle, did you see anyone outside the cabin?" I smiled and tossed a misplaced hair band to Carrie, who wore her long, thick blonde hair in a ponytail.

"No, why?" She climbed the porch steps.

"Just wondering what kind of privacy we get in our little haven." I laughed to dispel any tension. No sense in riling my girls into Nervous Nellies.

"None, if you leave the doors and blinds open." Eleven-year old Carrie smirked at me. My resident Laurel

Montgomery clone in the making.

I ushered the girls inside, locked the door, and closed the blinds. The four girls settled on their bunk beds, talking quietly, yawns suppressing their anticipation. I checked my alcove again, searching for signs of an intruder or missing belongings. I swept my eyes over the girls and their stuff, not sure if they'd noticed anything gone or disturbed. Ultimately, I chalked it up to the day's paranoia *du jour*.

Fully clothed, including shoes and hoodie, I switched off the light and lay on my bedspread. I waited for the whispering to cease, and breaths of deep sleep soon pervaded the cabin. Mental and physical exhaustion claimed me, and despite my best efforts, I dozed off, awakening later to tapping on my window. I nearly brained myself on the rustic log headboard to peer out the blinds. Landscape lights illuminated Logan, not that I needed the dim lights. I'd recognize his silhouette anywhere.

I checked on the girls before joining him outside. Laurel watched from her porch in her PJs, arms crossed against the night air. I waved to her.

A twig snapped and I swung my head toward the sound. An owl hooted, wings flapped out of a tree, and shaking, I clenched my neck. In familiar settings, darkness didn't bother me. At the unfamiliar campground, every little sound set my teeth on edge. When Logan extended his hand toward me, I didn't hesitate to take it. I think I would've taken Dante's hand. Well, not without major heebie-jeebies.

"Do we pass the offices?" Twangy country music drifted to us from the breakroom.

"No. I know a way around the back." Logan squeezed my hand, and we followed the path. "Allie?" he breathed out.

The lit paths ended and full darkness cloaked us. Cautious, we slowed our steps. A rock border defined an ill used pathway leading into the woods above the administration buildings.

"Yeah?"

"About today. This." His silhouette stood slightly hunched over and tilted to the right, the way he always stood. "It's weird."

No shit, Sherlock. I snorted to hide my surprise. "Thanks a lot."

"You know what I mean." He flicked his finger at my shoulder, a three musket-rats move. "We haven't hung together in a long time."

"Well, duh. Whose fault is that? Now you're my freaking *bodyguard*." Despite that half of me was *now* glad he'd come to camp, I was still ticked my parents thought I needed babysitting. "Right? The three musket-rats reunited for one last blast from the past." Sarcasm dripped out with my words.

"It's not like that. I wanted—" He snapped his mouth closed, and a long hush followed.

"So what is it?" I blurted out.

"I don't…know," he stuttered. "Being around you reminds me of our old summers when the three musket-rats used to goof off at Golden Gate Park and on the piers. Remember those days? They were a blast."

I didn't expect much more from him on our first day. One day together didn't solve the chasm of four years apart. Or his desertion in the mall that fateful day, his abandonment afterwards, his avoidance. My epic avoidance. "Yeah, I guess." We resumed our hike. I ducked behind trees and bushes, following his lead. "Are we friends?" I held in the pungent scent of conifers and redwoods, filling my lungs with freedom, fearing his answer.

"Sure." He stumbled over a rock, righted himself. "You think otherwise?" His smooth voice splintered.

"No. Yes." I had no clue what to think. He owed me a lot more than an explanation. *Holy crap.* We should've hashed this out when he'd first returned to town. *Don't dredge up the past now and ruin your summer. But how can I have a summer with him around me every stinkin' moment, along with the reminders he dredged up?*

"'K. Whatever." Reluctance edged his voice.

What did he mean? *Argh.* I needed to concentrate on the task at hand and not my stupid past life horror show. We approached the eight cabins where the camp workers lived during the summer, and I dropped the subject.

"Down," Logan whispered. We crouched behind ferns surrounded by several trees above the backyards of the cabins. A light flicked on in the second cabin. "The first one belongs to Mrs. Amadori and Martina."

The first and biggest cabin hulked in the shadows, set back from the others. "Think they've gone to bed?"

"One way to find out." Logan pointed uphill. "We go up, then down to the patios. Looks dark enough now."

A smidge of anxiety seeped into my bones. I zipped my hoodie to my chin to keep the dread at bay. "What happens if they catch us?"

"They'll cut us loose."

A football-sized rock littered the path, and I stumbled, yelping. Falling to the pathway, I clapped a hand over my mouth. A tree branch stabbed my butt, and I sucked down the pain.

"You okay?" Logan knelt to my level.

I jerked at the branch sticking into me and flung it aside.

He massaged my lower spine, surprising my mouth closed. "I think so." I leaned against his warm hand. Eyelids closing, I started melting until my sanity paid me another visit.

I flung away from his hand. “Let’s go before I lose my nerve.”

We continued our silent trek up the small hill and down to the backyards. Every few steps we took one of us stepped on a twig, and the snap in the quiet night about had me zooming into an epic freakout. Darkness shrouded the cabins except for a light deep in the interior of the second and fifth cabins. We slunk to the side of the first building.

The blinds slanted enough to allow us to see inside a bedroom. A nightlight lent a round glow inside the room, giving us a boon to our stalkerish activities. A made bed, tidy dresser, and neat computer desk met our curiosity.

“Mrs. A’s bedroom.” Logan’s voice had grown icy.

“Where is she?” I scanned the room. A word of the day calendar sat next to the desktop computer on a pristine desk. The date read June 26. “Calendar on the desk.”

“Oh, man. Not good.” His body tensed. “Follow me. Stay low.”

Slinking around the corner, we remained below the windows, hidden behind bushes in the surrounding planters. Logan hunched beneath the front window of the second bedroom. The bed was unmade and empty beer bottles littered the dresser next to lotions, makeup, and perfumes. Martina’s clothes were scattered across the room. No Mrs. Amadori. Other than a TV droning from an end cabin, quiet and darkness met us. Until a woman moaned from inside the first cabin.

Crouching low to the ground, Logan and I crept to the next window. Martina and a dark-haired guy lay on the couch making out. A blanket half-covered them. Hard to identify the man in the candlelit room, he laid on top of her, macking on her hot and heavy. He had the same height and coloring as Marco. *Marco?* Heck, who was I to judge?

"Maybe she's in another cabin?"

Logan scanned the row of cabins. "Doubt it. It's the only one with a wheelchair ramp." The portable ramp connected the wood deck to a stone walkway leading to the administration building at the front of the campground.

Tree branches scraped along the side of the house, endangering our stealth. The porch light flicked on in the cabin next door, illuminating our patch of darkness. We hugged the ground.

"Who's there?" Dante yelled. A screen door squealed open, banged shut.

The loud beating of my heart in my ears didn't drown out the click of a gun hammer cocking. Fear seized me, and my breath caught in my throat. Footsteps crunched in the gravel between the cabins.

"Sis, that you?" Dante called, closer.

I threw a handful of pebbles at his cabin. They pinged the log siding. Dante swung toward the noise.

"Go!" Logan half-dragged me toward the hillside where the brush grew thicker. I tripped over something hidden in the bushes of the planter, my foot catching between strips of metal. As I bent to ease it out, I realized my foot was stuck in the spokes of a wheelchair flipped on its side under a tarp. *What the what?* I freed my foot and crawled to Logan hiding in the hedges. We hid within a close circle of trees to gain our bearings. Skin crawling, I stared at Dante's silhouette framed under the porch light of his cabin, a gun engulfed in his hand. I cupped my hand over my mouth to halt the scream dying to trip out.

Gunshots cracked the air, and I jumped nearly into Logan's lap, my heart like a caged eagle beating at my chest to escape. The gun fired again, and from the sound of the bullets spraying the ground in the spot we just vacated, I knew Dante had fired a BB gun. I recognized the muffled clang of the small BBs. A year before my abduction, I had gone camping with the Montgomery family, and Logan had let me fire his BB gun a few times. At least dumbass Dante wasn't using a real gun with kids running around. Not that BBs couldn't hurt someone.

Lights flickered on outside Mrs. Amadori's cabin. "What the hell, Dante?"

"Someone's spying up here."

"It's probably kids or raccoons. Put the gun away," Martina yelled at him from the porch.

"Shut up. I don't want any bratty kids snooping. You know what'll happen if—" He put a sock in it, as if he'd spewed out a secret. He stomped to the sideyard, following our route.

My heart banged my ribcage harder. As I slowly turned to Logan to gauge our next move, someone streaked through the woods about twenty feet to our right.

"Hey," Dante shouted, his footsteps racing toward us.

"Roll to the left," Logan said into my ear as he propelled me down a slight incline. We rolled against a decrepit log that cracked apart at our impact. We hopped to the other side and stretched out behind it. My hand tangled in soggy leaves and pine needles. As much as I wanted to wring my hand of any spiders hitching a ride, I didn't dare move a muscle and risk spending another lonely summer at home if we got caught snooping.

Dante raced past the hedges up the hill separating the campground from the lake. Was someone spying on us, or was it a random coincidence?

"I'm gonna get you, asshole. You can count on it." His snarling drifted higher as he climbed the hill.

Once Dante ran out of range, we sprinted to the path we'd followed from our cabins. I ran blind behind Logan, wishing the stars lit our path through the thick trees. I wanted to escape before Dante shot a BB into my ass and turned it into grass. After running in the dark woods for eons, tree limbs lashing my clothing, we found the lighted path to the Dragonfly Lily cabins in the clearing. Panting, we passed the tree houses and three-sided cabins.

The sky hosted a million twinkling diamonds, and I thanked my lucky stars for the person who sidetracked Dante's attention off us. Silent, we hid in the shadows behind my cabin to corral our wits.

"When I tripped, my foot caught on a wheelchair hidden beneath a tarp in the bushes. Why would her wheelchair be turned on its side in the backyard?"

Logan kicked at a stone border. "I think you're right. Something's happened to her."

A long shiver worked up from my feet and traversed to full blown shakes. Logan wrapped me in his arms, his face buried in my hair. He inhaled deeply like he was memorizing the scent of me. Three long lost musket-rats be damned, he was warm. Not wanting to touch him any further, I kept my arms locked to my sides, a strange discomfort creeping up on me, creeping me out. This stranger wasn't the Logan I had known four years ago. Yet he was all Logan. And it was easy to pretend my old friend never existed…at least the parts I wanted to forget.

"Hey." Laurel intruded upon our freaky mysterious moment. "What's up with you two?"

We jumped apart so fast we plunked our guilt on a Twilight Zone platter. Laurel let it slide in the smirk she bestowed upon us. I'd receive her grilling in the morning.

Logan regaled her with our peeping Tom escapades.

"Mrs. A's a stickler about changing her calendar every day. I mean total OCD. Maybe she's in the hospital and left on June 26." Laurel tugged her jacket over her chest, hiding her PJs and her dread.

"But Dante said she's recuperating in her cabin." I opened my mouth, shut it, reconsidered. "I think she died on June 26," I said with a slow confidence I hated. "I think Dante killed her."

"Whoa, that's a little sketchy." Logan held up his hand. "I mean, the guy's a trip, but what makes you think he's a killer? What's his motive?" He took my shoulders like he wanted to rattle sense into me.

"It's what I feel." I fought the gurgling in my stomach. "I mean, the idiot was firing a gun that could've hit anyone. Who does that at a camp full of kids?"

"Let's sleep on it. Life will look clearer in the morning." Laurel's teeth chattered.

"Yeah. Get some sleep." Logan scratched his head. "We'll talk in the morning. Feel out Martina when you pick up your assignment from the office. Keep your suspicions on the down low."

"Well, duh, dork. What's she gonna do, go up to Dante and ask where he buried the body?" Laurel swatted Logan's arm to release her tension.

Too bad it didn't ease mine.

We split up for the night. I slipped inside my cabin as quiet as a mouse. The girls slept soundly, snuggled under their blankets, soft snores rising from one of them. I closed the curtain to my alcove and flicked on the small nightstand light. I froze.

Banded in a black silk ribbon, a droopy, brown-edged white rose nestled in wildflowers and a tiny balsam branch sat dead center on my pillow.

CHAPTER 5

My heart skipped a beat. Hands balled in my pockets, I leaned down and sniffed the bouquet. The scent of rose and balsam prevailed over the mixed wild flowers, and I wrinkled my nose. Between thumb and index finger, I picked the posy up by the ribbon and set it on my nightstand. The familiarity of the bouquet tried to emerge through the messy thoughts snaking in my mind. One of the girls coughed in her sleep and I lost focus. Had someone left the flowers as a gift? Had all CLs received them? My summer of freedom was quickly skating into a voodoo bizarre summer.

No way did I plan to let it harsh my mellow. Tomorrow was a new day. I scrubbed my hands together, stretching my arms wide to embrace my freedom. When I drifted off to sleep, the cloying perfume of roses tailgated my nagging suspicions.

Morning brought a smile to my face. Birds chirped to their own songs, and the faint gurgling of a river turned my smile to a grin. I rolled on my side and honed in on the wilting fauna. Reality set in.

Rustling and whispers in the next room flung off yesterday's negativity. "Rise and shine, girls. We have an hour and a half to shower, dress, and eat." Stoked to take up my CL role, I hopped out of bed onto the cool hardwood.

"We showered last night," Carrie grumbled.

I joined the girls yawning and crawling from their beds, their enthusiasm on the sleepy edge. "Good. You have more time to pretty up, eat, and chill." I opened the blinds to rays of sunshine streaming in. I yelped. Four screams tailed mine as I surged back from Dante's leer in the window.

"Hey, didn't mean to scare you." He mock-saluted me, his black polo showing off a tan, muscular arm. Dante was cute in an older gruff guy way, but an undefinable light burned in his eyes that left my mouth going Baja desert on me. *Good morning, Princess Paranoia.*

I gripped my neck. "Um…hello. Do you need something?" The girls huddled out of sight of the window in various stages of undress.

He held up a doorknob. "Following up on repairs we didn't make before you all arrived. Your door lock's busted. I need to replace the knob."

I tapped my forehead, spurring my morning brain cells into action. "You must be mistaken. Our lock works."

"Intermittent problem I need to fix for good." He stepped toward the door. "Plus the keys are missing, and if you accidentally lock it when no one's inside, you'll lock yourself out."

I unlocked the perfectly fine lock. Easing the door open a hair, I said, "Can you wait until we head to breakfast? We just need a few minutes."

"No problem." He perched on the steps, setting the doorknob on top of his toolbox. "I'll finish my breakfast."

He held up a large travel mug. "Take your time. Didn't mean to interrupt."

Seriously? Seven in the morning? I shut the door, closed the blinds, and the girls finished dressing, babbling about their upcoming day. Before we left the cabin, I shoved the strange floral gift in my bottom nightstand drawer.

"See you soon," Dante said as we passed him on the steps. His hand grazed my ankle and icy prickles zipped up my leg. I resisted the urge to fling off his cooties and mash them into the ground.

The girls went inside Laurel's cabin to use the bathroom, and Laurel joined me on her deck. We both wore our green CL polo shirts and khaki shorts, the required CL uniform. Her shirt was a tight small, while mine was a loose medium. "What's he up to?" She flicked her thumb in Dante's direction.

"Fixing the door knob." I slanted my head to the side. "Does everyone here strike you as slightly shady?"

"Everyone as in Dante and Martina?" Eyes rolling to the galaxy, she continued, "You haven't met anyone else."

"True." I kicked the wooden pillar holding up the porch overhang.

Dante earned a long, slow perusal from Laurel. "I'll throw you a bone. It's weird seeing old Mr. Nottingham, who'd puttered around the camp for the last five years, replaced by *that*."

I smacked her arm. "See what I mean?"

"You ready to snoop inside the offices?"

"I guess." I lowered my voice. "Hey, did you get flowers on your bed?"

"No. *You* must be someone special." She flinched. "I got a spider."

"Eww. The bouquet reminds me of something I can't put my finger on."

Our girls sifted out of the cabin one by one, ending our conversation. A noisy gang of boys followed the trail to the fork in the path. Laurel rounded up the stragglers inside and we set off. Logan and Nick waited for us at the fork, and we hung behind to let the kids precede us. Logan was doing martial arts drills off the path. He saw me watching and blushed, stopping on a gangly falter.

"You're gonna do that here too?" Laurel crossed her arms over her breasts. "Every freaking morning at the butt-crack of dawn." Logan glowered at her.

"Ladies." Nick bowed, his shorts slipping three inches off his ass. "Nice to wallow in the presence of you lovelies again." He crooked his arm for Laurel. "Your breakfast awaits, milady." Laurel hooked her arm through his, smiling wide.

Guess I was chopped liver since the gallant and cheesy Nick was on the scene. Wistful, I stared after them, scoping out Nick's fine rear end. When had I become such a butt whore?

"Guess that leaves us, huh?" Logan strode beside me.

"You laying down the gauntlet for me?"

Logan snickered. "I'll lay down my life, how about that?" His cheeks reddened. "What's a gauntlet anyway?"

I stopped my eyes from widening into shockerville. "No idea. Medieval armor?" A slant of sunlight through the trees lit my face, sobering me. "Did you leave flowers in my cabin?" I asked hesitantly, not caring to open the door for personal conversation yet. I still needed to get my bearings around camp…around him.

"Huh? What do you mean?"

"A white rose on my pillow."

"Did Laurel get one?" He scratched his head, the tips of his fingers disappearing into his messy damp hair.

The path narrowed, forcing him to bump his elbow against my arm, his skin oddly electric. My tension alarmingly drained to my toes, and my left foot stuttered. "No."

"Huh," he grunted, rolling his thumbs on his imaginary video game controller the way he always used to do in deep thought. After an uncomfortable pause, he asked haltingly, "Why'd you think I left it?"

Ten degrees of heat slithered up from my toes. "They looked familiar, like flowers you gave me once."

"Like the roses I picked from your mom's garden for your eleventh birthday?" He grimaced comically. "Man, was that ever dumb."

Unstoppable, the memory surged forward. "My mom wanted to kill you after you razed her prized rose garden." It was the happiest birthday I'd ever had, and offered my first inkling that I liked Logan as more than a second best friend. He'd given me the flowers and made a picnic lunch for us in his backyard with all my favorite snacks.

The path ended onto a large clearing near the front of the campground. The kids scattered toward the dining hall. The office building loomed, inciting a nervous jig in my empty belly.

"Does she still garden?"

"My mom? A little. I help a lot in the garden now."

He pointed at an expansive fern in a shady planter. "So what's that bush called?"

"A fern, you know that." I play-slapped his arm.

"I mean what kind." Genuine interest animated him as if he wanted to know how I spent my time, not so much the fern species.

"Australian tree fern."

"Allie," Laurel yelled over her shoulder. "You coming, or are you planning on eating pine nuts?"

Thank the dragonfly gods. Impeccable timing as always. Pine nuts may be more palatable too.

"Hey, Logan, Allie," Marco greeted as he and Jesse

joined us. "Dude, let's plan strategy for beating the girls today." He winked at me. Jesse gave me the slow perusal under his shades, then burped.

Pinhead. I hightailed it toward Laurel waiting for me at the dining hall door. Nick lifted her hand to his lips, kissed it, and bowed. My heart fluttered. Part of me wished he liked me that way, but I'd never begrudge Laurel his attentions. Neither of us have had a steady boyfriend. We've had boyfriends, but no real serious long-timers. I was open to serious. Laurel had been dying for a steady relationship since summer started.

Nick joined Logan and the other CLs, and her gaze never strayed from him. I pretended to wipe drool off her chin.

"You hate him, don't you?" I knocked my shoulder against hers. "He's a disgusting pig, not worthy of you. In fact, I bet you're hot on Jesse," I teased.

A dreamy smile on her frosty pink lips, she hugged her notebook close to her chest. "Isn't he fine?"

"Sizzling." I slid my wistful gaze off him. "Let's eat. We have a long day ahead. You'll have time to worship him later."

We loaded our trays with watery scrambled eggs, drippy oatmeal, cold half-burnt toast, and sat at the table with our girls as instructed. I took a head count to make sure all girls were present before digging into the not so stellar breakfast.

I sprinkled an unhealthy dose of salt on the bland eggs, then added a dollop of ketchup to mask the flavor. "Tell me this isn't normal camp food," I whispered.

Laurel choked down a mouthful of dry toast after slathering it with fake butter. "It's beyond pathetic. Nick said the cook is Dante's friend who used to cook at fast food joints in Vegas."

"So you're saying we *might* get a decent burger." I

picked up the small bowl of pale, lukewarm oatmeal to drink it down. No sense in dirtying a spoon on the thin gruel. Despite the slop, I needed my protein.

"More like taco."

"Even better." I gagged down my last mouthful, adding fuel to my sarcasm.

"Nick's gonna be his sous-chef. He said he can cook circles around the dude." Laurel purred at Nick's supposed talents. I might have to do random drug testing on her soon.

"Good morning, girls." Dante's voice behind me escalated above the racket in the dining hall. My back drew rigid. "Allie, don't forget to grab the scripts for the games from Martina." He tweaked Carrie's ponytail and handed Jasmine a polished quartz rock. "For your collection." Both girls cooed over his attention and the shiny, egg-sized gift.

"Be right there." I felt his presence for the longest moment. When I turned, he skulked behind me, tapping on his tablet device. "Will we see another video from Mrs. Amadori later today?" I couldn't resist baiting him. "I hope she's doing better."

His tone turned somber. "She's under the weather today, staying in bed."

"In her cabin?" I quaked inside.

"Yes. Poor gal. At least her cabin's in the setting she loves best in the world." He patted my shoulder, his fingers strong and warm, comforting like a predator. "Thanks for asking about her. She'll appreciate it." He swiveled around. "See you girls later."

The moment he left earshot, Laurel and I leaned against each other. "He's lying," I whispered.

"No shit, Sherlock." Emotion scarred Laurel's voice. "We need to find out what's going on. She's the sweetest lady in the world." Her throat hitched. "If he hurt her—"

I swatted her hand to save her from fraying her polo hem, the next step in her agitation. I don't know how many T-shirts she'd tattered over the years to maintain her calm. "I'll find out. Count on it." I tossed my napkin on the table. Dante soon had the kids roaring in excitement as he explained the day's activities. "I'll be in the office. Take notes."

Logan caught my eye and nodded. As I made my way to the back of the dining hall, the quickest route to the breakroom adjacent to the office, I felt him watching me. Dante's last statement to the crowd parked me in the doorway.

"Each Cabin Leader will bring their group to the Dragonfly Trading Post at the appointed time on your schedules later today. We've created a points system for your purchases. Everyone bring your spending money to deposit on account. Points will be worth more than cash."

The kids whooped and roared as they learned they'd receive more bang for their buck. I had a WTF moment. Our money was to spend at the Post and at offsite excursions, which Dante and Martina had struck off the schedule and replaced with other "exciting" events that didn't cost diddly.

"We'll put any leftover funds at the end of your two weeks in a camp raffle. Each time you purchase an item, you'll earn raffle tickets. How does that sound?" Dante's enthusiasm set off another round of applause.

Sounds like BS to me. I slammed the door shut behind me, more determined than ever to unearth some nefarious plot. It wasn't the camp experience Laurel and Logan gushed about every summer. Yet, I had to admit whatever was going down was far more exciting than my usual summers. Rather than sleuthing my day away, I'd be at home encouraging skin cancer at the pool in solitary confinement.

When I snuck inside the CL breakroom, I found it empty. As I marched down the hallway, Martina's agitated voice filtered out the first door standing ajar. I tiptoed closer and pasted myself to the hallway wall. No one said I couldn't be a dragon*fly* on the wall.

"Dante took her to a convalescent hospital. She's getting good care," she said defensively. "I don't know where," she whisper-yelled. "Some place in Auburn her doctor recommended."

My hand closed over my mouth to stifle my outrage. *Lying liar who lies!*

"Sure, Sherrie, I'll find out and you can call her. Sorry we didn't let you know sooner that all the positions were filled here. Dante and I wanted to stir things up. Plus I got my RN certificate in the spring." She giggled. "No, I didn't mean that you're old. But you know Carla had a hard time making changes. We needed to save costs by employing younger, less experienced employees."

"Allie?" Marco startled a life out of me, and I banged my elbow against the wall. "What are you doing in here?"

Stars wavered and my stomach flip-flopped. Rubbing my throbbing funny bone, I stepped closer to him away from the door. "Hey, Marco. Came to snag my scripts." No lie there. Martina slammed down the phone, and the crunching of papers replaced her voice.

"Right. A female Jeff Probst." He gave me a lewd wink. "Shall I call you Jeffra Probst?"

Martina joined us in the hallway, wiping her swollen, red eyes. "Hi. You must be Allie." She smiled, hiding her emotions. "I have your scripts here with the inside scoop on the games we've designed." She returned to her office. "Come in."

Well, you didn't have to ask me twice. "See ya, Marco."

He blew me an exaggerated kiss and unlocked the storage room across the hall. Shelves packed with shirts, binders, office supplies, tools, and a private cache of snacks lined the walls.

"What's Marco's role?" I didn't hesitate to grill Martina. Was he the dude she'd hooked up with last night?

"He's the oldest and has attended camp since he was ten. He's our assistant. My aunt adores him." She studied the floor for a second, eased behind the desk, her hands flitting from one item to another.

Martina fumbled with a binder, inserting pages, some with drawings and maps. A bulletin board of rules and regulations, activities and work schedules hung on the wall to her left. Relatively tidy, her desk held the usual paraphernalia like stapler, pens, and laptop. Nothing to run up the flagpole. Until I ogled the file with my name and birth date written on it sticking out from under a magazine. My heart skidded to the curb. Martina must've noticed my eagle eye. She slid a stack of magazines on top of the green folder, failing in her clumsy attempt to hide it when she knocked half the magazines on the tile floor. She knew I'd seen the file.

Why did she have a file on me? And why did it alarm her that I'd seen it?

CHAPTER 6

Pretending I hadn't glommed onto the file, I focused on the binder Martina was compiling.

"Here are all the game instructions, rules, and scripts." She handed me a green binder with a gold-stamped Dragonfly Meadows logo emblazoned on the center. "You'll assist Dante, fill in for him, manage the immunity idol and rewards. Game props are in the storage shack at the meadow."

Excitement buzzed me as I rifled through the binder. "Awesome."

"All kids meet at the meadow in an hour. Gives you plenty time to read the scripts for the first game. If not, don't stress, Dante will be there to guide you."

"I'll read through it now." I paused. "I read on the schedule that we'll have an offsite on Tuesday. Does that mean we won't be doing scheduled excursions that day?"

Flustered, blood drained down Martina's neck. *Vampires, get ready for the gusher.* She turned and groped her medical books on the shelf beneath her window, pretending to straighten them. "We have a fun excursion planned for Tuesday for the whole camp."

My eyebrows hiked up my forehead. "Gotcha. Anything else I need to know?"

A half-full water bottle tumbled to the floor. "We're good." She spun around, forcing a smile. "Sorry if I seem disorganized. I miss my aunt. She usually takes care of this stuff."

"I hope she's doing okay. Sorry I'll miss her this summer." I held the binder to my chest, blocking my heart from beating through it. "Maybe she'll watch some of the games in the meadow later this week."

"Maybe." Her brow crinkled.

The storage room door shut, the lock clicked in place. Marco popped his head in the office behind me.

"I'll walk you out." He held a foot-tall statue of a dragonfly. Carved of wood, the dragonfly fluttered on a wooden fence post, incredibly detailed down to the bulging eyes, blue-green serrated body, and sparkly gold wings. "I got the team immunity idol." He grinned. "Wanna touch it?" He inclined his head to whisper in my ear. "I got chocolate too."

A wave of heat enveloped me. Was he coming on to me? "Thanks, Martina."

"Have fun." Her distracted voice elevated to an unnatural pitch.

Martina, her aunt, the camp, the whole enchilada oozed weirdness. I hated that Martina or Dante had a file on me. Did they have files on all the teens in the Camp Leadership program? *Yeah. That's it.* But I wasn't ready to give up on my suspicions.

The moment the door to the breakroom shut behind us, I traveled a path of questions meandering through my brain. "Laurel tells me everything that goes on here every summer. How do you like it so far this year? The same as you remember?" We walked toward the dining hall to gather our campers for a short break before hiking to the meadow. He unwrapped the chocolate bar and handed me a hunk. Milk chocolate melting on my tongue and feeding my stomach was bliss after my crappy breakfast. I owed my stomach big time.

We sat on a bench along the edge of a lush greenbelt circling three fire pits. Freedom stared me in the face as I absorbed the warm, rising sun.

"Things are whacked." Marco licked chocolate off his full upper lip, in a slow sensuous move. "I think it's because Mrs. Amadori's not directing the show. Martina told me the new workers are getting in the groove but need ramp up time."

"No kidding. I could cook better."

"Me too and I suck in the kitchen." He chomped on another hunk of chocolate and handed me the rest of the bar.

I declined. His pleasure in the chocolate captivated me, leaving me strangely breathless. Despite his wide nose and caterpillar eyebrows, he wasn't bad looking. Not Nick gorgeous, but his personality more than made up for his deficiencies in the godlike category. Tall and lanky, he reminded me of Logan's build. His Italian tan arms put Logan's pale skin to morbid shame, though.

"Apparently, the chef's a friend of Dante's who needed a job."

"At our edible expense." I scattered pea gravel over a trail of ants marching toward the dining hall in their own dance of freedom. "Ants will even hate the food."

He crumpled the wrapper and slam-dunked it in the trash barrel. Kids were gathering in their age-marked areas to await the activities.

"Hey, do you want to eat lunch with me? You know, sit together at the CL table."

I blushed. Did he just ask me out? "I think we're picnicking in the meadow."

"Even better." His wide grin was sweet, his teeth so white, I almost fell into the chocolate kiss of his eyes.

"Sure. That is, if Dante doesn't have a special project for me."

"Nah. You're allowed lunch. Don't let him fool you." He twisted his black watch band around his wrist, and I followed suit, twisting my leather band. He jolted his head up as Logan, Jesse, and Nick strode over.

"Later. Time to gather up my girls." I skimmed my arm against Logan's arm. He pinned a dark glare on Marco. "Talk later," I murmured to him.

Laurel exited the dining hall, our girls in tow to gather backpacks from the cabins for our hike to the meadow. I jogged to catch up to her.

"What'd you score?" she asked.

I told her what Martina had said on the phone and about the file on her desk, but creepy Dante was sitting on the porch of my cabin slurping down more coffee. Did he have a clone?

"Now you don't have to worry about locking yourselves out." He dangled a ring of keys, scaring off a pair of chipmunks frolicking in the nearby woods. The chipmunks disliked him too.

"Thanks." I stomped on an ugly brown spider, wishing it was Dante.

The girls scattered, and I hung behind to watch him leave, positive my trust meter had taken a hike. I scoured the cabin, seeking signs of disturbance. My belongings were off kilter in the drawers beneath my bed. Earlier, I had deliberately left a T-shirt sleeve folded over. The sleeve was now straight. Alarm shot up my back. The lamp shade was angled to the left after I had straightened it in my slight OCDness before leaving the cabin for breakfast.

The girls and I gathered outside with the other DragonLily Flyers. I waved Laurel off to the side underneath a towering redwood.

"I think Dante pawed through my things. Nothing's missing, but did you notice any disturbance in your cabin?"

Laurel tugged on her hem, and I wanted to tuck it inside her shorts. "No."

"I didn't fess to the girls. I don't want to alarm them. If they see something missing, they'll come forward."

"Thank God you're here, Sherlock."

"No kidding. You'd never see beyond the back of your eyelids if not for me, or a cute boy, like Nick."

"Well, I saw you hanging with Marco. What's that all about?" Her lips pursed in an exaggerated smooch.

I blushed. "He wants to eat lunch with me."

"What?" Laurel screeched. "And you wait until now to tell me?" She play-punched my shoulder.

"We're going to be late." Carrie tugged Laurel's backpack.

I counted heads. "Let's go."

Laurel blew her whistle. "Move 'em out, Flyers."

"We're not cows." Carrie's sarcasm stretched the word *cows*. Moos charged the air as they scuttled off to join the older girls on a pathway beyond the tree houses.

Laurel and I brought up the rear. "You're not off the hook. Spill it."

Blue jays squawked in the trees above us, the epitome of free. A breeze rustled the limbs and rained needles down upon us. We brushed them off, and I crammed my binder in my backpack with my required refillable water bottle, sun lotions, and baseball cap. The day's early heat meant that sunscreen was on the menu. I shoved my sunglasses on.

"It's just lunch. You and Nick can join us too."

"What about Logan?"

"What *about* Logan?" A pinecone dove onto the path and I drop-kicked it into the woods. It split apart on a boulder.

"Will he eat lunch with us?"

"Free country."

"You know what I mean." Laurel toed the side of my sneaker. Hard.

"He can eat wherever he wants. We can't be the three musket-rats surrounded by all these kids. Duh."

Laurel sighed. She wasn't digging any more out of me, not that there was much to dig where Mr. Disappearing Act Montgomery was concerned.

"Laurel, Allie," Carrie shrieked, piercing my eardrum. "It's Jasmine. Hurry!"

The girls formed a circle in the path. Eleven-year-old Jasmine was one of the four girls in my cabin. Tall and lithe for her age, she had beautiful, smooth mahogany skin and the prettiest long red and black dreadlocks I'd ever seen.

The girls parted to let me in their circle. Jasmine lay on her hands and knees retching into the bushes, her shoulders heaving as she hauled in air.

I pulled my water out of my backpack and crouched down. "Honey, what's wrong? Laurel, get a counselor." Laurel ran ahead to catch up to the other groups. "Girls, step away. Give her some air, please."

I stroked her clammy neck, rubbed her shoulders while she upchucked her breakfast in the bushes. Nausea mounted, and I fought it down to handle the situation, to be the responsible person. Tears streaming down her cheeks, Jasmine sat on her knees on the path.

"Your tummy?" I asked, offering her the bottle. I made sure she took a couple sips. Serena handed her a napkin to wipe her eyes and blow her nose.

"No." Horror rode the gaze she pinned to her backpack. She abandoned the bottle and folded her hands over her middle, scampering to the side to escape her nightmare.

Carrie bent to pick up the backpack.

"No, let me." I snatched the purple and green checked backpack from her before anyone else tossed their cookies on my watch. The watery eggs and oatmeal did a perilous sloshing in my stomach. Did I want to see what was inside? I held the bag, indecision forcing my attention on a hummingbird dipping into impatiens along the path. The pink, red, and white flowers soothed me, painted their vibrant colors over my reluctance. *Just do it.*

I knelt on the ground and edged the bag open a skosh. Swallowing hard, I shifted so the girls couldn't see inside. My fingers trembled as I opened the pack farther.

The beady, blank eyes of a dead rat drilled into mine.

The rat hadn't just slunk inside the backpack. The rodent had no lower body.

CHAPTER 7

I snapped the bag shut and averted my head to check myself from puking out the memories the rat forced to mind. My breath rasped in panic. *It's a joke, a joke, a joke.* I pressed on my leather band, pushing the tiny pin in and out of my skin, focusing on the prick of pain instead of the nightmare memories.

Michael Kline, the man who'd kidnapped me, had a pet rat named Beni Hana. Yeah, dumb name after the infamous TV psycho rat from a gazillion years ago. From close range, he'd fired air pellets at Beni, telling me, "If you try to escape, you'll share the same fate." At the end of my tenth hour of captivity, he'd laid the rat on a cutting board, took a cleaver to its neck, and left the head dangling by an ear from a hanger as a reminder. I couldn't see a rat without remembering Beni, and thoughts of the rat always brought Kline and the abduction to the forefront. I swallowed hard several times, put on my game face, and forced my attention to the here and now.

The girls whispered in groups, casting leery glances at the backpack. Counselor Nadia, one of the two girls' counselors jogged into our midst. Logan followed Laurel, his gaze sweeping me up.

Nadia handed Jasmine a ginger ale from her pack and wet a small towel with bottled water to wrap around the back of her neck. "What happened?"

"She opened her backpack and freaked." Carrie rubbed Jasmine's shoulder. "Said something about a rat. Made her blow chunks." Carrie whispered soothing words to Jasmine as Nadia assisted her up. Jasmine was fine, no harm done, except to her psyche and empty stomach.

Nadia studied the bag sitting in a dark spot of shade. Her long brown hair fell around her face. She appeared early twentyish, almost less ready than myself to handle this trauma. "Did you look inside?" Her voice quivered.

"Yeah." My eyes implored her to ditch the subject for the sake of the girls. *For my sake.* It was then that I noticed the University of Nevada, Las Vegas patch on her hoodie. Was she another one of Dante's friends? It boggled the mind. According to Laurel, most of the camp workers from previous years were local college students or friends of Mrs. Amadori's. Had Martina told the truth on the phone about saving costs?

Logan scooped up the backpack. He held his hand out to lift me off the needle-strewn pathway. I took his damp hand in mine and gained my feet.

"It's a rat head," I murmured for his ears only. "I didn't want to hunt for a body, if you know what I mean." His gaze raked over me for an expected reaction. I wasn't sure if I displayed what he wanted to see. Did he know about Beni Hana?

"I'll take it over there." He nodded at a clearing surrounded by decaying logs and small boulders. Not that I wanted to see the contents again, I followed him. I needed to know. Someone had been in our cabin. The only other person who'd hung around it was Dante. Was he creepy or immature enough to play a prank on an eleven-year-old girl?

Logan spread the contents of the pack on the ground. The rat head fell onto a pile of dry, crackling leaves. No body followed. Little blood residue remained on the severed rat's neck. I clutched my stomach and turned away.

"Who do you think did this?" he asked. "Is there someone who doesn't like her?"

"She's the sweetest girl. If anything, someone would target her best friend, Carrie, who kinda grates on everyone's nerves."

"Maybe they mixed up the backpacks?"

The girls huddled on the path, waiting for us to make a grand pronouncement of guilt.

"Dante was in our cabin during breakfast fixing," I did air quotes, "a perfectly fine doorknob."

Jasmine's backpack had been in my alcove. I wanted to disappear inside my snow globe and fought the compulsion to make a run for it.

"What about the flowers?" The zipper rasped closed. Logan hid the backpack behind his leg.

Bars on the cage circling my heart dissolved under his empathy.

"Only you and Laurel know about that. Flowers are harmless. This is flippin' evil. Who does this to a little girl?"

"No clue. We need to bring this to Martina's attention."

"What about our other suspicions? Dante creeping about, the lousy food, absentee Mrs. Amadori."

"Stays between us for now." He pinched a pine needle out of my hair, his fingers lingering on my ear for a second. "Let's regroup at lunch. Tell me what you saw in the offices."

I shifted my backpack to prevent the strap from digging into my shoulder, to hinder my mind from freaking out or my legs from flying to my cabin. "I'm eating lunch with Marco. I'll try to get out of it."

A muscle ticked in Logan's jaw. "Whatever. Don't change your plans." He kicked at pine needles, watched them scatter. "He might know something. He's close to Martina and Mrs. Amadori."

We returned to the group and relayed our findings to Nadia.

Frowning, she seized the backpack from Logan, holding it at arm's length. "I'll take it to Dante. Logan, walk with the girls." Nadia hiked up the trail, carrying the backpack as if it were loaded with rat turds.

Logan's presence calmed the storm brewing inside me even though he was half the cause of that tempest. Why did my having lunch with Marco upset Logan? We weren't destined for each other. That ship had sunk four years ago.

Laurel slung her arm across Jasmine's shoulders. Jasmine held out my refillable bottle.

"Keep it," I said. "I'll get another."

"Was there anything else in my pack?" Jasmine's skin turned ashen again.

"No. Hang tight. We'll get to the bottom of this hoax."

"So disgusting," Carrie added her two cents. "Who'd punk us like that?"

"A sick joke. Probably the boys pranking. I bet they didn't know who the backpack belonged to."

"Yeah," Logan piped up. "When we find out who did it, I'll help you pay back the boys. Deal?"

"Deal," Carrie shouted and fist-bumped the air. Excitement in their voices, the girls all agreed. A couple gave Logan sly looks of wonder. *Oy vey*, to quote Laurel's fake Jewishnish. Young girls grow up way too fast in the midst of boys. *Jeepers, I sound like a mom.*

"Thank you." I squeezed Logan's arm. "That was perfect."

"No problem. If I find out my boys punked them, there'll be hell to pay." A long beat of silence followed. "Now that we have time, tell me what happened in the office." Finger on my arm, he slowed to put distance between the girls ahead of us.

I gave him the skinny on my sleuth-fest. "Why do they have a file on me or any camper?"

He rubbed his cheek, tracing the light sunburn he'd received yesterday. "Mrs. A always kept her life on her computer."

"Maybe Dante and Martina aren't computer savvy."

He sneered. "Martina is and Dante carries a tablet."

"Well we know someone's lying. Dante told me this morning that Mrs. A's in her cabin. Yet Martina told whoever was on the phone that she's at a convalescent hospital."

"He probably doesn't want it to leak out to the parents that Mrs. A's not here. I mean, your mom will go ballistic when she finds out. She'd never have let you attend camp if Mrs. A wasn't here. How many other parents feel the same?"

Unconvinced, I said, "Or he's lying to Martina too and he killed her."

"Back to murder again?" Logan hip bumped me.

"I never left *murder*." I repaid the hip bump, except my hip knocked his thigh as his new height registered. Another surprising reminder of the changes four years had wrought. Not wanting this budding *thing* between us to progress, I moved a foot away on the path, a safe distance between casual friends.

The woodsy path took us downhill, dumping us into a sun-dazzling carpet of tall grasses and a rainbow of wildflowers bordering a lake fed by a river at the far end of the meadow. Red, yellow, and blue dragonflies flitted about, landing on plumes of marshy grass, their glittery wings gyrating wickedly fast. The meadow and lake sat in a canyon surrounded by tree-peppered hills, a small slice of heaven on earth. I tipped my face to the sky, the sun bathing me in reckless abandon. I soaked up the liquid gold, trying to forget my freaky morning.

"Hey?" Logan intruded upon my bliss.

"Umm, yeah?" I opened my eyes and found him checking me out, the softest expression I'd ever seen on him. The sun lit up happy green flecks in his eyes, flecks I hadn't seen in four years.

"Just wanted to know if you were dead or alive." His mouth quirked up on the left in his crooked goofy grin.

I blushed. "Is my green ignorance leaking out?"

He tugged my hair. "Green's healthy on you."

"Musket-rats," Laurel yelled. "Get your hineys over here."

Whew! Saved by the Laurel. *Head. Bury. Sand. That's me.*

The kids gathered around the trees at the far end of the meadow. Weathered picnic tables sat in the shade of the woods. Drinks and snacks jammed a couple coolers under one of the tables. When I spied the whiteboard I realized I hadn't read up on the day's games.

"Shoot. I need to skim the game rules fast." I tugged Logan to a bench close to the whiteboard where Dante and Martina stood.

Laurel joined us. "While you were blooming under the sun, Dante told me to keep quiet about the rat. He'll investigate, but he doesn't want to rile up the kids. He thinks it was a prank by the older boys." She flicked

Logan's head. "He wants to talk to you, Jesse, and Marco at lunch."

There went my lunch date. Part of me was disappointed, the other part relieved that I wouldn't end up bugging Logan by having lunch with Marco. For some odd reason, I didn't want Logan annoyed. Was I messed up or what?

Laurel and I joined Dawn and Lupe, the CLs for the youngest and oldest groups of girls. Dawn handed out paint and flags, and Lupe tossed Laurel the purple bandanas, the cheap equivalent of *Survivor's* spandex tubes they called *buffs*. Each group snagged their designated tarps and spread out on the meadow grass to paint their team flags.

I wrapped my buff around my right wrist. Even though I wasn't playing in the games, I'd cheer for my girls. I studied the binder while Laurel supervised the art work. After an hour, we attached our team flags to poles, and then each team gathered around their poles. Six teams in all, all girls or all boys.

Dante drew abreast of me, closing in on my personal space. Spicy, woodsy cologne wafted off him, amazing and similar to Logan's deodorant. I breathed deep until he spoke, his raspiness ending my moment of lunacy. *Eww.*

"Hey, Allie. I'll announce the games and give the rules. You coach and cheer. Do you want me to call the first game, or do you have it down?"

I smiled and tapped the binder. "No prob. The scripts are easy to follow."

"Good, good. My aunt found the game over the winter and it impressed her."

He slung his arm over my shoulder. He didn't pull me close in a hug, but his touch shot creepy crawlies down my spine. Martina flailed her arm, and her eyes pleaded with him before he removed his arm.

"Sorry about that." He winked. "I have to be good around the girls. Let's get started." With that, he sauntered toward the gathering kids to start the game.

Should I add child molester to his repertoire of potential crimes? I caught Logan's attention. Suppressing his gaze of black death certainly wasn't one of his talents. He watched Dante climb the portable stairs to a small platform, hexing him with his stormy mask. Dante gestured at me.

Oh, crap. I jogged to the platform and hopped up the six steps to join him. Leaning against the safety bars on the right side, I left as much distance between us as possible on the four-by-four calling platform aka lifeguard station. The dragonfly immunity idol sat on a pedestal below us, waiting for its first victor.

The first game included three knockout competitions until a winning team was crowned.

"Each team has 6 bags. You can only bring back 1 at a time," I yelled.

Dante blew the whistle.

"Let the games begin! Immunity is up for grabs!" I shouted. "Jesse takes the lead for team Dragon Slayer." Six teams raced from the starting point by the platforms through an obstacle course to the river where each person had to snag bags of puzzle pieces. One team member raced at a time until the team retrieved all six bags. "Jesse is the first to claim his bag!" I called.

The remaining team members then assembled the puzzle pieces to spell out Dragonfly Meadows. Jesse's team of puzzle dunces quickly fell behind other teams. Once I approved each puzzle, the team rammed their flag in the holder next to the immunity idol.

"DragonLily Flyers win the fourth slot by a millisecond. Better luck next time, Dragon Slayer." Clapping, I jumped up and down. "Woohoo!" There were slots for four flags. First four winners escalated to the next leg. DragonLily Flyers entered the next leg against the middle girls, oldest boys, and youngest boys. "The rest of the teams have been eliminated. Sorry, kids." I gave the losing teams my most sympathetic smile, but I might have mimicked the Wicked Witch of the West by the scowls I received.

As the games continued, I called out encouragement, corrections, and stats the way the host did on the real *Survivor*, mimicking his commentary. I had a blast. Chugging down OJ from a bottle, Dante stepped aside and let me have at it, until the end when he announced the teams advancing to the next level. Before I stepped off the platform, he patted my back.

"You're a natural." He squeezed my shoulder in that familiar way he enjoyed, his eyes suspiciously bright. He listed to the right. "I picked the right person for the job."

"It was fun. Thanks." I grew warm and fuzzy from his praise. Maybe he wasn't such a bad guy after all. Like fire and ice, he confused me.

"I might have another job for you tomorrow if you're up for it. We're heading out on an overnight treasure hunt. It's one of the fun events Martina, Aunt Carla, and I came up with in place of the same old, same old excursions. We're hunting for gold in an old gold mining operation in the lower foothills."

"Awesome." Excitement exploded within me. "What do you want me to do?" After all that research I had done on the California Sierras and the old gold operations from the 1800s, I was raring to check out the local historical sites. *Yeah, I know. I've become a history nerd during my four year exile.* The next best thing to visiting those places was to investigate them on the Internet.

Logan wandered near the platform. Since his team had lost, he was done for the day. He waited while Marco and Jesse finished up their team pep talks and congratulatory speeches. While Logan organized the puzzle pieces, he listened in on my conversation, watching me.

Dante spun me around and pointed out a trail leading up the canyon beyond the lake and into the forest. "See that trail? We're hiking it to the campground."

My mouth dove open, and my leg muscles twitched in defiance. The trail carved into a steep incline, half rock and half thinning tree terrain. "Seriously?"

"Kidding." He twisted my hair like Logan used to do. His laugh was infectious, and I giggled. "The old mine is on the other side, in the lower foothills where the gold was more plentiful during Gold Rush days. We'll take the vehicles. But we can't take everyone at once. The first group will start setting up camp. Would you like to be treasure hunt leader and handle the map?"

My hand flinched on the binder. How'd he know I had a map fetish? I didn't write my stupid hobby on my application. Laurel, Logan, and I used to organize scavenger hunts, and I always sketched the maps. Everyone loved them because I aced the details.

Logan cleared his throat. "I'd love to help too," he interjected amiably. I almost felt him seething beneath his skin. The sun had burned him despite the baseball cap and sunscreen Laurel had coaxed him to apply to prevent him from turning into a lobster and embarrassing her.

A grim smile quickly masked Dante's displeasure at Logan's interruption. "I'll have tasks for the older boys to manage the campers while I set up the perimeter. What do you say, Allie? If maps aren't your deal, just tell me."

"No. I mean, I'd love to do it." My enthusiasm propelled me forward, my hand brushing his arm.

"Perfect. You were the last job I needed to fill." Dante patted my hand. "Let's head in for lunch." He bounded down the steps. "Logan, we need to talk about that prank."

"Um, Dante, about that prank." I followed him down the steps. He turned, a questioning slant to his eyebrows. "The girls are uneasy. Can you give me a key to the cabin?"

He scratched the nape of his neck and his left eye spasmed. "I don't have an extra key. If anything else goes wrong, we'll get another key made."

Bingo. There goes the lying meter, full tilt throttle. He'd dangled two keys in front of me earlier. I waved at Logan as they left. Marco mock-pouted as he picked up puzzle bags.

"Another time?"

His grin lit up his swarthy face. "You got it."

Laurel and our girls joined me, and we followed the trail of campers to camp, counselors Nadia and Tessa bringing up the rear, doing the flirting dance with the scummy men counselors, Marty and Alan.

Laurel flexed her arms. "I'll have the best tan."

"You always did come home with killer color." Envious, I checked my honeyed arms that barely reached the middle of the tan department.

We had a half hour free time before lunch. Everyone was supposed to bring their money to deposit at the Trading Post. I still thought that was weird, but I planned to keep some moola behind, just in case. They wouldn't expect more than the amount I contributed.

I took a slug of water from Laurel's bottle since Jasmine had mine. The poor girl had mostly recovered after we'd switched her mind off the rat. My own nervousness had abated, but warning flags fluttered one by one inside my head.

"That credit system is weird. Have they done it before?" I played my first hand.

She fanned her face in the shade. "No, and I'm not handing over my money. I never bought much in the Trading Post. My mom thinks I came home empty-handed. Heck, no. I always brought home a wad of cash that tided me over for a while."

We passed the three-siders. As we approached our cabin, Jasmine worked her way between us.

"Honey, don't worry, Mr. Amadori had one of the counselors watching the cabins while we were gone." Laurel draped her arm around Jasmine.

Seriously? Who? All the counselors were at the games.

None of the girls wanted to enter our cabin first. I took the bull by its wicked horns and hoofed it inside. Everything seemed normal at first glance, but who knew what had been crammed into a drawer? The girls soon followed, tense and white-faced. But as they sifted through their belongings, their tension drifted into the air and floated away. I checked all the surfaces, cracks, and crevices.

The moment I stepped inside my alcove, the feeling that someone had been there again propelled a slow creep of ants up my spine. Another bouquet of wildflowers sat on my pillow. A note accompanied it. Fingers gripping the card, I flipped it open. Black scrawling text read: "*When you least expect it.*"

Scrawled below the handwritten note was a pencil etch of a severed rat head.

CHAPTER 8

The bouquet of flowers drooped in my fist. Who had sent them? I wanted to scream from the highest mountain and cower in the deepest hole. *This is getting ridiculous. Who the heck is chasing me? I'd rather spend the summer alive sitting at home under Mom's thumb than put up with threats that remind me of The Incident. This wasn't part of my freaking freedom plan.* Ready to bail, I tossed my empty suitcase on my bed. Was I ready for the big, bad world or not? I sank onto the stiff mattress, my face buried in my hands.

I had to quit running from myself, my apprehension, and paranoia. I needed to run to my future free of all the bad stuff. A mystery needed solving. I had to solve it, or I'd never live with myself. I'd never have a life.

I kicked the suitcase into the corner and stomped through my curtains. "I'll be next door. Clean up, then we'll eat lunch. Bring your money for the Trading Post." Mashing the stems in my hand, petals dripping on the ground, I strode to Laurel's cabin. She stepped out to the porch to meet me.

"Another one." I waved the mangled bouquet and note in her face.

"I got one too." Her voice wavered. "What does your note say?"

What the what? I opened the note for her to read while she did the same. Hers read, "*The line forms behind*," above a drawing of a kitchen knife with blood dripping from the blade.

I took her note. "I'm taking these to Dante."

Laurel grabbed my arm. "Wait." She fingered the side of her nose. "I think it's a puzzle."

I blinked up a breeze. "Are you nuts? They're threats, plain and simple."

"You think someone's trying to scare us off?" She liberated my arm, and I smoothed the red moons her fingernails left behind. "Let's see if the other CLs are *special* like us."

We stared each other down. I'd never told her about Beni Hana, but I'd confessed it in my statement to the police. It was no secret to perverted news reporters. She'd read the articles and just hugged me afterward. "I'll do more *digging* at lunch. I swear this vacation has waltzed into Weirdsville."

"Nah. You're just not used to socializing." Laurel play-punched me, but the notes had dumped the hazy fear in her beautiful blue eyes.

"Suck it. I think you're in denial that your perfect camp is anything but." The truth stared her in the face, but my teasing wink defrayed her unease.

"Lunch first. Then we decide. 'Kay?"

"Be ready in five."

"Yes, master," she flung over her shoulder as she flounced inside, her happy-go-lucky attitude warring against my distrustful nature.

I foamed at the mouth on the way to my cabin. I stuck the notes in my rear pocket and tossed the flowers in my backpack. In five minutes, we gathered on the path, joining the girls from the other cabins. Dawn and Lupe chatted away like best friends as I approached them.

"Hey, did you or your girls receive any gifts in your cabin?" I winked.

"No rat heads." Dawn fake-gagged.

"Nothing, thank God," Lupe replied, her oversized boobs bouncing with her exaggerated shiver.

"Nothing unusual, then?" I pressed her.

"A spider cling-on." Lupe fluffed her long black hair. "Ugh, I hate spiders. But I refuse to wear a hat."

"Or go without hairspray?" Laurel piped up.

"Hey, hairspray makes the world go round." Lupe took a lank of Laurel's clean, straight hair in her fingers. "You could use a spray or two."

"And round and round." Dawn fluffed Lupe's wild, big hair some more.

"Did you get any flowers from a secret admirer?" Smugness remade Laurel's face.

Oh, yes, let's be obvious about it Miss Open Book Laurel Montgomery.

"Wait." Dawn stopped, wide-eyed. "Did Nick give you flowers? How romantic."

Here we go. Did she think Nick left the bouquets? He did work in the kitchen and had access to knives. Whatever that meant.

"No. But we spied Jesse hanging with you during the games earlier." I nudged my elbow into her side. "Fess up."

"Jesse? Eww. He's gross. He thinks he wants a piece of this." Dawn wanded her hand up and down in front of herself. "He tries every year."

Everyone scattered toward the dining hall. Laurel

and I hung behind in the woods.

"Dude, what happened to playing it down?" I asked.

"I was playing it down, duh."

Mental head smack. "Oh, right. Why didn't you shove the bouquet and note in their faces? It would've gotten the same effect."

"Chill out, Nancy Drew." She pushed me toward the dining hall door. "I'm starving. According to Nick, we're in for a treat."

"Human food?"

We entered the teeming dining hall, the deafening noise of the kids echoing off the walls. Kids rushed out of the food serving line, smiling. Turkey, ham, or tuna salad sub sandwiches, fresh fruit salad, deep colored punch, and assorted chips lined the serving counters. I salivated.

I grabbed a tuna salad sandwich. "Did they fire the chef?"

"No. Nick did this. He's good, I tell you. He made the sub rolls from scratch." Laurel snagged a turkey and Swiss and two fruit cups. "He said they have decent supplies, but not what we're used to from previous years." She dropped her voice. "There's a locked storage room he thinks holds better food for the workers, the type of food they used to serve the campers."

I pondered that tasty morsel. "Can Nick snag the key?"

Laurel halted, shocked. "What's taken over your body?" Heads swiveled as we walked to the table where Dawn and Lupe sat next to a random group of younger kids. Now that the kids were renewing friendships or getting to know the newbies, everyone sat wherever they wanted.

I gave the air a pat to force her to dial it down. "Who has the key?"

"Chef. Big burly guy by the name of Eddie." She

pointed at the kitchen doorway.

Over six feet tall, Eddie's shoulders filled the doorway, his potbelly preceding him by a foot. Clean-shaven, he wore a white chef's cap over a buzz cut. He appeared to be in his late twenties. Another one of Dante's friends, I presumed. *You won't catch me assuming. I'm not ready to be an ass yet.*

"We'll chat up Nick later. I want inside that room. I want proof."

"So what'll that prove?" Laurel took her right hand off her wavering tray and fingered her polo shirt hem. Her constant agitation promised to leave her topless soon.

"That they're stealing our money and feeding us cheap slop." We sat opposite Dawn and Lupe, who had their mouths buried in their sandwiches, moaning in ecstasy.

I bit into my sandwich, gelling on the spot. The bread was soft, fresh, and mouthwatering.

"I've croaked and gone to heaven riding Nick's shoulders," Laurel mumbled through a mouthful of sandwich.

"You better marry that boy. You'll never get a good meal if your husband relied upon your less than stellar cooking skills."

"Hey, I make a mean pot of boiled water."

"Your specialty." Logan slid onto the bench beside me.

Bending to my insatiable curiosity that overshadowed everything Logan represented, I shifted to face him. "What'd you find out about the rat?" I forced down the memories of Beni.

"No one's fessed up."

"Well, no shit. Did you think they would?" Laurel stole a taco chip off his tray.

"What will Dante do?" I picked out the fresh grapes from my fruit salad and dumped them in Laurel's bowl.

She picked out her pineapple chunks and dumped them in my bowl.

"Nothing for now." Logan scooted closer to make room for Jesse to sit on the other side of him. Stealthily, I eased a few inches away from him. I had a hard time reconciling our unspoken past and this new paradigm. A little physical distance helped.

Nick sat across from Laurel. "Good?"

"Paradise," Laurel said dreamily, her foot sliding up and down his ankle.

"Where's Marco?" I asked, looking at his empty seat at our table.

Logan stiffened. "What's the deal with you two?"

"Jeez, bro, she asked a simple question." Laurel took a handful of his taco chips. He whacked his fork on her hand.

"Um…yeah, just asking. He's the sole CL missing." Logan was acting all weird about Marco, jealous even. What was up with that?

He shoveled a handful of chips in his mouth, chewed slowly while I tapped my foot, waiting for his answer. He washed his food down with a double gulp of fruit punch. "He's eating with Martina." A smile ghosted his mouth. "I think they have a thing going. Know what I mean?" He nudged my leg.

So it had been Marco slobbering all over Martina in the cabin last night? I drummed fingers of curiosity on the table. "Martina? She's scraping the cradle. Or she needs his blood."

A few minutes later, Dante stormed into the dining hall and hovered behind Marco in the seat next to Martina. Arguments rose from the table.

"I said that's my seat, punk." Dante prodded his tray into Marco's upper arm.

"Take it easy, man." Marco pushed Dante's tray off

him. "Martina and I are reviewing schedules. Give us a minute."

"Screw you." Dante tried to lower his slurring speech. Epic fail. He listed to the left, drunk off his ass. I'd noticed him during the games earlier sucking down OJ. Had it contained easily hidden, no-scent vodka?

Martina stood and clamped her hand on his arm. "Let's take this outside. You're bothering the kids."

"Bothering the kids?" He sneered. "I'm only bothering Marco."

"Man, take it out of here." Marco sprang up and tried to steer him to the door. "Go sleep it off."

Dante wound back his arm and slammed his fist into Marco's gut, his tray of food clattering to the floor. Grunting, Marco doubled over, hands pressed to his stomach.

"Don't you tell me what to do, punk. This is my camp now. It doesn't belong to Carla's pet boy toy."

Silent and rapt, the kids watched the most excitement to happen since they'd hit camp. More exciting than a decapitated rat.

"Shut up, Dante," Martina whisper-shouted. She took his arm. He wrenched from her grasp, not buying her efforts to appease. "Marco's right. You need to sleep it off."

Logan stood up in his lethally, graceful way. He took up Marco's left wing. A frisson of excitement swept up my spine. Four years ago, Logan would've run the other way to avoid engaging in a physical or verbal altercation.

Kids talked among themselves and repositioned their chairs for a better view. Where was the popcorn when you needed it?

"What's Logan thinking?" Laurel fingered the side of her nose. "He's gonna get in trouble. We'll end up shipped home to die and wither in our backyards."

I shook my head. "Logan's a black belt. He can handle

himself."

"My point exactly. If he engages, he becomes a lethal weapon."

Nervous jitters perilously plagued my stuffed stomach.

Dante stepped back, showing a healthy respect for Logan. He held up a splayed hand. "Okay. Okay. Let's take this outside."

Logan pressed his shoulders forward. "Nothing to take outside. We're cool here. Marco will eat at my table."

Marco hadn't regained his composure from the blow to his gut. He glared at Logan first, then Dante. In a gravelly voice, he said, "Let's take it outside."

Dante picked up a bowl of fruit salad and slung it at Marco, the bowl bouncing off his forehead above his left eye.

Fruit juice dripping off his face, Marco charged forward, ramming his head into Dante's middle. Noise in the room exploded as kids whooped and jeered. Dante pummeled Marco's head and shoulders, while Logan tried to pull them apart. The two planted fists and kicks wherever they could land. I sprinted to the scuffle, Laurel shouting at me to stay put. I pulverized a slimy pineapple wedge into the tile floor, sliding to an ungraceful stop against the table.

"Do something, Martina," I yelled.

She wrung her hands, lamely screaming, "Knock it off. Come on, not in front of the kids."

Logan landed a well-placed karate kick in Dante's middle, sending him to the floor, moaning in pain.

My mouth hung open. Logan's guilty horror nearly spurred me to his side to soothe it away. Yet, I felt no horror at seeing what he'd done. Strange pride and respect mingled with my shock, leaving my warmth edged in ice. Instead, I rushed to Marco kneeling on the floor and held a napkin to his bleeding nose.

"Everyone, finish your lunch and return to your scheduled activities," Martina shouted over the frenzy.

The din died down, Dante rose, hands splayed in surrender. "Sorry kids, this won't happen again. Marco was disobeying my orders." He smiled his crazy, fake sweet smile that didn't mollify anyone. The snake in the grass smile remained plastered to his face as he challenged Marco. "Stay away from Martina or you're home bound."

CHAPTER 9

Lunch ended on a strangely sour note. Martina cancelled the afternoon *Survivor* games, and handed the campers free time at the lake or in the craft room, assigning a counselor to each activity. Dragonfly Lily girls agreed on swimming at the lake after our appointment in the Trading Post.

Subdued, the girls huddled and whispered as they trailed Laurel to the small store, with me bringing up the rear. Laurel ushered the girls inside the old-fashioned 1800s trading post replica. Built out of fake logs, the inside smelled musty despite the open windows. The shelves were sparse, but it contained a decent selection of snacks, sodas, drugstore items, clothes, hats, books, and games. Dragonfly Meadows postcards, key chains, and T-shirts packed a corner. The girls flew from one corner to another, touching and eyeing everything. *Shopping is a girl's best friend.*

Every item on a rack of snacks was marked with points. Three points for most regular-sized candy bars.

"Everyone line up at the counter and deposit your dough into your accounts," I said.

Martina took up her perch behind the counter and gave me a grateful smile. A floral wreath circled her dark hair, the flowers gathered from the meadow. Charlie the Tuna churned in my gut.

"Thank you." She waved. "My other role as purveyor of small goods." She wore a funky billowy top with ruffles down the front that may or may not have belonged to the 1800s. The hickey at the top of the neckline belonged to any century. She logged the girls' deposits in an old-fashioned, leather-bound ledger.

"How's Mrs. Amadori doing?" Sue me for being curious.

Laurel kicked my shoe. I met her kick and upped it a glare.

Martina didn't bat an eye. "Still not moving too well, but she's healing."

"You're taking care of her?" Laurel asked, now that I'd opened the door.

Martina stowed a wad of cash inside a metal lockbox on top of the counter. A small key dangled on her plastic spiral wristband, clinking against the box. "I care for her when I'm free from my duties. She has everything she needs."

"Can we go see her soon? I've looked forward to spending time with her this summer." Laurel laid it *on*!

"That would be awesome. I've been dying to meet her," I chimed in, dazzling Martina with a beauty contestant smile.

"It's up to Dante." She squinted, cool as a cucumber.

"Oh, sure." Dejected, Laurel's shoulders hunched forward.

I thumbed the side of her hand, our secret sign of commiseration. I hadn't thought much about Laurel's feelings in not getting to see Mrs. Amadori. The woman was special to a lot of kids, like their favorite aunt. My determination to bust open the inconsistencies at the camp became a rock inside me. Cliché or not, failure wasn't an option. *Been there, done that.*

A couple girls called Laurel over to scope out the T-shirts. I wanted to talk to Martina further and waited by the price board while she finished logging in the girls' money. The point system on the board left me bristling. Each point was worth a dollar, which meant those candy bars were three bucks. Unbelievable. I bet it was Dante's grand scheme to gouge everyone and pocket the change. I doubt he intended to award the leftover money as raffle prizes. Add another item onto my growing list of random curiosities.

Serena and Michelle were the last to make their purchases.

I handed Martina the money I'd brought, half my stash, and leaned over the counter. "Love your flowers, fits the motif here."

She touched her fingertips to her floral crown. "Thanks. Dante gave it to me this morning. He thought it matched my costume." Martina locked the box.

Laurel clapped her hands. "Flyers, get in line. Time's up. We need to move out for the next group."

For the shysters to con more unsuspecting innocents.

I noticed a new backpack in Jasmine's hands. "Put Jasmine's backpack on my tab."

"No need," Martina said. "It's free for her."

Jasmine squealed and hugged my arm. I might gain some minions, after all.

Speaking of, I stepped toward Laurel, nudged her arm. "Swimming next?"

Laurel lit up like a Christmas tree. "Yesss. I'm dying to parade my new bikini for Nick."

My head lolled backward. "While I continue working my angles."

She whacked my arm. "No one said you have to play Nancy Drew. You can let it go, you know?"

I triple-blinked. "Really?"

"For an hour or so, I mean."

"That's what I thought." More than anyone, Laurel wanted Mrs. Amadori to be okay. After the day's events, hanging by the lake under the sun sounded like heaven. *No, it won't remind me of sunbathing by the pool at* Casa *Bailey*. Not by a long shot. I had too much to see in the surrounding hills, the canyon, the lake, too much people watching.

Too much Logan.

The girls were bursting to reach the lake, their chatter drowning out the sounds of nature. They'd donned their cutest bathing suits in all colors of the rainbow, and all levels of coverage from barely there to granny overkill for the chubbiest girl. I changed into my new halter-top bikini, checking myself in the full-length door mirror to make sure my tiny poochy stomach didn't make me look chunky. Laurel and I had gone shopping a few weeks ago, a tortuous experiment in stupidity on my part. She preferred skimpy bikinis, while I preferred not to show my entire birthday suit. She talked me out of buying the purple tankini and boy shorts, but I bought them later with my mom. I wore the bikini to avoid a ration of crap from Laurel if I didn't wear it at least once.

Laurel stomped up the steps. "Ready, Freddy?"

Her tiny fuchsia patches and strings made her board straight stomach and long legs look amazing. Her bordering-on-a-C-cup boobs overflowed her halter-top.

She plucked at my top tie. "Thought you were wearing that lame tankini."

I hid a smile. "You saw that?"

"You can't hide clothes from me."

"Except when they're your clothes."

"Hey, I knew you had my T-shirt all along. It looked better on you."

"Oh. Well, thanks." I slipped on my gossamer short-sleeved cover-up Laurel had coaxed me into buying instead of the over-sized T-shirt I wanted. "So you'll fork it over?"

"I didn't say that." She picked through the open drawer beneath my bed, checking out the other clothes I brought that she didn't know about. "You *seriously* need a makeover. I better give you the shirt."

"It's a good start." I shouldered my beach bag. "Let's go before the sun burns away." I stuffed the rules book and a notepad in my tote since Laurel's tiny bag had only enough room for lip gloss and a mirror.

The hike through the woods on the marked path was uneventful. Standing at the top of the last hill before descending to the meadow and the lake beyond, I stopped to take it all in. Private cabins dotted the woodsy land on the other side of the lake. Boat docks jutted out on the deep blue lake. The campground's long pier ended at an old boathouse. Sunlight sparkled off the placid water, a coating of rippling diamonds. The heaven of independence was gorgeous.

The day had grown warm, and I wanted to dip my toes into the cool water. Laurel waved to Nick as he sauntered over, drooling over Laurel in her next-to-nothing bikini.

"Ladies. You are visions of perfection." Nick's eyes never strayed from Laurel's boobs. "I saved lounge chairs for you." He jerked his thumb over his shoulder.

Mr. Mach*eese*mo wore long checkered trunks, and his bare chest was tan, firm, and delish. I left them to wipe the drool off each other's chins.

Marco suffered in silence on a lounge chair on a brick patio adjacent to the boat dock. The bruise over his eye had turned amazing shades of purple.

"How are you?"

"I'll live." He patted the empty chair next to him.

Two counselors sat in lifeguard chairs at opposite ends of the pebbly beach. Kids splashed along the shore, others swam or played on floaters up to the buoys marking the swim boundaries.

I dumped my bag next to the lounge chair and slipped off my cover-up. Marco whistled. I blushed to my toes. "Stop."

"No." He grinned, his bushy eyebrows drawing together comically.

A loud splash off the dock and hollering boys ended my acute embarrassment. I followed Marco's gaze to Ricky, one of the older boys who'd cannonballed into the lake. Ricky was a tree house boy, which made him at least fifteen. Tall and muscular, he could give Dante a run for his stolen campers' money if *they* ever engaged in a fight.

Settling in the lounge, I rolled on my side to confront Marco. "Can I ask you a question?"

"Ask all you want. Doesn't mean I'll answer." He waggled his eyebrows.

The heat of a watchful sun warmed my skin. "Do you have a thing for Martina? I don't understand what happened at lunch."

"Do you need to understand?" A dark edge accompanied his words.

"Guess not. It's your business."

After a long beat of silence, he relented. "Martina

could've run the camp by herself. She didn't need to bring Dante in. But apparently he's saving the family money to pay for Carla's medical bills."

"Did you antagonize him?" My curiosity refused to die.

"Martina and I go back years. Carla and my mom are friends, attended college together." Sweat popped on his brow, and he swiped it off, hesitating as if to weigh his words. "He doesn't want me hanging with her. He hates that I'm working the offices. I think Dante's abusing her."

CHAPTER 10

Laurel tore off her cover-up and raced Nick to the lake. "Chop, chop, Allie, Marco," she yelled. I picked up the sheer white cover-up puddled on the brick patio.

Marco sat up. "Don't go." His mouth pressed into a grim line.

I hadn't planned to, not since he'd opened the gates of disclosure and threw down his bombshell. I sensed more confession to come. "Sure."

"I trust any friend of Laurel and Logan, and I want an unbiased opinion. Can you keep this between us?" He balanced on the edge of his wooden lounge chair.

I sat, our knees gently knocking. The sun or my anticipation began burning my face, flushing in a heat wave down my chest. "I won't repeat anything, unless you want me to. Not even to Laurel. You know how she is." I winked.

"My biggest fear." A smile curved up his lips to match mine.

I traced a cross on the back of his hand. "Swear on the cross."

He traced a cross on my hand. Somehow, the gesture became a little unnerving and a lot exciting, intimate even.

He leaned closer, our knees mushed together. "I promised to bring some private documents to Mrs. Amadori. But neither Martina nor Dante will let me see her."

My pulse raced. Maybe it hadn't been Marco macking on Martina Saturday night. He would've known Mrs. Amadori wasn't in the cabin. The one other person remotely resembling that dude was Dante. *Eww…creeptastic.*

"Do you want me to sneak up there with you?" I was dying for another run up to the cabins now that my suspicions seemed to be panning out.

"No. I want you to keep Dante and Martina distracted at the campfire tonight while I sneak up there. I need to do this before we leave for the gold mine."

I pressed on my wristband. "What do you want me to do?"

Shrill whistles filled the air, and the lifeguards called a twenty-minute water timeout. A troop of girls bounced by, reaching for a pile of colorful beach towels near us.

"I'll snag a pair of two-way radios from the storage room. You keep Dante and Martina occupied at the campfire."

"Will you let me know how she's doing, so I can assure Laurel? I mean, I won't divulge what you're doing," I amended, rubbing the goosebumps chasing up my arm. Will he find Mrs. A in her cabin?

"Yeah, I guess. Depends on what Mrs. A says. The whole camp's supposed to watch another video of her tonight in prep for the treasure hunt tomorrow."

"Thought you were coming in the water?" Laurel said, as she toweled water off Nick's back.

"After break. Marco and I were getting acquainted." As I reclined on my lounge, I gave Marco a discreet thumbs-up.

Laurel plopped down on a chair beside mine. "What's up with you two?" Her voice fell to a purring conspiratorial level.

"Zip it. We're just talking." Marco was kinda cute once you slid past the caterpillar eyebrows and the honking cave nose. Glittery gold flecks speckled his chocolate kiss eyes when he smiled, leaving me drowning in warm, bubbly sweetness.

"You could do a lot worse. He lives nearby in San Jose too."

Logan strode toward us in his new catlike way. No strut in his stride, all grace. His gaze fixated on me, then Laurel, bouncing to me, raking his eyes from my head to my fuchsia colored toenails. Once again, I heated under his scrutiny rather than from the sun burning me to a crisp. This bodyguard act had turned weird.

Logan wore a tank, a frame from the TV sitcom *The Big Bang Theory* screen-printed on it, his shoulders already burning. I nicked a tube of sunblock out of my tote.

"Logan?" I held out the bottle.

He extended grubby hands, palms out. "Will you rub it on?"

"Jeez, bro. Were you playing in the mud?" Laurel held up her hands and flinched in her chair.

"Martina had me loading dirty tents and camp gear in the truck for the gold mine excursion tomorrow."

He sat on my lounge chair, his back to me, wiping his hands on a wet rag. I poured a dollop of lotion on my hand. The second I touched the hard plains of Logan's shoulders, feelings I'd buried crashed forward. Touching him reminded me of when we used to slather lotion on each other as kids after the parental smackdown about skin cancer. I worked the lotion into his shoulders, down his arms. Before I realized what he was doing, he'd reached down and towed his shirt over his head, exposing his pale back.

"I'm next," Marco teased, draping a T-shirt over his head as he reclined.

"Then me." Nick grinned at Laurel, raising his left eyebrow in his trademark wink.

Laurel cast him a withering glare. "*I'll* take care of your back."

"What about the rest of me?"

"I got that covered too." She arrayed herself over his arm, rubbing herself against him, stretching her leg across his thighs.

Nick's deep skin didn't need sunscreen. However, he did need a jar of oil to slick on his muscles, and then he needed to parade in front of us so I could enjoy the show.

I squirted lotion on Logan's back and he winced. As I spread my hands over his flesh, the solidness of his muscles sent my insides buzzing in surprise and so much more. As much as I wanted to continue working toward his chest, I knew I had to stop. I didn't know what my hands would do if granted the chance to touch him further. I'd either caress my fingers over his chest or gouge my fingernails into his heart. Feelings I'd never experienced for Logan battled within me. I'd stumbled into a major chasm on the path leading to adulthood. Escaping it was a nebulous notion. Before he turned around, he slipped on his tank, covering up his paleness that called out Martina's vampire complexion for an epic challenge.

"Al, what's percolating in that brain of yours?" Laurel

rolled on her side, her boobs practically popping out of her bitty top.

"Hmm...thinking about the gold mine."

"Ugh. Not sure I'm down on the idea of creeping through a gold mine or digging for treasure."

Marco left to play catch with his tree house boys. Logan sat and dumped a graphic novel on the table beside him, a teen girl and boy defending themselves from a pack of wolves on the cover. Maybe I should learn self-defense to defend myself from pack leader Dante?

"You doing okay?" he asked.

"Better than that sunburn on your face." I handed him a bottle of aloe vera. Our fingers touched, electric and so very strange. I yanked my hand away, wiping it on my bare stomach.

"It'll tan fast. You know this always happens to me." He set the aloe aside for later.

"I don't remember," I lied.

"Yes, you do," Laurel piped up.

"Whatever." I closed my eyes and drifted off, the sounds of cheerful play lulling me toward sleepy time. This was so much better than lounging poolside at home with birds and my black cat, Bella, to keep me company. I don't know how long I slept, but Logan's hand on my shoulder awoke me.

"Time to head back." He blocked the sun, which had made a distinct plunge from the sky toward the surface of the lake. A fiery orange-red ball streamed coral beams onto the lake, rippling in all directions. "I told Laurel to take the kids back."

Three stragglers hiked up the path to the woods, the beach now deserted. Scrambling up, I gathered my scattered belongings and shoved everything in my tote. It only took me a second to realize that Logan hadn't abandoned me on the beach when everyone else had. He'd stayed behind...for me. *Atonement?* Still not good enough, but it gave me pause.

Hesitating, I kicked a piece of driftwood, burying a spider crawling along our path. *Death to all creepy crawlies.* "Can you...teach me some self-defense moves?"

Startled, Logan's eyes stretched wide. "I guess. You *should* learn self-defense. Both you and Laurel. She ignores me every time I bring it up."

Despite his implied comment that attempted to dredge up memories, warm and fuzzies erupted inside me from his voice and the eagerness dancing in his light-flecked eyes. More memories emerged like the undead, and I mentally stuck wooden stakes in their hearts.

I plunked my tote onto the table. "Awesome." Self-defense might come in handy later.

"First, the best defense is to run if you have a clear path and you know you can outrun your attacker."

"Seriously?"

He rubbed his thumb and index finger together, his classic "thinking" habit. Or had it grown to a nervous twitch?

"Why engage and risk hurting yourself if you can just run away?"

"If I can't run, then what? I don't have a man's strength."

"You don't need brute strength. You'll have seconds to defend against an attacker. You'll use parts of your body to cause enough pain to incapacitate him to make a getaway." He took a defensive stance, his long legs and surprisingly solid torso more lethal than I ever believed they'd make him. "The upper block is the easiest to learn. Watch this." Logan lifted his left arm and bent it at a forty-five degree angle to his head, his palm facing away from his face. He slashed his right arm out in an upward crossing movement the same time he brought his left arm down across an imaginary face before rotating to the ready position. His arms flowed through the motions again, agile and dangerous. Perspiration filmed the nape of my neck. Who was this Logan?

I'd seen his moves mimicked in movies, but never thought I'd ever practice them. Logan kneed my legs apart, then rested his hands on my tense shoulders.

"You do this every morning?"

"Yeah. Keeps me in shape. It's relaxing, redirects my energy, helps me focus."

"Awesomesauce." All I pictured was women twined in yoga pretzels.

"Keep your shoulders in a relaxed position. Make sure your right arm's in this ready position." He shifted my right arm into position, tucked under my shoulder, my forearm parallel to the ground, palm facing up. "Try it."

I swung my arms, following his instructions, royally screwing it up, and jabbing the air at a mystical man's crotch. I giggled. "That would hurt, right?"

"Yeah." He laughed. "But it'll land you in trouble before you make contact. The point is that your right arm should make a complete twisting motion, rotating the attack over your head." He demonstrated a few more times. Stepping beside me, he said, "Shadow me."

I followed his slow steps, time after time, feeling a familiar camaraderie. When he thought I'd had enough, he played attacker, and I successfully blocked him several times.

Sweat dripping between my breasts, I clapped and grinned. "Flippin' brilliant."

Logan massaged his arm where I'd thrust him off me. "You did good." His smile engulfed all of me into the warm depths of his deep hazel eyes, and his praise caused adrenaline to pop in my blood.

He showed me a kickass kick move. I practiced it,

loving the connection my foot made, able to knock an object out of a person's hands to give myself time to escape from an attacker. Foot aching, I stood, grinning like a fool.

"Practice it every day and you'll have it memorized in no time. Next time, I'll show you the elbow strike and the palm heel strike."

"Thank you so much." Before I could stop myself, I lunged against him and hugged him. No one had ever spent time to teach me something so sacred to them. That was, no one since Logan had taught me tricks he'd slaved to learn to beat his latest video games when we were kids. Confused tears welled. His arms enclosed me. None of yesterday's awkwardness plagued us for several long moments, until I dropped my arms and Logan released me.

"I can teach you—" What? What could I teach him? I had no hobbies of interest to him. Why did I feel compelled to spend more time with him?

"Photoshop? Do you still take photos and create digital pictures?"

Surprise lanced my heart. "Sort of. I designed the logo for my mom's law firm." Her firm had held a contest to update their logo. All entries had been anonymous, and she hadn't known I'd entered until after I won. She gloats over my creativity to her partners who all hired professional designers to create their entries.

"That'd be cool. I haven't used Photoshop since—" Since the day before my kidnapping when he'd drawn a cartoon picture of the three musket-rats. I picked up my tote. The single use camera in the bottom of my bag—all they allowed at camp—was all but forgotten in the happenings at camp. I had totally forgotten to snap photos of flowers, dragonflies, and whatnot to use in my fun designs. I took it out and shot a couple snaps of the sunset on the lake, and a red and gold dragonfly helicoptering over some reeds in a shallow pool.

Silence descended as the sun sank closer to the lake, fiery amber shimmers stretched out to touch the edge of the shadowy woods. We trudged to the campground path side by side.

Logan coughed, announcing his intention to break our companionable silence. "Watch yourself around Dante. I hate how he's glommed onto you. In fact, I'd rather you weren't alone with him. Anywhere."

"I know. He gives me the skeevies." Well, that might toss a wrench in my nighttime plans. *Dare I tell Logan? No. Don't jeopardize Marco's trust.* Regardless of our martial arts bonding, Logan remained a mystery. I still had that aching question mark dancing inside me. Before I could stop myself, I said, "Logan? Can I—"

Halting and freezing on the path, he quieted me with a finger to his lips. "Did you hear that?"

Murky light ghosted the darkening woods. Twigs crunched underfoot. Birds took flight, wings flapping into the twilight sky. Ice prickled at the base of my spine. A stick snapped to my right. I swung toward the sound, meeting more trees swaying in the breeze cutting through the woods. The sensation of someone stalking me joined the eerie crawl now a biting wave across my shoulders. Another twig snapped loud and disconcerting, booming in the dead silent woods. Where had all the animals and birds vanished to?

"Someone's trailing us," I whispered, peering out the corner of my eye, not wanting to give any indication we'd noticed the noise. Guards up, we increased our pace. Logan's defensive moves repeated in my mind from start to finish. I fought to keep my arms at my sides rather than form the positions he'd taught me.

A shadowy shape streaked from one tree to another to

our left.

"Who's there?" Logan demanded.

I curled against his side and he took my hand in his. Sweaty palm or not, his hand comforted me as he sought his own degree of comfort.

No answer. No big surprise.

Something zoomed within a foot of our heads, a whisper of air in my ears. An arrow stuck out of a tree to my left. Another arrow whistled, piercing the next tree to my right. Unable to hide my fright, I yelped, staggering against Logan.

"Duck." He pushed me down, covering me with his body. A third arrow whizzed by, well above our heads, and struck another tree. The archer deliberately missed in an apparent attempt to scare the bejeezus out of us. His aim hit the center of each tree trunk.

Trees and bushes rustled as the archer fled toward the lake. My instincts kicked in, and I bolted in the direction the mysterious archer took, jumping over rocks, scrabbling through lashing branches.

"No! Don't chase." Logan's low-voiced shout stopped me cold.

One lesson in self-defense was not a death wish in the making. I halted so fast, I stumbled against a tree, scraping my upper arm against the jagged bark. Logan caught me against him before I took a header into a half-dead, thorny bush that could use my blood in a resurrection ritual. Steadying myself, I clung to his arms, willing my heart to dip below stroke zone.

He inspected my scraped skin, picking out bits of bark.

"Well, rock my world," I said, attempting to lighten my anchor of fear.

"Let's check out those arrows. Could've been a random hunter who wandered out of bounds."

"No, Logan. It was a lunatic campground director who needs to visit a padded cell." I stepped to the side. Part of me wanted to stay near him to feel his body heat forever. The other part needed to visit her own padded cell and beat my head against the walls.

"Taking it a bit far, don't you think?" Determination fed his stride to the tree, and he wrenched out the first arrow by the time I reached him.

"Do I have to spell it out?" I retorted to his ass end, marveling at the strength hidden beneath his pale lankiness. "Dante Amadori's hiding something. Freak flags are flying high. It's not my paranoia." I stamped my foot on a branch, pulverizing it into the ground. "It's not my imagination. They're not tricks campers are playing on other campers." I kicked a sugar pinecone into the forest, launching my anger with it. "Don't I have a right to be wary?" *Say what? Why'd that come out?* I vowed never to say anything like that to Logan, at least not until I called him on the carpet. "Never mind," I added. "We're reporting this to Martina and Dante."

Logan stepped to the second tree and yanked the next arrow out. The muscles on his arm popped. I licked my lips. Who was this Logan Montgomery? Where had the scrawny geeky boy I used to know gone? Was he hiding behind the shell of the here and now geek?

He turned to me, holding the arrows in his fist, a scrubbed mask on his usually descriptive face. "You have a right to a ton of things."

CHAPTER 11

Mired in deep thought, I hurried to the campground, scanning the woods with every step. Logan trailed me, tangled in his own head. He'd always tended to zip it rather than confront issues head on. Guess I'd been doing the same, lost in the torment inside my head. I twisted my leather wristband, scratching at my tiny scars. Along the edge of the woods above the main campground area, I waited for him to come abreast of me and stared at the newish store-bought arrows. What I knew about archery filled a molecule.

"Do you really think they were aiming for us?"

"Yes." Logan gripped the arrows tightly, his fingers an angry red.

"To kill us?" I splayed my hand on my stomach, trying to hold together the mystical chinks in my armor.

He shook his head emphatically. "Scare us. He knew what he was doing."

"What about next time?" I hugged my tote bag, willing it to morph into an arrow-proof vest.

"Won't be a next time." A dark edge hardened his face and his resolve. "Not on my watch."

I touched my index finger to his wrist, smoothed it up his forearm, shivering from the resurfacing memories from before The Incident. "You might not be able to avoid it."

A muscle in his arm twitched against my touch. "I won't let anyone hurt you." He leaned in, whispered, "Never again."

My body had a mind of its own, and I closed the distance, shy of touching him. He pressed his lips to my forehead for the longest moment. Flames licked my stomach. I laid my palm flat on his chest, feeling the heat of his sunburn or something far greater through his thin tank. His lips brushed mine, the barest touch of all that was Logan. Enough to make my breath clog my throat.

Shocked silent, he drew away, and I touched my fingers to my lips to hold him in, to erase our hesitation, or to put the unspoken words on the table. We'd failed the test of full disclosure. I didn't know whether to be furious or stoked.

A bubble of anger floated to the surface, and I kicked myself into that sphere of loathing. What the hell was I doing? *Logan? Hell to the big fat no.*

A new air of awkwardness showered us in the slight breeze whispering through the clearing and into the darkening woods. Groves of kids heading to the dining hall penetrated our strange cocoon.

"Let's hit the office from the front before kids see the arrows." Logan led us down a path behind the dining hall to the front door of the offices.

I slid my tote onto my shoulder, scraping it along the hallway wall. The noise caught Martina's attention, and she scurried out of her office. It appeared she'd just arrived, an unwrapped sandwich and frosty glass of soda on her desk.

"Dante here?" Logan asked.

Her gaze zinged to the arrows clenched in his hand. She froze, narrowed her eyes. "In the dining hall. Where'd you find those?"

"Someone shot at us in the woods while we were hiking back from the lake." I stepped closer to Logan, blocking her from escaping. Blood drained from her face, not that her corpse face had much to drain. She looked ready to flee to her coffin.

She tapped her fingers on the doorjamb, twisting her mouth. "Are you sure they were shooting *at* you? Could have been poachers. We've had trouble with hunters on our land."

"*Your* land?" My fury spun out. "Where kids roam?" I sneered.

"Carla's land." Her lips pinched tight and she held out her hand. "May I have them? I'll need to call the sheriff."

"How about, *are you okay*?" Logan's disgust rolled off his tongue, and he held the arrows tighter to his torso.

Martina's shoulders lifted, elevating her guard. Annoyance drew her mouth into a tight line. "I see that you're okay. Sorry, of course, I should've asked that first." She stepped aside. "Sit and give me a complete statement. I don't want anyone else getting hurt. We take safety here with complete seriousness."

Reluctantly, I sat in front of the desk. Logan perched on the other chair and relinquished the arrows to the desktop. Never allowing my gaze to rest in any one spot long, I scanned for that Allie Bailey file, or a file on anyone else. Supply requisitions and old gold mine operations files sat among the crap teetering on her desk.

Logan spoonfed her the details of our incident while she typed notes on her laptop. Paper files my flat ass. A dog with a fatty, meaty bone had less determination than

I did to find that mysterious file.

"I want Dante to know what happened," I demanded.

"You can count on it." She tapped her short fingernails on her keyboard. "He found the poachers the first time and warned them off."

He'd probably beat the mythical poachers to a pulp and they'd returned for revenge. A sudden release of tension drained down my shoulders knowing none of the kids were in the woods. They might not have ducked in time or might have run off and gotten lost in the woods.

"Did you file a police report?" Logan leaned forward, elbows on his knees, clasping his hands together, probably to prevent them from wringing her scrawny white neck.

"No. Happened off season. We figured the hunters got the message." Martina rustled in her top desk drawer. "I have the sheriff's card." She set a white business card against her computer screen. Snatching the arrows off the desk, she tossed them on her credenza behind her chair as if to get the evidence away from us.

A bit of familiar dark red between her credenza and tall file cabinet in the crowded corner captured my immediate interest.

Rising, I gave Martina my attention. "Thanks. Let us know if the sheriff wants to question us." Logan stood, towering over me, and I was grateful for his presence. More so when he blocked Martina's view of me while I checked out that corner. *Yep. Lying sack of cow dung.* Half a dozen arrows with the same red plastic feathers nestled against the wall in the corner.

Logan and I left the offices. Landscape lights flickered on outside and someone had lit dozens of tiki torches surrounding the three fire pits in the center green.

"The arrows came from someone here." I drew Logan

under the eaves of the dining hall.

"I saw them in the corner." He stuck his hands in his front pockets, jangling a pocket full of pebbles he'd gathered earlier for the craft room.

"Coincidence?"

"Arrows and fletchings come in all sizes and colors. The local sports store probably stocks them."

I adopted the Stance, hands on hips, curl to my frown. "Get real. Who hunts with a bow and arrow in the 21st century?"

"Poachers who don't want to risk the sound of guns."

"Seriously? There're some screwed up people at this camp."

"It's so farfetched, Al."

"What about this?" I dug in my backpack and showed him the crumpled wildflowers and note cards. "Laurel got one too. No one else got one, but Martina wore a hair wreath today in the Trading Post with the same flowers. Random or not?"

"Do you want to leave camp?" His intense gaze riveted me to the spot.

"No way. 'Cause I want to see Mrs. A and get to the bottom of this flippin' freakshow. These aren't random events, poachers, or hoaxes."

"You think you're a target?"

"Not really. I think we've been too accessible, though. As if we're in the way, or they're inside my head reading my thoughts. I can't imagine any camper or CL being a target. For what?" I tossed up my hands. "Can you think of any weirdness from your past summers here?" I refused to believe I may be a mark a second time in my life. Once was more than enough.

"Nah." He shuffled his feet between mine, knocking his shoe to the side of my checkered sneakers. The touch of his shoe infiltrated the intangible armor I'd thrown up around me.

I flicked the beads on my leather band, taking comfort in my smallest suit of armor. Laurel had given it to me from a class trip to San Francisco three years ago which I was forced to miss. It was a survivor band with ten beads to add for each year of survival. Little did she or anyone know how important it had become to me. “We need to rejoin the routine before Dante mows us down with his bad-ass BB gun.”

The dining hall had mostly cleared out as kids finished their dinner. They milled around the fire pits, awaiting the campfires and the promised surprise. As I handed a tray to Logan, I spied Laurel and Nick by the kitchen door.

“Where’ve you been?” Laurel rushed over in her skintight jeans and midriff-baring, second skin T-shirt. Her boobs stretched the T-shirt out so far, her pink bra was visible through the thin material. “I brought you a change of clothes. Didn’t look like you’d made it to your cabin.”

“Thanks. Tell you later, ’kay?” I loaded mushy Spanish rice, canned refried beans, and spicy ground hamburger on my tray, then spied the empty plate of tortillas. “Shoot,” I grumbled.

Logan handed me another plate with a cold flour tortilla on it, and I dumped the rice, beans, and burger onto the tortilla. “Thanks.” The cheese bowl held dry crumbs. “Suppose there’s no more cheese, huh?” I asked Nick.

“Ask and I shall deliver, my fair lady’s best friend.” Nick loped into the kitchen and brought us a bowl of fresh grated cheese. “Saved for Dante.”

“In that case.” I scooped up a huge handful and sprinkled it on my burrito and on Logan’s burrito. He loved cheddar cheese as much as I did. We left mouse-sized morsels for Dante. I topped my burrito off with tomatoes and scraggly lettuce. Must get in my veggies. The serving counter was as bare as Mother Hubbard's cupboard on a good day. "No dessert, or is it all gone?"

"Well, hon, if you'd been here during announcements, you'd know that we'll have dessert at the campfires tonight," Laurel mimicked my mother. Not sure why, but it sounded weird. Mom used *hon* when annoyed with me. Was Laurel feeling left out? I glanced at her flirting with Nick. *No dice. She had her hands full.*

The tables had emptied. Some kids had left their plates and empty glasses for the cleanup crew. Not good. Everyone was supposed to clear his or her places to help out. I gorged on the tepid burrito. My belly rumbled, searching for a better host. The bland burrito should appease it.

While Logan and I ate, Laurel and Nick regaled us with the announcements we'd missed. The most important was that we were set to leave at ten tomorrow for the gold mine and had to be ready to travel in shifts since the camp only had four vehicles.

Twilight descended and landscape lights created amber puddles, scattering ghostly shapes in the murky woods surrounding the lawn. Through the front floor to ceiling bank of windows, I spied Marco with the older boys carting wood to the fire pits. The boys had already built kindling teepees in each pit. Other kids spread out on blankets on the grass, all in innocent and carefree fun.

A gulp of milk cleared the taste of dinner from my mouth. At least they couldn't screw up milk. I glanced at the expiration date on the cartoon, satisfied it was still fresh. I picked up my plate and gathered the other discarded dishes on the table. Nick sprinted over and took them from me. "Thanks, Chef Nick. I take it you weren't part of the gourmet crew tonight?"

His wicked grin lured me in, and I liquefied a little on the spot. Lucky Laurel was one stoked girl for a reason. I envied her a little, but I didn't deny her. Life was too short for those emotions and petty peeves between best friends.

"My creativity needs a break. Wait for tomorrow, though. Chef Nick will blow your socks off." Nick winked, hiking his eyebrow comically, then he scuttled away, dishes and trays loading down his arms.

"Let's get close to the fire." Laurel sidled to my side, mesmerized by Nick's escape.

"Keep close," Logan said behind us.

Laurel threw her hands in the air. "Now what? Can we slide through a day without new intrigue setting up shop in your paranoia?"

"If you weren't gaga over Chef Nick, you'd already be in the know."

Laurel flushed from her forehead down to her toes. *Laurel blushed? Did hell freeze over?* "Well, we did come here to scope out the boy situation." She sniffed to enhance her point.

"Scope them out. Not lose yourself completely." I didn't aim to sound mean, but my voice held a tinge of sarcasm I didn't quite feel. My own absences and suspicions had sucked me in more than I'd planned. My summer camp fun had spun into summer camp creeptastic territory. At least I'd retained my freedom. And not one phone call from my mom. That was almost worth the price of bow and arrow target practice.

Logan slung his arm around our shoulders. "No fighting, musket-rats. The campfires await your lovely presences," he mimicked Nick.

"Nick Constantine doesn't sound well on you, karate dork." Laurel ducked out from under his arm, leaving Logan and me hugging. In that moment, I wanted to escape the twisted jumble my mind and hormones had adopted. First step, slinking out from under Logan's arm and putting proper distance between two people who were nothing more than acquaintances. Right? I pressed my wristband into my hip, my left eye flinching from the sting of the tiny pin.

Marco approached, Jesse in tow. Odd that we all hung out in one group, yet the other girl CLs, Dawn and Lupe, had their own agenda with Neal, Jeff, and Richie. Just as well that I didn't have to hide the inside of my brain from a gaggle of other untrustworthy souls.

Marco patted his belt loop, his polo shirt covering a small bulge. "Allie, can I talk to you?"

Logan made a clicking sound in his throat. "We have a short leadership session before the campfire."

"Cover for me?" The leadership training material was in the manual we'd already gotten. As far as the Teen Leadership Program, Dante and Martina had given it the figurative boot into the lake. No big deal, I didn't come to camp to be their puppet-in-training.

Logan's eyes bored into my backside all the way from the dining hall. The mystical holes pierced my skin in a mix of guilt and triumph.

White fairy lights lit up the enclosed patio, scrolled around the poles, and laced the lattice cover. A small table with four chairs filled the small space. Unlit candles decorated the center of the table, and potted hydrangeas filled the corners. Someone had transformed the previously bland patio into a magical romantic setting.

"Wow. It's gorgeous out here. Did you do this?"

"Part of Dante's surprise tonight. It's nice in the daytime too, when the waterfall's flowing and you can see the vines and blooms in the lattice." He plucked a walkie-talkie off his belt and handed it to me. "These don't have vibration mode. You'll have to leave it turned low. If you need to call me, find a private place," Marco said.

CHAPTER 12

Nervous goosebumps chased in a wave down my arms. "You sure it's safe hiking up to Mrs. A's cabin? Is it that important?"

"My mom's a lawyer, and Mrs. A had her do some legal research." Marco patted his waist, and paper crinkled beneath his shirt. "She wanted me to hand deliver it and not say a word to anyone. Didn't want to send by email either. Not sure why." He lifted his shoulder in a half shrug. "I'm just the messenger."

"Did you think all the secrecy a little weird?"

"I thought it might be a surprise for Martina. But ever since I met Dante and saw how much Martina has changed, I've had a bad feeling." He blew out a breath as though his exhalation cleansed his soul. "Don't rat me out to anyone."

"Things aren't kosher here, are they?"

He combed his fingers through his unruly black hair, leaving it more tousled. "You sense that when you've never been here before?"

"I feel like I have by the way Laurel describes it every summer." I'd always lapped up her every word like a flower in the woods starving for sunshine.

Marco opened the gate to the private patio. "Here's the plan. I'll make an appearance at the fire. Once I split, keep Dante occupied. Martina won't go to bed until the kids go to their cabins. If Dante leaves for whatever reason, call me."

I slipped through the gate, and it clicked shut with a quiet snick. We scattered in different directions, guided by the glow of landscape lights trailing to the center lawn.

Three fires burned, flames shooting toward the sky as the fire devoured the kindling. Kids circled the fire rings, all attention fastened on a picnic table supporting Dante standing on the tabletop and Martina standing beside the table next to a large covered rectangular object. The heavenly aroma of fresh popcorn pervaded the air. Huge bowls of fluffy white kernels, snack-sized candies, and troughs of ice and soda covered a table. Talk about treats. They'd broken out the precious hard stuff.

"Hey, kids," Dante yelled. The din died to a dull roar. "Tonight's movie night!"

Martina tore the cover off a large outdoor monitor. "Tonight we have a great feature." She held up *Space Nerds*, a PG-13 movie that came out on DVD last Friday. More excitement swelled the warm night. "Plus we have movie theater treats, and later we're having a raffle. Nick and Jesse will hand out tickets in a minute. Three winners will have the chance to pick three friends for a separate private dinner, games, and movie of your choice on the exclusive Dragonfly Café patio."

The kids lined up for their treats as I hid behind trees and slipped on the jeans and hoodie Laurel had brought down from my cabin. I stuck the two-way radio in my hoodie pocket and zipped back to the girls. I counted heads to make sure all were present.

"You sitting with Nick?" I tossed my tote on the ground near the girls, keeping Dante and Martina in view.

"No, we're supposed to sit with our groups. If you'd graced us with your presence you would know the rules." Laurel munched on popcorn and tossed a handful at me to lighten her words. "Tell me what's going on with you and Marco, where you and Logan disappeared to earlier, Nancy Drew."

"We're just getting to know each other." The snick and hiss of my cola tab drowned out her rude titter.

"What. Ever." She rolled her eyes, not buying what I was selling, but respecting me enough not to pry...too hard. "Why'd you and Logan hang behind at the lake? That's an about face from your earlier stance on him."

"You're not gonna believe this." I wanted to keep my self-defense lessons to myself. Laurel and I told each other everything, but once in a blue moon I needed to keep something mine for a while before she blabbed it to the world. "Someone shot arrows at us in the woods."

"What?" she shrieked loud enough to wake the dead. Heads swiveled, and she crammed a wad of popcorn in her mouth. Chewing furiously, she took a swig of grocery store brand lemon-lime soda. "Did they hit you?" She felt up my chest and arms, her hands grazing me like a cop frisking a kleptomaniac. "Did they hit Logan? Talk to me." Her voice rose hysterically.

Patting the air to force her to take it down a dozen notches, I recited the story and my suspicions.

"Holy crapola." She tapped the side of her nose. "Al, I'm scared. This is getting real."

"You don't want to go home, do you? Logan asked me the same."

She hesitated a moment, her brow going all frowny.

"Not for this, but I'm freaked out."

I patted her leg, my finger catching in a fashionable hole in her skintight jeans, poking my fingernail into the soft flesh of her thigh. "Oww," we both said in unison.

The monitor flickered on. Mrs. Amadori filled the screen, as Creepy McCreepy had promised. I craned my neck to see every corner of the monitor, to find a discrepancy as I had the first time. Mrs. Amadori sat at her kitchen table, hands in her lap, encouraging the campers on our *Survivor* games, telling us she missed us and would visit later in the week. Most kids hardly paid attention as they chatted and whooped it up. The beloved camp director had already been replaced in their minds and hearts by Dante. I choked on a piece of popcorn, and coughed up the offending piece, barely surviving Laurel's thumps on my back.

The screen blinked, and the sound system chased away our talk time. Dante sat surrounded by Chef, Jesse's boys, Neal and his minions. They bantered and joked as the movie's opening credits and previews rolled. I palmed the silent walkie-talkie in my pocket.

Marco skulked along the fringes of the lawn by the tree line. He slinked into the dark woods, where he became the ghost of a shadow.

The girls circled us, and I tuned one eye to the movie. My other eye remained glued to Dante, unsticking long enough to eyeball Martina. Ten minutes later Dante picked his way through the close-knit kids. My heart seized up.

I jumped up, stepping on fingers. A couple girls yelped. "Sorry. Sorry. Be right back."

Ducking, I half-waddled, half ran toward Dante, trying to avoid tromping on more hands. I hid in the shadows where Marco had stood before he'd vanished into the darkness. Dante stopped to talk to Martina sitting with the oldest girls, then took off toward the dining hall.

Smoke blew in my face. My eyes watered and stung, but I managed to trail the tree line to the dining hall without boinking my face on a tree trunk. Dante slipped inside, and I flew through the gate leading to the private enclosed patio. Someone had turned off the fairy lights and darkness cloaked me. A light glowed inside, enough to make out the kitchen.

Dante kept peering over his shoulder as he slid into the kitchen. *Crud on a cracker.* My pulse beat so loud in my ears I figured he'd hear it and bust me. I stole into the dining hall and crouched behind the serving counter, inching my way to the kitchen. Hefting his massive keychain, he unlocked that storage room Nick had told us about. A minute later, he strode out carrying a bottle of booze. Then the unthinkable happened. He walked toward me.

Easing into the darkness, I banged into a rolling cart, my rear knocking a discarded spatula onto the floor, where it clattered so loud, they probably heard the noise on the other side of the lake.

"Who's there?" Dante demanded, his footsteps pounding on the floor.

My escape vanished. I stretched to my full height and made it appear like I'd just entered the room. I doubt I fooled him. "Hey, Dante. Came in for a glass of water." I retrieved the spatula, setting it on the counter. "Sorry, I didn't know anyone was here."

He narrowed his eyes and hid the bottle at his side. "The kitchen's off limits after hours. Campers are to use the water dispenser outside." He trod to the refrigerator and returned with a bottle of water. "On me."

I took the bottle, meeting his grin. "So what's with the wine? You sneaking it into the movie theater?" A nervous trill flitted in my bloodstream.

"Actually, I was taking it up to Aunt Carla. Helps her mood."

His right eye ticked. Seriously, did he have a nervous eye when he lied? *Well, hello precious.*

Racking my brain, I lurched forward, crooking my arm through his, forcing down a shiver. "I could use a drop or two." I cooed seductively, although I think it came out tacky beyond belief since my nervous high-pitch sounded like Miss Piggy.

Dante's spine grew rigid, and he disentangled his arm from mine. "We don't do things like that here. We could get shut down."

"I'll never tell." I fake-pouted. Wow, the dude seriously had a conscience. Had I underestimated him? But contributing to the delinquency of a minor and murder were two very different crimes.

He winked. "I know. As your elder, I'm responsible." He held the bottle up high.

"Okay." I imbued my words with enough fake dejection as I could suffer without up-chucking my dinner.

"Good girl." He patted my head, and I suppressed my urge to bark. "I need to go before Carla dozes off. I promised her this special treat tonight since she can't join you at the movie." No eye tic followed his words.

"Can I go with you and meet her?" I held my breath. "I'll keep you company on the walk."

"Not a good idea. She's not up for much company. You know, drugs and all." He stepped toward the door. "Go enjoy the movie."

Drugs and alcohol? Give me a break. I have a brain. At least half a brain. His eye didn't need to twitch for that moronic lie. "Sure, see you at the movie."

After he left, I sprinted to the enclosed patio, fumbling for the walkie-talkie. I rotated the dial on to crackling static, cursing as I muffled it under my clothing against my waist. The darkness pressed in on me, but I felt safe in the small enclosed patio…until tiny footsteps scratched across the brick floor. Stifling a scream behind my fist, I leaped on a chair, planting my butt on the table. The rodent scurried along the periphery of the patio, its eyes catching the light from inside the dining hall. It stared at me, twin glowing pinpoints willing me to breathe. I hauled my knees up close to my chest, losing myself in a major moment of weakness. The rat broke eye contact and scurried into the dark.

Hands numb, I spoke into the two-way radio. "You there?" Dead silence greeted me. Marco had already set the radios to the same channel, so I thumbed the volume up just in case. "He's on the move to Mrs. A's cabin," I whisper-shouted. More silence. *Come on, dude, answer.*

Smoke drifted over from the fire pits in a gray cloud, and I buried my face in my sleeve. Laughter rose from the kids enjoying their movie.

"Get out now!" I hopped off the table and followed the landscape lights to the office building. Screw the radios. Dim lights lit my way up the hill path, past the offices, down another hill. Hard rock music drifted out of a middle cabin, which I assumed was assigned to one of the mysterious workers I'd never met.

Dante rounded a bend in the woods, his frame silhouetted by the blazing porch lights of the first four cabins. Lights radiated inside the first two cabins, glowing through the slanted blinds. I crouched in the woods off the path overlooking the clearing above the cabins, fighting the darkness stealing air from my lungs. I feared using the walkie-talkie now in case Dante heard it. He sauntered to his cabin.

A shadowy shape crashed into the bushes in front of Mrs. A's cabin, the same bushes Logan and I had hid in the first night. Marco lost his balance and fell against the wall with a shattering thump.

Dante spun around. "Who's there?" He set the bottle on an accent table and wielded a flashlight. "Show yourself now. Kids aren't supposed to be up here. Anyone caught may be sent home. You know the rules."

Actually, I didn't know that rule. Maybe I needed to do a better job of reading the CL manual. For the moment, I had to help Marco escape. I scrabbled into the debris carpeting the ground, feeling for pebbles.

"What are you doing here?" An unfamiliar man's New England accent behind me sent my body twitching. So close I smelled his musky cologne.

"Girl, I asked what you're doing here." A large hand clamped onto my shoulder. "This area's off limits. You're heading home now."

Terror rooted me to the forest floor like a hundred-year-old oak. Before I knew what I was doing, I ducked beneath his hand and fled into the woods. Branches lashed at me, catching on my clothes.

"Damn girl. Get the hell back here," the man shouted, his accent growing thicker as if he'd just stepped off the bean town plane.

He crashed through the woods and threw himself at me, his arms wrapping around my torso. I thrashed my body and kicked various parts of him to no avail. His hand covered my mouth as he lugged me upright.

"How 'bout you and me have a talk?" he growled in my ear. He jerked on my right arm, and I stood stock-still.

"What do you want?" I panted, trying to calm my thundering pulse.

"This is no place for a smart girl like you, if you know what I mean. Time you headed home. Understand?"

A bewildering fog swirled in my brain. "Why do you care if I stay or go?"

"Oh, I care, all right. You're interfering in my

business." He yanked my hair, forcing my head back.

I pinched back a yelp. I wouldn't give him the satisfaction of knowing he'd hurt me. "What if I don't go home?"

"Then you may end up like that rat. Know what I mean?" He tugged my head again and let go. I tumbled forward, falling on my hands and knees in a patch of crunchy leaves and twigs. His threat shot shockwaves down my chest.

As I lifted off the ground, he vanished. Not a shadow indicated he'd ever existed. Boulders stood like stalwarts a few feet away, and I hid behind them. Campground lights dotted the distance. I shivered more from the unknown than from the cooling night. Numb, I waited five minutes to ensure the man didn't return before inching my way toward the lights so I didn't end up face-planting into a tree trunk or trip over the million branches and rocks carpeting the forest floor. The slight scent of burning firewood calmed me. Would that man make good on his threat? What did he mean that I was interfering in his business? What would happen if I didn't go home? Questions peppered my head like sodden snowflakes, melting onto my epic confusion.

Squirrels and other animals I didn't want to name crashed through the forest, grating on my last nerve. Arms to my sides, the night enveloped me, and I wished I'd brought a flashlight. Even though the campground was close, I stood alone in a foreign world. I could get lost out here and no one'd ever find me. Of course, my survival skills needed a brush up. Logan's self-defense lessons only traveled so far. They didn't do a lick of good against Mr. Boston Tea Harbor reject.

I walked for what seemed like hours in the dark woods to find a path to the campground until the radio woke up. "Allie, you there?"

The last voice in the world I wanted to hear squealed through the tinny speaker.

CHAPTER 13

Ducking into shadows behind the kitchen, I pulled the two-way out and thumbed down the volume before Dante became the town crier.

"Allie, I know you're there. Answer me now." His pissed voice lacked any semblance of concern.

"Oh, mother trucker." I gritted my teeth. *Did Marco give me up? Did Dante's No-Neck friend narc on me? Think, think!*

"Answer me," Dante yelled. "Who's on the other end?"

I turned the two-way off and threw it far into the woods. I hated losing the gizmo, but I refused to let it sell me out or dump me on a bus heading for home.

The lighted path took me past the girls' cabins to the center green. I followed the dark edges, creeping within the shadows, until a man-sized silhouette engulfed my path.

"Where've you been?" Logan ground out, folding his arms over his chest. "I've been searching everywhere."

"Bathroom." My lying had become epic. I wasn't ready to confess what'd happened. Logan would glue himself to me, or call my mom. Laurel, the current Town Crier, might unwittingly blurt it out. I couldn't risk Marco getting in trouble, or the law coming down on me in the form of Logan or Dante.

"Alone?" He reached out to touch me, withdrew his hand.

Turning the tables, I gripped his wrist. "If Dante or anyone asks, tell them I was with you all night. Do it for me, Logan. Please. You owe me."

"I don't like the sound of that." He grunted out a caveman sound.

His protective growly voice hit a strange new button inside me. Had Logan seriously come to camp to atone for his desertion of me in the mall and after The Incident? "Logan—" I started to ask the inevitable question, stopped. It wasn't the right place. We needed privacy for the conversation that would end and begin me. Instead, I returned to my present conundrum. "Have you seen Marco?"

"Haven't seen him since dinner."

In my uncontrollable jittery avoidance, I kicked pine needles over his sneaker. I steered him around and walked toward the lawn. We slipped to the ground next to Laurel.

"You found her," Laurel said. Heads rotated.

"Shhh!"

"Why'd you rush away?"

"The bathroom. I wasn't feeling well, if you catch my drift." I hated talking about bathroom habits, but I was shooting blanks from my arsenal of fibs.

The rest of the night flew by uneventfully. Neither Marco nor Dante returned to the movie. I wanted to make sure Marco was okay, but the Logan & Laurel Watchdog Company refused to let me out of their sight.

After a restless night of agonizing over everything under the sun revolving around Logan, Marco, Dante, and the mysterious caveman, morning came too fast and not fast enough. I had big enough bags under my eyes that I didn't need to bring a bag on our overnighter at the gold mine. The girls awoke way too early, eager to pack. We were about to head down to breakfast when a knock shook our door in its frame. The girls quieted as I peered through the blinds on the door window.

Dante. Blood drained down to my toes. I was screwed to hell and back. I'd made one decision as I tossed and turned over night: going home wasn't an option.

Slipping out to the porch, I shut the door behind me. "Did you need me?" I hugged my arms to myself, covering my nightshirt, trying to kill my nervousness.

"We need to talk. Tell your girls to go to Laurel's cabin." His brusque tone brooked no nonsense.

My heart thudded as I went inside and shooed the girls out. They all greeted Dante like he was the second coming. Outdoor movie night had been a big hit, and the kids clamored for a repeat. It erased their memories of Dante's brutality against Marco in the cafeteria. One of my girls, Nicole, won a dinner and movie date too. All my girls were on cloud nine.

I hung on the porch while Dante teetered on the ground two steps down, probably suffering from a hangover from his bottle of booze. I rocked back on my heels, feeling a degree of superiority standing above him. I hoped he didn't make me sit.

He held no punches. "Were you and Marco using two-way radios last night?"

I decided to come clean. Sort of. "We had a pair

earlier in the day at the lake. You know, goofing off. I lost mine in the woods when those archers shot at Logan and me." I sniffed hard, half faking my radiating tension. The target practice incident was my get out of Dragonfly jail card.

"You weren't lurking around the staff cabins last night?" He raked a hand through his damp hair, his exasperation riding the waves of the citrus shampoo he emitted into the air.

"No. I've never been there with Marco." True that. "I haven't seen him since after dinner at the campfire." Had Mr. Strange Brute in the woods ratted me out?

"Why'd you leave the movie?"

A blush torched my face. "Umm...if you must know, I had nervous stomach issues...from being shot at in the woods." I forced my blame upon him.

He glanced down at his shuffling feet. When he lifted his head, a grim line tightened his lips. "Sorry about that. Martina called the sheriff, and we're doing everything to prevent it from happening again." He paused as if he wanted to say more. "Hunters are forbidden in this area due to the kids. Someone was playing a game."

"A deadly game." I retorted. "I mean, I could call my parents and report it myself."

Capitulating, he held up a splayed hand. "Not necessary," he said too quickly for my tastes. He was deflecting, and I highly doubted Martina had called the sheriff. Heck, I hadn't seen anyone drive to the property since we'd arrived on Saturday.

"What's the deal with the two-way radios?" I asked.

"They're off limits."

"I didn't know that."

"Marco knows it, yet he got caught red-handed." Dante scoured the area. "You're off the hook." He smiled his charming smile that lured in all the campers, girls and boys both. The smile of a pit viper...or a kidnapper. Or a mad killer.

"May I go now? The girls are waiting for me."

He stepped aside. "Find me at the gold mine and we'll go over your map duties."

A half hour later, I waited alone at the *T* in the path for Marco. Logan and his boys sauntered down the trail first.

"Waiting for me?" His smile broke across his sunburned face, beguiling, encompassing, and unnerving to the nth degree.

Mental head bang. "Actually, I need to talk to Marco. Something Dante wants us to do."

His smile evaporated. Relief trickled through me as Marco trotted down the path behind his racing boys. Whistles and catcalls followed as the oldest boys caught up to Logan's gang. There were a couple cute sixteen-year-olds in the group, but my hands were shackled dealing with the two boys glowering at each other beside me.

"I'll save you a seat." Logan fired a pointed stare at Marco and stomped off.

Marco lured me off the trail into the woods, his pale face haunted, as though he'd slept in a cave of hungry bears last night.

"What happened? I tried to warn you when Dante left the kitchen."

"I know. I had to keep a low profile. Someone was tracking me around the cabins." He slid his hand underneath his polo and massaged his ribs. When he winced, I rolled his polo up from the hem.

Purple and black bruises climbed the left side of his torso. Every muscle in my body tensed.

"Who did this?" I breathed out. "Dante?"

"One of his goons, right before Dante showed up." He

pulled his shirt down. "I'd never seen him before. He might be a contractor working on the two empty cabins."

"You okay?" I took his hand in mine, linking our fingers, hoping to transfer healing vibes, or at least my concern, in our touch.

"I'll live." A muscle flicked in his jaw. "Mrs. A wasn't there. Lights were on in her cabin, but it didn't appear like she's been there for a while. Her day calendar—"

"Still on June 26," I finished for him.

He didn't display any surprise. "I saw you and Logan there the first night. I was the one who ran off and sidetracked Dante's attention."

"What?" My surprise knew no bounds.

"I tried to take the envelope to Mrs. A the first night."

"Were you hooking up with Martina that night?" I asked slowly, unsure how he'd respond.

"Martina?" He staggered back, disgust screwing up his face. "Hell no. We don't have *that* kind of relationship."

"Maybe it was that dude who beat on you, then."

Marco gripped my shoulders. "Tell me what you suspect."

I didn't want to go there, but I had already spilled too many madly jumping beans. "Did Dante find the envelope?"

"No, thankfully. After that asshole pounded me into the ground and took off, Dante told me I had two choices: either go home or obey the rat bastard."

"You chose the latter."

"I want to find out what's going on. So do you, if I'm not crazy off my ass." His thumb caressed the side of my neck.

Needles followed his touch, and I eased away. What would Logan think? I sucked in air. *Whoa...did I just ask myself that?* Both my investigation and my non-love life had wandered into Complicated.

"We need to chill. Dante's no-neck caught me in the woods last night." I regaled Marco with my story. "Why would Dante let cavemen beat up kids?"

"I'm not exactly a kid."

I pinched his arm. "You know what I mean."

"Dante says Mrs. A's in her cabin. She's not. You willing to help me work it out?"

"You kidding? I've been trying to do that the minute I heard Mrs. A had hurt herself." Marco let go of my shoulders, his own shoulders slumping as his tension drained out.

He tapped his watch. "We better go before Dante sends in his commandos."

Side-by-side, we headed toward the dining hall. "We shouldn't be seen together. Let me go first. You follow a few minutes later through the enclosed patio." We hung in the woods before splitting up.

"I'll try to use the landline in the office before we go to the gold mine," he said.

Dare I tell him I have a contraband phone? I twirled my leather band around my wrist. "What will you tell your mom?"

"That Carla's not here and ask her to find out where she is. She'll be discreet."

"Have her check the local nursing homes. Martina told someone on the phone that Dante took her out of here for better care."

"Then he's lying to all of us."

"That's what I've been saying." I bobbed my head. "Catch you on the flipside. If you can't get to the phone, wait until I can help."

I found Logan at a table in a corner of the dining hall. He'd already bagged my breakfast, another gourmet meal of scrambled eggs, toast, and an oatmeal chaser. Not the

Chef Nick gourmet kind either. The meal appeared as appetizing as the first day.

"Where's Laurel and Nick?" I covered my eggs in ketchup, salted, and peppered them. I needed the protein for a long day ahead and forced the first bite down.

"Packing the perishables for camping." He'd eaten his meal already. Watching me, he stacked three protein bars by my plate. "Nick found them in the locked storage room."

A buoyancy flowed over my limbs. "Awesome. Thank you." Logan eased closer, revving up my pulses. He remembered how much I liked protein bars for quick pick-me-ups. At this rate, I may need them. I dowsed my oatmeal with brown sugar and stirred it in to thicken the thin Goldilocks fare.

Logan tensed. "What's Marco's deal?"

Expecting the question, I decided to bring Logan into a tiny bubble in my circle of trust. Laurel's membership was pending approval at the door, a loose cannon I'd rather not involve while she was fixated on Nick. Multi-tasking was not one of her talents. I downloaded what Marco had done and about being on the receiving end of Dante's smackdown. Logan's seething body and fisting hands inspired me to withhold the tidbit where the man caught me in the woods.

He grunted angrily. "This is screwed up. I'm calling my dad."

"Then what? We all go home?"

"At least we'd be alive." Storm clouds swirled in his eyes, and a *V* shaped line formed on the bridge of his nose.

"Do you honestly believe our lives are at stake?"

"Someone shot at us." He pounded his fist on the table.

"Shhh." I cupped my hand over his mouth, a gentle

touch he took strength from by the unclenching of his fist. "We'll catch more flies with honey. Remember my grandmother used to say that?"

"You're having fun." The truth dawned on him, and his jaw hung open, forcing my hand off him.

Tears sprang to my eyes. "If I leave, who'll figure this out? It's better than sitting at home all day, picking cat hair off my legs. This experience will get me out of the house more, once my parents see that I can handle myself out in the big bad world again."

Air whooshed out of him, and he trembled once against me. It felt as if he wanted to say more he couldn't dredge up from the depths of his soul. Without pressing him further, I luxuriated in the calm companionship he offered. Memories of my tween crush didn't try to boot out these fresh, new feelings. Feelings I still had a hard time naming. Logan and I had a history to dig through, uncomfortable truths that needed baring. Would he bare them? Did I want to hear the truth? Was I better off just taking my anger and walking away from him at the end of our two weeks, none the wiser? *Head smack. I'm so freaking lame.*

Laurel entered the dining hall from the kitchen door behind the counter. "Hey, musket-rats." She ruffled Logan's hair. "What's the haps?"

"Where's Nick?" I pocketed the protein bars.

"Loading the truck." She settled her hip on the table. "You two good? No more target practice?"

I nodded. "Girls ready to go?"

We were in the first troop to head to the gold mine, part of the tent crew. They must've picked our crew to learn a new task. I think I was the only one with tent-building experience. I doubted any of DragonLily Flyers knew how to erect a flagpole, let alone a tent.

"Playing outside." Laurel turned to Logan. "Your

troop's following us, right?"

"Yeah. Keep an eye on Allie, will ya?" Logan stood so close behind me, my hair lifted on the top of my head with each breath he took.

I spun and grabbed his hands stuck in the bunny ear position over my head. Our fingers entwined as I pressed our tangled hands against his shoulders. His goofy, crooked grin grew strangely intense, and I pressed forward against him, playfully wrestling his hands. "How about some respect here? I'm the paranoid one."

"We need to ground your paranoia in reality." Logan pretended to trip me, but I anticipated his classic move, one step ahead like back in the day.

"No. You need to side with my cracked ideas." And not so crazy ideas.

Laurel whacked her brother's arm. "Allie's the queen of crazy. Let her go before her cooties jump ship and you wind up giftwrapped in a straitjacket."

Reminiscent of old times, we tangled, giggling, barely standing upright. The three musket-rats together again. I wanted to cry for the four years of separation, and glory in the nebulous new pact we'd made.

A black spot soon marred our cotton candy cloud.

Logan stiffened. We stood in a line in front of Dante, straightening our clothes and tousled hair like good soldiers in front of their domineering commander.

He shot me a stony glare. Had I worn out my welcome with my earlier threat about calling home? I sidled closer to Dante and caught a gander at his tablet screen.

"Allie, you're off map duty," he announced matter-of-factly.

A picture of a mine shaft situated along a creek under the headline, "Hidden Gold in Amadori Hills? Amadori or Cardona? Myth or Reality?" flashed on his tablet. Before I could read any further, he turned and pounded away.

CHAPTER 14

On the way to snag our gear, Laurel prattled about her über (not so) secret obsession with Nick. Half of me listened with appropriate responses. I tried, I really did. But a volcano sputtered to life within me.

Laurel sensed my moodiness. "I think you're on Dante's shit list."

"You're observant," Logan replied, shifting aside to avoid Laurel's smack. She ended up hitting my shoulder. I deserved it for not paying attention to her rave about Boy Wonder.

"I threatened to call my parents about the shooting arrow debacle if he didn't back off." I cringed, ready for Logan's outrage.

"You what?" Logan stopped and rounded on me.

"His pea brain worked out that Marco and I used walkie-talkies last night." I gave them the down-low.

His hand fisted in an uncharacteristic move. "You need to tell me this shit."

Oh boy, when the curse words fly, I knew I'd hit his

buttons. But it incensed me, infringed upon my freedom.

"You're not my father," I exploded, clenching my head. I plunged through my annoying bodyguards.

"Al," Laurel cried behind me. "Don't be this way."

"What way do you want me to be? Tell me, so I can get it right."

"We're just looking out for each other," she replied.

I spun around. "No. You're babysitting me." I thumped my chest. "I can handle myself pretty well out in the big bad world. No one's kidnapped me yet. You wanted fun, and you're having a blast with Nick."

"Are you saying you're not having fun?" She chomped on her bottom lip, tugged her shirt's poor defenseless hem, *and* rubbed her nose. *Oy vey, I'd done my best to upset her.*

I took her hand to soothe her ruffled feathers. "I'm having fun. I dig this intrigue biz. I mean, check this out. Dante was reading an article on his tablet about gold in the Amadori hills. I bet that's why we're having an excursion," I did quotes in the air, "to the old Amadori gold mine."

"Wow, you're a sponge today." A healthy dose of respect flanked Laurel's voice.

"You've always known about my overkill observation skills." I gave her a quick hug.

"What do you think?" I let Logan in, but I refused to apologize for my reaction or my secrecy. Not everything was meant to be shared. I had Marco's trust to maintain.

"About the gold mine?" He stroked his jaw, his sunburn already fading into golden tan, coloring the edges of his geekiness. Or was I seeing Logan in a new light? "I'm sure other Amadoris from the past have already found the gold," he added.

"Then why read the article now?" Laurel asked.

"Exactly." I beamed her a smile, glad her curiosity

had hooked up with mine. "We'll find out later." I hiked up the path before Dante the Dragon swooped out of the sky and lit a fire on our rear ends.

It didn't take long for us to round up our gear and kids, and return to the loading zone in the campground parking lot. A contagious eagerness hung in the mountain air under a crystal blue sky. As we loaded the girls onto the tiny bus, we all buzzed with excitement.

The drive to the gold mine took fifteen minutes, situated in the lower foothills near the river where gold was once plentiful in the 1800s. The camp workers had already set up two large canopies for gathering places between the tree line and the river. Someone had dug fire pits and stacked wood near each pit. Supplies lined the walls of a decrepit log cabin, and portable toilets and sinks sat off along the woods enclosed by hanging tarps.

"Gotta give the Amadori siblings credit here. They've done a half-baked job at setting this puppy up," I said. We caught our sleeping bags as counselor and driver Marty tossed them off the van's rooftop cargo hold.

"Probably took lessons from Mrs. A." Laurel dusted her hands on her skimpy denim shorts.

"Or covering their butts, keeping everyone happy," I muttered. "Making sure no one buys a ticket home."

"No doubt, oh wise one." Laurel tossed the last two sleeping bags to Serena and Carrie.

Marty sped off to transport the next group of campers. Two more vehicles drove in, carting the oldest boys and Marco. I waved and he gave me a thumbs up. Had he contacted his mom?

"Where do we set up?" Serena asked.

Mud brown and hunter green tarps lined the ground in a checkerboard pattern, fifty feet from the river. Tent bundles lay on each tarp. Our team flags marked our tarps. "Aha." I pointed at our purple flag. Our group's space was on the interior side closest to the woods.

"Hey, girls," Marco greeted us. "Let's work on your tents, then we'll do the others."

Carrie draped herself down his arm. I remembered my own puppy love days at her age. At that moment, I yearned for Logan's presence. I'd come to rely upon his nearness, and being apart from him left a weird vacancy in my chest.

Marco directed while the girls erected two room-sized tents. They unrolled their sleeping bags, and Laurel tossed out commands, in seventh heaven directing her minions. Admiring our handiwork around the camp, Marco and I walked toward the river to escape the increasing crowd of kids. We remained in plain view so it didn't appear like we were planning a heist or using illegal walkie-talkies.

"Did you call your mom?" I picked up a flat oval rock and skimmed it across the river, watching it touch the surface four times before it sank in a ripple of water.

"No." He watched my stone skip a calm pool of the river. "You're good at that." He found another skipping stone and threw it. It plopped into the water and sank.

"Logan taught me. I used to camp with his family before—" I covered my mouth with my hand. "Before he went to boarding school," I finished, muffled behind my hand.

"You don't like talking about it, huh?" He tossed another stone across the river, skipping it three times.

Water rushed over boulders in the river, gurgling near the shoreline. A hawk swooped and dove into a placid pool ahead of us. Within seconds, it soared into the sky, a small fish tucked in its beak, fins and mouth flapping. The same sense of doom left a frosty spot in my gut for the briefest moment.

"You know?" Did everyone know about my

kidnapping?

"Laurel told me the summer after it happened. We used to talk a lot. I was having a hard time with girls, boys, life."

Incredulous, I handed him two smooth, round stones. "Laurel? You're talking about *the* Laurel Montgomery?" I teased. When it came to the big things, Laurel was a great sounding board. The little items stumped her the most.

I liked his warm and non-threatening hearty laugh.

"She *can* spend too much time in her own tunnel." He rested his hand on my arm. "She's there when it counts."

The sun dappled speckles of amber into his chocolate eyes, buried in puffy and purple skin. "She helped me live through the kidnapping more than anyone else. She spent all her free time at my house. We went everywhere together. She's always watched out for me, even when you think she's not paying attention. I don't know what I'd do without her."

"Speaking of." He launched another stone across the river, flinched from the pain of bruises on his torso. "If anything happens to me, will you grab that envelope?"

Jaw hanging open, I stared him down. "What? What's gonna happen to you? Did Dante or his thug threaten you again?"

He scraped his sneakers in the rocks, digging for another skipping stone. "I don't trust that asshole. He's playing Martina somehow. One minute, she thinks he walks on water. The next, she shies away. He's like a snake oil salesman."

"If you think he's dodgy, let's call home." I gripped my leather band, feeling the prick of the pin pierce my wrist. Blood seeped, and I shoved my hands into my pockets, trying to hold onto my warmth in the frost that suddenly enveloped us under the afternoon sun. "I think he's been inducted into the Criminal Hall of Fame."

"We need proof. I don't want to call home first. He'll cover his tracks if he suspects us investigating him."

"What do you mean if something happens to you?" Life and the Mysterious Mystery just got uglier.

He shrugged, a dire movement that didn't answer my question. "I'll do whatever I need to avoid breaking the rules, to keep him from sending me home."

"Me too."

"Deal." He stuck out his hand. When I clasped it, he towed me into a bear hug, like hugging a brother. Nothing like the tingly acute awareness I felt when Logan so much as looked at me now.

We picked our way along the shoreline back to the makeshift camp. Martina was directing campers. The closer we progressed to her, I noticed a dark shadow between her neck and shoulder blade. A bruise climbed down her shoulder beneath her short-sleeved blouse, easy enough to make out on her über pale skin. Had Dante hurt her? Mystery goon?

Logan jogged over to us. "Dante wants a Leadership Training session to go over the rules. He wants to talk to you first, Al."

Marco returned to the tent construction zone. Logan's complexion turned chunk-spewing green, his mouth pulled into a pained grimace.

He opened and closed his mouth twice. Finally, he asked, "Are you into him?"

I cupped my mouth. Did Logan *like me*, like me? Was our relationship truly speeding down that mystical speedway? We'd never had that kind of relationship even though I'd wanted him in the hardest way a twelve-year-old preteen experienced. Our friendship had meant the world to me, and I'd feared upsetting the balance of the three musket-rats. I was the only one of my friends who'd had a boy as a friend. A boy who didn't fear peer pressure from hanging out with his little sister and her best friend. A boy who did what he pleased no matter what anyone thought, regardless of whether it defined his geekiness or lost him friends he might otherwise have made. Not that he necessarily wanted those friends. He'd been content with his small circle of guy friends, his video games, me, and Laurel.

"Will you answer my question?" The pain in his strangled voice became more evident.

I stared at him as if he'd grown bear claws and planned to dip me in honey. I decided the truth would set me free, as they say. At least a partial truth. Maybe Logan would learn something from it. *Mental snort-fest.*

"Marco thinks something happened to Mrs. A too. He tried to deliver a package to her last night, and one of Dante's workers beat the crap out of him." The same man who threatened to decapitate me. *Chop, chop, bye-bye, Allie.*

Logan's mouth gaped open. "Are you serious?"

"Dead."

His fists furled at his side. "We need to report this. Who was it?"

I pressed my palm on his chest, the heat of his skin through his red "come to the nerd side, we have Pi" T-shirt giving me an acute feeling of rightness. "No. He's working with me to solve this mystery. We want to trap Dante before we tip him off and he hides evidence or worse. Marco thinks the mystery guy is Dante's friend working on the staff cabins."

"You're walking dangerous ground." He spread his legs in a defensive stance, pressing forward against my hand splayed on his chest.

"Please just go along." I skated my hand over his heart. "Do it my way."

He gloved his hand over mine, linking our fingers, holding them to his chest. “If anything happens to you, I’ll never forgive myself. Not this time. Not ever.”

“There won’t be anything to forgive. Okay?” I propped my forehead on his chest, and his chin found the top of my head.

We stood there for the longest time, silent, contemplative, comforted by a new awareness surrounding us. I wanted more than that moment. Did Logan? Did I have the ability to forgive *him?*

The sun beat down upon us. My stomach gurgled, intruding upon the moment. Logan and I laughed. The river babbled by, charged with adventure and the great unknown.

A scream rent the air, dispelling our tranquil moment of bonding, and so much more.

CHAPTER 15

Gathered inside the giant tent circle, kids whooped and hollered, louder than the situation demanded. Grunts and growls joined the fray. Sounds of kicking followed the soft and firm sound of fists hitting skin. *Ah, jeez. Now what?*

Logan rammed through the tightknit crowd to Laurel. “What’s the racket?”

“Dumbass Neal and his bitches were harassing the girls. Marco tried to stop them. Neal attacked him.”

“Help Marco, Logan.” My eyes implored him.

“Stay together and stay back.” Logan shot through the gaggle of kids toward Marco.

“Where’re the counselors?” I searched the crowd for an adult.

“What freaking counselors?” Her sarcasm didn’t fall on deaf ears.

Dante and a dark-haired man stood on the fringes of the crowd. Mystery Mammoth? Slightly taller than average height, the man had a wrestler’s tree trunk arms and legs and a barrel chest. His dark hair rivaled Marco's shaggy mane. We locked gazes. A wicked grin took his face into slasher movie territory, and he sliced his index finger across his throat. Shocked, I broke eye contact, pressing on my leather band, not caring that I missed the pin, and hardly noticing the lack of pain devouring my dread.

"Finally. Dante's going in." Laurel peered over the heads of the boys in front of her.

Someone from behind shoved me forward. I fell against Jeff and Richie, Neal's bitches who'd chickened out of the fight. They hung onto me, grinning, acting like they ruled the world. Laurel grabbed me, missed as Jeff yanked on me harder, tipping me off balance.

"Hey, assholes," she screamed. "What's your problem?"

"Who you callin' assholes?" Richie made an obnoxious gesture aimed at his crotch.

They grabbed my breasts and butt, pretending to pull me up, but really just looking for a chance to manhandle me. Richie slobbered kisses on me, and I scratched his cheek, digging my fingernails in his skin. He snarled and yanked on my hair, licking my cheek.

"Leave me alone!" I jabbed my elbow into Jeff's gut. My jab served to egg his hands on in their exploration of my boobs. Most of the kids around us hardly paid attention as they were riveted on the fight. The others seemed to think we were playing a game.

"Babe, you fell on *my* lap." Jeff leered, tugging on my shirt, trying to slip his hands underneath it.

Laurel shouted, yanking on Richie's shirt and scraggly hair. The crowd noise died as kids directed their attention to me and my pseudo-attackers. I guess I was much more exciting than watching Neal and Marco pound each other into dust. I realized in the scuffle, my blouse had rolled up, exposing my sports bra.

I tried to tug it down, but Jeff's hands were deliberately in the way. He and Richie brayed like hyenas, as they each grabbed one of Laurel's arms, gripping them behind her, holding her back from helping me. Older boys egged them on, while the Dragonfly Lily girls screamed for them to leave me alone. The space was too tight for me to lift my arm to try out my new self-defense moves. My intangible armor fractured, and a wintry numbness coursed up from my toes.

Jeff's rancid breath and Richie's ripe armpits assailed my airway. I gagged a little in my mouth and my head grew woozy. As my throat closed up, Dante's mysterious friend tossed the two boys off me. My knees buckled, and I slumped to the ground, heaving in air.

With a mere flick of his hands, he'd thrown each boy to the ground. They cowered, his shadow a demon blight ready to descend upon them. Laurel surrounded me, touching me everywhere.

"Allie, Allie," she cried. "Did they hurt you?"

Unable to do more than wave at her, I tried to gather my scattered brain cells and whatever else I had lost in those few tumultuous moments. I wanted to hide in the top of my snow globe's lighthouse, my safe haven. For the first time since I'd arrived at camp, I wanted Mom. Worst of all, I wanted the safety of my home prison.

I pressed on my leather cuff, pushing the pin into my wrist repeatedly, relishing the prick of pain. "Get Logan," I whispered.

"Carrie, go find Logan," Laurel flung over her shoulder.

Before I knew it, Logan enclosed me in the safety of his arms. I folded my arms around his waist, burying my face in his chest, shaking up a tempest. "Get me out of here." Blood dripped from beneath my leather cuff down my arm.

A soft hand alighted on my arm. “Come with me, please.”

“No.” I lashed at Martina. “Don’t touch me!”

Logan’s arms tightened. “I’ll take care of her.” He rolled my blouse down since my half-hearted efforts only served to tug it to my belly button.

“I need to tend to her and take a report,” Martina insisted.

“I’ll give you a report,” Laurel ground out. “Those asswipes attacked Allie and practically raped her.”

Mystery brute’s shadow held Jeff and Richie cowering, captive on the ground.

Logan half carried me away since my noodle legs had their own uncooperative brain. A gray, weathered picnic bench in the shade of the woods seemed as good a place as any to regroup.

After a long moment he asked, “Was it seriously an accident?”

“Someone pushed me, I fell, they swooped in.” Fog stuffed my head. “Will they get sent home?”

“Probably. Neal too. This is a no-bully camp. Cardinal rule.”

“That was then, this is now. It’s Dante’s rule.” I knuckled my nose, sniffing hard, wishing for a tissue. *Gross, I know*. “Neal and his buds hang with Dante. They worship the ground he walks on.”

Marco strode over to us, Martina in tow. They seemed to be arguing, Marco’s fists clenched at his sides. The cut above his eye had opened again, dripping blood onto his eyebrow, giving his bushy black brow a red tint.

“Allie, Dante says it’s up to you if you want the boys to go home.” Marco unfurled his fists. “They *should* get kicked out.”

“Say the word. If they stay, they’ll be reprimanded

and an immediate report emailed home to their parents." Martina gripped her clipboard. "One more infraction and they're out. Okay?" She gave me an odd look of triumph. "You also have the option to leave if you want. We'll give you a full refund." Her voice encouraged, and I got the odd sense that she wanted me to go.

"That's not what Dante said." A muscle ticked in Marco's jaw.

"It's what I say," she challenged. "Dante doesn't make all the rules."

"What about Neal's fighting?" Marco's brows merged in one long red caterpillar. "It's his second time."

"It's your second time too. You ready to go home?" Martina tapped his shoulder hard. "You're all on notice now."

"I want an apology. And I want you to keep them away from me." I glanced up at Marco, their cabin leader.

"Done," he replied, all frowny-faced and not at all happy that Martina and Dante were allowing the bullies to stay.

Dante led Jeff and Richie over. "Apologize." He thrust them forward.

They hung their heads in contrition, hands stuck into their front pockets. Had lynch mob mentality gotten to them?

"Sorry, Allie," Jeff and Richie said in tandem.

"We didn't mean to hurt or embarrass you." Jeff's shame met my crimson fury.

"It won't happen again." Richie shoved his fists deeper into his pockets.

Marco rode their butts back to tent building.

Dante knelt in front of me. "You okay?"

"Yeah." His friend watched us over his shoulder. "Who's that guy?"

"Rambo. Friend of mine. He's retrofitting cabins

vandalized by winter vacationers."

"Rambo?" I snickered for the sake of diverting my roiling emotions.

"Long story." Dante smiled. "The boys lost their map duties. It's back in your hands if you're up to it."

He handed me a cardboard tube containing rolled maps for the treasure hunt. He explained that I'd lead the leaders. Each team received incremental maps. Once they unearthed a treasure, they earned the next map, and so on until a team found the grand prize. *Yippee.* From public mauling to map leader. I was on a roll.

Martina hung behind after Dante split. "Logan, stay with Allie if you don't mind. I need to talk to the kids about what happened. Some of the girls need reassurances and consoling."

"I'm not leaving her side." The wintry, calculating look he landed on her sent her rushing away.

Logan had seen the dark side of Dragonfly Meadows and wasn't merely coddling my paranoia. He climbed another notch in my esteem. This time, he wasn't obeying my mother and playing watchdog. The respect in his eyes told me a different story.

Kids avoided us for a while, except Serena and Michelle. They brought me water and a bouquet of wildflowers they'd scrounged from somewhere. I hugged them and told them we didn't need to speak of what had happened. Their solemn nods and silence informed me they were more than happy to oblige. The wildflowers set off a noxious roiling in my stomach. They held too much hidden significance.

After all the tents were erected, we sat with our sack lunches. Nick had prepared his special homemade bread again. Paradise in the form of a salami sandwich soothed my empty churning, while Logan and Laurel instilled the relief of an age-old camaraderie in my bubble. Neither left my side. Logan spellbound the girls while he practiced his martial arts forms. He mesmerized me, awakened my numb soul.

Marco came bearing a basket of painted rocks. "For picking the treasure hunt teams." He sat opposite me, clutching his middle. No one else noticed his pain.

A whistle blew and the games began. We gathered in the center of the tents. Teams were chosen by picking colored rocks from my basket.

I'd spent time at our late lunch studying the professionally drawn maps. Well-marked, they encompassed much more area than what Dante had marked off for the hunt. I handed each team leader the first map, a blow up of one small section of the larger map.

Dante blew his whistle, a shrill sound above the excited din. "Everyone listen up. You each have a wide area to search. Take each clue one at a time until you figure it out, then progress to the next clue. If you solve each clue in order, it will lead you to the treasure and the final clue that'll carry you on to the next site. Each site has three hidden treasures in different spots. Last two teams that don't find a treasure will be eliminated."

"Grab shovels and rakes. Take gloves too," Martina shouted.

"Jeez, are we landscaping?" Laurel grumbled as her team took off to grab tools.

"Check this out." I finagled the large map to block Dante and Martina's view. "This is a copy of an old map."

"So?"

"Dante was reading that article on his tablet about buried gold in the Amadori hills. You think gold treasure exists here?"

She tilted her head to the side, finger tracing the mining camp on the map. "Mrs. A mentioned the mining operation when she talked of her family's history, but nothing about hidden gold."

"Did she ever bring campers on a tour?"

"No way. The family didn't want to spoil the land. They used to do tours with the off season people who rented the campground for large events."

"Why did they stop?" I rolled the map up and stuck it into the tube.

"They quit the tours ten years ago. Her father was strict about preserving the land, hoping it'd become a registered historical landmark."

"You remember a lot and you hate history," I kidded.

"Because I think you're right that Mrs. A might be in trouble." Her playful smirk melted into a frown. "Do you want to call someone?"

"Marco's gonna call his mom. She's tight with Mrs. A." I didn't feel bad about giving up the goods, as long as I didn't divulge the real secret about the papers. Laurel was too freaked about Mrs. A and she needed reassurance. "Don't tell anyone. He's gonna sneak into the office when we get back to camp."

"Can he use your phone?" she whispered.

I patted my purse for my rogue cell phone and realized I'd left it hidden in my alcove. "Crap. I meant to bring it. I bet reception's better here too."

"That's not like you."

I scrubbed my head. "I know, I know. If Marco can't sneak into the office, I'll offer it to him. He'll have to hike for reception."

The game whistle blew. Laurel's team, comprised of several of our girls, hurried to the yellow-flagged section to hunt. The well-spread hunt areas made it harder for the teams to sneak glimpses at other teams. The game might keep the kids from asking why they'd cancelled our paid excursions. Logan waited on the other side of the tent ring. Laurel followed her team, her map flapping in the wind, her boobs nearly flapping against her chin. Her rack needed more support than her bikini top beneath her T-shirt, like an industrial grandma bra to keep those puppies in place.

I zigzagged around the chairs and blankets covering the ground. "Where's your team?"

"Sector four. Coming?" Logan asked quietly, digging his hands in and out of his pockets.

"Yeah. Gotta direct the teams." I shoved the map tube under my arm and stuck my left hand in my pocket, trying to wipe the blood off my wrist. I brushed Logan's hand and his fingers tangled in mine. Deliberate, unfettered. A lifetime careened into our knotted fingers. It left me reeling, wanting to absorb his touch into my skin.

"Marco's hurt, isn't he?" Logan broke the spell.

"He's bruised, but doesn't want anyone to notice."

"I did."

"I already told you that goon pounded on him, plus the cafeteria fight, now this." I walked toward the old shack Marco and I had stood near earlier. Dante's eagle eye on Logan's team of bullies didn't escape me. "Oh, goody, you get Dante supervising. Where's your map?"

"Gave it to Serena. She seemed trustworthy." He chuckled.

"'Cause they learned from me." Giggling, I darted forward, spying a perfect skipping rock. "Remember when you taught me how to skip rocks?" I needed more to occupy the dregs of my mind from my mauling.

"How could I forget? Dead fish litter my nightmares."

I shoved a stone against his middle and we laughed. "I didn't kill any fish." Skirting past him, I sailed the stone across the river, skipping four times. Each touch upon the surface of the river barely made a dimple in the grand scheme of life. "Beat that, sucker."

We skipped rocks and kidded like the old days. That made me sound old, reliving my youth. But when one had been kidnapped and held at gunpoint for a day, the time, no matter how little, morphed into a lifetime of lost youth. I rarely dwelled on my life's events before the kidnapping. Once I'd slid past pre-abduction times in my memories, it always revolved to that fateful day in the mall, to Logan abandoning me in his quest to best the latest and greatest video game. The memories always carried with them a slash of hatred. Sometimes that hatred was greater than the loathing and pity I felt for Michael Kline. And I hated myself for having those emotions, wrong on so many levels. In a way, I had forgiven Logan, but I'd never told him. Honestly, I didn't know how to broach it after our four-year hiatus. I'd already tried twice and couldn't get the words out. It ticked me off that he hadn't fessed up. I needed him to vent a spleen, and part of me wanted him to do it on his initiative, not at my prompting. But since we'd already skated into an effortless familiar pattern, I didn't want to upset the fragile tableau. We were becoming new friends, different from our twelve- and thirteen-year-old selves. A new and different sameness.

Grinning, Logan wrangled me around my waist, preventing me from skipping him into oblivion. He'd taught me too well. It was obvious we were becoming so much more than friends. Yet, I didn't think I could go much longer without dwelling on the past, without confronting him.

CHAPTER 16

Dante called me to join Logan's team. I avoided the bullies as Logan ran interference and tossed out clues for Serena, Michelle and some younger boys. Five paces this way, ten paces that way, traverse under a gnarled oak tree, dig through layers of mulch that dated to the Gold Rush. The kids were having a blast, scrounging through the debris, digging up dirt, plants, and rocks, not paying attention to the clues.

The clues were so random I had a hard time believing they led to anything more than dirt. I checked on the other teams, finding the same clueless turmoil, same fun, some frustration, and a few sulking kids. Laurel and Jesse called me over to consult on their map in sector five.

Laurel pointed to an *X* with the citation: *cross the creek, then double back five paces*. "There's no creek here."

Navy blue flags marked off sector five from a slight slope in the woods, tapering down to a small gulley.

"Did you search in the gulley?" I asked.

"No creek there." Jesse scratched his head.

I slapped his arm. "Dude, ever hear of a dry creek? Are there small river pebbles?"

"Maybe." He turned tomato red and loped off to gather straying kids.

"*You* so smart." Laurel faked an Asian accent. "No wonder Dante made you his pet map bitch."

"Ya think?" I sat next to her on a boulder, watching the kids scramble, dig, count off steps, throw leaves at each other.

Scents of pine and moldy mulch competed in the air surrounding us. The moldy mulch won, and I breathed through my mouth. The kids scared off the birds and squirrels, except two blue jays scolding us from the high branches of the trees.

"The shade feels nice." I fanned my face.

"Nick wants to go off tonight and…you know, make out," Laurel threw out casually.

I jack-knifed upright. "Seriously? You gonna do it?"

She rubbed the side of her nose, and I wanted to slap her hand away. "I want to. It's getting serious."

"It's only been a few days. How serious is serious?"

Emotions stormed her expression in the wrinkle of her nose, the scrunch of her forehead, the twinkle in her eyes. She was falling hard and fast, blonde head over flip-flop heels.

"I didn't think I'd ever experience these feelings. People say you know when you know, but I've never known."

"I get it." It freaked me out. We'd both waited years to discover our first love. Earlier with Logan, butterflies had danced in my middle when he touched me. Some nameless bug had bitten me. Infatuation, love, wariness? "Does your middle feel all weirded out when you're with him?"

Laurel's nails dug into my sunburned forearm. "Yes!

Isn't that what people say happens?"

I drew a stick in the dead leaves blanketing the ground. "I've held you back, haven't I?"

"What? No." Laurel ruffled my hair. "Al, you know I wanted us to both have this experience. I'm free for Nick. You're free for Marco." She beamed me a radiant smile, and I knew she wasn't yanking my chain. I adored her for it.

"Allie, can you give us a clue?" Carrie tromped over to us. "This is ri-donk-u-lous." She tossed her gloves on the ground.

Jasmine stood behind her, holding a shovel. "We've dug stupid holes everywhere."

"Dig deeper," Laurel snapped, so unlike herself.

I opened my clue page to their sector. "Did you do the five paces in the dry creek?"

"A gazillion times in every direction." Carrie plummeted to the ground in a desolate heap.

"Found it," Jesse yelled.

Like bats on fire, the girls flew away, returning with the clue for the next sector and a small cloth bag of commemorative Dragonfly Meadows coins and real dollar coins.

"Where did you find it?" I nonchalantly scrutinized my map.

Jesse unfolded his crumpled map and tapped the spot within a trio of trees. "No clue pointed to that location."

My map indicated the various treasure locations marked correctly, but he was right. The clues didn't make a lick of sense. The kids blindly dug holes and scrounged the vegetation, as if searching for real hidden treasure. Surely, Dante didn't have them out here digging for the mysterious Amadori gold?

"Can we move on?" Carrie bounced on her feet, antsy for the next dig.

"Wait for the rotation signal." I explained that once each sector found their treasure, all groups rotated to the next sector. "Take a seat, rest. Drink water. Stay hydrated."

After everyone scattered, I gave Laurel my renewed attention. "Why snap at the kids? I don't blame you if you held your former lack of boyfriend against me."

She exhaled heavily. "I need to talk to you. We never have a free moment."

I gawked at her as if she was batshit crazy, and then realized I was the batshit crazy one for chasing my paranoia versus being there for her. "I'm listening." I rested my head on her shoulder.

Laurel bumped her head against mine and we twined our pinkies. "It's Nick, he's so—"

My back stiffened. "He's not pushing you, is he?"

"No. Not going all the way. Jeez, I'm not that hard up, or dumb."

Phew. She had me shaking in my sneakers for a second.

"He's out of my league." Her bottom lip quivered.

"What do you mean?"

"His family's über rich. He's had country clubbers and smoking hot girlfriends."

"And you smoke every one of them." I gripped her arm. "Don't sell yourself short. You don't think he's playing you, do you?"

She waved my words off. "No. I just don't stack up." Doubt flattened her like a damp blanket.

Aghast, I gave her our wonky stare. "You're flippin' cracked. He's lucky you give him the time of day, let alone cozy up to him."

Preening, she pushed out her perfect boobs, her full, pouty lips, flipping her long blonde-highlighted hair that matched Logan's hair over her shoulder.

"You're gorgeous, smart, and funny with excellent taste in clothes. You don't need Daddy's money and stupid clubs to land him." I rose off the ground and tugged Laurel up. "We need to hit it before Dante's tighty-whiteys twist him up."

Red-faced, the maestro in question glared at the kids in sector three, who were the last to unearth their treasure. No one progressed to the next sector until all teams succeeded. Laurel's team waited outside sector three, egging team five on. By the number of holes dug, it was evident the team had given up on the map and clues.

"I need to help them." I wagged my head. "Remember, Nick's lucky to land you. Don't do anything you're not comfortable with. Don't let him get you drunk."

We traded stilted giggles. Alcohol could kill her ability to say no. Been there, done that. I ended up with half her wardrobe because she couldn't say no after we got tipsy at her cousin's wedding last spring. She had awesome taste and a bigger clothing allowance than I did.

Mom and Dad didn't shower their only child with nice things, but they set limits, despite the trauma I'd endured. They wanted me to earn my way through the mall. Sometimes, it sucked after enduring the kidnapping and the ensuing years of emotional distress. It's not like they couldn't afford to buy me an extra T-shirt or two and a used car. Nope. No car. The bars on my prison included never owning a car. I'd be lucky if they allowed me to get my license. Ever.

Laurel interrupted my trip to Negative-ville. "Will you cover for me tonight?"

"You know it, sista." I looped my arm about her waist, hugging her tight. I had become the leader, when she normally usurped that role. I'd expected her to lead me at camp due to her familiarity. My confidence soared with this knowledge.

A cheer rose in sector three as the team scored their treasure.

"Gather 'round," Dante shouted, standing on a boulder. Once all the kids had closed in, he continued, "There're two more prizes in each sector before you move on to the final round tomorrow. Everyone take a twenty minute break."

The kids scattered, many heading for the river. Counselors Marty and Dawn were stationed along the banks as lifeguards. Hail to safety.

Logan, Nick, and Marco had disappeared. "Where're the guys?"

"Nick said they had to gather firewood during the breaks."

"What, like go into the forest and chop wood?"

"I guess." Laurel twisted up her mouth. "Nick's scoping out an old cabin for tonight. He saw it on the drive in."

"Eww. What if it's swarming with spiders, snakes, or rabid chipmunks?"

A shudder rippled up from her feet. "That's what I said."

A tingly chill swept up my spine. "You *should* stay near camp. You could get lost."

"I trust him." She chewed on her bottom lip, her last source of food.

"I don't know him well enough."

"You don't trust anyone. Lighten up."

"What's this about trust?" Dante startled us as he stalked up behind us.

"Nothing. Dredging up old stuff." I kept my back to him, hoping he'd find a sinkhole to step in. He didn't.

"Let's talk map strategy for a minute," he said. "Laurel, go join your team."

Laurel cast me a wary glance before tromping off to

her team playing in the river.

He crossed his arms over his chest, the way my dad did when he was pissed. I stood there like a possum playing dead. "Marco told me you were with him last night. He said you planned to make out in the woods, but he wanted to spy on my aunt first." He tipped forward. "Why are you all so interested in my aunt?"

Map strategy, my flat butt. I blinked back my surprise. Marco would never rat me out. Right? "Umm...I was following Marco. I didn't want him to land in trouble." The tube slipped from under my arm, and I bent to retrieve it, avoiding Dante's black look, hiding my lies.

"I've been watching you two lurk."

What? *I don't lurk. Much.* I straightened, my expression a blank slate. Kids squealed and laughed while I wallowed in my tangle of emotional crap.

"I'm sorry." The best strategy for getting out of this reprimand was to act like it really bugged me. I mustered up a fake blubber and hoped he'd buy the crocodile tears. "It won't happen again."

"You're a smart girl. I'd hate to see you follow the bad habits of others. Be your own individual and you'll go far in this world. I don't want you to go home. It's your first time at camp. Don't make it your last." An arrogant strut fueled his long-legged stride toward his tent. He sat in a lawn chair under a tree and swiped his finger on his tablet device, shooting furtive glances my way.

I wiped the real-fake tears off my cheek. He had a bull's-eye on my forehead, and I needed to scrub it off fast.

The ground rumbled and vibrated below me. Cries and hollers rent the air, leaving a new foreboding spinning in my brain.

CHAPTER 17

Dante barreled out of his chair, dropping his tablet. The ground quit quaking, and a plume of dust ascended into the air near the rise above the old mine shaft.

Kids jetted toward the mine shaft. I shot forward and picked up Dante's discarded tablet, using the bottom of my polo shirt to keep my fingerprints off it. I snuck behind the nearest tent. Excitement swept through the crowd, and I wanted to see what'd happened, to make sure no one was hurt. California occasionally experienced earthquakes in this part of the state. Torn in two, I gnawed on the inside of my right cheek. The lure of Dante's tablet, without needing a password, enticed me horribly.

His email was open. Except it was Mrs. Amadori's account, all her emails filtering into his account. "Un. Believable," I whispered. *No wonder Marco's mom didn't want to send email to Mrs. A. Someone had shot her with a clue gun.*

Keeping an eye peeled for Dante, I skimmed several articles about the hidden gold on the Amadori property and a couple emails. Voices escalated nearby and panic gripped me. I returned to the page Dante had discarded. Jeff and Neal hobbled Jesse between them to the first aid station by the makeshift kitchen area. I set the tablet on the ground near Dante's chair and dashed off to the crowd gathered on the other side of the mine shaft.

As inconspicuous as possible, I threaded through the crowd and stopped behind Serena and Michelle. "Hey. What happened?"

Serena swiveled toward me, dancing with excitement. "The ground collapsed. Jesse and a couple boys fell into a hole. They're okay. Jesse may have sprained his ankle."

Shock impaled me. "Stay here. I'm heading down to see if they need help."

"No." Logan chest-butted my back. "No kids allowed."

I spun, my eyes bulging. "Is it an old mine shaft?"

"Yep. Dante's all excited." He leaned in close and whispered in my ear, "He told Rambo he's hunting a hidden passage. He thinks he just found it."

"There's buried gold here," I said. A couple of Logan's boys sidled closer to us, waiting for Logan. "I'll tell you what I found out later."

"There you are," Laurel yelled at me. "Jeez, you disappear—"

I whacked my palm over her big, fat mouth. "Shhh. Keep it down. I was taking care of business." I cricked my head at the portable potty setup. The lie rolled off my tongue. Sheesh…when I went home, I'd need to do a million Hail Marys.

"You got the squirts?" Carrie sniggered.

I ignored the twit.

The cave-in instigated rampant rumors about real gold. Kids aren't stupid. We loved to fantasize about finding sacks of cash hidden in ditches along highways or tossed in bushes in our front yards.

The boys who'd tumbled into the hole were okay, besides a few scratches and Jesse's sprained ankle. Martina bandaged it, and he was walking with barely a limp.

After scoping out the outside of the hole, Dante dove into it with Rambo, pretending to inspect the damage. He didn't fool me. He *was* searching for gold. He pegged the area off limits for everyone. The treasure hunt continued, and the kids soon tired of digging useless holes. I sat in the shade waiting for the last team to find the third clue. Laurel and Nick sprawled on the ground near me, all touchy feely and giggly. Logan sat next to me.

"What'd you find out?" He shook grit out of his hair.

"I read an article on Dante's tablet. There once was lost gold. People have questioned whether it belonged to the Amadoris or their blood enemies, the Cardonas, since the 1800s. Apparently, there was a feud over ownership of the mineral rights in the gold mine. The Cardonas claimed it belonged to them. An Amadori girl and a Cardona boy fell in love and absconded with the gold. A train derailed with them on it, and the Cardonas believed the Amadoris stole the gold and hid it. The Cardonas have always claimed that the Amadoris caused the train derailment." I sucked in a breath. "I think Dante rigged this excursion to force us to find his hidden gold."

"Wouldn't put it past him." Logan lay on his back, sweat glistening on his brow. "A lot of the ground has already been dug up, leaves and debris scattered to camouflage it. At first, I thought the upturned ground was to throw us off to where they buried the clues. But it's not random."

From our distance, I could tell that the tilled ground was marked in a distinct pattern of rows. "See the grid of what's been dug up." I traced the grid in the air, corroborating Logan's theory.

Nick tackled Laurel flat to the ground, climbing on top of her, tickling. Screams erupted out of her, luring the curious. Laurel lapped it up. She was having the time of her life and deserved every minute of it. I'd always felt guilty holding her back due to my forced home life restrictions. She told me she didn't mind going along with what my parents allowed me to do. The best friend ever and I had never taken her for granted.

Smiling, I sagged in my chair, realizing how much fun I was having with all this intrigue, dodging Dante, spying with Marco. It didn't bother me that someone had used me and Logan for target practice. Most of all, I was having fun with Logan. I'd missed him so much over the last four years. In my furious fear, I never realized how much I'd counted on his presence in my life. Until that summer.

"Logan?"

"Allie."

"Are you glad you came to camp one last time?"

"I had nothing else planned this summer." His lips kicked up in a knowing smile.

"Shut up. You know what I meant."

"The three musket-rats rule." Laurel came up for a breath and fist-punched the air.

"Screw that. Four musket-rats." Nick tackled her again. More squeals drowned out the sounds of nature, the sounds of freedom and fun.

Hollers eclipsed them as the last team found their prize.

"Finally. Now it's grub time." Logan skirted my question.

Not sure why I asked the question, I let it go. I didn't want to put him on the spot or hear him say no. *Yes, Allie*

Bailey needs her brain returned to the store.

Laurel and Nick took off for KP duty. I held Logan behind.

"I read an email between Dante and Mrs. Amadori from March. She was ticked he wanted to work at camp this summer. She told him she'd report him to the sheriff if he showed up on the property."

Logan bolted upright. "Serious?"

"Dead."

Thought lines created that soon-to-be ingrained *V* between his eyes. "Let's step this up. Is Marco calling his mom?"

"Yeah. Soon as he returns to camp."

He jumped up. "Let's go spy on Dante."

I sprang up so fast I bowled into his arms. "Whoops. Don't have to ask me twice."

His intense gaze pierced me, reaching into my soul, his hands hot on my arm, strong and secure. I traced the veins in his forearm, surprised again at how solid he'd become from his martial arts. Not like football player muscular, but strong.

"You asked if I was glad I came."

"Oh. Right." I ran my thumb down his arm, already on its way to a nice even tan. My heartbeat sped up. He rested his hands on the small of my back, his touch infusing me with a warm calm.

"I'm glad I came." His voice was low and seductive. He tilted forward, his breath tickling my cheek.

A thread of heat unwound in my stomach, mushrooming lower. I couldn't halt the tremble rising up from my toes. When his lips landed on mine, I inhaled sharply and parted my lips. But he brushed his lips over mine and they traveled to my ear. I fisted his polo shirt. My legs weakened, and Logan's arms supported me before I drowned in melting, bubbly lava. What was wrong with me? I lifted on my toes, fingered Logan's face to mine and my lips met his again. I pressed hard, wanting to devour him, wanting to drive him away and leave me to die in peace.

Without breaking contact, I maneuvered us out of view of peeping Toms. I thrust him against a tree, and he cupped my cheeks, his hands possessive, hard, but gentle. His lips never left mine. I didn't want them to. Ever. Our lips parted at the same time. And sanity paid me a visit. Before I could draw away and slap sense into myself, he shifted his mouth and trailed nibbling kisses to my ear.

"I came here for you," he whispered in my ear. "For *us* to have a chance."

I fingered my lips, holding onto the taste and feel of him, salty and sweet, the softness and firmness of his lips pressed hard to mine. "Okay."

"What do you want?" He dropped his hands, settling them on my hips.

I tried not to think. We had baggage. I couldn't just say I wanted him, move forward, and not open and explore the inside of that baggage. His disappearing act times two had tortured me for four years. I had to tell him how I'd felt every day since that moment in the mall when Kline had snagged me at gunpoint, then forced me into his car and into his home. I had to tell him what that had done to me, and what Logan Montgomery had done to me when I received his get well card and withering wildflowers the day after the police had rescued me. I never saw him again until the beginning of the recent spring semester. We'd passed each other in the hallways at school or in the Montgomery's house, pretending not to see each other or squeaking out a random *hello*.

Say what? Withering flowers? Nausea bloomed. I shoved away from Logan. Doubled-over on the other side of the tree, a fern was about to receive an unwelcome gift.

"What's wrong?" Logan pressed his hand to my back.

I plunged to my knees. Dry heaves settled in. Logan kept massaging my back. "Laurel," he yelled. "Bring me some 7-Up."

Within a moment, Laurel stuck a bottle of lemon-lime soda in front of me. "What'd you do to her, karate dork? What did you say?"

"Nothing. Nothing," he shouted.

I'd never heard him shout in anger. I waved my hand to forestall their pending fight. "The flowers we received. I just figured out they reminded me of the kidnapping." I swallowed the bile threatening to rise again.

Laurel choked on a sob. "You got flowers from jerkwad Kline."

From the confusion written all over Logan's face, I didn't think he remembered.

"Why would we receive something that reminds me of *that*?" I gripped Laurel's arm and leveraged myself off the ground.

"It's got to be a fluke." She held onto my soda until she was sure my stupid moment of weakness passed. "Flowers are dime a doz. Plus, Kline didn't give you dumb notes."

I tried to recall the words on the cards, but they were jumbled in my head. I didn't believe it correlated to my kidnapping. I'd read them again to make sure. I needed to rule out Logan like I needed to breathe. He'd already said he didn't give us anything. *A coincidence, right?* I racked my brain to recall the flowers Logan had given me versus the ones Kline had brought me. The ones left on our beds were definitely the same type as Kline's flowers with the rose and the balsam branches. Not the same as Logan's bouquet. A wellspring of peace permeated me. Or the soda had done its job.

"Let's spy on Dante before we lose our light." Logan

seized my hand. Had he remembered the flowers and wanted to keep it in the vault? *Whatever*. I wanted off this topic before I lost my head in the sunken mine shaft. I didn't mind his weird shift in the conversation.

"No." Laurel stamped her foot. "You're gonna get busted and booted home."

"Cover for us," Logan said. "I'll keep her safe. Dante's not shipping her home. He wants her here."

Shock stuttered my foot on the uneven ground. "You picked up on that too?"

"Yeah." He scratched the nape of his neck. "I don't like it."

"It's not like he's gonna hook up with her." Laurel gagged. "Eww. Just eww."

"Not that way." I tapped sense into Laurel's temple. "He wants something from me. Not sure what, though." Who tried to scare me off with Kline mementos? My head swam in the world of Mystification, a new galaxy of my own making.

"He's bluffing. He's not sending anyone home. You're too smart for him. You might tell your parents something that'll land him in deep."

Laurel contemplated Logan's words, bypassing the nose rub and shirt hem routine. "Fine. I'll cover. Don't get caught."

"Sure you're okay?" Logan asked as we headed toward the cave-in.

"I'm fine." I bit my tongue to prevent myself from shouting. He didn't remember his get-well gift. I wanted to beat them across his chest and make him remember it was the last item he'd given me before he split town. *Flipping flowers. Freaking Logan Montgomery*.

We crept up the butt-crack side of the old mine, hiding behind trees and rocks. The cave-in wasn't much larger than coffin space. Dante and Rambo's conversation drifted up from inside it along with the thunk, thunk of their shovels hitting the dirt. Everyone else had scattered since he'd called the unsafe area off limits. The ground might cave, so Logan and I stayed well off the trajectory of the old mine shaft.

I nudged Logan in the side, a quick jerk of my elbow. "They're not filling it in."

"Exactly. Can't wait to see where he's gonna have us all dig tomorrow for the final prize."

Plumes of dust clouded the air. Dante and Rambo grunted and groused for a while longer, until they scampered out of the hole and roped it off limits.

After dinner, campfires blazed and Laurel signaled me to watch the girls while she and Nick snuck off. Nick had taken a bottle of wine he'd smuggled from the campground pantry. I hoped Laurel stayed sober and sane.

Marco steered clear of me, throwing Dante off.

After gorging on S'mores, the girls and I fell into exhausted heaps in our sleeping bags. Sleep had just claimed me when Laurel bumped my foot.

"Allie," she whisper-shouted loud enough to wake the dearly departed.

I fisted my groggy eyes. "What?"

"Check this out." Excitement elevated the pitch of her voice.

I crawled out of the tent, wearing sweatpants and a hoody to fend off the nippy night air.

"You'll never believe what we found." She led me to the portable bathrooms.

Nick waited behind them, a flashlight lighting our path, an old, yellowed plastic sleeve protecting a map as old as dirt in his hands.

CHAPTER 18

Nick slid the map out of the envelope protecting it from the ravages of air. In mint condition, it was western days old on thick parchment with yellowed edges.

"We found this tacked inside a loose wallboard in the cabin," Laurel explained. "I doubt anyone would've found it until they tore the cabin down. We found it by a fluke 'cause our flashlight reflected off the plastic."

Nick steadied the light on the map. "It's a map to buried gold."

"I knew Dante was up to no good. Again." I told them about my sleuthing on Dante's tablet, the article about gold in the Amadori hills. The emails I'd read weren't a topic for public consumption yet.

"Do you think he has a copy?" Laurel asked, a slight lisp in her voice.

I leaned forward and sniffed, not smelling a trace of alcohol on her breath. I blew out a relieved sigh. "Doubt it. I get that he believes the map he gave me is an authentic copy. Similar to this one, though." I followed the light as Nick flicked the beam across the map. "This one has different pathways and roads." I outlined two lines that veered off in altered directions than our treasure hunt map. "Here and here. A few other differences."

"Do we give it to him?" Nick asked.

"No way," I said.

Logan's "no" eclipsed mine, as he stealthily came up behind me.

"Well, that's final." Nick chuckled. "What's the deal? What're you hiding from me, girl?" He quirked his eyebrows at Laurel.

Her hand flew to her chest in indignation. "Not me."

"Look, dude, can we trust you?" Logan asked him point blank.

"I just made out with your sister for an hour. Do you trust that?"

"Nick!" Laurel clamped her hand over his mouth until he licked it, and she burst into a fit of giggles.

"Shhh," I hissed. "You'll wake the psych ward, then we're all screwed."

"You'll give up your secrets?" Nick slipped the map into the envelope, thumbed off the flashlight, and stuck both underneath his shirt for safekeeping.

"Secrets? I'd love me some secrets." Rambo's booming voice spurred us into action.

I nearly peed myself. "Go!" Darkness hiding me, I bolted into the woods. No way would I incur the trespassing police again. Mulch and twigs crackled underfoot, snipping my frazzled nerves. Steady breathing revealed Logan on my tail. I ducked behind a trio of close set trees, before I crashed into a tree trunk. "Over here," I whisper-shouted.

Logan stumbled beside me. Nick and Laurel followed, all panting heavy enough to alert the forest rangers in town.

Thrashing sounds through the woods and a flashlight illuminating the area gave Rambo away. *Criminy.*

The light swept the spot we'd just vacated. "You kids don't want to get lost out here with the bears, do you?" Rambo growled out. "Best return to your tents. I'll go easy on you, let you off the hook. Not tell Dante."

My sight adjusted to the dark. Laurel's teeth chattered, and Nick slipped his arm over her shoulders, hauling her close.

"He's baiting us," I whispered.

Darkness pressed bristly fibers all over me. A creepy-crawly sound rustled the bushes to my left, and I recoiled, landing on Logan's bent knees. He took the brunt of my weight, his arms holding me so close, the pounding of his heart echoed through me.

"Shhh. He's leaving," he said.

Rambo swept his light into the woods and headed to the tents.

"We're just kids. He doesn't give a crap about us," Laurel whispered.

Logan and I gazed into each other's dark eyes, a palpable foreboding riding the air. If they knew we possessed the map, would Dante celebrate it or off us? My mind spun into the morbid.

"Don't know about that," I answered Laurel. "Shady is as shady does."

"You lovelies need to tell me what's going on in your pretty heads." Nick fisted Logan's shoulder. "You too, Montgomery."

Another light bobbed toward us. Busted for real. I contemplated bolting deeper into the woods, but the dread of bashing my head or snapping my leg in two proved greater than being caught by whoever held the second light. My educated guess pinpointed Dante.

A quick plan blossomed. "Follow my lead. You guys stay hidden. Laurel, stand with me."

A blinding beam lit us up. "You found us." I tromped into the light, recognized Douchedick Dante's silhouette. "Laurel didn't return from the potty, and I went hunting for her. We got lost." Laurel erupted in an Academy Award winner crying jag. She hugged my arm, jiggling against me. I think she was giggling.

Dante followed the beam of light. "Where's Nick and Logan?" Exasperation set up shop in his voice.

"They're looking for her too. Took off that way." I pointed to the porta-potties. "I told them to meet me near the potties in five minutes." I snatched Laurel to my side, leaving Nick and Logan hidden in a depression behind the thicket of trees.

"She's lying," Rambo's words preceded his bear-shaped shadow. "They're up to no good. I say send them all packing tomorrow."

"What?" I uttered, stunned. "We didn't do jack."

Dante slanted his head to the side. "You're already on thin ice, Allie. Laurel, do you want your friend dragging you down with her?"

"No. But if Allie goes home, I go with her, and so will Logan, Marco, and Nick. Who will you have left?" she demanded. "Who'll transform your crapass meals into gourmet delights? Who'll take care of the kids since you didn't hire enough counselors? I'll tell my mother how run down this place is, how you cancelled all our excursions and took all our money. She'll be on the phone to Mrs. A and other parents within seconds."

Whoa. Laurel. I squeezed her arm hard to shut her up, afraid to tip us off if I cupped my hand over her mouth, which I was raring to do.

Dante advanced on us. A frisson of panic touched my chest. *Holy mother. What did Laurel do?*

"Back to your tents." Dante batted his flashlight against a tree, his rage barely controlled. "Now."

That was one command I obeyed without thought. Laurel and I fled.

Outside Laurel's tent, she said, "I'm sorry. I couldn't check myself. This garbage just got real."

From the glow of the lanterns, I saw tears glistening in her eyes, heard the catch in her throat, and reined in my wrath.

"I know. Go to bed. It'll be okay."

"What about Logan and Nick?"

"They ran off before Rambo showed up the second time." I seethed so hard, I wanted to hit something. Not Laurel. No. This was typical Laurel. Most times, she used a filter. Other times, her filter had massive holes. I was used to compensating for her.

When I climbed into my sleeping bag, tears wet my cheeks. If Dante shipped me home tomorrow, I'd dry up and die. My parents would never release the shackles until I was eighteen. Shudders rolled up from my toes, and I wanted my snow globe so bad I almost tossed my cookies. Unsuccessfully, I pressed on my leather cuff. I had to force myself to take deep, even breaths to end the strange mix of rage, fear, and confusion that bound me.

Serena's arm flung out over my stomach, and I hugged her. The girls needed me still. I was here for them. Not me. Not solely for my freedom. I refused to let them suffer from Dante and Martina's machinations. I'd do whatever it took to stay at camp for the kids. But I refused to quit investigating Dante and trying to find Mrs. Amadori. At least once before I left the campground, I would see her in the flesh.

The morning brought a new perspective on life at Dragonfly Meadows. Before I headed to the crude bathroom, I hunted down Logan. He met me in the middle of the tent circle.

He took my hand, stroked his thumb across my palm. "You okay?"

The touch of him on my skin launched jolts of electricity across my palm. But reality had risen with the sun, and I eased my hand out of his clasp. Too soon, too fast…chock full of memories I'd labored to bury for so long, that kept rising and crapping on my freedom. It was easier to just pretend he wasn't Logan Montgomery. "Yeah. You get caught?"

"Nope. Nick hid the map. I kinda filled him in on the haps."

"You mean Laurel hasn't blurted it out to him?" I laughed to defray my lingering annoyance.

"Not a peep."

"Thank the masters of silence." I wished her distress had blurted it out to Nick rather than Dante. "I need to clean up. See you at breakfast?"

He smiled. "I'll save you a spot."

Neither of us budged. My tangle of emotions fed my heart. The moment filled with life and promise, full of Logan and Allie. It represented a new paradigm.

"Allie," he breathed out. "What's—"

Silencing him, I dipped my index finger into the little dimple on his chin, the way I used to do. I didn't want the moment to change, but I left him standing there gob-smacked.

Dante stood along the bank of the river. He motioned me over. I held up a finger, the one-minute finger, not the screw off one, and did my business in the bathroom area. As soon as I repacked my cosmetic case, I took hesitant steps toward our psycho leader. Laurel stood beside him.

Nick and Logan walked toward us. *Stay or go time.*

When we circled him, he gave us a good-natured smile. He appeared calm for the most part, despite the white knuckles gripping his tablet.

"If you want to leave the campground, you're free to go after we return to camp." He held up a hand. "However, if you think," he glared at Laurel, "camp is different from previous years, you need to tell me rationally. Not that I need to tell you this, but with my aunt out of commission, I'm doing the best I can to run this place. Martina knows more about administration and organization. I'll talk to her about the food."

"I'll still help out in the kitchen," Nick offered, scuffing his sneakers in loose river rocks, jangling them, drawing Dante's glare to the ground for a second, as if he spied a gold nugget.

"I'd appreciate that." Dante shook Nick's hand. "Chef is green, but he's trying. We're on reduced staff since money's tighter this year. Instead of raising rates like other camps, we kept our rates the same as the last couple years. As for the excursions, it cost us bank to set up this camp and we'll return next week for hiking. We had to buy extra gear for other outdoorsy excursions too. Believe me, you kids will get your money's worth."

Silent, we listened, knowing one negative response might set him off. He excused us and we dashed off. I wanted as far away from the prick as my leash allowed. His smarmy germs coated me, and I fought the urge to take a dunk in the river.

"Let's talk at lunch. Not now. Not here," Logan said. "Nick, go back to kitchen duties. Everyone stay separated, do your assigned tasks."

As soon as breakfast ended, the final phase of the treasure hunt commenced. I was still map leader and had to make contact with Logan and Laurel as part of my duties. They took their maps and clues, and skedaddled.

"What up?" Marco approached.

I handed him his map. I told him about getting caught and Dante catching on to things that might not be right in the lala-land of his own making. "You still gonna call your mom?"

"You bet." He scratched his head, leaving his messy dark hair more tousled. "I have office duty when I return."

An idea whammed me. "Hey, does office duty include answering the phones?"

"Yeah," he said slowly, then he palmed his forehead. "Oh, man. Martina had all the phones forwarded to her voicemail. I haven't had to answer them."

"Oh, hell in a hand basket." Another piece of the puzzle. They're fielding parent calls.

"Dante's watching us. Catch you on the flipside. Hey, soon as I make my call, I'll hunt you down at dinner."

The treasure hunt teams were allowed to search in any sector. The final map held vague clues, and most of the search included digging beyond the cave-in area, far enough away to stay safe. The winning team earned the coins in the final treasure and a special movie night alone, extra free time and other privileges at camp.

After an hour of digging, kids grew annoyed, and they sat on the ground complaining and tossing leaves at each other. In a foul mood, Dante scolded them. Fights broke out when fake treasure was found and kids fought Neal and his bullies over them. Weirdo Rambo separated them. What role did the no-neck play at camp? He did some digging, helping the kids here and there, but for the most part he acted like he was filling in the cave-in, while digging up more ground.

I was dying to study Nick's map. We played it safe and hung onto the map for Mrs. A. She owned it and the gold, not Dante or Martina. The four musket-rats agreed on that.

Laurel sat across from me on a tarp covering pebbly ground.

"You didn't tell me how last night went." I pinched leaves from her hair.

She blushed. "We made out, you know, just kissing. I got nervous being out there. Nick tried to calm my jitters by sweeping his flashlight in an arc so I could see the cabin was harmless. That's when the light reflected off the sleeve of the map between wallboards."

"Were you nervous with him?"

"Not really. He's so easy to be around. Despite his corny lines, he's smart, fun, and nice."

I bumped her shoulder. "You're falling for him."

"No. I've *fallen* for him." She gave me the evil-eye. "Speaking of. What's up between you and karate dork?"

I fought the flush blazing up my neck. "Honestly, I have no clue."

She made a smooching sound. "Thought you lusted after Marco?"

"Marco? No. We just hang together. He's too complicated. I get the impression he's into both boys and girls, if ya know what I mean. Didn't you tell me that he liked *everyone*?" I sprawled on my back, arms extended.

"He never came out and said one way or another." Laurel shrugged her hands. "I've always wondered."

Some of our team members joined us, tired of the endless treasure hunt. They flopped on the ground.

"This is dumb." Carrie flung a handful of leaves in the air. They floated down onto her legs. "I don't give a hoot about winning some stupid prize."

"Can we go into the river?" Jasmine asked. "I'm hot."

"Not until the treasure is found." I spritzed water on her red face.

Dante growled. Tomato-faced and steaming, he held

Jesse by the scruff of his neck and stuck a shovel in his hand. "Keep digging. You'll stop when I tell you to." Despite Jesse's lame ankle, Dante threw him into a heap on the ground. "Quit whining," he screamed. "It can't be this hard to find buried treasure." He kicked at a decrepit tree stump, sending chunks of decaying wood flying into the air. "No one goes anywhere until the treasure is found."

"Holy macaroni." Carrie's jaw dropped. "Why're his shorts in a bunch?"

Jasmine sat up straight. "There's no treasure. We've searched everywhere. And he's making everyone dig randomly, really deep, pointing from spot to spot."

"It's stupid. He's making everyone dig in dirt that hasn't been dug up before." Carrie tossed up more leaves. They fluttered to the ground as if falling from autumn trees.

Another loud burst erupted out of our smoke-billowing Dragon Lord. He'd gone off the edge, using the kids to hunt for his family's lost gold. *This is a nuclear disaster, a gift that keeps on giving.*

Martina stomped over to Dante and pulled him aside. A heated argument ensued, then Martina jabbed him in the chest. Half the kids witnessed this breakdown in leadership. *Brilliant, Maestro.*

"Campers," Martina called. "The hunt is over. Everyone take a break, pack up, and we'll return to Dragonfly Meadows. We'll draw for a winner later."

A few campers were upset over the change in plans, most glad to be done with the endless digging.

Under a tense pall, we headed to our tents and packed. Marco's group rode on the first bus out of camp. Before he left, he secretly gave me a phone gesture. Shit just splattered the fan. It was time to call his mother.

CHAPTER 19

Dragonfly Meadows Campground looked like paradise when our mini-bus crunched onto the gravel parking lot. After grabbing lunch bags from the cafeteria on our way to our cabins, we had the afternoon free until dinner. A dreadful excitement fueled my steps to the relative sanctity of my cabin, despite Dante and his stalker key to our door. The gold mine camp experience had been a momentary blip on the ride to sanity, or insanity as the case may be. Most of all, I was dying to take a real shower, dying to find out what Marco discovered from his mom.

We rejoined the others in the cafeteria for dinner. I set my tray on the table next to Logan. "Seen Marco?"

"Not since the gold mine. Think he made the call?" he murmured.

"Hope so. I brought my phone, just in case." It was nice that I could talk about Marco to Logan and not find myself on the butt end of that growly jealousy.

Dinner was food barely fit for rabid dogs again. I

choked down the bulk store generic mac and cheese and shriveled weenie hotdogs. At least the bread was semi-fresh and the punch had flavor. What flavor remained to be named. How hard was it to screw up bags of bland-with-no-butter frozen corn? Pseudo-dinner ended and still no Marco. None of his campers had seen him since they'd arrived at camp either.

Thank our lucky stars, Dante skipped dinner, probably planning his next freakout or killing spree. Martina hopped on stage and tapped the microphone, sending thumps through the speakers in the corners of the hall. She'd gained color at the gold mine, despite her sunken cheeks and red-rimmed eyes.

"You'll have a free night. No campfire tonight." Grumbles emerged from the kids. "I want all campers to head to their cabins and remain in or near them. You can visit other cabins until nine. Tomorrow we'll continue the *Survivor* games and other activities you signed up for." She pointed to trays of half-decent brownies. "Everyone grab a brownie and your drink of choice on your way out."

Still no sign of Marco, I sat with the girls on our porches to eat our brownies until they scattered to play hide and seek.

"I'm hunting down Marco," I announced to Laurel. "Cover for me."

"Think he got caught calling his mom?" Laurel whispered. Her guilt over blurting out my suspicions last night left her vulnerable. Whispering was a learning experience she might benefit from.

"I hope not." I wiped my damp palm on my thigh, tripping out inside. If Dante had caught him, there was no telling what he'd do. A thought dawned on me. "Where did Nick hide the map?"

"Behind the mirror in his cabin."

Perfect. At least I knew where it was in case I needed

leverage. I checked my pocket for my phone and headed up the path to the boys' cabins.

Marco's tree houses sat farthest down the path. At Logan's three-siders, his boys played wiffle ball behind the cabins, making a racket of fun. He sat on the front steps as if waiting for me.

"I knew you'd come." He stood, tracing his fingertips from my wrist across my hand, feathers brushing against my fingers.

I flipped my palm up, and he pressed his hand to mine, prodding my fingers apart until our fingers entwined as one. His touch electrified me, causing my pulse to buzz. We both took a step forward until the toes of our sneakers touched.

"Allie," he whispered. "Are you okay with…us…like this?" Anguish dragged his voice down, catching me off guard.

Whoa, what? Our spell fragmenting, I detangled my hand from his. I wasn't one-hundred percent okay. He must know that. *Hells bells.* How could he when my head was so screwed up whenever he was near me. Or had he chosen to ignore, forgot, or not care? In our past life, he'd never had trouble talking to me. Now a universe separated us, and I didn't know how to cross that chasm trying to push us together. I desperately wanted him to address that glacial space in the between.

I pulled my hand out of his and took a step backward, locking my hands to my sides to halt their freedom march. "Not really. Are you?"

He stood rooted to the ground, his thumb and index finger going to town on his dumbass air controller. "What do you think?"

A long silent moment enveloped us as I waited for him to say more. His lips became a tight pinched line. My ire met his, and I booted the mess into a mental corner due to bad behavior.

"I need to find out if Marco contacted his mom." Seriously, I wanted to sneak into a burrow in the woods and cry or scream. These feelings overwhelmed me to distraction. My stupid hope that I could ignore my dredged up feelings had vanished the minute I had laid eyes on Logan at the school before we boarded the bus.

"He's gone, had an emergency at home. Apparently, he left after we returned. Nick's in charge of his cabins."

I blinked rapidly. Marco went home? I absorbed this late breaking news. "The only cars that had materialized at camp were the vehicles bringing the kids back. He didn't leave with any of them either."

"I know." Logan rose and paced along the path across the front of the cabins.

"They're lying like a rug. You're thinking he got whacked too?"

Boys' innocent whoops as they played ball tried to blow the convoluted clouds hanging over our heads into normalcy. But the clouds hung tough. The thought of Marco getting caught calling his mom or Dante finding the package meant for Mrs. Amadori refused to budge from my head. A feeling of doom centered me. If I caused Dante to expel him or worse, I'd never forgive myself.

"Hey." Logan tipped my chin up. "He's okay. We'll find the truth." He snaked his arm around my waist, drawing me to him.

I felt his hard planes against my soft curves, a hidden strength I never anticipated. I clamped my arms to my sides, refraining from returning his hug, and he released me. My armor had broken and I needed an overhaul. Did Logan possess the right tools? Is that where all this *stuff* between us was leading? My gaze darted around like a dragonfly, looking for a sand dune.

I sighed. "Can we check the tree houses? I want to see

if his stuff's there and find that envelope."

"Did he tell you where he hid it?"

"No." I mentally kicked myself for not asking that one important question when I'd asked so many others. "Hey, we'll search for his mom's phone number and call her."

"Thinking the same."

"We may have to sneak inside the office."

His spine stiffened. "I know. Shit's weird now. We might think about calling your mom."

"What? No." I shook my head so hard I about gave myself whiplash. "She'll make me come home. You know she's hunting for any excuse to keep me at home *all* summer."

"She's a lawyer. She can help."

"Sure. After she makes me go home and talks your mom into bringing you and Laurel with me." I scrubbed my face, cleansing away the dire thoughts. "Let's see what we unearth." Arrows aiming for me wouldn't send me home. Until I saw proof of the wrongdoing pudding, I'd keep my suspicions to my small group of sidekicks.

"I'll walk you to your cabin. Stay with Laurel. I'll check out Marco's cabin, then ask Dante where Marco went."

"Take me. I can gauge Dante's response better than you."

"Right." He sneered.

"You know I'm good at reading people." Disdain laced my words. Except where kidnappers with the name of Michael Kline were concerned. And the Logans who refused to vent their spleens. A perfect storm. *Duh.*

"No. Let's go." He tailgated me. Either he was ticked or didn't trust himself next to me.

Fine by me. What the hell ever. I needed a clear head, not one clouded by all things Logan Montgomery. By the time we reached Laurel's cabin, I decided Logan definitely needed a tagalong. I wanted to see what Marco had left behind. I feared Logan might sugarcoat things for the sake of keeping me safe. We caught up to Laurel coaching a game of tag behind our cabins.

"Nick told me Marco had to go home. Emergency," she said.

"*Right.*" I scowled.

"You don't think so?"

"Did you witness a car carting him away?" I sat in a lawn chair, kicking my sneakers through the wild grass, wishing it was deep enough to flit around in like a dragonfly to find answers to all my nagging questions.

"Nick thinks the same."

"Bingo."

"You think Marco went the way of Mrs. A?" Changing her tune, she genuinely seemed interested in my paranoia.

"If you see Nick, send him to the tree houses to run interference." Logan stomped away as if he was heading to a firing squad.

"I'm going with you. You occupy the boys. I'll search Marco's alcove," I declared, trailing after Logan.

CHAPTER 20

Logan groaned and kept on walking. The boys continued to play behind the three-siders, and we whizzed by them to escape their notice. The tree houses sat empty.

"You look out. The boys won't question seeing you outside rather than me." Not giving him a chance to argue, I hopped up the first step at the base of a giant tree leading to a wrap-around landing about sixteen feet off the ground. Logan's hand alighted on my butt to steady me. Shoes and gear cluttered the landing, reminding me of Logan's bedroom. Except this gear was athletic versus Logan's geeky tech gear.

"Hurry," he said. "Marco's alcove's to the left."

Boards creaked underfoot in the doorway. Dodging the crap littering the floor, I zipped inside the inner sanctum of stinky boys. My nose tickled at the underlying stench of dirty shoes lingering in the main room, glad the windows were open to let in fresh mountain air. The CL alcove had a curtain similar to mine. I swept it aside, my palms growing damp. Marco's bed was neatly made, clothes strewn across the foot of the bed. His watch sat on the windowsill next to an alarm clock. I'd never seen him without the black-banded watch. All his belongings had been left behind. Major willies plagued my spine in a frigid wash. What kind of emergency had taken him home? Was he planning to come back? I hoped everything was okay. But I had a bad, bad feeling things weren't okay at camp. Once again.

Clothes hung on pegs along one wall, some of which I recognized as Marco's. I dragged his suitcase out from under his bed, hunting for the envelope from his mom. I tore the room apart, but found nothing. Out of the corner of my eye, I spied a blue object sticking out partway from under his bed by a front leg. I gathered up his nylon wallet and stared at his driver's license. Who'd leave their wallet behind?

As I raced to the doorway, I caught a fleeting glimpse of my pale, stricken face in the wall mirror inside the alcove.

"Logan, catch." I tossed him the wallet. He missed, and it clunked onto his shoulder, and then bumped down his arm to the ground.

"Hurry. Dante and Nick are coming up the hill."

A wayward thought jiggled my memory, then the light bulb flicked on. "Stall them."

Backing into the alcove, I fingered the mirror away from the wall. Nothing behind it. *Crap on a cruddy cracker.* It clinked against the paneled wall. As I was about to leave, a framed print of a man fishing along a mountain river, the Amadori gold mining operation in the background, caught my attention.

I pried the print away from the wall, pulling the bottom nail out. Adrenaline sped through my veins. *Bingo.* First-aid tape secured the envelope to the flipside of the print. I peeled the envelope off. Voices neared the tree houses, and I buried the envelope under my blouse and bumbled down the steps the same time Neal and his minions rounded a bend in the woods. They caught me red-handed, poised to run, with Dante coming at me from the opposite pathway. My stomach dove for my feet.

"Hey," Neal yelled. "The hell you doing?"

The three bullies strutted toward me. Too late to run.

"Come back for more?" Richie taunted. "Dudes, told you she liked us." They all laughed as though he'd won comedian of the year.

"Please." I scoffed. "I'm looking for Marco." My brain told my mouth that Dante, Nick, and Logan would crash the scene any second.

"What's wrong with us? Marco's a wimp. He doesn't even hit girls." Neal tugged my hair as if girls liked having their hair pulled. I knocked his hand away.

The three boys circled me as if I was tuna to a starving cat. "Here's a tip for you. Dante and Nick are hiking up the hill. If you leave now, I won't tell Dante that you were harassing me."

Scuffling sounds wafted to us. Dante, Nick, and Logan had reached the top of the incline.

"You better scram." Relief surged, and I thrust through Jeff and Richie, prompting them to scatter the way they'd come. I zoomed into the woods in front of the tree houses and hid in a thicket of young scraggly pines.

"I'll pack up Marco's things. Then you can move in, Nick," Dante said. They stopped ten feet from where I crouched. I held my breath, afraid Dante would hear me.

"I can do it," Logan offered.

"Go back to your boys. I'll handle it."

"So what happened at Marco's home?" Logan asked loudly for my benefit.

Go Logan!

"Family stuff," Dante said. "Nothing to worry about."

Seriously? Marco leaves every lick of his belongings behind, including his wallet and the envelope, for "nothing to worry about family stuff?"

"Why'd he leave in such a rush?" Logan pressed onward. I wanted to kiss him.

"His parents wanted him home ASAP. I offered to pack and arrange for delivery of his things."

Get real. The only delivery Dante planned was into the kitchen dumpster. I felt up the papers against my torso, dying to open the envelope. But the papers belonged to Mrs. Amadori and weren't mine to open. Would they help me in my quest to find her safe and sound? The conflicting ideas burned inside my brain, leaving my head aching.

Dante and Nick climbed up to the tree house. With a backward glance, Logan took off toward his cabin. As soon as Dante and Nick vanished inside, I sped after Logan, tripping and coming within inches of my face becoming one with a tree. I fell to my knees, my hands catching my fall. Road rash burned my palms and I stifled a cry.

Instantly, Logan was by my side, helping me up. Tears stung as he inspected my palms and picked out pine needles.

"I'm normally the klutz, not you," he said to brighten the moment.

I swiped the tears threatening to cascade. My hands burned, my knees hurt. The pain in my heart hurt the most—the pain of four years of an emptiness Logan's desertion had created.

"I was trying to catch up to you."

"Because I'm a great catch?" He hugged me to him.

No. Yes. The darkness of twilight enclosed us, and I burrowed in his arms. The crinkle of the envelope intruded upon our moment.

"You found it?"

"Yes. He wouldn't leave it behind *and* his wallet." I rubbed my palms on my shorts to clean the dirt off them, stifling a whimper.

"Dante's lying." Logan's thumbs and index fingers rotated on his mental game controller. "He wouldn't let me and Nick pack Marco's alcove. I think he knows Marco hid something for Mrs. A. He's looking for it."

"Do we peek inside the envelope?" I patted my hand over my stomach. "There might be clues to Mrs. A's whereabouts."

We walked down the path, Logan's hand on the small of my back as if to steady me. It was comforting, and no longer made me want to detonate into a twitch storm.

"I want to see what's inside."

Shocked, I said, "You do?"

"I believe you, about everything. We may have to make some calls tomorrow. Tonight, let's plan our attack."

Part of me had thought he was humoring me for the sake of getting closer or returning to our old friendship. Now I knew for sure how wrong I had been. I melted a little inside in that moment.

Without warning, he crushed me to him and captured my mouth between his lips in a hard, pressing kiss. A funny whimper emanated in my throat, and burning butterflies flitted low in my awakening body. My mouth parted and Logan's tongue speared inside. How did he learn to kiss so good? Who cared, as long as he didn't stop? I raked my fingers through his hair, absorbing the burn on my palms, tugging his head closer. Finally, my tongue tangoed with his, eliciting a moan from him, his fingers trailing up my sides to brush his thumbs alongside my tingling breasts for a nanosecond.

An eon crawled by with my lips crushed to his, touching wherever my skin made contact, hearing his halting breath amid the distant sounds of frogs croaking. Air diminished to short supply, and I had to draw away to end the hot as sin kiss.

"Logan," I whispered. "What's going on?" He puzzled me from my curling toes to my prickly scalp.

He kissed my lips, my nose. "What do you think?"

Despite the encroaching darkness, I ducked my head to avoid his frank stare. A tense silence trembled up my spine.

"Okay. I get it." Logan shrugged back his shoulders, and freed me to head up Allie's Spying and Investigating, Inc.

I'd lost the moment and didn't feel right seizing it back. "You don't get it." I walked my fingers down his wrist. "Can we table this conversation for later? My investigation is more important, you agree?" Despite my incessant craving to get him to fess up, my head was too twisted to deal at the moment, and the case had taken a bizarre turn that took precedence. And I wanted to savor that kiss. *That holy guacamole kiss. Oh, my shit, I'm messed up six ways to Sunday.*

He laughed a carefree happy sound that reawakened those incessant butterflies in my lower region. "So now you're a detective?" He flipped his hand and clasped mine in his long, firm grip.

"Well, someone has to own it. May as well be me." I steered course for the Dragonfly Lily cabins.

Laurel and the girls were scaring each other telling ghost stories around a portable lamp in front of her cabin. The fake fire enthralled the girls.

"Keep them occupied," I whispered to Laurel. "We're going fishing." Logan ruffled her hair and gave her a thumbs up, meaning all was well, at least for her small world.

Logan joined me in my curtained alcove. He perched

on the edge of my bed, and I sat across from him, holding the envelope.

An unspoken assent passed between us. I slid my index finger beneath the gummed seal. It gave way easily. My pulse raced as I fingered out the printed pages. The first page, a letter from Marco's mom to Mrs. A took my breath away. Apparently, Mrs. Lorenzo had done research on Dante. The package contained a dossier, a petty criminal record of theft crimes, and a credit file.

"Dante's up to his eyeballs in debt." I handed him the credit file that contained multiple pages of credit card debt and collection efforts.

"Why would Mrs. A care about this?" Logan scanned the pages.

"He was shaking her down for money?"

"I doubt she had any money. She owned the campground and whatever money her husband left her after he died ten years ago. From what I remember, she used that to keep the campground afloat."

"And Dante tells us he came here to bail her out financially."

My eyes bulged at a will and probate file. I skimmed over the pages. "Oh. My. God. This is it." I showed the pages to Logan. "Mrs. A's brother is Dante's father. Dante Senior and kids were cut out of his father's will. Check this out." I pointed to the line in the write-up Marco's mom had compiled. "If Mrs. A dies, the property goes to her children. If she has no children, the property goes to Martina and Dante equally."

"She has no children." Logan leaned over my shoulder, reading more. "But the gold mine property goes to the county historical society—"

"When Carla Amadori dies," I finished for him. "Including all mineral rights *and* hidden gold."

CHAPTER 21

Logan and I stared at each other for a long, horrifying moment.

"It's motive for murder." I clutched the papers until my fingernails made moon-shaped dents in them.

"Hide them." Logan gathered the papers, crumpling them in his haste. I stuffed them in the envelope, scanned my room for a hiding place.

"Where?" I whipped my head about. "I don't want this in my cabin."

"I'll hide it in the woods. He'll never know who read the contents if he finds it." Logan took the envelope from me.

My mouth dried up like a sun-bleached prune. "I'm freaking out now more than ever," I confessed.

"Play it cool. Stay out of his hair. Don't antagonize him or ask about Marco. Do whatever he says."

"Should we call our parents now?" My gaze flitted to the nightstand where I'd hidden my phone underneath it.

"I'll find Marco's home number first. Let's do this

right."

Acid roiling in my belly, I nodded. I didn't want to go home, but I wanted to live more. I wanted Logan, Laurel, Nick and all the kids safe from this monster that lurked in our midst. I didn't think he wanted to hurt any of the kids, if what we feared was true. I think he wanted the land and gold and had to kill Mrs. A to get both.

"Why would he off Mrs. A for the hidden gold? Why didn't he search for it himself?" Logan mused.

"There may've been bad blood between the families. Mrs. A probably wanted the goods on him because she didn't trust him."

"But she trusted Martina." Logan secured the envelope in his waistband under his shirt.

"Brothers and sisters aren't equally trustworthy." The meaning of my words hinted at the contention between us. Despite his awakening—the awakening of us—Logan still had to earn my renewed trust again.

He tilted his head. "Act chill. Join the girls. We'll touch base in the morning."

Logan rushed out of the cabin. I decided not to tell Laurel anything to keep her from stepping off the ledge.

Bedtime came too soon, and I lay awake for the longest time trying to corral my chaotic thoughts. Unable to sleep, I grabbed my flashlight and crawled out of bed to snag my snow globe.

I dug into the drawer underneath my bed all the way to the back where I'd wrapped the globe in my sweats, touching the wooden rear of the drawer. "What the what?" Opening the drawer all the way, I shined the flashlight from side to side, chucking my clothing every which way. Then I searched the other drawer. Panic clogged my throat. Forcing myself to move, I searched my alcove top to bottom. Someone had nabbed my snow globe.

A cool sweat popped on my neck. I double-checked to

ensure the cell phone was intact. It remained taped to the underside of the nightstand next to the charger. For the first time, I was glad Mom had forced me to bring a first-aid kit with medical tape…and the phone.

I flicked the flashlight over the sleeping girls, checked all their drawers. No globe.

Climbing into bed, I gathered the covers close, the flashlight in my hand. Thoughts tangled in my head. I fought the rising agitation, tamping it to the ground, but it kept rising like the walking dead.

"Stop it," I whispered to myself. "You're investigating a murder that has nothing to do with you. If you can do that, you can slide through the night."

A vision of Logan soared to mind, and I focused on him first, but it was painful and mystifying. My mind traveled to my investigation, making a mental checklist of the trouble and contradictions I'd stumbled upon. Soon, my panic abated, and I fell asleep, memories of Logan's silky warm lips on mine, holding me close. The snow globe became a distant memory.

Morning delivered a new surprise. Dante asked Logan to fill in for Marco doing his and Martina's gopher duties, which meant Logan had ready access to the office. *Holy flippin' cow.* Luck dallied on our side. Or Dante and Martina wanted to keep their enemies closer. *Whatever.* I wasn't looking a gift donkey in the mouth.

Cereal with sliced bananas and strawberries constituted breakfast. Not sure where the fruit came from, but it was decent enough, if somewhat pathetic. Food choices were sliding downhill fast. Logan joined me at the table with Nick and Laurel. I'd bagged him a bowl of cereal heaped with overripe fruit and milk before breakfast disappeared from the limited selection. He nodded appreciatively.

"I have keys to the storage room, but no computer access," he whispered. "Martina keeps her office locked. Dante's office was always locked according to Marco."

"Dante gave you keys?" I blinked my surprise.

"Stole them. I think they were Marco's. Dante still has his. None of them fit Dante's office."

Awkwardly, I high-fived him. High-fives weren't in our normal arsenal, but the moment deserved it, even though half our hands hit air.

"What about Marco's home number?"

"No dice. His wallet's clean. I even called info for San Jose. Number's unlisted."

Dante and Martina hopped on the stage, and the room quieted. We gave them our most rapt attention, dutiful campers once again. They announced that we'd finish the *Survivor* games after breakfast, attend craft sessions after lunch, and then free period before dinner.

"One last thing." Dante waited for the noise to die. "Marco has been called home for personal reasons. Logan Montgomery will take Marco's assistant duties and Nick Constantine will take over as Cabin Leader for Marco's cabins." Dante and Martina left the stage. The dining hall erupted in speculation.

"Any idea why Marco got called home?" I asked Nick.

"No." He leaned in conspiratorially. "The boys are wondering because no one saw him leave. He went to the offices after his group arrived from the gold mine and he never left."

My mouth hung open, enticing flies. "Surely he caught a ride on one of the vehicles carting kids back from the gold mine."

Nick shrugged. "No one saw him."

"Are his boys freaking?" I asked.

"Nah. I told them not to worry, that it's all on the up and up."

"But you don't think so, right?" Laurel piped up, tapping her fingers on her chin, excited to join in the conspiracy theories.

He shrugged. "Lovely Laurel, don't fret your pretty head over it."

I about tossed my churning breakfast on the table as Laurel cooed and drooled all over Nick.

Breakfast period ended, and Laurel, Logan, and I headed to our cabins surrounded by our kids. We had to keep our suspicions on the down low due to elephant ears.

At the fork in the path, Logan skimmed my hand, a safe outward sign of our lingering friendship. It's not like he could bend me over his arm and plant one on my mouth, which is what my mouth was dying for. I trudged behind the girls next to Laurel, thinking about my next steps.

"Everything good with you and Logan?" she asked out of the blue.

"I don't know. Why?"

"You two are acting weird. Together, but not, but not friends either."

"He kissed me," I blurted out.

Laurel screeched. "What?" She dug her fingernails into my arm and tugged me to the side of the path. "Did you kiss him back?"

"I think so." A flush worked up from my chest to my neck.

"Either you did or you didn't, missy." Her hands settled on her hips.

"Okay. I did. More than once." Insects buzzed nearby, and I swatted at a fly, wishing to bat away this conversation as easily.

Laurel's mouth formed a big *O*. I'd rendered her

speechless. Yay, chalk one up for an Allie first.

"You know I'd always liked him."

"As a friend, until he left."

"Those feelings...returned." I sucked in my bottom lip. "But it's wrong, so wrong right now."

"Did he tell you why he went to boarding school?"

"No. That remains a source of conflict." My challenging gaze met her curious one. "You still have no idea, do you?"

"No. You know I would've told you the minute I found out. Guess you'll need to force him to fess up if he won't spill on his own. Stupidass brother. Do you want it to go any further?"

I shrugged, wobbled my head, and narrowed my eyes, all in my dance of avoidance. "He's so freaking complex. I'm complicated. *It's* thorny." I couldn't think up any more words to describe our problematic—aha, another one—situation. "He's different, but the same, if you know what I mean. Nothing goes further until we hash this out. Then who knows? I may hate him forever." My shoulders slumped. "Do you mind if we progress, *if* we progress?"

Laurel took my hand in hers. "I mind if he doesn't come clean. You know I love you both, and didn't have a problem when you liked him during our three musket-rat days."

I hugged her tight.

"You're...killing...me," she fake-gasped.

I freed her, and we continued onward to the cabin.

"Wasn't so bad he came to camp, after all," she gloated, wagging her eyebrows.

I bumped my shoulder against hers. "At least he's been helpful with my mystery." I grinned. "What about you and Nick?"

"I know. It's freaking awesome." She skipped a jig.

Our campers captured our attention as we gathered

towels, lotions, and totes for the afternoon at the lake, ending our awkward conversation. We'd needed the conversation. Relief loosened knots in my shoulders knowing that she was okay with Logan and me. *If there is a me and Logan. Big-ass if.* Her relationship with Nick helped matters, or else she'd take a shovel to my business.

The girls were excited to resume playing and glad the doomed treasure hunt had ended. I promised them a trip to the Trading Post later for a treat on me due to my neglect. I hoped I had enough credits to make good on my promise. Numbers rolled in my head until I remembered we didn't have Marco's home number. And I'd left my phone in my room.

I tapped Laurel's arm. "I forgot my book. Be right back."

She pushed her sunglasses up, trying to hide a nose rub. "Not a good idea to be alone."

"Just running to the cabin." Before she slipped a word in edgewise, sideways, or any other way, I dashed down the path toward my cabin.

"Yo, my lovealicious Allie," Nick called as I dodged around his group of rambunctious boys. "Where're you heading in such a hurry?"

"Forgot something. Catch up to Laurel, she's up ahead."

He herded his boys up the hill. The coast was clear to the cabin.

The door hung ajar, and I froze halfway behind a tree. As the last one out, I had shut and secured it behind me. Kids were not allowed in other cabins without permission. Another prank? Another fake repair?

The girls' room had windows on the side and front, but not the back, and they'd left the blinds shut. I snuck to the rear of the building to peek through my alcove window and lifted on my toes along the edge of the window. At first, I didn't see anyone, but low thumps on the floor gave my intruder away. Dante pulled the drawers open beneath my bed. *Whoa, Nelly.*

He rummaged through my clothes, discovered my stash of bills, and stuffed the money into his front pocket. The money didn't satisfy him, and he continued rifling through my belongings, maintaining my natural neat order. Had he stolen my snow globe? I pressed on my leather band, my arms crossed over my chest. *No, no, not my phone.* If he found it, I was up crap creek without a paddle.

Without another thought, I flew around the cabin and tiptoed up the wooden steps. Logan's self-defense moves revolved in my head. I opened the door, glad that it didn't squeak. Dante had closed the curtains separating the alcove.

Silent, my sneakers ate the short distance on the hardwood floor to my alcove. Through the gap between the curtains, I watched him scavenge my room. So far it didn't appear that he'd found the phone. Just as I was about to back up to the doorway and pretend I was just entering the cabin, a pinecone thunked onto the roof. I froze.

Dante slipped through the curtains, his toolbox in hand. We came face-to-face.

I mentally zipped through the self-defense steps one more time.

"What are you doing here?" he demanded.

"I could ask you the same." I gripped the doorway molding until my fingertips hurt.

His lips ruffled up in a furious half-sneer, half smile. "Just doing my routine cabin inspection. We can't always count on the CLs to report repair items."

I spread my feet apart in preparation for defense. "Do you make it a habit of snooping through campers' belongings?" I couldn't prevent the question from tripping out of my mouth any more than I could stop eating a slice of my favorite key lime pie if shoved in my face.

"Don't know what you saw, but I was checking a loose floorboard," he said as if crunching on glass.

I tensed, ready and willing to put him in his place. "Funny, I don't recall packing floorboards in my dresser drawers."

He took a step toward me. "You saw wrong, little girl. Now get out of my way and get back to your group."

I held my ground, confident in my ability to take him down a notch. Enough of a notch to escape him. "Not until you hand over the money you stole, and my snow globe."

A dark evil crept across his face as he inched another step toward me. "You were supposed to hand over all your money. This is to pay for extra excursions and events." He patted his pocket. "You disobeyed the rules. I'm correcting your behavior."

"What extra excursions am I paying for?"

"I think it's time you went home." He reached behind him and tore a clunky satellite phone off his belt. "Shall I call your mother now and ruin the rest of your summer? The summer you paid dearly for after four years of shackles?"

Shock liquefied my knees. What did he know about that? Had my mother said something in her overprotective way? Is it in that mysterious file Martina possessed?

"That's right. I know all about why you were able to attend camp this year, why Logan came. Logan and I've spent free time talking about you, getting to know one another."

My knees buckled. My death grip on the doorjamb was the sole support holding me upright.

"Why're you spying on me? You know you've broken

so many rules. What would your parents say?" He moved so close I smelled the hazelnut coffee on his breath. "You think they'll lock you up for another four years?"

"Stay the hell away from me. You're talking smack."

"You sure about that? Ask Logan how much I know about your past."

I spun around to run, but he was quicker and yanked my arm behind my back.

He whispered in my ear, blowing my hair onto my cheek in a tickling wave. "You gonna cause more trouble for me, or do you want to go home now?"

"I'm good." I squeezed the word out from the bottom of my gut.

"Good, good." He patted my head as if I was a puppy. I wanted to turn on him and gnaw on his hand, give him a case of rabies. "You keep quiet about what *you* think is suspicious here and we'll be fine. Nothing happening here except your overactive imagination. But maybe I can help you sort it out. Your friend Laurel was wrong yesterday."

My spine drew taut. "Leave Laurel out of this. She was merely repeating me." I wouldn't endanger my best friend over my suspicions. "She's clueless."

"Well then, you'll keep quiet and all three of us will be fine."

His threat didn't fly over my head. "Sure." With all my strength, I rammed my heel into the toe of his sneakers. He yelped, releasing my arm. I shot out of the cabin, not stopping at GO, not collecting $200. Not collecting my useless phone.

CHAPTER 22

Dante bounded down the three wooden steps in one leap. "Allie! Get back here," he yelled.

Running away, I focused on the path heading up the hill toward the lake on the other side of the hill. He gained on me, his huffing and puffing growing louder.

"Damn it, Allie! We're not done."

"Dude, we're done. I'm joining the kids." An old overgrown path to the left lured me. Wary, I resisted the depths of the unknown woods, afraid to get lost. Nor did I want to go to the meadow and drag a fuming Dante to the happy kids. I needed alone time to regroup, to lay my thoughts and sanity back on the rails.

Making a mental note of the old pathway, I sped onward, pretending to run to the meadow and lake. At the top of the hill, I glanced down at Dante chugging toward me and streaked into the woods on my right, a fake-out toward the main campground. The no-slouch jerkoff lumbered after me, but I remained a couple hundred feet ahead of him. Tree branches lashed at me, and I swatted limbs at head height, gaining stinging scratches on my arms. I stumbled in a hole and crashed my shoulder into a tree, jarring my head. Pain radiated across my shoulders.

"Oww." I kneaded away the thudding pain, rotated my ankle. Panting, I froze behind a thick tree. Birds squawked in the highest trees, scolding us for infringing upon their peace. Dante's crashing in the woods ceased, but I felt his presence nearby.

"Come on, girl. This isn't what you think," he cajoled from behind a grove of cedars about fifty feet away. He stepped around them and we locked eyes. "I thought we were good?" He took three steps closer. "Come back, let's talk."

"About what?"

"What you think is going on? I'll set you straight."

"I think nothing." Stealthily, I scanned the woods for another pathway to lead me away from him.

"We both know that's a bald lie." He advanced another step.

I bolted toward the front of the campground, dying to warn Logan and Laurel. And I needed my phone. Losing my mind and anxieties in my snow globe nagged the edges of my conscience. Even if it were in my cabin, it wouldn't help me. I was stronger than it now. Pressing on my leather band of armor no longer held any power over me in that moment either.

Dante sprinted hard behind me. I weaved through the woods until I spied a wedge of the parking lot and halted, bent double to catch my breath before a final sprint out into the open. Dante must've known how close we were to the main campgrounds and hovered behind a copse of pines before either of us became visible to others below. Just as I believed the marbles had come home to roost in his head and he'd gained his senses, he feinted to the left, then right and charged me. He leaped at my ankles and barreled us both to the forest floor, nearly knocking the wind out of me. Barely avoiding a face-plant into a pinecone, I caught my fall on my hands. I was on a roll of bodily destruction. *Yay me.*

"Let me go." I punctuated the last word with a rear kick, landing my foot hard on his head.

"Knock it off," he ground out. "Let's talk civilly. We can find common ground."

Not sure what common ground he meant. Tell him my suspicions and then what? He kicks me out of camp, kills me, hurts Laurel or someone else? *No can do.*

Gathering a humongous burst of energy, I twisted around, tearing my ankle out of his hands, and jetted into the woods in the direction of camp. I didn't check to see if I had hurt him, or if he gave chase. As if the forest bogeyman aka Dante Asshat Amadori hunted me, I ran for my life, for my future. Sweat dripped down my temples. I rubbed it through my hair and flung slashing branches out of my way. The obscure pathway I'd seen earlier loomed ahead. I slid behind a gnarled tree trunk, gasping for air, peeking around the rough exterior. No Dante, but I gave him plenty of credit in the surprise department and took no further chances. Crouching low, I zigzagged behind boulders and trees on the overgrown path. Once I hit the scraggly trail and regained diminishing air, I jogged for a while, keeping tabs on landmarks to find my way back. The downhill path petered out, and I sprinted through the woods until it grew so thick I was forced to a walk as I squeezed my way through thickets, around boulders and trees. I had no clue where I was.

I dropped to my knees, sucking in air like a Hoover. A squirrel scurried across the pine-strewn ground, another one chasing it. The woody rodents reminded me that Dante might be lurking around the bend. Yet I hadn't heard him for a while and hoped he'd given up. Giving up meant many things. He could be calling my parents to arrange a trip to the Bailey Prison, or making plans to murder me. A snicker slipped out between heavy breaths. I was sunk any way I looked at it. I hoped Laurel and Logan didn't get the boot out of camp or a boot to the head.

After hiding in a burrow of ferns for five minutes, I scoped out the area to ensure Dante didn't have a bead on my forehead through a rifle scope. Coast clear, I darted behind a tree and gathered my bearings in a foreign world of trees, rocks, and decrepit logs. The faint stench of skunk drifted to my nose, completing my crapass day. If I screamed, would anyone hear me?

Dappled sunlight leached through the tree branches, splattering light on the ground, highlighting a rock here, a patch of ground there. I checked the sun's position. One item we'd learned in our one and only Team Leadership class was to detect time by the position of the sun in relation to the campground. Too bad they didn't hand out compasses. Vaguely, I knew which direction the campground lay. I pressed on the thread of panic blooming in my belly, studying the area to deflect my increasing alarm.

An intriguing plant caught my curiosity on the edge of a small incline. I picked my way through the clumps. More of the plants grew in dense rows on the floor of the tiny valley. My horticulture education ended in my backyard at home, learning about whatever plants Mom bought from the local nurseries. But I remembered reading about "mountain misery" in preparation for camp. The white rose-like flowers with yellow centers imbued the air with its pungent floral fragrance. I touched the stems and drew sticky fingers away. The name fit the gummy leaves and the dense knee-high thicket that strangled out any other plants. The misery plant grew in profusion in the ravine.

Distracting myself before I figured out how to escape this jam, I slid down the incline and kicked at a hollow log poking out of clumps of sticky mountain misery.

A clinking noise emerged from the pieces of soft wood I scattered. I squatted, careful not to kneel on the overgrown bushes, and studied the spot from where the sound emanated. Finding a foot-long stick, I raked leaves and twigs in a pile until I found the object that'd made the noise. I picked up the gold dangling on a plant limb, a beautiful and expensive dragonfly pendant on a broken chain. About two inches wide, multi-colored gems crusted the dragonfly's wings, and diamonds sparkled in the eyes.

Shock coursed through me, crashing me to my knees. Slightly dusty and sticky from the plants, the pendant hadn't been in the woods long. It appeared familiar. Had I seen too many dragonfly pictures in my research on the camp? I shoved the pendant in my front pocket, and double-checked to make sure Creepy McCreepy wasn't lurking like a rattlesnake in the choking bushes.

I needed to snatch my phone before he discovered it. If I had to hike ten miles to get reception, I planned to call home. Laurel and Logan were probably having epic freakouts wondering if I'd fallen off the face of the earth. But a weird sense of peace overcame me, and I slipped down the small ravine. Tension drained out of me, leaving a hollowness inside my core. It was the same feeling I'd experience when the bullet ended Michael Kline.

Dante couldn't ruin that feeling. Unless he walked to the edge of the dropdown, he couldn't see me.

Bushes and wildflowers grew in abundance, and I wondered if a stream flowed nearby or underground. Leaving my spot, I investigated until my foot sank into loose dirt covered with leaves and fir needles. Inspecting the ground, I found several depressions where someone had dug up plants, then attempted to cover up the leftover holes.

Slowly, I spun in a circle until I found several half-dead mountain misery bushes in a deep thicket of lusher plants along the ravine twenty feet away. No one needed to call me twice. Without knowing why I was wasting time, I rushed to the brown, droopy plants. My gut was bugging me to investigate. The dry, crackling plants appeared recently planted, as if transplanted from the other spot. I dug through the sticky stems and discovered the ground had been turned up there as well. It reminded me of Mom and me removing all the plants from one planter and moving them to another spot in our backyard.

I floundered in the middle of a flippin' forest in the California Sierras. "Who digs up and replants plants in a forest?" I whispered. I found a thicker, sturdier stick and began digging up the freshly upturned ground. Knee deep in plants, I gently shifted the transplanted ones so as not to totally uncover the dig spot. The sun beat down on me, and sweat dripped along the back of my hairline, but a wintry numbness worked its way inside me. The cloying scent of the blooms incited a dizzying dance inside my senses, the stickiness coating my hands and clothes.

What the living bejeezus was I doing? I sat on a bare patch of ground, my back against a tree, staring at the suspicious ground tempting me in ridiculous lunacy. A grubby protein bar wrapper stuck halfway out between clods of dirt. The same brand as the ones Logan had given me from the kitchen storage. I stared at the wrapper for the longest time.

Beyond the wrapper, a bit of dark green plastic fluttered in the breeze between two bushes a yard away from the ground I'd dug up. I lunged forward and yanked at it, unable to budge the plastic without it tearing.

Wielding a stick, I drilled through the dirt until I exposed more of the green plastic, then more as the dirt easily came away from it.

The smell of decomposing, rotting flesh hit me, and I flung back, covering my mouth. "Oh God, oh God. No." Bile climbed fast. I tossed my cookies in the bushes to my right, trying to simultaneously cover my nose and press on my erupting stomach.

Glacial fingers trailed up my spine, injecting common sense into me, enough to handle what I needed to handle in a half-assed calm manner. I wiped my mouth on my shoulder, wiping the smell of death on my polo shirt, though it pervaded the air. The implications of my discovery remained in its own shallow grave in my head. If I dredged them up, I'd unravel into a million strands of fiber, powerless to knit myself back together. The leaves and limbs of the mountain misery would snare me in their web, suffocating me from its pungent scent, the sticky residue my new prison.

Reluctance and dread engulfing me, I poked a hole in the plastic for a secure grip. One hand over my mouth, I narrowed my eyes to slits of avoidance. I ripped open the bag, exposing lank and lifeless locks of red hair. Carla Amadori's red hair. I recognized the slightly decomposing features of the woman I'd seen in many photos Laurel had brought back from camp over the years. Photos where she wore the gold dragonfly pendant.

Incapable of planning my next step or figuring out how to breathe, I froze, visualizing pacing in front of my lighthouse in my snow globe, shuffling my feet in the warm sand even as snowflakes drifted down from the light of the miniature spire. My right hand instinctively reached for my leather bracelet, my small suit of armor. Between it and the snow globe, they were my last safe havens. Sticky from the mountain misery, I fingered the four beads. One bead for each year I'd lived after escaping Kline. I pushed on the tiny pin, closing my eyes as it pricked my skin. I counted to ten, dropped my hand. I felt no better. The leather band absorbed the bead of blood, one of many before it. I sat, clutching my head.

Had Dante killed her? How had he done it? Did she suffer much? Was it an accident? Tears welled, fell upon my cheeks, and the scent of decay forced me to wipe my cheeks off on the inside hem of my shirt.

A bird trilled, warning me, startling me into movement. Logan. I needed to snag Logan. Breathing through my mouth, I covered the body—Mrs. Amadori—with the dirt I'd unearthed. The way the plants disguised her grave, I knew it was meant to be a permanent burial spot. I diligently positioned the sticky mountain misery in their holes, burying the broken stems and leaves. I brushed over my footprints and made the area appear undisturbed once again.

Ten feet away, I dumped a reddish rock next to two brown rocks to mark the spot so I'd find my way back. Limbs weary, I climbed the hill, slinking to the top to scan for signs of life, studied the ravine and burial place. I wiped tears off with the back of my dirty hands, and ended up using the hem of my shirt again. In a moment of unfathomable grief, I had to hug a tree trunk to hold myself up and lamely dreamed I was hugging Logan. Not a tree. Not the lighthouse in my snow globe. Not that small piece of armor I needed to abandon in order to live again. When had I let go of my snow globe? When had this changed? My armor had splintered. It didn't seem feasible to visit that safety net again. I needed to travel forward and leave my havens behind to live.

"Just do it." I stamped my foot on the ground.

Cold determination adrenalized my legs, and I began to jog toward the campground, following the sun dipping lower in the western sky over the lake. I passed few recognizable landmarks, lost my bearings twice, and had to double back once. Between jogging and walking, it took me over an hour before I found that obscure trail leading to the meadow and lake.

I hadn't crossed paths with a living soul. Occasionally, a scream or laughter from the meadow where the *Survivor* games continued drifted on the air currents. One person hadn't survived whatever games Dante Amadori played. My grief and apprehension persisted below the surface, waiting to surge to the forefront again if I let them. Yet I couldn't afford the distractions they caused. I had to focus on reaching my phone and finding Logan. Avoiding Dante.

Slowing to a crawl, I hid in the shadows of trees and boulders as I descended the hill to the cabins. Relief had no place within me. I'd gotten my wish to see Mrs. Amadori once before my two weeks was up. I hated that stupid wish now.

I probably resembled a slasher victim, but I stepped onto the path in front of the girls' tree houses and passed the three-siders. Familiar male voices floated to me from outside my cabin. With my waning energy, I scooted behind the last three-sider, hugging the outer wall, my weighty head resting against it, seeking support to hold myself up.

Dante flopped in the wooden chair on my porch. Logan reclined on the steps, as if he had no cares in the world. Like long lost buds, they bantered.

I banged my forehead against the wall, my fists against my thighs. *Take a hike to hell, Dante*, I willed inside my head.

Instead, Dante chuckled at something Logan said. "Keep your girlfriend under control and away from the cabins."

"Will do. She gets obsessed and suspicious easily. Stems from the kidnapping, know what I mean?"

"Girl's got some loose marbles." Dante smirked.

"Totally." Logan did a loser *L* on his forehead.

How dare Logan agree with Psycho Jerk? How dare he mention my kidnapping as if they jabbered about the latest video game? Bad enough the entire incident had been plastered across every U.S. news outlet. Had Logan played me all this time? Is that why he refused to open up to me? Was he just trying to slide past summer without addressing the thousand-pound gorilla between us? Heat burned behind my eyelids, forcing my powerlessness of the past into fuel for the future.

CHAPTER 23

Brushing tears off my cheeks and while Benedict Logan occupied Dante, I rushed to the offices. I didn't think I'd get reception on my contraband cell anyway and wanted to try the office landline.

The main campground area was deserted, everyone hanging by the lake. The offices were locked tight, except a window in Martina's office.

Hidden by a garden shed and bushy hydrangeas loaded with blue pompom blooms, I jiggled the screen off the back window and laid it against the siding. Standing on a plastic chair, I climbed through the window, landing on the desk.

I clicked on the cordless phone from the base. Dead silent. I pressed on the laptop, but I'd already seen the red light flashing on the modem, and the nape of my neck prickled. No connection.

This can't be happening. A scream climbed up and I stomped it down. Ear to the door, I listened for activity in the rest of the small building. Not even a rat stirred. The offices were truly deserted. Dante's office was locked as well. Voices murmured on the front deck. I peeked out and saw Rambo and Martina eating at a table on the porch. Good. Tiptoeing away, I began to scout out a way into Dante's office.

The front door behind me opened, then clicked shut. Who was that? I staked out the front deck again, and only Martina remained. *Criminy.* Rambo.

I dashed into Martina's office. The door clicked shut behind me so flipping loud I thought I was a goner. I practically fell through the window to the outside, crushing a hydrangea bloom along with a skosh of hope. But I replaced the screen and hid behind the storage shed. A white phone line stuck out from behind the shed. A second cable line lay loose on the ground, snipped clean through.

"Are you kidding me?" Who'd cut phone and Internet access?

Heart hammering into stroke zone, I streaked back to my cabin. I had to lead Dante away and snag my phone. I hid between the three-siders and peeked at my porch. Dante and Logan sat where I'd left them. Had Logan leaked all my secrets to Psycho Freak?

No. He's playing the ax murderer, not me. Right?

Dante rose and hopped down the steps. "See you at the campfire tonight."

While waiting for Dante to clear the area, I wrangled with the scene, unable to wrap my head around it. Just when I thought I'd conquered yesterday, along came today. I gave up and trudged down the path to where Logan paced.

"Where've you been?" His concerned gaze raked me up and down. "What happened? Did *he* do this?"

Biting my tongue, unsure what to say or do, I sagged onto the first porch step, plopped my face into my hands.

"Talk to me." Logan sat beside me, flung his arm over my shoulder to pull me close. "When you didn't show up at the lake, I came searching for you. Dante was creeping about, said you were incoherent and babbling weird BS, and when he tried to calm you down, you kicked him and ran off."

"Then why didn't you track me down?" Lifting my head, accusation blazed in my eyes.

"Been trying to escape him for a half hour. He kept talking me up." He hugged me closer. "What did he mean?"

"I heard your conversation."

He paused as if mentally processing that revelation. "You heard me give him a ration of what he wanted to hear." With a finger on my chin, he rotated my face toward his. Gently, he used his T-shirt to wipe grime off my cheeks. "I'll destroy him if he hurt you, you know that," he said fiercely. "Please tell me you understand that."

A haunting darkness floated in his eyes. Too dark to trust or understand. It burned me up and joined the ache of my discoveries. Maybe I'd read more into this new Logan than met the eye, or I was only seeing what a subconscious part of me hoped to see. Will I ever be able to trust him again?

The dam to my momentary lapse of judgment flooded open, and I broke down sobbing, inhaling the clean scent of laundry detergent. He held me like he'd wither up and die if he let me go. It took eons for the tears to dry up. I didn't have forever to waste.

I wiped my nose on my sleeve. "She's dead, Logan." I hiccupped. "Mrs. Amadori's dead. I found her...her body." Rendered speechless, he froze, his spine steel rod straight. I showed him her dragonfly. "I remember seeing her necklace in Laurel's photos."

Logan studied the pendant in silence.

"I need to clean up," I said. "Then we need to make tracks before that asswipe returns."

Before he uttered a word, I jumped up, sprinted into my alcove, and tipped my nightstand to the side, the lamp and clock crashing onto my bed. My cell phone was gone.

Logan found me wilted on my knees grappling with something unattainable.

"My phone's gone," I whispered.

"I figured." He didn't appear surprised. "Dante was doing more than skulking."

He picked me up and tenderly cleaned the dirt off my face and my hands with a wet washcloth. When he finished, he kissed me, his lips warm against my cool and unreceptive mouth. Numb, my mind was a tempest of emotion and thought. Normally, I'd bury myself in my snow globe, pretending to exist inside it until I calmed down. This time, I plowed through the storm, shoved past him, and ran outside.

Logan followed me into the woods and we hid behind a thick copse of trees. I told him everything that'd happened since morning, every detail of finding Mrs. Amadori's body.

"We need to alert the sheriff," I said calmly, not knowing how we'd manage it.

"Can you find the body again?"

"I marked my trail and the ravine."

"I want to see her."

Ire twitched my shoulders. "You don't believe me?"

"I believe you. But Dante now *thinks,*" he did air quotes, "you've gone off the deep end. I think he's capable of convincing the sheriff to send you to the loony bin."

Through all this mess, I managed to laugh, cupping my hand over my mouth to stifle the sound. It felt good. It calmed me to think Dante believed I'd lost my marbles.

Let him believe the worst. He was going down for murder.

"Allie? Where are you?" Laurel's voice floated to me. Apparently, I'd become the lost once again. She hadn't seen us yet.

"Wait here," he said. "We're all hiking to the ravine together. The kids are at lunch now. We can get back before free time's over."

"They'll miss us all. Dante's on the prowl for anything outside the norm." I jumped up, brushing off the back of my shorts.

Logan took off. Within seconds, Nick and Laurel crashed into the woods behind him. Laurel enclosed me in the biggest hug ever. I felt horrible that she'd panicked big time after her unwavering vigilance due to my kidnapping.

"I'll kill you if you ever do that to me again." She wagged her finger close to my mouth. "What's up? You don't look so hot." She thumbed dirt off my nose. "Why are you so dirty?"

After repeating my horror story, we agreed that I'd take Logan and Nick to the burial site. Laurel needed to stay behind and cover for us. She assured me that the only words she'd utter were, "I don't know."

I had to believe her. She knew as well as I did that every child in this camp was in jeopardy. She was the first to admit aloud that Martina may not be as innocent in her corpse bride role, and we'd have to tiptoe on eggshells around her too.

"I think Dante's cowed her," I said. "She fears him. Maybe he pounded those bruises onto her."

"She reports everything to him," Nick offered. "I stole a candy bar from the kitchen bunker. She caught me. Dante deducted it from my Trading Post points and gave me a warning strike."

"He didn't have Rambo beat it out of you?" My

pathetic attempt at levity in the somber moment earned grim smiles.

"Chef wouldn't let him." Nick scoffed. "They need my impeccable cooking skills."

With his final attempt at normalcy, we took off, leaving Laurel behind. The second trip to the gravesite didn't take as long as before. I loathed the idea of seeing Mrs. A again. But this trip was necessary. I needed witnesses. I needed to ensure I hadn't hallucinated the entire morning.

Halfway to the ravine, I noticed a black object sticking out of Logan's left cargo shorts pocket. Casually, he secured the button on the pocket. *My phone?* If it were, surely he'd be checking for reception. Not wanting to tip my hand, I shelved the question until I figured out his deal.

No big surprise, the body was right were I'd left it. The mountain misery grew stickier in the afternoon heat. It took Logan and Nick a few minutes to unearth Mrs. A's gruesome head and for Logan to verify her identity. Silent and somber, covering their noses, they reset the burial site the way we found it.

"This is messed up. Now what?" Nick folded his arms over his chest, grooves of uncertainty denting his pale forehead.

"We call the sheriff." Logan's calmness encouraged me.

"Can't." I stomped down on loose dirt, giving it a more secure appearance. "Phone and Internet lines were cut in the office."

"What?" Logan's jaw dropped.

"I snuck into Martina's office, found phone and computer dead, saw the cut lines outside." I spoke rapid fire and made a snipping motion with two fingers.

Lost in thought, we all turned to head back to camp.

That cold encasing my body iced over. Dante stood halfway down the hill leading to the ravine, a gun engulfed in his hand, aimed at me sandwiched between the boys. My stomach plummeted to my knees, taking my lungs for the ride.

"Going somewhere?" He advanced down the hill and stopped six feet away. The gun didn't waver in his hand, and his focused determination settled on me.

Who would he risk shooting first? I poked my elbow in Logan's side and took the chance, slicing out my arm and kicking my legs in the self-defense motions he'd taught me.

"Run!" I knifed my arm down on Dante's forearm, refocusing the gun barrel at the ground. Logan kicked Dante, his blow sending the deranged killer to his knees. I lunged behind a tree, Logan and Nick on my tail. We scattered up the incline on the other side of the ravine. Dante recovered quickly and followed, the ominous gun silent. He had the chance and didn't use it. Was he bluffing?

We zigzagged through the forest, tree branches lashing our arms.

Dante screamed, "I swear to God, I'll shoot one of you."

A gunshot blasted the air, and the hair on the top of my head lifted higher as the bullet whooshed over my skull. I came to a screeching halt. Logan and Nick stopped, arms raised over their heads, panting. *Guess he wasn't bluffing.*

"Turn around. Now," Dante demanded.

On cue, all three of us pivoted on our heels. Logan dropped his arms to brush mine held to my side, a sign of our allegiance and camaraderie.

Memories of my kidnapping flooded back, and I took comfort from that small touch, his nearness, so absent that first time. So alone at Kline's mercy when he led me at gunpoint to his car in an ill-used section of the mall parking lot. It had been twilight and no one paid us much attention as he'd stabbed the gun into my back, his jacket covering his arm and gun, looking like a father leading his daughter to his car. How horribly wrong that scene played out in so many ways. No one had noticed my stricken expression or the words that'd lingered on my tongue but failed to bear sound. No one had cared.

"What do you think you've found here?" Dante asked. Rays of the sun painted red slashes across his face. Sweat dripped down his temples and pit stains swelled under his arms, his hair all skewed and his eyes unnaturally bright. He'd stepped over the line into a twisted territory I had no desire to visit. I might have once been there in another capacity. Never again.

I answered in a small, weak voice, "We were hiking. Took a break." I gave a stiff, nonchalant shrug.

Dante laughed, a cruel sound rising from the depths of his gut. "Don't fucking play me, girl."

"What do you want me to say?" I took the lead. Nick and Logan bracketed me, lending me their physical support. I had a kneejerk feeling they weighed ideas for escape in their heads, and I gave them that opportunity, with a stern internal admonition to bite my tongue before I triggered even deeper evil inside Dante.

"What you know," he replied. "You're too smart for a sixteen-year-old girl. Guess getting kidnapped does that to a brat. Gives you a suspicious edge, right?"

"Exactly." A shiver worked its way into my voice. "Once one becomes a victim of a crime against their person, life looks different afterward." I expressed a feeling I'd fought since the police rescued me four years ago. Although I never saw Kline's dead body, any kind of death didn't sit lightly with a person. The man didn't deserve to die for his crime. It'd haunted me for four years. And now, faced with another crime, more disturbing and wrong, the horror of it quenched my weaknesses, powered my strength. This time, the perpetrator deserved to die for killing Mrs. A. An eye for an eye.

But I refused to let another person die at Dante's hands.

"Look, man, we don't want any trouble," Logan said. "You wanted me to watch Allie and I did exactly what you asked. I found her phone, you have it now. I followed her out here to make sure she stayed out of trouble."

Hard acid gushed into my middle, breaking me apart. Was Logan deflecting? Projecting? Tricking Dante? Or me? Confusion churned that acid into molten lava. If Dante had my phone, what did Logan have in his pocket?

"You brats really are too stupid to live." Dante sniggered. "I've been watching you for the last twenty minutes. You uncovered a body, reburied it, covered up evidence and you were innocently stealing away." He waved and pointed the gun where Mrs. A was buried. "Where does that leave us now?"

"Let us go and we won't say a word," Nick suggested.

Dante spewed out another evil cackle. He didn't utter a word for a long moment. Eagerness brightened the gold flecks of his whiskey brown eyes. "I want Allie. You two can go."

A sudden freeze iced that lava in my gut.

Dante cackled again. "Not like that. I'm not into doing teenagers. I meant, Allie goes with me. We'll have fun calling your daddy. Just like Michael Kline."

I listed sideways against Logan, this time his strength and stanch presence boosted my own. During my abduction, I had disappeared into a subterranean part of myself I never knew existed. I'd gone numb, my feet and legs moving by the machination of that foreign part of me I never wanted to visit again. And without my second best friend Logan at my side, it zapped more out of me. And knowing Logan had abandoned me in the mall where Michael Kline so easily tricked me had struck me mute and hollow inside that black hole. No one would ever exploit me like that again. *Hell to the never ending no.*

"You can't have me," I growled out in a low, lethal tone I'd never used. "No one will *fucking* ever take me again against my will." Steel strengthened my legs, adrenaline powered my arms, and the fog evaporated in my mind. "What do you know about Michael Kline, anyway?"

Logan kicked my foot from the side, trying to shut me up. Still needing to earn my trust and respect again, he had no right to silence me. Not ever again.

"It's not hard to Google it. I recognized your name." An evil smile was plastered on Dante's face. "Logan's a good source of info too." His eyebrows peaked, and his sadistic hoot transformed his dark good looks into evil incarnate.

I refused to lay complete blame on Logan, but a thread of doubt continued to wind through my head and flick my heart. *Innocent until proven guilty? In Logan's case, guilty until proven innocent.*

The file. Had Dante planned this all along? *No, no, no! I'm not a target of his nefarious criminal brigade, right?* His plans had to include getting his sticky fingers on the gold and the property. Why else did he kill Mrs. A? Was I a byproduct of his criminal activity? A foil? Criminal terms kept rising to my mind as I tried to hatch our escape plan.

"Take me instead." Logan nudged my arm, his muscles taut.

"Take me too," Nick offered.

Whoa. Furtively, I checked out Nick's blank slate.

"Shut up. All of you." Dante waved his gun. "Move it. Back to camp. Now!" He strutted behind us, gun centered on my back. "You make one move other than to set one foot in front of the other, she's dead."

My heart pounded like a gorilla trying to burst through my ribcage. I wanted to run and hide into my snow globe and never ditch it again. Logan's karate moves jumped into my mind, along with the simple breathing technique I'd seen him do. I took several deep breaths, calming my racing pulse. We had to get the upper hand. No ifs, ands, or skinny flat butts. I elected myself puppet-master and motioned for Logan and Nick to advance forward.

"I'll trip on the hill," I whispered. "Then run."

"Cut the talk." Dante butted the gun against my back.

Nick, Logan, and I climbed the short incline. Halfway up, I stumbled and fell forward, deliberately catching myself on my forearms. Loose rocks and dirt cascaded down the hill behind me as I scrabbled to catch my balance. "Now," I murmured to Logan on my right.

Pretending to stand, I kicked my right leg back, knocking Dante off balance. Logan flew into a martial arts stance, and in a smooth lethal arc, he kicked the gun out of Dante's hands. It slid perilously close to my head. As I scrambled to seize the weapon, Dante grasped my ankle and wrenched me down to the ground, thumping my chest hard against the loose dirt, sending us sliding toward the ravine. Before we slid farther, I managed to wrap my fingers on the gun's barrel, twisting my index finger on my right hand in the process. Stars wavered and I gulped down bile. I'd break all the fingers on my hand to best him.

Dante wrangled me flat onto the ground, and I

twisted my upper body to escape his lethal grip. He was fast, though. Heavy and rough, he slithered over me and slapped me hard across the face. Those dozen stars exploded into hundreds, and my fingers loosened on the gun. Logan and Nick screamed at him. Soft thumping sounds of their fists punching him ceased. When my vision cleared, Dante hovered over me, the gun stuck in my face.

The world collapsed into a thick hush. Not even birds trilled. Only the sound of Dante breathing as he lay half on top of me met my ears. Only his sweaty treachery permeated my nostrils. The forest stilled as we contemplated our next moves.

Endorphins burst in my blood. I hauled up my knee and bashed his family jewels, hopefully killing his right to procreate.

"Son of a bitch!" Dante wheezed. Groaning, he fell to his side. I leaped up, snagged the gun from his loose grip, and touched the barrel to his temple.

"Bat an eyelash and you're a goner," I gasped out. "You think you had me, asshole?" I kicked him hard in the left shoulder, dying to kick in his nose, but I didn't want the kids to see him battered and bruised.

"Hands behind your back." Nick thrust a knee into Dante's spine, forcing him face down in the dirt. He'd removed his T-shirt and wound it into a short rope. It was enough.

Logan's hand engulfed mine on the gun. "Let me have it." His presence entrenched me to the present, stabilized me.

"No," I gritted out. "He's mine."

"Allie." Logan exhaled my name. "Let me do this for you."

"This doesn't make up for…for that other time." My voice had gone to that frosty, emotionless tone I'd heard before…and hated.

"That has nothing to do with the here and now." Though his tone was calm, the pain was unmistakable.

My feral gaze never faltered off Dante. "It has everything to do with *me*."

CHAPTER 24

Nick finished tying Dante's wrists behind his butt and goaded him to a quaky stand. I hoped I'd caused serious shrinkage to his man package to cow him for a while.

"Hit it. Back to camp." I dug the gun barrel into Dante's back, mimicking his not so suave gun wielding moves on me. Except I jabbed him a few extra payback times. Logan remained vigilant by my side. He looked ready to either bolt or bang one down on Dante if the dickbag moved within an inch of me.

Dante took the lead, Nick and Logan ready to tackle him if he stuck one toe out of line. He didn't say a word, probably planning how to escape this jam he'd created. Screw him. A ride in a sheriff's car was his one-way ticket out.

"When we close in on camp, take the path toward the staff cabins," Logan said. "We'll put him in one of the closed cabins for now."

"Stuff him in the kitchen storage room," Nick said.

"No windows, the door locks. There's ventilation and a bathroom."

"You kids've thought of everything." Pain twisted Dante's sarcastic voice into a nasally song. "What's gonna happen when Martina or Rambo come hunting for me?"

"Shut the hell up." Logan whacked him upside the head.

"You won't get away with this." Dante chanced it and received another light glance off the head from Nick.

"Just like you won't get away with murdering your aunt." I poked the gun into his back.

"Who said I murdered her?"

I held my finger up to prevent Logan and Nick from their pending smackdown. "Did she wrap herself in a garbage bag and dig a hole on her own?"

"You think you have it figured out?" Dante stumbled, tried to escape. Logan was faster. He leaped on the killer freak's back and barreled him to the ground, a loud thudding jolt, hopefully knocking out a few brain cells.

I shoved the gun at Dante's skull. Logan's gaze swept over the weapon, appreciation spilling across his expression. He'd just realized the other reason why I wanted to hold the gun. I didn't possess the brute strength to ram Dante down. After a moment to get Dante back on track, we continued ever more vigilant toward camp.

A thick, tense hush reined over our motley crew as we hit the periphery of the main campground. We skirted the girls' cabins. Nick jetted ahead to clear the kitchen and snag Chef's hidden keys.

My injured finger ached, and I kept it as straight as possible, despite the radiating pain down my hand. My arm became leaden, but I held steadfast, the end of the barrel touching Dante, giving me leverage to counteract my waning energy. A few longer than necessary minutes later, Nick returned toting a grim expression and a baseball bat.

"I had to knock Chef out. He found me stealing his keys."

"Getting out of hand, much," I mouthed to Logan behind Dante's back.

"He's Dante's friend. He would've let him out of the storage room. He sleeps in there." Nick swung the bat in the leaves carpeting the ground, knocking the toe of Dante's shoes. "I locked him in."

Dante swore up a string of blue curses. "You kids are insane," he shouted at the top of his lungs.

Logan clamped a hand over Dante's mouth. "One more word and I'll *knock* you out. Hear me, asshole?"

I prodded Dante forward, and we entered the kitchen without incident. The musty storage pantry was a decent-sized space. Food overfilled the shelves and crammed a large refrigerator. The type of food that wasn't being served to the kids. *Un. Freaking. Believable.*

Nick tied Chef's wrists and ankles. We secured Dante to a chair and transferred the food to the kitchen. The kids would eat well that night.

The pantry was huge once we removed the food and cleared Chef's sleeping area. Another foldup cot was buried in a corner with two old plastic lawn chairs. We left them water bottles and protein bars. I checked the adjoining bathroom. It held a vent, but no window, no escape. This scenario was created perfectly for our bizarre coup.

We helped Nick store the food, giving the kitchen a semblance of order. Once finished, we stared at each other. I'd entered a new freakout zone. Not merely at finding Mrs. Amadori's body, but by what we'd done to Dante and Chef.

"Someone needs to drive to town, alert the sheriff." I

ended our silent standoff.

"Surely Dante, someone, has a cell phone." Nick hugged the bat to him, like his personal lifesaver. "Chef doesn't have a cell 'cause he hates them."

Logan held up a phone, the one I'd seen in his pocket. "I picked Dante's pocket. It's broken."

The satellite phone Dante threatened me with that morning. "Where's my phone?" I studied his emotionless eyes.

"Don't know." Logan shifted his head, avoiding me.

"Did you give him my phone?" I demanded.

After a long, long pause, he replied, "Yes."

Kill any puppies lately too? I stamped my foot on the floor. "Why'd you do that? I trusted you." The lie rolled off my tongue and splatted on my toes. My mind went sideways.

"It's not what you think." He clamped onto my forearms. "He provoked me. He was searching your cabin, and I went along with him, trying to open him up, keep you safe."

"Then where's the phone?" Nick challenged warily. "I emptied his pockets."

"He must've lost it in the woods," Logan defended, not at all convincing.

I wrangled out of Logan's grasp. My trust meters spat out duds. *No big surprise there.* "Someone needs to leave this god-forsaken campground and head to town. I don't trust anyone here, phone or not." My narrowed gaze landed on Logan's face. "We'll try whatever phone we can find, but I want someone to drive to the nearest town."

"You want me and Laurel to go?" Nick asked. "I'd feel safer having her with me."

"Yes. Thank you." I heaved out another sigh, relief tagging along. Keeping the kids safe became my number one priority.

"All car keys are in Martina's office, except Rambo's motorcycle keys," Logan contributed a crumb to the convo.

Before we left the kitchen, Logan wrapped my pinkie to my ring finger and I slammed ibuprofens. The pills would help keep me alert, even though I wanted to curl up in a ball and sleep, pretend this nightmare had never happened.

Kids streamed down the hill from the meadow, their steps slow after a long day playing. Dinnertime loomed. Who'd fix dinner with Chef tied up and Nick gone? *Wait, I possess minor cooking skills! I wouldn't kill anyone...at least not too quickly.* Barbequed hamburgers and hotdogs sounded perfect.

Once again, after assuring the offices were empty, I climbed through Martina's window and grabbed every key ring off the pegs by her door. Stupid place to leave them if an emergency occurred. I tossed the keys out the window to Nick.

Logan gripped my hips in the window frame and supported me until my feet touched ground. "What about Martina and the counselors? They'll find Dante and Chef missing."

"We'll head them off. Fake them out somehow. We can hold them off until Nick and Laurel return," I replied.

"Martina doesn't ever enter the kitchen, she butts heads with Chef," Nick replied. He'd lost his lame come-on lines and wisecracks. This had become real for him, which led me to believe that his Mr. Cheeze-mo act was a front. Maybe he possessed more substance than I'd given him credit for. Lucky for Laurel.

Logan secured the window screen, then raced off to find Laurel. Nick and I sprinted to the deserted parking lot. Hiding along the gravel lot in the boughs of trees, we searched the key rings for the four vehicle keys. All were identifiable by either the manufacturer logo or a key chain. Nick chose the smaller, more agile SUV.

"This is some insanity going down." He unlocked the SUV, stuck the key in the ignition, leaving the door ajar.

"From day one, I noticed things weren't right. Laurel knows a little." I kicked a pinecone into the woods where it crashed and broke apart against a tree. I launched another huge sugar pinecone and pretended it was Dante's head.

"She told me. She was worried you weren't having fun after The Incident." He dipped his head as if he feared my wrath that Laurel had fessed up to him.

"She told you about my kidnapping?"

He tapped my hand. "I won't tell anyone."

I had him on the hook and yanked the line. "So what're your intentions toward Laurel? She's my best friend, you know."

His Adam's apple bobbed. "It's all good. We're tight and I plan to keep it tight when we go home."

"Just don't hurt her." I fake-growled and cast him my most evil-eyed glare.

He held up his hands in surrender and gave me his heart-skipping grin. "Or you'll kill me?" We both laughed awkwardly.

Laurel muffled a cry as she rounded the corner of the offices. "Logan filled me in." The pale white of snow colored her complexion. "God, Allie. I'll never doubt you again."

I arched my eyebrows. "Since when did you doubt me?" I teased, trying to defray the crap storm brewing.

She slapped my arm. "You know what I mean."

"Let's hit the road." Nick gave Laurel's hand a quick squeeze before they climbed inside the car.

Logan and I remained halfway hidden on the other side of a mini bus. Laurel rolled down the window and waved. Nick turned the key in the ignition. No click, no sputtering, no juice. The engine didn't make a sound.

He climbed out. "Let's try the Suburban."

We tried the Suburban, the minivan, and the mini bus. All were dead. Nick checked the batteries to make sure they were all connected, all he knew about cars. Logan knew even less. Someone had sabotaged the cars to foil anyone from leaving the hellish campground. Had Dante screwed us over while I was gallivanting through the woods, stumbling over dead bodies? Had Rambo done it before he'd split? What was the mysterious man hiding up his sleeve?

"There might be another satellite phone in Dante's office," I offered, dampening my horror. "Marco said they don't remove it unless for emergencies. Maybe the one Dante had earlier was a spare."

"One of the adults has to have a cell." Laurel molded herself into Nick's side like a leech.

"Who's left?" Logan asked.

I counted each person off on my fingers. "Martina, possibly Rambo, and the four counselors."

"All friends of Dante's," Logan replied. "The second one of us asks to use a phone, the jig is up."

"Any of those keys go to Dante's office?" I asked.

Nick handed me the keys. "Give it a shot."

"What are you thinking?" Logan turned to me, crinkles fanning the corners of his eyes.

"I bet he has another weapon or satellite phone in his office."

"Nick, you and Laurel stand guard in the breakroom while we check it out." It was only a matter of time before Martina returned.

Logan blocked me as I fruitlessly tried key after key on Dante's lock. I knocked my fist against the door in frustration.

"Nick, Laurel, you two chilling out?" Martina's voice

wafted to us. The French doors in the breakroom clicked shut as she entered the building.

Not that I needed the prompt, but Logan pushed me toward the hallway bathroom. We scrambled inside. I fell on the closed toilet seat. Logan tripped over me and took a header into the bathtub.

"Oww." He groaned, rubbing his head.

"Let me see," I whispered.

He knelt down to my level. A red mark painted the side of his forehead, the birth of a nasty bruise. Moving fast, he lifted his head and caught my lips to his. His kiss was swift, hot, and possessive. My head prevailed and I drew away. Something alien dribbled inside me, so wholly inviting, I wanted to experience it again. The rush of adrenaline, fear, and passion, all overriding my long-seated anger.

"Are CLs allowed to use this bathroom?" I asked to defray my jacked emotions and to enable me to get a grip.

"Not together. She catches more than one person in here with the door shut, we're in deep."

"Seriously. You're concerned about trouble?"

He grinned. "Guess not."

I mussed my hair and wrenched my polo off my shoulder. "Follow my lead. Let her take her best shot." Pretending to straighten my blouse, I opened the door as Martina was unlocking her office. I stroked my hand against the gun wedged in the rear waistband of my shorts. The foreign object had become a comforting boost to my confidence. I patted my shirt over it, trying to draw Logan's attention to the forgotten weapon. I scared myself.

Clutching a bag to her chest, Martina flinched. "You startled me." A dark mask descended over her face. "Logan. You know the rules."

"Hey, Martina." I patted down my hair. "I need to call

my mom. Can I use a phone?"

"Phones are off limits." She entered her office, leaving the door open. "Is it important?" She plunked her tote behind her chair and located her tablet device.

"Yes."

"Reason?" Her strained lips brought attention to her hollow cheeks.

"I don't fit in here. I'm having anxiety attacks." I forced a weakness into my voice, knitting my fingers together in a sign of agitation. "I need to go home."

"Really? This's the first I've heard of it." Her eyebrows knitted.

"Dante knows. What do you expect when someone shoots arrows at me?"

Logan gasped, an imperceptible sound. He closed the distance between us, and my skin tingled when his hand touched my back beneath my shirt.

"Okay." Martina stretched out the word. "Let me talk to Dante first. Can you hold out for a while? Do you want to be excused from tonight's activities?" Her voice had grown condescending, losing any semblance of sympathy.

"I need to call my mom now. I'm sick." I wilted against the wall. Logan slid the gun out from my waistband.

"You should lie down." Martina approached me. "We'll see how you feel later."

"Are you kidding me?" Logan shouted. "She needs to call her mom."

"Get out, both of you," Martina demanded. "No one's calling anyone. The phone's not working anyways."

"Then give me a cell or the satellite phone." Arrogantly, I held out my hand, shifting to the right, giving Logan space in the doorway.

"Cell phones don't work here. Dante has the satellite."

"Unlock his office then." Noise exploded behind me as Logan forced me against the wall and hoisted the gun to Martina's face. Nick and Laurel crowded the hallway. "Do what we say, and no one gets hurt. I just want the satellite phone."

Martina held stock-still. Red-hot anger engulfed her corpse-white fear. "Where'd you get that gun? Where's Dante? What'd you do to him?"

"Turn around, slow and easy," Logan demanded.

Slowly, she pivoted on her heel, then lunged toward her desk. Anticipating her move, Logan leaped forward, elevated his arm and cold-cocked her. Bam, right across the neck. Not with the gun but with his arm, a smooth, suave martial arts move that drove her dripping into a puddle of jean shorts and green Dragonfly Meadows polo to the floor.

"Dude, that was totally subhuman." Nick carried a roll of duct tape into the room and went to town taping Martina's wrists and ankles.

While he and Laurel searched the desk, Logan and I found the key to Dante's office and scoured it. It seemed Dante had never been in the office. The small room was a sham, stuffed with old files, books, and outdated office equipment. Not a phone or computer to be found. When my fingers trailed over paper taped to the underside of the desk, an excited tapping scrolled across the nape of my neck.

"Well, what do we have here?" I tugged at the tape and was rewarded with a large envelope. Breathless, I gazed up at Logan, eyes meeting. Was this ammunition to use against our psycho camp director? Not waiting another minute, I ripped it open. "Whoa, check this out." I skimmed the papers. "An offer to Carla to buy the property including the gold mine dated June 1, expiring on July 31. It includes all mineral rights. Worth millions of dollars." Logan leaned over my shoulder, and I continued speed-reading the documents. "Any signs of excavation in a marked area surrounding the gold mine deem the offer null and void."

No wonder Dante had Rambo filling in the gold mine cave-in. I doubt the small holes the kids made hunting for treasure counted, but I bet Rambo was at the mine filling them in too. *Dante's riding the elevator to the top level of stupidity.* Any expert would know the dirt had been disturbed, and some of the holes the kids had dug were pretty deep. Heck, I was no expert and I'd figured it out.

"You think he was hunting for the gold and planning to sell the property?" I asked.

"Hell, yeah. These people making the offer know gold is here. I doubt the property's worth this much alone. The fact that they're asking to buy mineral rights might mean there's more gold to be mined."

"Obviously, they didn't know about the will. Or Dante's scamming his way out of it." I stuffed the envelope under my shirt, and we rejoined Nick and Laurel.

No phone materialized.

"Let's lock all the adults in the storage room, and take over the camp until we get help." The extreme idea had percolated in my head for the last half hour. Laurel looked at me as though I'd tripped through the one-way door into crazy town. Logan rubbed his fingers, working his mythical game controller.

"I'm not knocking out anyone." Laurel threw her hands up into the air. "This is freaking insane."

"You got a better plan?" I asked. "Who knows how far their loyalty to Dante goes? Obviously, he'd told them enough, gave them plenty of incentive to run this racket with him. You think they'll willingly go along with us? Or believe us?"

“We can show them Mrs. A’s body.” Laurel folded her arms around herself.

“What if one or more helped Dante kill and bury her?” I quirked my eyebrow. “We can’t take the risk.”

“I agree with Allie. She’s been right from day one,” Logan said.

Laurel gave me our wonky smile in conciliation. “How do we get them in the pantry?”

“We’ll tell them Dante’s having a surprise *adult* party in the kitchen, wink-wink, offer them booze,” Nick suggested. “I’ll be in the kitchen prepping dinner. They won’t know what’s up. Laurel can help me block the doors once they’re inside.”

“Logan can lay in wait with the gun. We’ll wait until dinnertime when they’re all in the cafeteria. Then I’ll round them up for a trip to Storage-ville.” I scrubbed my hands together.

CHAPTER 25

It was insanely efficient to knock people out and plan to lock others in the storage room. Didn't stop my quaking in my booties every step of the way. People always say things are easier said than done. So far we'd tricked the odds. How long would it last? My guard was up and not falling anytime soon. Every move we made cut like a knife through my heart. I hoped I didn't hate myself after this nightmare ended. I'd spent four years too long on that boat and look where I'd washed ashore.

Logan and Nick had gagged and tied Martina to a chair in her office, closed the blinds, and locked the door. We'd drag her to the kitchen storage room once we secured all the adults. Nick and Laurel remained behind for dinner prep to fake normalcy for the kids.

I joined my girls in the dining hall, pretending my world hadn't flipped on its axis. Logan and I waited for the call to grab a burger from the grill behind the counter. The girls bought that Laurel was helping Nick in the kitchen. They all knew about her infatuation and gave her a small ration of envious crap behind her back, while going gaga over Nick "Cute on a Stick" Constantine. The topic kept them occupied. Keeping my eyes peeled for the four counselors, I maintained a steady chitchat with the girls.

"Where were you this afternoon?" Carrie asked, smugness reforming her cat-like expression. "I noticed Logan was gone too." She made googly eyes at Logan. Love triangle in the making? *Not.*

"Funny." I gave her a fake mad-dog look. "Doing errands Dante—Mr. Amadori—gave me last night."

"Hey, where is he?" Serena eyeballed the dining hall. "He promised to sit with us tonight. He has some special presents for us."

Crap on a crazy cracker. Her question hit the one hollow in my brain.

"Haven't seen him since we talked at the Dragonfly Lily cabins." Logan pretended to search for Dante. "You asked me where he was earlier too, remember, Allie?"

"Duh." I smacked the side of my head. "He'll be around soon." I vowed to stir up my brain cells for ready excuses. "We don't need no stinkin' adults, do we, girls?" I uttered with enthusiasm, sending them down another path of conversation involving sneaking out of the cabin one night to scare the youngest boys.

The side door to the dining hall hung ajar. Nadia and Tessa walked in. The two men counselors, Marty and Alan, followed, shutting the door behind them. I think the two dudes had hard-ons for Nadia and Tessa. They seemed overly friendly toward one another. Had they known each other before this summer? The counselors changed every year or two as the college students went on to grander jobs. Occasionally Mrs. Amadori hired an older adult for one of her low paying interim summer jobs.

"Now?" Logan asked.

"Yes." The burn of trepidation killed my wandering thoughts.

As he walked to the serving counter, my senses devoured him, his lithe, graceful movements melting my heart. If he got hurt...or worse, I didn't know what I'd do. And I'd never abandon him.

Whatever the outcome that day, I needed to stand on my own. No Logan, no snow globe. Just Allie Bailey, amateur sleuth, with a wrist marred with scars. *Will the real Allie Bailey please stand up?*

I trailed Logan to the kitchen. He took his position behind the door, flat against the wall. Uncharacteristically, Nick was burning burgers on the indoor grill, and a grim Laurel stacked buns in the plastic bins neat and tidy, so unlike her normal random chaos. I gave them all a thumbs up, noticed the loads of canned goods on the rolling cart blocking the far door in case someone had a key.

I stopped in front of Logan. The scent of his fear, like sweat and fresh forest, concealed his spicy cologne.

"It'll be okay." He caressed my cheek. "Just get them in here and lock the door. They won't put up a fight." He held up the gun. "Not with this."

"Or this." Nick held up a huge chef's knife.

"Or this." Laurel held up a cheese grater.

We all laughed. I needed that.

I left the kitchen. The battle games officially kicked off.

As usual, the four counselors sat in their clique. Luck rode piggyback on my shoulders. I shivered, hoping Lady Luck didn't fall off and get trampled into dust.

I approached the table near the front windows. "Hi." My beauty contestant smile pinched my cheeks. "Dante asked me to fetch you. He has a surprise for you in the kitchen. Wants you to eat in there, adult style, if you know what I mean?" For good measure, I winked. "The CLs will keep tabs on the kids."

"What's the surprise?" Tessa pushed her chair in, scraping the legs on the floor, a nail on a chalkboard screech.

I cringed, my last nerve taking a hike. "Surf and turf are cooking on his private grill, with expensive booze on the table. Not that I'm a judge of alcohol." I giggled for good measure.

The guys popped up like I'd offered them a vault of cash. Women, food, and booze. The trifecta of man porn worked.

"What's the occasion?" Nadia asked. "I haven't seen Dante all day. Didn't know he was planning this."

Like he told you anything. I managed another wink. "Where do you think he's been all day? He wanted to treat you to a good dinner, thanking you for your hard work. But hey, if you don't want it, I'll tell him—"

"Hell, yeah, we want." Big Alan salivated, caressing his beer belly.

"You'll watch the kids?" Nadia studied the room. Kids played, sat, and waited for the dinner bell.

The noise level blossomed as usual when all the kids were in the dining hall. I envied their cheerful excitement, when they didn't care what the dinner menu brought them. For the most part, the kids loved being at camp, escaping the doldrums of home, adults, school, and life's typical humdrum existence. I hated to see it end. At least we owed them one more night of fun before the law crashed the party and shipped everyone home.

Mentally, I hitched up my big girl panties. "The CLs got this. Soon as I return from the kitchen, we're on double duty." And then some. After we locked up the counselors, we'd agreed to bring the other CLs into the fold. We planned to tell them the bare minimum to sway them to our side. After all, the dark side had the cookies of freedom.

I weaved through boys playing tag between tables, glanced over my shoulder to ensure the four counselors followed. They bumped and rushed me in their eagerness. Jacking them into the plan was easier than blowing cocaine at an addict.

Hesitating near the swing door, I inhaled a deep breath, opened it. Knowing Logan was on the interior hinge side, I blocked him and held the door for the adults to enter.

"Hey," Nick greeted them. "Dante set your party up in his special room."

"What special room?" Nadia asked with a heap of skepticism.

Nick gallantly waved his arm at the prize door. "Milady, the special room beyond that lovely door. Dante's secret getaway. Tonight it belongs to you lovely guests."

I shut the swinging door, exposing Logan to the backs of the adults. As I slid the other loaded cart in front of the door trying not to make a sound, Alan glanced over his shoulder to scope out the squeaky wheel that ratted me out.

"The hell?" He stepped toward me. "Dante doesn't have a *special* room here." He did air quotes with one hand. "You kids are yanking us."

"Back off." Logan darted in front of me, the gun stuck in the rear waistband of his pants.

Laurel opened the hallway door to the pantry. Nick picked up the cleaver and held it to his side behind the counter.

"Where's Dante?" Nadia sidled closer to Tessa. Distress lines bracketed her eyes.

I stepped from behind Logan to eye the group better. "Waiting for you. You want to keep him waiting?"

"Where's Martina?" Short Marty asked, his fists bunching at his sides. "She coming to the ball?"

"She'll join you later. She's tied up in the office." Logan's back grew stiff as a board.

Hiding a smile, I wanted to high-five his play on words. "I'll show you the way." As I edged away from Logan, he grunted. Laurel took two steps from the hall door.

The unthinkable happened. A thud hit the interior storage room door. Chairs scraped the cement floor. Dante shouted unintelligible, muffled words.

Alan zoomed forward, knocking Laurel against the wall and grabbed me from behind. "Don't move." He locked his arm around my torso, dragging me close to him, clamping my wrists behind my back in one giant paw. Spinning me in his arms, he faced Logan. "I smell a rat. Dante never showed up to direct the games. Martina was to meet me a half hour ago. Where is she? Marty, check the pantry."

"You're not going anywhere." Logan advanced, his right hand sliding toward his butt. "Let Allie go."

"Or what, kid? You gonna wreck me with your martial arts?" Alan's belly rumbled against my bound hands.

"He's a black belt, you moron. A lethal weapon," Laurel spat out.

Good going, Laurel. A lethal weapon good for assault and battery charges if he engaged. I gave her a stink-eye. She knew that black belts could be held to a higher standard in a court of law during the commission of an assault. Well hell, what was worse, a black belt or a gun?

I tried another tactic. "Who has a phone? I'm sick and I want to call home. Martina won't let me. Can I just use a phone?" I wailed, drumming up phony tears.

"Cells are banned." Nadia wrung her hands. "Besides,

there's no reception here. I've tried to use Dante's tablet and he gets no bars. Martina's a nurse. Why didn't you go to her?"

Did you carry his flipping tablet all over the campground? I wanted to scream at her. "He banned *you* from bringing a phone?" I glared at her.

"It's an electronics free camp." Her voice dove to pipsqueak level as she realized how dumb she sounded after mentioning Dante's tablet. "What's wrong with you anyway?"

"Get real. The kid's lying," Alan said. "Marty, go fucking check the pantry."

My stall tactic had given Laurel time to move out of the way and Nick to take position to rush the counselors. The click of the gun hammer deafened me before Logan pointed it at Alan's head towering above mine.

"Let Allie go." He spoke in a steady and deadly voice. He even scared me.

Alan's hand tightened on my wrist before he flung me forward, slamming my head into a stainless steel counter. Stars flickered as I tumbled to the floor. Logan and Nick rushed the adults. Screams, shouts, and scuffling feet grew muffled. The stars winked out, and the darkness of oblivion captured me and took me for a lonely spin.

CHAPTER 26

A cold compress wet my forehead, and I recognized the feel of Logan's sinewy legs beneath my shoulders as he cradled me on his lap. How I recognized the feel of him stretched beyond my comprehension. Battling the blinding, hammering headache took all my focus. I wanted to time-travel to four days ago and transform our dragonfly disaster into a dragonfly paradise.

"Wake up or I'll kill you." Laurel pierced the dense hush.

My incapacitation could be a coup if it cowed Laurel's high-pitched voice. *My mind became a tilt-a-whirl on steroids. Avoidance, much? The story of my life.*

"What happened?" My eyelids refused to open. "Can you dim the lights?" Logan twined his fingers in mine.

"What light?" he asked.

Where did they put me if there's no light? "Where are we?"

"Out in the enclosed patio," Laurel said. "Had to get

you out of the kitchen so the kids didn't see you conked out on the floor when we opened the serving windows."

"How long have I been out?" Hysteria bubbled in my chest.

"Fifteen minutes," Laurel replied. "Are you all right? Martina said to keep you awake in case you had a concussion. You wouldn't wake up." Blabbering now, she tried to hide her mounting hysteria.

I touched the washcloth. "Did I break skin?"

"No." Logan shifted slightly. The pain shifted with him. I moaned. "Sorry. My leg's asleep."

"Are they in the brig?" I fingered the egg-sized lump growing on my forehead. By midnight, it might be bigger than my own head. A two-headed Allie Bailey. *Gah.* I sucked down the pain. Logan sifted my hair, leaving tingles on my neck where his skin made contact.

"All the adults are locked up," he replied.

Pans and utensils clinked on the stainless counters as Nick prepared dinner. Dining hall chatter drifted in through the pass-thru windows. The scent of charred burgers lingered, despite the aroma of brownies baking, stirring my thirst.

"Everyone okay on both sides of the door?" I finally managed to crack my eyes open.

"Except you." Laurel kneeled beside me, a bottle of water to my lips.

I took a sip, managed a second gulp with two aspirin. "We need to search for phones."

"I sent Jesse to check cabins." Logan scraped his thumbnail along my palm.

I stiffened. "What did you tell him? Do you trust him?"

"We have to trust someone. I told him you found Mrs. Amadori's body in the woods, and we locked up the adults because we discovered they were scamming us."

"He didn't question it after I showed him Marco's file on Dante," Laurel added. "He's no fan of Dante's."

"Does he think Marco met foul play?" Logan helped me sit, bracing me between his legs, my back against his chest. I loved the feel of his solid body supporting me and fought my untimely desire dissolving me and my ire.

"He does now." Logan wrapped his arms around me. I clutched his forearms, resting my head on his shoulder, feeling right with our tiny world in that moment, ignoring the larger picture of us as usual.

Kids lined up outside the kitchen, banging utensils on the counter, jabbing lightning bolts in my skull.

"I need to help Nick." Laurel drifted away.

"You should help too." I feathered my finger up Logan's forearm. The warmth of his sunburn made my skin sting. "I'm wrecked." Perspiration dotted my upper lip, and I wiped it on my arm. "I'll sit in the kitchen and hand sharp knives to Nick."

Logan made an annoyed grunt, but he helped me up onto a stool behind the counter, propping me against a wall to prevent any unforeseen clash with the floor.

Jesse hurried through the door and locked it behind him. "Found these two phones." He placed them on the counter. "One in Dante's cabin, one in Mrs. Amadori's cabin. Hey, you alive?" He smiled, showing his gapped front teeth.

"Barely." We exchanged smiles, and I picked up one phone. As dead as Mrs. A. Same with the other one. "What gives?"

"I couldn't juice them up, not even with a charger." Using a thin blade knife, he opened the phones to reveal their guts.

The batteries were missing and the circuit boards were fried. Jesse and I traded looks of absolute horror.

"Tell me Dante didn't have a big fat crime spree in

mind here?" I mocked.

"That dude's whack. Damn, girl, why didn't you fess up to his crazy-ass BS earlier?"

He earned my most baleful glare. "Are you kidding? Until I found Mrs. A, I didn't know if I was suffering from delusional paranoia. Nothing made sense, but it all pointed to the land of sour milk and rancid honey. Marco knew it too."

"Unless someone knows how to fix a vehicle, we need to find another way into town." Logan joined us again, his arm curling around my shoulders.

I wanted to take his strength and fill my empty holes, to banish my headache and a boatload more. Whatever was going on with him and Dante still bothered me, though. No way was Logan colluding with Dante to cover up a murder or any other crime, no matter how much Logan had changed. Sly as a shit storm, Dante had been playing us all from day one. Yet I felt unease around Logan due to Dante's friendliness. Dante knew more about my kidnapping than mere newspaper articles or a school file provided.

"Is there a boat in the boathouse?" I asked.

"Just canoes." Eyes suddenly brightening, Jesse slapped his hand on his thigh. "We can row across the lake to the vacation homes!"

"Ding, ding, ding, we have a winner." My smile prepared to tear the skin off my face.

"It's getting dark, but I can manage." Confidence gave Jesse a new lease on his gimpy life.

"Do you want to take one of the other campers?"

"No. I'll take a small canoe. Easier to row. Splitting now while it's still light." Jesse turned, halted. "We're doing the right thing, right?"

"Do you want to see Mrs. Amadori's body?" I asked, not unkindly.

"*Touché*." He wagged his head and limped from the kitchen, slamming the door behind him.

Dinner service went off without a hitch. Nick and Logan managed to transfer food to Dante and crew without earning bonks on the head. We also threw in blankets and pillows to make them comfortable. My sense of right and wrong battled over comfort versus punishment. Humanity won out. After all, Dante's friends might not know the full extent of what he'd done. Yet I refused to trust them.

The aspirin kicked in and my headache abated. Wrangling what little energy I'd harvested, I felt okay standing and walking. I helped Nick clean the kitchen, while Laurel and Logan set the kids up with campfires and a movie, and to answer their questions about the missing adults. My attention never strayed far from the eerily quiet storage room.

The door to the kitchen banged open, sending me jumping, bouncing my headache to the forefront again.

Jesse entered, his eyes manic, fists clenched. "The canoes are gone. I've looked everywhere hoping Dante stored them somewhere else."

My heart dove to the bottom of my stomach. "What the hells?"

"He could've sold them before summer to scare up cash." Nick's hand curled in the washrag he was using to wipe down the last counter.

"I think he sold a lot of stuff." Jesse slunk down onto a stool. He drummed his stubby fingers on the counter, picked at the bandage on his ankle. "All fixtures are gone on those two cabins being repaired. The staff cabins are bare bones compared to last year. All Mrs. Amadori's paintings are gone, you know, the Kinkade ones she loved so much. Her collectibles and jewelry are gone." He reached into his pocket and tossed a checkbook on the table. "Dante made a bunch of deposits after May. After each deposit, he cut a check to a credit card company. I think the dude was up to his eyeballs in debt."

"Major debt. That's why he killed Mrs. Amadori."

Nick gave me a sharp warning look. Jesse looked at me as if I held a crystal ball.

I held up my hand. "Hey, I had more than a little access to the office." I wouldn't fess up to having the papers from Marco's mom, not to Jesse, who I knew about as much as I knew Dante.

Logan returned, and Jesse brought him up to speed. Logan insisted on hoofing it out on foot through the mountain terrain to town at first light. We had no other choice. He'd slyly questioned the other boys and no one had a clue how to repair a vehicle. *Bunch of sissy boys!*

The boys set up a rotation schedule to guard the impromptu jail cell for the night. We were about to join the kids when the kitchen door burst open. Neal and his minions sauntered in, gazes sweeping the kitchen.

"Where's Dante?" Neal took a defensive stance. "The others?"

"Went to their cabins. We gave them the night off," I managed to say with my last dose of energy. It wasn't every day a maniac chased me through the woods, I stumbled across a dead body, and planned and executed a coup to take over a campground full of kids. And kept my sanity on this side of Crazyville.

"Don't lie, you stupid cow." Neal advanced toward me.

Logan stepped between us, taking up a defensive stance, feet spread wide and arms in position. "Back off."

"Or what, pansy nerd?" Jeff threw in his two-cents. He earned a chuckle out of his bitch, Richie.

I took a different tactic with the bullies. One called truth. We needed them on our side. We needed their help in watching the kids. How long would it take Logan to reach town and convince the sheriff to believe him?

"Hold on a sec." I conferred with Logan and Nick on the side. They agreed with me, not that they liked my plan.

I faced Neal. "How would you like to be general in charge of the brig? Richie and Jeff can be your lieutenants."

Neal's forehead furrowed into dumb territory. "What do you mean?"

"I know you guys are buddy-buddy with Dante. But you all loved Mrs. Amadori. You don't like seeing her hurt, right?"

"Yeah, I guess," Neal said slowly, his forehead going all scrunchy.

"She was like a fun aunt." Jeff scratched his head, taxing his pea brain. Neal and Richie nodded.

"She hurt again?" Richie asked, pushing forward.

I'd hooked them. "Dante hurt her first," I said conspiratorially. "He broke her leg." I guessed at that logical speed bump on the road to murder.

"No freaking way." Red exploded over Neal's face. "Dante's cool. He wouldn't do that."

"How do you know?" Logan stabbed his fist into Neal's shoulder. "She's not here. We've searched all the cabins. Dante's been lying since day one."

"What about the video messages?" Richie's lips quirked up.

"Taped last month." To their flycatcher shock, I explained the date inconsistency on the TV in the first video, then I dropped the bomb. "I found Mrs. Amadori's body buried in the woods this morning."

CHAPTER 27

Neal and his buds didn't take the news well, but I'd deflated their wings and they agreed to staff the guard contingent. They believed me about Mrs. A's body. Who'd lie about the murder of a beloved camp host? At first, they thought I was lying to cast Dante in a slant of tarnished light. I showed them all the phones, and then we walked out to the disabled vehicles. I offered to show them her body, but with green faces, they drew the line. I agreed to never speak of their assault on me, nor report it to their parents and remove it from their camp records, not that I believed camp records existed at that point. When I showed Neal the probate papers, he barfed up his double burger and fell into line. Where he fell, Jeff and Richie tumbled. We agreed to keep a twenty-four hour guard on the Pantry Prison until help arrived. Neal took up first guard. Nick stayed to ensure Neal wasn't playing us.

After the movie ended, kids dragged their feet, talking quietly, yawning on the way to the cabins. They were too tired to question the absence of the adults. Every noise in the woods grated on my nerves, and I expected Dante to lunge at me with every step. Although freer than ever, I felt trapped in a horrific disaster of my own making, and I kept perspiring out my freakout. No snow globe or pinprick could flip the table on me this time.

A hot, sweaty sleep took a long time in coming. A plan to force Dante to confess his crime kept revolving in my head. I don't know why I felt the need to hear his confession. Forensics and DNA should fry him. But I needed validation.

Even though Kline had shot and killed himself during the police standoff, I had wanted a trial. I'd wanted to see him admit to the world what he'd done to me and why. Although I had lived it, I burned with a need for the world to know he'd abducted me, and that I hadn't gone with him willingly. I'd lost part of myself during that time and let him lead me to the slaughter, so to speak, too numb and small to engage in a fight against a full-grown man. The other part of me hadn't done enough. He'd conned me in the mall, gave me the flowers, said another gift awaited me in his car. After all, I knew him from my father's firm, company picnics, and parties. He had always been nice to me. And he'd known that day was my birthday.

Logan had abandoned me, leaving me ticked at him. I blamed him in part for my abduction. For four years, I'd yearned for him to admit why he'd left me alone in the mall. Where had he gone? I'd assumed back to his beloved video game store. Why did he go off to boarding school without a word? Truth set a person free. I wanted Logan to have his freedom, whether I loathed what he had to say or not. I needed it to set me free one way or another...with or without him.

I wanted Dante to download the truth about everything he'd done at the campground. Not that I wanted him to go free, but because I needed it to set myself free. To hear how my paranoia paid off.

An exhaustive, bone-weary sleep claimed me around two o'clock. Morning arrived in an eye blink. In a surprising shift of roles, the girls woke me up.

"We're gonna miss breakfast." Carrie jerked the covers off me.

Hammers went to town in my head. Fingering my scratchy eyes, I crawled out of bed. "I got your back. Nick won't let you starve."

Speaking of the devil, Nick and Laurel arrived to take my girls, leaving me alone until Logan showed up.

Dressed for hiking, long pants, hoodie, backpack loaded, he handed me the gun. "Keep this hidden on you."

I shook my head. "You take it."

He gave me his goofy, crooked smile, a smile that now drowned me in all of him. "Don't need it."

I touched my bulging forehead. "Right. You're a lethal weapon. I forgot."

"I have a knife." He parted my messy hair. "Swelling's gone down. Nice colors. Great battle badge." Chuckling, he enclosed me into his arms. I was too exhausted to fight his embrace.

"You sure about this?" Numb, I returned his hug and let him go. He gave me no comfort. Too much history and old memories had jammed my rattled head overnight. Our day of reckoning was a hop around the next grove of trees. As soon as this mess was over, Logan and I would have a serious conversation. Until then, I had to keep my distance to remain rational.

I stuck the protein bars he'd given me in a pocket of his backpack. "Do you have food, lots of water? How far is town?" Unable to zip it, I studied his well-worn hiking boots. "You doubled up on socks for extra cushion? You have sunscreen, sunglasses?"

He rested his finger over my lips. "I'm set." His all-encompassing smile was worth my anxiety. It wicked away my terror.

His grin lit his face, and I noticed how tanned his skin had become from a few days in the sun. He was handsome in a way I'd never seen before. Square firm jaw, vibrant hazel eyes that changed from green to gold, honeyed skin with a faint shadow along his jaw and chin since he hadn't shaved that morning. His hair was mussed haphazardly. Man, he looked like light and airy sunshine. And freedom.

"Be careful," I said.

"Don't worry about me. Keep an eye on Neal and his buds. I'm not sure they're a hundred percent on board."

"I know. They accepted it last night, but in the light of day, who knows. Maybe I need to take one of them to Mrs. A."

"No. It's a crime scene now. We've already disturbed it enough."

I nodded. "We'll keep searching for a phone, see if we can repair a vehicle, or find a canoe."

Before I could stop myself, I rose on my toes and his head descended. His lips fell onto mine before I reached his. Our kiss was soft, then hard, firm lips to firm lips, minty toothpaste fresh. Our lips pressed together, not budging, just breathing each other in. His woodsy cologne cocooned me. After what seemed like eons, we eased our mouths apart, our gazes locked onto each other until I broke contact and gently pushed him away.

I brushed hair back from his eyes. "We're burning daylight."

"One last thing. Watch out for Rambo. He might come back."

"I know." I shielded my face from the rising sun.

Mentioning Dante's friend propelled it out there like

a bad omen. Yet I was glad. I hadn't forgotten about the caveman and his intimidation. Threats I hadn't fessed up to anyone. What happened if he never returned? Had I screwed everyone by not confessing his threats? I didn't want to admit that he might have sent the flowers and notes to Laurel and me. Time for a war meeting with Nick and Neal, to plan our counterattack in case Rambo returned.

I accompanied Logan to the front of camp. We slipped between trees to avoid contact or line of sight with any campers.

Logan's final words were, "Don't let Dante out of the room. Only Martina if someone gets hurt."

Wistfully, I watched him hike down the driveway until he vanished. A deep well of emptiness flooded me, and I slumped against a tree. All I'd suspected had come to fruition, and the excitement of the chase drained out of me. I felt alone on Cutthroat Island. This time, I refused to let Dante hold me hostage in any way, shape or form the way Kline had. Not my mind, not my body. Not one child at this campground.

A glittery object catching a glint of sun on the ground to my left dragged my gaze to a perfectly formed dragonfly. About three inches long and equally wide, its four iridescent wings caught the sun, sparkling in shades of blue green, its body a teal blue. Eyes bugged out, scoping its prey. I toed it. The dragonfly had frozen in time, its life leeching into the ground under my feet. Dead. One wing representing each year of my imposed incarceration. I tensed from the ominous prediction, a dragonfly's worst nightmare, to live a short life and die in the woods, before it had a chance to experience all the meadows and lake had to offer. Or it'd flown to the darker, somber woods to die, a fitting receptacle of death. Now that I'd battled for my freedom, I wasn't done living.

I refused to die in the troubling forest of my mind.

Another dragonfly flitted in front of my face, then dived down to the carcass on the forest floor. A life for a life.

Twigs and leaves snapping behind me spun me around, hand on the gun at my back.

"Laurel." I exhaled my wariness on her name. I vowed to be more vigilant and not drop my guard again.

She peered down the driveway, pulling on her frayed shirt hem. "He's gone now?"

I snaked my arm around her waist. "He'll be okay."

"I know." Her laugh was stilted, concerned. "I'm more worried about us."

"How are Neal and his minions dealing?"

"Lording over the flies. They take to guarding like they were born to it."

"That's what I'm afraid of." I shifted us toward the dining hall. "I better check on them."

"You know they like you, right? I think they respect you."

"Right. Sure."

"For real." Laurel tripped on a root and practically separated my arm from its socket as she righted herself.

Zipping it, we entered the kitchen. Kids sat in their seats eating scrambled eggs, bacon, and toast by the smells wafting in the room. Dawn, Jesse, Jeff, and Richie were monitoring the dining hall. Jeff saluted me and I waved.

Lupe was helping Nick in the kitchen, and Neal was still on guard duty.

"What did you tell Lupe and Dawn?"

"Same load we dumped on Neal's gang. We had to tell them something. Nick put the wrath of God into them. They're on our side."

"Are the kids asking about the missing adults?"

"Well, duh."

"And?"

"We didn't know what to tell them, so we brushed them off with pancakes."

To wait for me. Since when had I become the leader of this Dragonfly Meadows revolution, or freaking dragonfly nightmare?

"Guess I need to give them something concrete." I waltzed out to the dining room and hopped onto the stage. "Hey, kids," I yelled, not needing the microphone. I motioned for Laurel to join me on stage.

Forks clinked on plates, glasses clunked on tables. The room quieted.

"We have exciting news." An animation I didn't feel elevated my voice. "As part of the Teen Leadership Program, the CLs have been given the exciting challenge of running the camp for a day. By ourselves."

"Dude, that's brilliant," Laurel whispered.

Animated voices elevated in the dining room, and I tailgated the eagerness, ignoring a few dubious barbs. "The adults will be planning awesome events for next week. You won't see them for the day. How about that?"

"It's kids' day," Laurel yelled, inciting momentum. "We have special events and treats in store for you all day." She winked and clapped.

I clapped and stomped my feet, riling up the kids. The noise deafened until Laurel clunked her hand on the microphone and thumps pounded out of the speakers. I grabbed the microphone.

"Finish your breakfast, then we'll give you free play time for two hours. Two hours, can you believe it? During your two hours, you'll go to the Trading Post and get whatever you want up to a limit of ten dollars, no charge to your account."

Kids cheered so loud and long you'd have thought I'd

given them Christmas. Screw Dante and his stupid-ass overpriced points system.

Laurel and I returned to the kitchen. Neal approached me, wearing a yellow scarf sash and homemade badge that revealed his rank as general. *Oh, my Lord of the Flies.*

"Neal, you look great." I spoonfed him compliments, not wanting to engender more animosity from him or his minions. I fingered the sash stretched tight over his barrel chest and fat stomach.

He puffed out his chest, his back steel-straight. He stabbed the bat onto the floor, then shouldered it like a rifle. I wouldn't trust him with a rifle if my life depended upon it. His usual frowny face was all arrogant, badass business.

"Reporting in, General Bailey," he said. I smothered a grin. "The prisoners are cooperating. They've been fed and special needs handled."

"Special needs?"

"Vitamins and Tylenol, ma'am."

Ma'am? Jeez, did I look that old? "No trouble?"

"My men and I handled them."

"Such as?"

"Chef was demanding we send in booze if we didn't release them. He stormed the door. We subdued him." Self-importance inflated Neal's chest even more.

A thread of alarm wound in my gut. "How?"

"I slammed the door against his head." He preened, stroking the bat. "Dumbass deserved it. He almost escaped."

That dread burned, and I thought I was having a heart attack. My mouth gaped.

"Chill. Dude's an alcoholic. We tossed in two bottles of booze. Shut him up good."

"Next time you open the door, I want three guards

there."

"No prob." He clicked his shoes together. "Did Logan leave?" He usurped his voice to the young kid inside him, serving up his vulnerability.

"Yes. He'll get help."

Jesse joined us. "No luck finding the satellite phone." He tossed a video camera and a wireless gadget on the counter. "Found this surveillance camera."

"Can you jury rig the phone or Internet cables?" I'd seen my dad scrape the plastic off electrical wires to expose the wires on a lamp then twist them together.

"Good idea." Jesse limped over to an open toolbox we'd salvaged from the pantry and scrounged for tools.

Why had Dante incapacitated the entire camp? Was he über afraid of me? Or was he planning another crime that involved the campers? A lot of campers had rich parents, including mine, as publicized during my kidnapping for the world to drool over. Had he planned to keep us all hostage? Jeez, my paranoid mind was working overtime now.

It felt good commanding Operation Dragonfly Occupation. For the first time in my life, I had purpose, strength, and the ability to conquer fear my way.

I snagged a pancake. Foreign sounds drifted in from the open windows, the burble and chugging of a Harley Davidson.

CHAPTER 28

Every cell of my being froze, and my pancake plopped onto the floor, stealing my brief moment of strength. The loud Harley screamed past the offices to the staff cabins beyond.

Laurel rushed me. "What are we going to do?" Her voice reached the level of dog training whistles.

"He'll be looking for Dante," Nick offered the obvious.

Neal joined us, his nervousness mingling in the air with mine. He'd gotten chummy with Dante, but that friendship didn't extend to Dante's friend. For the most part, Dante kept Rambo away from the kids. He'd never joined the campground experience until the gold mine visit. Was he selling Mrs. A's belongings to line Dante's pockets? Had he used Logan and me for archery practice?

"Neal, you chummed up to Dante. Did he ever mention why Rambo's here?" I asked.

Scowling, Neal shrugged back his shoulders. "So what if Dante and I got friendly?"

I held my hand up to forestall his defensive rant. "I'm

not accusing you of dirt. Rambo will bust this wide open unless we subdue him. I need to know his vulnerabilities."

"Oh. Kay. Dante didn't talk much about him. He's a contractor friend working on the two damaged cabins."

"What else?"

"Dante said he's into Martina."

That explained the mystery hook-up on the first night. An idea bloomed. "Neal, go spy on Rambo and stay hidden. Make sure he stays up at the staff cabins. If he starts looking for Dante, Martina, or anyone, run back and let us know so we can head him off."

Neal peeled a walkie-talkie off his belt. "We found these in the storage room." He handed me the radio, a different set from the one Marco and I had shared. "I'll snag Jeff's."

"I've got guard duty." I walked to the hallway door. "It's awfully quiet."

"They made a ruckus earlier, then put a lid on it." Neal tapped his bat against his hand, as if he wanted to bust some heads. "You gonna be okay alone?"

"Sure." I pulled out my gun, warm from resting against my back all morning. "I have Mr. Glock to keep me company."

Neal licked his lips. "I should take that while I watch Rambo."

"I doubt you know how to use it." I stuck the gun back into my waistband.

He sneered. "Seen my dad handle one. I can do it."

"No. End of story. Don't let Rambo see you." His sneer turned uglier, and I added some sugar to sweeten his mood. "Later we'll guard together and you can hold the gun." *Fat chance.* "For now, it's code red, top priority to keep Rambo under control. You're the best man for the job, general."

Neal shambled away, his bouncing strut taking on a

new importance.

Laurel and I perched on the stools by the counter while Nick cleaned up from breakfast. He'd shooed away our efforts to help.

"Should we try to hide his motorcycle?" Laurel asked.

"No. If he thinks all is A-okay, he may stay in his cabin and out of our hair. At least until Logan returns. We need to kill his curiosity and keep him from cruising over here."

"When do you think Logan will come back?" Laurel wiped a tear off her cheek. "Will he be okay?"

"If he can reach the highway and flag down a car, we'll be good."

I hugged her close. "You and Nick go set the kids up with their activities. Give them lots of attention so they don't miss the adults."

"Are you sure? I don't like leaving you alone."

"I'm not opening the storage door." Releasing her, I smiled our smile. "Have one of the boys stay in earshot."

Reluctantly, Nick and Laurel left me alone in the sparkling kitchen. If Laurel didn't marry Nick in the far future, I might. The boy was a wizard in all things kitchen.

I lugged a chair in from the secluded patio and collapsed onto it, setting the gun on a stool next to me. The storage room was suspiciously quiet for another five minutes. Then Dante yelled and pounded on the door.

"Let us outta here," he slurred out the words. *Great.* Dumbass Neal should've never given them alcohol. At least it made them stupid and slow-witted to the point they might not try to force their way out. I hoped.

I banged on the door. "Shut up, killer. We'll let you out when the sheriff arrives."

"Allie? That you? You've got it all wrong."

"You sure about that?"

"Carla fell off a cliff. I didn't kill her. You gotta believe me."

"Right. And I'm the president." I flung up my hands. "Did her zombie body dig a hole and bury itself too?"

"I don't know how she got there." He smothered a fake sob. "Look, I was drunk after I found my poor aunt's broken body. I don't remember what happened. Swear it."

"Screw you."

"You know people do dumb things when they're traumatized, drunk, feeling grief. You of all people know that." I barely heard Martina.

I propped my shoulder against the wall, shriveling into a puddle of memories and grief, thoughts of Logan. *Was she talking about me or Logan?*

"What do you know about that?" The question dripped out of my mouth. "You don't know me at all."

"We know all about your kidnapping." Dante scoffed. "I know Logan left you because he felt so much guilt for abandoning you at the mall. He couldn't confront you and confess how his video game obsession contributed to your kidnapping."

My fists curled. How did they know about Logan and his guilt when I barely suspected his true reason for going away to boarding school? I thought Logan didn't want anything to do with me because I was too traumatized and our parents were ticked at him for leaving me alone when we had strict orders to stay together. At first, I believed Logan assumed I'd gone with Kline willingly and he was ticked at me for leaving *him*. I'd thought his parents had sent him away, to keep him safe from me. I hated Logan for leaving me alone due to his stupid obsession. I still couldn't look at a video game without thinking of his betrayal, his direct defiance. I hated him for abandoning me when I needed him the most after The Incident. I hated him for never telling me why he left.

Worst of all, I detested hating one iota about him. Especially now.

"You know it's true," Dante said, his words deliberately enunciated. "Logan confessed to me at the campfire. He needed an unbiased opinion, someone who didn't know either of you. I fit the bill. He trusted me enough to tell me why he left you for boarding school, why he couldn't tell you."

I pounded my fist on the wall. "Shut up. You don't know jack." Tears cascaded down my cheeks.

"Logan and I are buds now. I know his deep, dark secrets about your kidnapping. He would've rather bury his head up his ass than face you. *He* chose to go to boarding school, not his parents. He chose to leave you alone for four years. He came to camp hoping to make amends and still doesn't know how to do it. And you're letting him get away with it."

"Shut up," I cried, unable to move or to cease listening. Dante was like a twenty car pile-up on the freeway. You had to ogle even though you should look away.

"I told him to cozy up to you, hook up if that's what it took and you'll forget all about what he'd done. It's working, isn't it?" Dante guffawed.

"Shut up, Dante," Martina shouted. "Allie, don't listen to him. He's drunk."

Not drunk enough. I seethed, lamented, hashed out every moment I'd spent with Logan since we'd arrived at camp. I wanted to smack him, kiss him, knee him where it counted. I wanted to slap myself upside the head for dropping my guard where he was concerned.

Resting my forehead against the wall, I breathed in and out slowly, gathering my strength, corralling my crazed thoughts. Was Dante telling the truth about buddying up to Logan? Did Logan really try to convince

Dante to spill about Mrs. Amadori? Had Logan confessed his secrets to Dante? Willing the questions to take a hike, I gripped my head, squeezing sense into my brain. I should just cut him loose after all the history or lack thereof between us. Life might be so much easier. But something inside me refused to give up so easily.

"Let me out. I can help you," Martina cajoled. "You keep the gun on me at all times. I just want to talk, girl to girl, okay? We'll sort this all out and call the sheriff."

"Bite me, Martina," Dante bellowed. "You call the sheriff and you'll land in jail too."

"Shut it," Martina screamed.

A scuffle ensued. Not one peep emerged from the other five people in the room. Were they putting on a show for me?

How much did Martina know about Dante killing their aunt? When she'd learned Mrs. A was dead, her horror led me to believe she didn't know squat. I believe she truly thought Dante had taken Mrs. A to a convalescent hospital. But she'd lied to me about taking care of Mrs. A in her cabin. Maybe Dante was manipulating her too. Was he tormenting her into her pale, anorexic self? Had he put that bruise on her shoulder? Did he hold a bucket of crap over her head to force her to hide his crimes?

Unable to listen to more puzzling smack from the peanut gallery, I returned to Dragonfly Nightmare headquarters. I spied the video camera on the kitchen counter where Jesse had dumped it. Another demented idea sprouted.

Static squealed out of the two-way radio attached to my belt loop, followed by sounds of an engine chugging through it. A Harley Davidson engine.

"Oh, hell no." I lifted the radio to my mouth. "Neal? Come in, Neal."

No response.

I sprinted out of the kitchen. Neal sat hunched on the Harley, zigzagging down the path from the staff cabins toward the center green. The motorcycle tilted precariously to the right, horror creeping over Neal's gleeful grin. Waving his fists and yelling, Rambo lumbered after his runaway hawg. A handful of scattered kids cheered Neal on and trailed alongside the bike. Neal hung on, increasing his speed incrementally as he managed to gain control of the beast.

I waved him on, and he grinned as he passed me by. He removed his right hand off the throttle to give me a thumbs up. The engine sputtered and the bike listed again. Neal aimed straight for an old oak tree.

I screamed, "Watch the tree. The tree!" Too late.

He veered to the left to avoid hitting the oak, and the bike crashed into another stand of trees, falling on its side. Neal managed to pull his legs out of the way from the bike's full weight, sacrificing his left shoulder in the process.

Screams of bloody murder poured out of his mouth. Black birds squawked and took flight, circling like vultures searching for their next meal. Rambo reached the bike and lifted it off Neal, cursing a blue streak.

Neal lay on the ground, left arm at a strange angle. I bolted toward him, sliding to a stop on my knees at his side.

"What'd you do?" I whisper-yelled.

"Tried to get…help," he muttered through his pain. "My shoulder—"

Rambo collapsed to his knees and tore away Neal's shirt. "Stupid kid. What the hell were you doing?"

Neal opened his mouth, and I put my finger over his lips. "Shhh." *Don't give us away.*

"Get Martina," Rambo gritted out between his teeth.

"She should be in the Trading Post."

"She's not in the Trading Post," one of the youngest boys said. "The adults are taking the day off."

A knot formed in my intestines. "I know where she's at." I jumped up. "It's a teen leadership training session today," I added to keep Rambo's suspicions in check.

I turned to one of the twelve-year-old boys. "Andy, take the kids to their activities with Laurel and Nick. Now." The kids scattered, glancing over their shoulders on their way to the dining hall where they'd set up a new craft room to accommodate all the kids.

As I rose to my full height, I noticed the golden trail of rocks from Neal to where Rambo had leaned the motorcycle on its bent kickstand against a tree. The map Nick and Laurel had found stuck out of the leather bag on the right above the tailpipes. How'd he find the map? Nick had hidden it, and only he and Logan knew where. *O.M.G.* Had Logan coughed it up? When Rambo diverted his attention to Neal, I scooped up a few nuggets and fled to the kitchen.

Excitement swept through me, not that I had much to do with the find of a lifetime. I shoved the nuggets in my pocket and drew out the gun. I had no choice but to let Martina out.

I knocked on the locked door. "Everyone move back. I'm armed and surrounded. Martina, I'm letting you out. Neal's hurt. You come to the door alone. No funny business."

Luck must've been on my side. When I unlocked the door, everyone lounged on the two beds and chairs against the far wall. I think they were all plastered. Martina took slow, sure steps forward. I held up the gun, far enough away to prevent her from making a grab for it.

"Out. Shut the door behind you."

She obeyed and I relocked the door. "Hands in the

air."

Martina extended her arms toward the sky. "I'll help you frame Dante. Let me go free."

"Why? He's your brother."

"I didn't want to anger him. He did this against my will. He forced me to go along with his plan. We know you kids found the map to the gold. Logan gave it to Dante, who gave it to Rambo, who's at the mine searching. You know Rambo will return anytime, don't you? He and Dante are tight."

No, no, not Logan. Please, God, not Logan. Everything pointed to the runaway Logan train. "He's already back." I gulped hard, fearing my actions may've dumped us all in a heap of disaster.

Red suffused her corpse coloring. "Then you need my help. If Rambo finds out what you've done, he'll go berserk. You can't fight him."

Jeff and Richie sauntered in for their guard rotation. Baseball bats lifted as they surrounded Martina.

"Stand down. Martina's coming out. Neal may have broken his arm trying to ride Rambo's bike. Jeff, guard the door. Richie, with me."

"Act normal in front of Rambo and he won't suspect anything. I'll do what you say if you don't hurt me," Martina suggested.

Call me an idiot, but I believed her. She wore her sincerity on her mottled, grim face.

"Who bruised your shoulder?" I asked. "Did Dante do that?"

"What do you think?" The scarlet blotches deepened on her cheeks. "Like I said, I'll help you frame Dante, then we're both done with him."

"Then what?" I asked curiously, spying the video camera. "How about you help me persuade Dante to confess to the murder and cover-up on video? Then you're scot-free. Will you do that?"

"Perfect." She gave me a tentative smile. "I'm sorry I let him manipulate me. Carla knew he was bad news, but he's my brother. Ya know?"

Richie and I sandwiched Martina as we hurried out to the crash site. I hid the gun under my shirt, not wanting to alert Rambo. When we arrived, Neal was alone, Rambo and the bike gone.

"Where'd he go?" I asked.

"Left. He suspected some weird shit going down." Neal winced. "I blew it," he wailed. "I saw the gold," his voice dropped to a whisper. "It all came out."

"What came out?" I asked slowly, deadly calm.

Martina sank to her knees and smoothed her hands gently over Neal's shoulder and arm. "It's dislocated. I can fix it." She glanced around, saw random gold nuggets Rambo had missed on the ground. Lunging for them, she scooped up a couple. "He found the gold?"

"Looks like it." I scanned the area for Rambo. "Richie, go back to the kitchen. Rambo may be looking for Dante."

"What did you tell him?" I demanded, gripping Neal's good shoulder.

He screamed, "Stop it. You're hurting me."

I snatched my hand back, mortification and guilt sweeping up my torso in a wide swath of heat. "Sorry."

"He asked why the camp was so quiet. I told him about the teen leadership day. Didn't believe me. He shook me, hurt so bad. It just came out." Tears streamed down Neal's cheeks. The bully had emotions I never suspected.

"What, Neal? What came out?" I asked gently.

"That Dante killed Mrs. Amadori. That he better run far and fast."

"Okay." I breathed out my relief. "He left the campground on his bike?"

"Think so. He headed down the driveway. I heard it start up closer to the highway."

Martina positioned Neal flat. "Allie, hold him down. I need to reset his shoulder. This will hurt. Can you handle it, Neal?"

"Do it." He clenched his teeth.

"If I do this and help you, you'll confess to the sheriff that Dante killed my aunt? You'll help me? You'll tell them that I helped you?"

"Yes. As long as you go along with us," I replied.

"Fine." She prodded Neal's shoulder, and he gritted his teeth from the pain. "Hold him down with your body."

I lay half on top of Neal. Within a few seconds, he screamed loud enough to disturb Mrs. Amadori's final rest and tried to buck me off. Martina pulled and manipulated his arm, snapping it back into the socket. The sickening crunch of bones forever etched itself onto my brain. Neal quit thrashing and began groaning.

I rolled off him, considered pulling the gun out. Martina had all the chances in the world to run and she didn't.

She helped Neal sit up. "Feel better?"

"I can handle it." Hand on his shoulder, he slowly rotated his arm.

"Where's the second satellite phone?" I threw Martina off guard.

She stood, brushing leaves and dirt off her jeans. "Dante hid it after he cut the phone and Internet lines."

CHAPTER 29

Martina, Neal, and I returned to the kitchen. Jeff and Richie were encouraging Dante to talk them through fixing a vehicle. But Dante acted like he didn't know what was wrong with them, and kept throwing out suggestions, repairs for them to check and report back. We wired Martina with the hidden video camera, gave her a tray of sandwiches Nick had made earlier and sent her back inside the room without incident.

I urged Neal to relax on the cushioned chair, but he wanted to contribute, feeling bad about what he'd done. He took a suggested timeout for a half hour first, guarding the kitchen door from any errant kids wandering about.

I kept an ear out for Rambo's motorcycle. The wait drove me batty. Sitting in front of the tiny screen, I watched Martina position herself in front of Dante and coax him to talk about what he'd done. He roared at her to shut up before he said something she didn't want to hear.

I wondered what he meant. If they were caught kicking puppies and killing aunts, the property was forfeited, bequeathed to another family member or elsewhere. Martina didn't spill a word about Rambo finding the gold or possessing the map. The map that Logan supposedly had handed to Dante on a silver platter.

Logan. Was he okay? Questions revolved in my head again, and I almost missed Dante telling Martina he'd hid the satellite phone in the woods where no one would find it.

At that moment, I knew we couldn't rely on Logan to save us. We needed a backup plan. "Jeff, get Dante talking about how to fix a car again."

"Sure, but what he was spouting didn't make sense." He pointed to Richie and Neal. "None of us know how to fix cars."

"Just do it." I slammed my hand on the counter. My anxiety flicked on my raving bitch switch. The mere thought of people using us like Dante and Martina had was enough to send me over the edge. The kids needed me to stay rational, with a side order of bitch to keep us on the right side of Dante's lunatic shenanigans. Otherwise, I'd melt into an oil slick of emotions. Only God knew what would happen if I disappeared into a snow globe created in my head, a meadow, dead bodies, dead dragonflies, a nightmare world encased in a secure bubble. Not gonna happen. I pressed on my leather band, jerked my hand away.

Jeff, Neal, and Richie took sloppy notes on napkins as Martina encouraged Dante to fork over car repair instructions. Jeff and Richie left to test them one at a time.

I walked over to the locked door. "Dante, why're you helping us?" I asked loudly.

"I want out. The sooner the sheriff arrives, the sooner

I can explain what happened. Not that you care to hear me out."

"Then explain it."

"Okay. Good." He took a few seconds to coral his lying brain cells. "So here goes. Carla fell and broke her leg. That part's true." He came closer to the door. "She didn't want me directing the campground with Martina. Bad family blood and shit."

Hmmm... I placed my hand on the door, opposite of where I thought his face was. So close it was creepy, but I felt somewhat connected by that thread of confession.

"Then I discovered how badly in debt she was. I told her I could turn the place around if she'd give me a chance, give me room and board. She agreed. But there were complications. Things I wanted to do she didn't like."

"Like digging for gold?"

"I knew you'd found out about that. I mean, Logan gave me the map Nick and Laurel found in the old cabin."

A wintry heaviness centered me again. *No.* "Right." I scoffed. "Why would Logan do that?"

"You'll have to ask him," he said with a dismissive edge. "He understood the map belonged to my family. He wanted to help Carla, I guess. He didn't know she was dead. He thought he was helping her by helping me."

My fist clenched on the door as his lies and half-truths tangled my mind. "Then what?"

"Rambo came to help me find the gold while Martina and I managed the camp. I promised him half my share if he found it. Carla liked him, knew his family, and knew he had construction experience. She hired him to fix the two damaged cabins."

"What does that have to do with killing Carla?" I waved my hand to hurry him along, fantasizing he'd see my gesture by osmosis.

"I didn't kill her," he gritted out. "Carla heard Rambo

and me talking about the gold and confronted us. Told us we weren't allowed to search for it. It was our grandfather's wish to leave the gold mine intact to preserve it for historical purposes."

"Who owned the gold?"

"Possession is nine tenths of the law. If it's on Amadori property, doesn't matter who it belonged to in the past."

Did it actually belong to someone else? Who was Rambo? Was he scheming to steal the gold from the Amadori family? How well did Dante know his friend? *Holy crapola. He's throwing his friend under the bus.*

"Go on." A sick excitement vibrated through me.

"Carla got into Rambo's face. He was drunk off his ass and took offense at her needling and refusal to let us search. He didn't know what he was doing and chest-butted her down a cliff."

"And you buried her instead of calling the cops?"

"No, Allie," Dante said with the right amount of solemnity. "Rambo buried her, tried to cover it up. I didn't find out about it until later. I swear. I just needed time to find the gold, then we planned to come clean."

Then you planned to sell the property and sell your friend out?

"You need to let Dante out. If Rambo returns, he'll go insane. No telling what he'll do to you or the kids," Martina pleaded.

Neal paled. He'd heard the whole story. "Do you believe him?" I whispered.

He wiped a film of sweat off his brow. "Rambo's kinda psycho."

Jeff and Richie flew into the kitchen like canaries the cat had nibbled on.

"Can't figure it out." Jeff slammed a wrench on the stainless steel counter, his hands black with grease, smelling of boy and fear. “We need Dante to help us. We have the battery cables connected, but spark plugs are missing.”

“Who disabled the vehicles?” I asked Dante.

“Who do you think? Rambo did. He’s trying to find the gold on his own.”

“He already did.” Agony charged Martina’s voice.

“The hell? Why didn’t you tell me?” Dante beat his fists on the wall. “Come on, Allie. I’ll get a car started, then I’m hunting down that son of a bitch. I’ll keep him from hurting you or the kids. Mark my words, he’ll come back to nab you as leverage. Or one of the other rich kids. Let me out. Everyone else stays inside.”

“Why bother coming back if he has the gold?” I rolled my eyes. Did he take me for an idiot?

“Because you found…Carla. His DNA’s all over her. Plus, the minute he tries to convert the gold to cash, they’ll nab him. Everyone knows that’s Amadori gold. He can’t hide it. It’s fucking legend in these parts.”

“Hang tight.” I drew Neal, Jeff, and Ritchie into the kitchen.

“If all four of us guard him, we can do it, right?” I asked. “Long enough to get a car running.”

Neal’s tired gaze kept flicking away. “We’ll do it. I trust him,” he said. “He’s been good to me. Talked me through some personal shit at home.”

“Jeff, tell Nick and Laurel to keep the kids in the dining hall. No one goes outside,” I said.

Laurel and Nick tried to talk me out of it. In the end, they agreed. We couldn’t sit on our butts and wait for Logan to rescue us. Every minute we kept the adults locked up ratcheted up our criminal charges count. I wanted the sheriff to know that we did everything to secure help despite Dante and Rambo’s machinations thwarting our efforts.

Drawing the gun, I stepped six feet away from the storage room door. Neal and Jeff bracketed the door. Bat in hand, Jesse waited near the patio door where we'd take Dante through so the kids in the dining hall didn't see us.

"Dante comes out alone. Anyone rushing the door will meet the blunt end of a baseball bat. Head on." I nodded to Neal to unlock the door.

True to his word, Dante slipped through the door alone, hands in the air. Neal tied Dante's hands behind his back with a zip strip. He whispered a few indecipherable words to Dante, then nudged his bat into the man's back. We escorted Dante through the patio to the parking lot. The boys had lifted the hood of the SUV and tools littered the ground.

Dante studied the engine, slowly walking from one side to the next, the three boys shadowing him. I kept the gun trained on him. Could I use it if needed? Or even shoot straight? I didn't know, but it gave me no small amount of comfort, especially if Rambo returned to exact revenge. That is, if Dante had told the truth about his caveman friend.

"Okay. See that right there?" Dante nodded. "Rambo removed three spark plugs and dislodged the distributor cap." He looked at Neal. "Did you find the plugs?"

"No. Didn't look for them." He gripped his arm, leaving a black smudge on his white T-shirt.

"Look inside the cab. Doubt he tossed them." On his best behavior, Dante leaned against a crusty tree trunk. Neal and Richie began searching the SUV. Jeff remained close to Dante, bat held at strike position, a bowie knife in a scabbard on his belt.

"Where's Logan?" Dante asked.

"Watching the kids," I replied, trading his level stare with one of my own. His smirk betrayed his disbelief.

"Kids okay?"

"What do you care?"

"Hey, I'm not the villain here." He grunted.

"You knew Carla was dead. You didn't call the sheriff. Cut the innocent act. Your list of crimes is ten miles long."

"Matters flipped out of control. We were trying to help Carla find the gold to pay down her debt. Logan was helping us figure it all out."

"You mean *your* debts?" Tilting my head to the side, I refused to acknowledge Dante as Logan's long lost pal.

He wagged his head as if flinging off mountain ticks. "My debt stems from helping Carla. I gave her a lot of money over the last couple years to keep this place afloat. Then she stopped me from hunting the gold when it would've saved her ass and repay me and Martina."

I contemplated his words. Was he telling the truth? Holy moly, I was bumbling to the crossroads of Confusion Circle and Suspicion Street. During my kidnapping, Kline had told me crap I wanted to hear. He'd told me he was helping my father's company, helping my father realize he needed to spend more time with his family instead of work. When he received all the money my father owed him, he said he'd give some to me to buy whatever I wanted for my birthday. He'd made me believe my mother would divorce my dad once she found out my dad fired Kline, because he was my father's top investment broker. He'd said my father's company would go down the tube without Kline bringing in the biggest and best clients. We'd end up homeless, living on the street, and all my friends would take a hike. I would lose Laurel and Logan.

He had my mind so fogged up I barely knew my identity. Some of his ramblings were true. Michael Kline had been my father's best investment broker, until he nearly destroyed my father's firm. The financial mess had strained my parents' marriage. The kidnapping made my parents realize what had become of our family, and that they'd let me become a latchkey kid too soon.

The weight of the gun dragged my arm down. A flurry of movement by the SUV forced my attention from my muddled thoughts. Dante had Jeff grasped in his arms, baseball bat tossed into the woods, bowie knife biting into Jeff's neck.

Son of a lying bitch. I pointed the gun at Dante's head, so close to Jeff that I couldn't shoot without risking him.

"Drop the weapons," Dante demanded calmly.

Richie and Neal charged the whackjob, knocking him and Jeff to the ground. A scuffle of pummeling bodies broke out. I froze, the gun wavering in my hand, unable to shoot, unable to move. *Stupid boys never listen.*

A slash of sunlight gleamed off the knife blade and cut through my sluggish mind. I jetted forward, toppling over scissoring boy legs and quickly righting myself. Dante was quicker. The knife disappeared in one hand, his other slammed a jarring fist into Richie's nose. He rose and punched Neal in the gut several times until Neal slipped into lala-land with Richie. He hauled Jeff up, the smallest of the three boys, and yanked him in front of his body like a shield, the knife once again at Jeff's throat.

"Toss the gun or I'll kill him." Dante gasped, blood dripping from a cut on his forehead, narrowly missing his right eye. Jeff stilled, shaking like a scolded puppy. A thin crimson thread dripped down his neck.

The blood knocked sense into me. He didn't say where to toss the gun, so I tossed it into the woods, then extended my arms skyward. "Go. Leave Jeff here."

Dante scowled up a storm. "Think I'm stupid?" He tapped the handle of the knife in Jeff's spine. "Move it." He forced Jeff to walk toward the empty staff cabins. "I'll let him go once I'm free of this stink hole."

Jeff sniveled. Pee left a dark stain on his board

shorts. Dante prodded him up the path.

"Okay." No way would I use my sketchy martial arts to take Dante down while he held a knife to Jeff.

The idea of Dante hurting a child immobilized me for a second. I gasped, inciting a freakout until Neal groaned. I clambered to his side. Richie lay unconscious next to him, but his pulse was beating okay.

I swept stringy hair off Neal's pale face, my eyebrows drawn tight as a storming anger filled me. "You helped him, didn't you?" I forced the words out between gritted teeth. "You didn't tighten the zip strip. You didn't believe me. He doesn't give a rat's ass about you. Do you see that now?"

"Sorry," Neal mumbled. "I'm gonna get that asswipe." He scrambled up, holding his head.

"Get help for Richie. Tell Nick and Laurel what happened. Tell them to watch for Rambo and not let Martina out unless it's a matter of life or death. I'm following Dante."

Dante and Jeff had moved out of view, and I tore into the woods to hunt for the gun. My eyes misted with too many emotions to count on one hand. It took forever, scurrying in circles, thrashing through the forest debris, trees, and ferns before dappled sunlight illuminated the barrel of the gun half-covered in needles and leaves. I dove for the weapon then sped to an obscure path I'd found in my cat and mouse game with Dante yesterday.

The gun felt oddly right in my hand, like a finger. I vowed to spend time learning how to use one when I returned home. If I made it home. *Criminy.* I hated the fact that twice in sixteen years I'd been the target of a crime. I refused to let it happen again. Ever.

The eight silent cabins loomed ahead. The door to Dante's cabin stood open, rustling sounds emanating from inside. Dante pushed Jeff out onto the front stoop, a bulging backpack strapped on his back. He guided Jeff to the backyard, and they climbed the hill behind the cabins. Using two zip strips, he'd tied Jeff's hands behind his back. Did he have another car or boat stashed away? *Whatever. That sucker's mine.*

Stealthily, I trailed them, keeping a good distance because it was hard to remain silent when every step crunched on a dead tree limb, a pile of dry leaves, or rocks and dirt clods that rolled me off balance as I climbed uphill. Soon, there weren't enough trees or rocks to hide behind, and I had to dart from one barrier to another as Dante headed down the hill toward the lake, lengthening his lead.

They reached the bottom of the hill near the shoreline of the lake, and took off to the right. I lost my cover and scampered uphill to trail them from where the trees hid me better. Fighting the woods as the forest thickened again, I prayed Dante didn't hear my pathetic covert stalking. When I tripped and pebbles clattered down the hill, I threw myself to the ground and rolled behind a crumbling log, holding my breath.

"What was that?" Dante's voice drifted to me.

"What?" Jeff's reply quivered as if he tried to suppress his emotions.

Another fist-sized rock tumbled down the hill, dirt and debris trailing it.

"Come out now, or he bites it," Dante yelled. "Allie, I know it's you."

I lodged the gun in my waistband, its second home on my body. It could cause serious damage if it ever went off. I had a flat enough butt already. My mind spun like a crazy hamster wheel to avert my pending unraveling.

Standing, I held up my hands and moved into the psycho's view. Just as well we confronted each other. The fear of following him and endangering Jeff stirred acid in my stomach, and I didn't know how long I'd hold out.

"Two for the price of one. Down here." Dante waved his knife, motioning me forward.

I picked my way down the hill to the pebble-strewn beach. Gentle waves lapped the shore, receding over rocks, free and unfettered. Boats the size of ants sped to nowhere along the far shore, too far away to make a difference in the here and now.

Jeff stood on Dante's left, a good enough distance to thwart a surprise attack.

As I took the last step onto the rocky shore about three feet from Dante, I kicked at his hand wielding the bowie knife, catching him off guard. The knife flew six feet down the beach. Dante bellowed and tackled me to the ground. I fell backward hard, my head hitting rocks, a searing burn radiating down my back. White light exploded in my head. I drew up my knee and kneed him in his junk and head-butted him, rolling him off enough for me to grab the gun digging against my spine. Stars wavered in my vision as my head exploded.

I jerked the gun out and brought the butt down on Dante's skull the way I'd seen in movies. He stiffened half on top of me. I squeezed out from under him, and Jeff kicked the knife out of the way, both of us staring at each other, our mouths gaping. It all happened so quickly, Jeff didn't have time to help. Didn't matter.

"Anymore zip strips?" I wanted to curl up on the ground and die from the pain seizing me in a searing grip. Instead, I grabbed the knife and sliced the ties on Jeff's wrists.

He rummaged through Dante's backpack and handed me two plastic strips. We bound Dante's wrists and left him lying on the beach. Grabbing the backpack, I had a moment to sit and think. Unlike the stupid people you see in slasher flicks, I sat well away from Dante to foil any attempt to attack me if he stretched out an arm or leg. Distance I'd failed to achieve in the mall when Kline parked on the bench next to me.

"Run to the kitchen, get Nick."

"I can't leave you with him." Jeff wrung his hands. The rivulet of blood had dried on his neck, his pee-stained shorts had dried, and he looked no worse for wear. But I knew otherwise. He wore bruises from his beating and invisible emotional scars. I knew those scars intimately.

"Go. Take the knife."

At that moment among the infinite moments of my life, I knew I'd truly survive better than ever. I didn't know how or why I knew it. Daylight emerged in the depths of the nightmare. Though my nightmare continued, the light burned away the edges. *Baby steps.*

"I'll be all right," I muttered, watching Jeff jet toward camp. I hoped.

CHAPTER 30

Gun glued to my hand, I glowered at Dante as he attempted to sit up. Waves lapped the shore and receded, towing the water down the river, its sole escape from the wide bowl of blue. I wanted more for myself, the challenge of choosing my freedoms, the challenge of living a normal life again. I thought I'd gain my independence by coming to camp. Justice had to prevail first. Truths needed spilling. Until then, I was stuck in a bottomless limbo.

Steadying my arm, I aimed the gun point-blank at Dante's chest. "Freeze, asshole."

"Let me go. I swear I'll leave you alone." Pain etched lines across his forehead.

"Take a hint, pinhead. I'm turning you in for murder, kidnapping, assault, fraud, whatever else I can make stick. Let's call this a citizen's arrest." I vaulted off the ground for better leverage, the rear of my shorts damp.

He emitted a guttural laugh. "Think you know it all. You don't know the half."

"Shut. It. Don't move or I'll split your nuts open."

"You won't shoot me. You aren't that kind of person." Ignoring my weak threat, he lifted off his knees, staggering from the blow to his head. His hair fell over his eyes and he whipped his head like a dog to clear his vision. Too bad I hadn't hit him harder.

"Try me." My heart beat so hard it deafened the world beyond the two of us.

"Untie me, let me go. You keep the gun. You'll need it."

"For who? Your lapdog, Rambo? Golum and your precious gold are long gone."

He shifted forward. I stepped back. We danced our dangerous standoff along the shore for a few more steps. Forward. Backward.

Then I tripped over a blasted rock. Falling backward, I pinwheeled my arms. Dante lunged at me, pummeling me with the full length of his body once again. This time I buried the gun barrel into his board-straight gut.

"Do it." He spit in my face, shoving his knee between my legs. When his knee connected with my crotch, I lost my breath from the force of the blow. Bright pinpoints of light blinded me. "You can't live in a bubble all your life. No lighthouse will save you."

Shock rippled up my chest. As he tried to bump the gun out of my hand, I struggled to keep my grip on it, to keep it pointed away from me. Dante screwed back his leg one more time to knock me silly, giving me a chance to regain my hold on the gun, and more.

I pulled the trigger.

The blast echoed in my ears and bounced off one side of the canyon to the others. The recoil bashed my head against the rocks. It was worth seeing the darkening red patch blooming on his thigh, the frozen *O* his mouth made as he fell to the side, out like a snuffed flame.

I crab-crawled away, scraping hands on rocks, tearing my shorts. In an epic freakout, I brought my knees to my chest and hid my face in them. The gun thumped to the ground between my legs, and I almost shook myself into oblivion. *Oh, vigilante hell. I shot him. I shot someone.* My arms trembled, but I managed to find my wrist to press on my leather band, but it was gone. The scars and the new abrasions met my terror head on. I started to scratch off the scabs. Stopped. I took ten level breaths, gazed down the shoreline, focused on a shiny piece of quartz the water rushed over. So much fear had swamped me the last few days, my newest horror met emptiness. Marshy air, warm enough to kill my chill saturated my nose. Maybe I had nothing left to fear.

"Allie? Allie!"

The familiar voice bumped around my thundering head, and my gaze fell upon my salvation. Logan knelt down and held me.

He smoothed my hair as I shivered in his arms, holding onto him tightly. The devil you know and all. Somewhere along the line, Logan had become my lodestone. I needed either to cut him loose or hang on for dear life. Now, I needed his strength holding me up.

"Al, what happened?" he whispered. "Are you okay?"

The vision of Dante's prone body woke up the part of me that tried to die.

"I…I shot him." I pressed against Logan. "Make sure he's out. He already surprised me once."

Logan withdrew a rope from his backpack and tied it around Dante's thigh to slow the blood. "Doesn't look like you hit an artery."

I whipped up my head. "Why do you care if he lives or dies after he killed Mrs. Amadori?"

Logan looked at me askance. "He needs to live to face the rap, to suffer the guilt of what he did. Come to terms with his crimes and guilt."

Whoa. How'd he know I felt the same inside?

"Dante said you gave him info about me and the kidnapping. You gave him my cell phone, the map." I needed so badly to know what Logan had done and more importantly, why. The *whys* bombarded my head, four years of them swirling and clanging against my skull.

"It's not what you think." He reached for me, but I stepped away from the hands I wanted touching me. His touch would incapacitate parts of my head and heart I needed lucid.

"Tell me what I'm missing. You told this bastard why you left me four years ago, yet you haven't even told *me*." I expelled the words through gritted teeth. Dante had booted me off the ledge of sanity. I floundered in the air toward the looney bin. "You owe *me* an explanation."

Logan trailed me up the beach, both of us keeping an eye on Dante. "I wanted to gain Dante's confidence in hopes he'd trip up or confide in me. I wanted to help you solve the mystery so you could enjoy your time at camp. I got close to him when he was hammered, and he talked about the history of the gold, selling the property. He kept saying he was doing all this for Mrs. A. They had a big offer to buy the property as long as the gold mine area was left intact. The buyer knew about the hidden gold, and mineral evaluations proved there was more gold to mine. Dante fessed up because he thought I might help him find it. He didn't say so, but he wanted to trick this investor. He hired Rambo to hunt for the gold while he managed the camp." The words hemorrhaged out. "I gave him your phone to earn his trust. He already suspected you had it and was searching your room. You remember. You caught him."

Logan had never uttered so much in one sitting. My head wanted to implode. "Okay. I get it, I guess." My knotted intestines loosened a smidge. "According to the probate papers, if Dante or Mrs. A sold the property, the gold mine goes to the historical society."

"Exactly. He was lying." Logan dug inside his pack and handed me crumpled papers. "I stole these from his file on you. Remember that file on Martina's desk?"

I unfolded the printed pages. My jaw dropped as I stared at detailed articles about my kidnapping and my father's investment firm. He'd highlighted specific information—my father's net worth, how much money Kline lost for my father, details about the kidnapping like the flowers Kline had given me. Proof in black and white.

"He got some info from Mrs. Amadori's Teen Leadership files. The rest was public info about the kidnapping. I didn't say a thing about your kidnapping."

After a long moment digesting this mind-bender, I asked, "Do you think he was pitting us against each other?"

"Yes." Logan grimaced. "To distract you from stumbling upon the truth. You were getting too close. I was afraid he'd target you the closer you traveled to the truth. I was steering him away."

I slid my hands over my face. "God. I don't know what to think anymore."

He stepped closer. "Trust me, please?"

Through my splayed fingers, I gazed deeply into his watery eyes. His pain and guilt nearly undid me. But I needed more, a crap-ton more.

"Did you tell him why you left town after the kidnapping?"

Thick tension descended upon another long hush.

Logan toed a dead fish carcass. "He guessed some of it one night. I couldn't shut him up. And *I* needed to talk." He reached out to touch me, then lowered his hand. "We were supposed to stick together at the mall. I knew it, but

I failed you. God, Allie, I couldn't face you afterward, knowing it was all my fault. I couldn't function while that bastard had you. When you were rescued, I broke down. From guilt, fear, failure. You name it."

I wanted to wrap my arms around him as if he were the kidnapped victim. But I held my ground, held my breath, hearing the truth I'd waited four years to hear.

"My parents thought it best I go away...and get counseling."

I blinked away tears. "What? You went to counseling too?"

He snorted like a honking goose. "For almost a year. I was in a rehab for a while too. The guilt destroyed me. I started drinking, stealing booze from the teachers' lounge, other students." He shrugged. "This isn't about me. It's about you."

Shock riddled my intestines, shooting holes in the reformed knots. "Laurel didn't tell me. No one told me."

"Only my parents knew."

"Oh, my God." I sobbed, my hand over my mouth. "Why didn't you tell me?"

"Shame, guilt, stupidity. Been trying to tell you since I came home. I was hoping we'd reconnect and I could fess up here. I didn't expect us to connect the way we did. I didn't know what to expect." His thumb and finger madly rubbed back and forth.

I stamped my foot on the rocky ground, ignoring the rocks poking into my arch. "I meant before. You didn't say goodbye. No note, no nothing. Flowers. You left me freaking wilted wildflowers."

He squinted, cocked his head to the side. "I gave you a card too, didn't I? So the flowers were similar to the ones Kline gave you, like the ones you and Laurel got here?"

Unable to speak, I nodded.

"I'm sorry. I was messed up. It's no excuse, just the truth." He approached me, cupped my cheeks. "I thought you hated me. I wrote you every day, but I never sent the emails. I came here to try to make it up to you, to keep you safe. I've failed you again. I won't blame you if you hate me all over."

I sighed. "I never hated you." A snicker escaped. "Okay, for a bit." The corners of my mouth kicked up in a tiny smile.

"Good. I deserve it."

I gripped his wrists. "You don't. I would've eventually forgiven you everything." And walked away forever.

"But I was stupid and thought it better to leave with the memories of our friendship rather than jeopardize you never returning my feelings."

"Feelings?" My heart compressed. "What…what do you mean?"

He craned his head and stared up at the heavens through the blue sky. "I had a major crush on you, and you shrugged me off. If you didn't return my feelings, I didn't want to ruin our friendship."

I laughed, bent double and laughed some more.

"Jeez, it's not that funny." Hurt shimmered in his eyes.

I stood to my full height, leaned forward, and feathered my mouth over his. "You dolt, I was twelve. I figured a thirteen-year-old boy had better ideas than liking his pesky sister's best friend." I pressed my lips to his cool lips in a brief kiss. "I had a mad crush on you then. Now you know why I was so hurt when you left without a word. I thought you were being a dumb selfish boy, who didn't give a wit about me. It destroyed me. You destroyed me." I swept my arm out, encompassing our mock-serene setting. "Then our dragonfly summer happened."

"How dumb is this?" He crushed me to him, our lips and tongues tangoing, unable to get enough from each other. He angled his head for a deeper liplock, and his kiss weakened my knees. Eons later, our kiss softened, and he drew away, his mouth brushing over mine. "I love you, Allie Bailey. I always have. When you warmed up to me a few days ago, I feared that if I told you the truth, you'd hate me. But I had every intention of coming clean before we left camp."

I grinned. "But you wanted me to profess my undying love first, right?"

"Something like that." He chuckled.

A mountain slid off my shoulders, down my arms, and I snuggled against his chest, holding onto my anchor. "I'm glad you did. I forgive you, ya know." He smelled of the woods, sweat, and my spicy, woodsy haven.

A dragonfly flitted near our heads, four iridescent blue wings never ceasing. It lived in the freedom within my grasp. I now had the chance to spread my wings and boot the last four years behind me. Not just because the air had cleared between us, but also because I had survived another nightmare. This time I did it on my own. *The real Allie Bailey has arrived.*

Now I had Logan beside me, dousing the fiery heat of my memories. I loved him for it even though he didn't know he'd become a fixture in my sanctuary.

Sunlight lightened the gold flecks in his eyes, and he grinned. "Cool. But do you love me? Or am I doomed?"

"You're gonna be doomed if you don't get me medical help," Dante said hoarsely.

Holy dragonfly nightmare. Would it never end?

Logan and I spun toward the Grim Reaper. Immobilized, he lay on the ground, wrists bound. The dragonfly had alighted on his leg, sniffing the blood. Its bluish body twinkled in the sunlight, its bulging eyes encompassing Dante, the dragonfly's next prey.

"We need to transport him back to camp." Logan strutted over to Dante. He took off his T-shirt and secured it around Dante's mouth, tying it at the back of his neck.

For the first time, I saw Logan's bare chest. A jagged, broken lightning bolt tattoo cut through his left pectoral, cutting his heart in half, drops of blood dripping down his chest.

My breath caught in my throat in a way that had become so darn annoying. "When did you get that?" I traced the tattoo. He shivered at my touch, and I pressed my fingers to his chest. We'd always been touchy feely, but I had identified it as comfortable friendship. Now, it was so much more. It tingled, exhilarated, left me reeling.

"Two years ago. My way of facing what happened every day of my life."

My heart skipped a beat. "You hate tattoos. How'd you stand the pain?"

"It was nothing compared to what I felt inside."

I kissed the lightning bolt, kissed his healing heart. His skin warmed under my touch and he rested his chin on top of my head.

"Let's get the hell out of here."

"Jeff took off for help. Don't know why he's taking so long." Looking up the hill, I gnashed down on my bottom lip. "Hey, why are you back so soon? Did you find a house, call the sheriff?"

Logan's face took on a grisly gray cast. "I found the satellite phone. It's dead, but the charger's with it. We can call from camp."

Relief swamped me, loosening those infernal knots tightening my intestines. "Why the grim look? Where did you find it?" I wasn't sure I wanted to hear the answer. Did I need to peel more pieces of crap out of the fan?

Logan touched my chin, his thumb tracing my lips. "I

found Marco in the woods. He's...dead." I sucked in my stomach. My knees grew spongy and Logan caught me. "I found the phone buried with him."

"No. No. No," I moaned against Logan's chest. Tears exploded down my cheeks, and something unnamed wound through my middle. I tore away from Logan and stumbled toward Dante. "You killed him, you stupid piece of shit. I hate you so much, you don't have a clue. You and Michael Kline will rot in hell where you belong." I kicked him in the gut with all my strength, the blow jarring my spine. As I prepped for another kick, Logan's arms enclosed me, inhibiting my assault. He let me fall to the ground in a heap of sobs.

He held me, allowing me a moment of grief for Marco. He was a better person for it, and I loved him a little more. I'd grieve alone later for this young man who knew who he was but never had the chance to share himself fully with the world.

I was hardly aware of Logan releasing me and tying Dante to a tree, tying his ankles together with rope he'd found in Dante's backpack. When he finished, I peered up at him through a veil of tears.

"Let's go." He picked me up, and I found strength in his arms, on my own feet.

Near where Dante had lain, I found my leather band. After staring at it a few moments, I shoved it in my pocket.

"Is he secure?" I asked.

"He's not going anywhere."

"What if Rambo comes back?"

"What do you mean?"

He didn't know all that'd happened. As we headed back to camp, I filled him in. "How'd he get the map to the gold?" I asked at the end.

Logan tore Dante's backpack off his shoulder,

rummaged inside it, plucked out surveillance equipment. "They bugged some of the cabins."

Shivering, I recalled things we'd said and done in the cabins. "That doesn't make sense. Dante never found Marco's mother's package."

"Marco found the video bug in his alcove. When I was searching it, I found the camera stuck inside a drawer, snapping pictures of his skivs."

I bristled. "Why didn't you tell me? God, Logan, half the time I don't know if you're coming or going."

"Damn, Allie. I was trying to help you stay safe, alive." He tapped my arm. "You were too close to the truth. Look what Dante did to you. If he'd hurt you, I don't know what I would've done."

I poked my fists into his shoulders, my irritation dissolving when he smiled, the smile I never wanted him to lose. I kissed him hard, forcing his mouth open, twining my tongue around his, nibbling on his bottom lip. Biting down softly.

"Oww." Logan fingered his lip. "You like rough play, huh?" He grinned. "I might love this new paradigm."

Absolute glee filtered through my convoluted emotions in a hot and cold wash. "I love you, Logan Montgomery. Always have, always will. Now let's go rescue the world, and end this nightmare."

Five minutes later, we reached the perimeter of the campground, eerily quiet, deserted. Where was Jeff? We hadn't passed him in the woods.

Rambo's motorcycle lay on its side in the grassy area in front of the dining hall, as if it'd skidded to a crash. "Ah criminy, not again."

CHAPTER 31

I half ran, half tumbled down the hill, landing in a pile of gnarly twigs poking into me like I was a pincushion. Logan and I reconnoitered at the rear of the empty offices.

"If he's back, he may've opened the storage. Not sure what part he plays, but he's hot for Martina. He was the one macking on her the first night."

Logan hitched the backpacks onto his shoulder. "Didn't think he was here then."

"The rat scurried about while searching the gold mine." I toed my sneakers in an ant hill, watching the ants scatter for their lives when I wanted to stomp on them. "He threatened to slice my neck that night he found me in the woods."

Logan's lips mashed together. "Why didn't you say anything?"

"He was blowing smoke, trying to scare me off, while Dante was trying to keep me here. Come on." Intentionally skating off our conversation, I took the lead, sneaking inside the offices. Martina's door hung ajar. Gun in hand, I inched it open to reveal an empty room. Logan plugged in the satellite phone and dialed nine-one-one.

A deadly calm entered his voice as he addressed the dispatcher. "This is Logan Montgomery. I'm a Cabin Leader at Dragonfly Meadows Campground. My girlfriend, Allie Bailey, found the body of camp owner Carla Amadori buried in the woods. We believe her nephew, Dante Amadori, killed her. He attacked some of the campers and we have him tied up. He cut phone and Internet lines and disabled the vehicles." I heard the sound of a woman on the other end of the phone. He growled. "This isn't a prank. There're other accomplices on the loose. You need to send a squad now. There're a lot of kids in jeopardy here." Another pause. "Okay. Good. Just get here."

My heart hitched at the word *girlfriend.* He clicked off and we stared at each other, willing this nightmare over.

A gunshot shattered the calm air, spurring us into action. I ran to the breakroom, hid behind the blinds. Sun reflected off the windows of the dining hall, creating a mirror effect, but I recognized the shadowy shape of Martina's slim body standing on the stage and the distinct shape of a gun waving in her hand above her head. A large lump of a man floundered on the stage floor.

"Holy crap. Martina's holding Rambo and the kids hostage." I inhaled and exhaled to the count of ten, trying to tie off unraveling nerves.

Logan paced, angry stomping steps. "We need to wait for the sheriff."

I shook my head violently. Without waiting for a green light, I tore out the side door of the office building, skirting the shadows. Logan trailed me, quietly calling to me.

Ignoring him, I continued into the secluded courtyard patio and peered through the open door. Rambo lay on the stage holding his leg, blood pooling on the wooden floor. The kids huddled in groups in the corners, some crying, most frozen in terror.

"I was falling in love with you, and you betrayed me, you son of a bitch," Martina screamed at Rambo and viciously kicked him, barely missing his man package.

"Put the gun down, Martina," Rambo said through gritted teeth. "I never pretended to be anybody else."

"You never told me your name was Richard Cardona," she screamed. "I bet you and Dante had this all planned. Manipulating me."

"I came back for you, Martina. Not Dante. He doesn't know I'm a Cardona." He groaned in pain. "I played *him*, not you. That gold belongs to the Cardonas, but I'm willing to share it with you, like our ancestors before us." He attempted to sit up, but pain held him in check. "Let's go before Dante or the cops arrive. Before that smart chick resurfaces."

My eyes popped. *Well, hello, murder twist.*

Silent and contemplative, Martina stalked the stage. She ignored the kids who ogled the unfurling scene.

"Pronto, Martina. Time's ticking." Blood loss had painted Rambo's skin snow white. I think she'd hit his femoral artery. "Help me up."

They make a great contribution to a corpse party.

"How are we going to escape, you stupid idiot? You sabotaged the vehicles so you could steal our gold." She nudged the gun at his head. "Isn't that right?"

"Dante did that to keep the older kids from leaving, ratting him out." Rambo coughed, hacking out a lung. "I'll get my bike working."

I handed Logan my gun. "I'm going in to distract her from the kids."

He blocked the door. "Can't let you do that."

"If she hurts one of the kids, I won't be able to live with it. This is my fault."

"Don't think that. They did this. They killed Mrs. Amadori. You exposed them. Don't take that guilt on."

"Okay. Okay. This time I'm not sitting it out and waiting for rescue that might not come for a while. She trusted me earlier. I'll distract her, talk her down while we wait for the sheriff. If I get a chance to incapacitate her, you rush in with the gun. Okay?"

"I don't like this." Logan dumped the backpacks on the patio, took the safety off the gun. "Okay. Nice kick on Dante yesterday. Not exactly how I taught you."

I whacked his arm. "It worked."

"Wait for the right opening, set it up the way I showed you. Stand down if you don't think it'll work or puts the kids in danger. Watch where the gun's pointed."

"Already used it once today, kicked a knife out of Dante's hands. Worked like a charm, kinda like my *other* kick did." I flashed a quick and shaky grin.

Logan hid between the door and window. I slid the door open and squeezed through. Hands in the air, pulse racing, I slunk into the dining hall to Martina's left.

"Hello, Martina." My exterior calmness belied my internal turmoil. Gasps and chattering rose among the kids before dying into the silence of terror.

Martina swung toward me, pointing the gun at my heart. "Where's Dante?"

I halted at the stage steps. "Tied up in the woods. He's alive."

Kids cried softly, breaking my heart. Their fun, exciting summer had gone so horribly wrong. This day would haunt them forever, as Michael Kline would always be the bane of my existence, right beside Dante Amadori. But where Kline destroyed part of me, Dante Amadori fixed that broken part, gave me back the backbone forced out of me on my twelfth birthday. Not that I felt gratitude toward Dante, I believed I'd live with this nightmare much easier than the aftermath of the abduction. Not if one more child got hurt, though.

"Dante's ready to confess. He'll take the rap." I refused to say murder in front of the kids. "I'll protect you. You were an innocent accomplice."

Martina wildly waved the gun. "Please, I'm not dumb. Doesn't matter what I did or didn't do. They'll lock me up."

"Then make a run for it. You and Rambo go. I'll distract the cops."

She laughed maniacally, a flush giving the color of life to her thin, pale complexion. "None of this would've happened if you hadn't butted in. I tried to warn you away. I shot arrows at you hoping you'd get a hint and go home. I planted the same kind of flowers on your bed your abductor gave you four years ago. That rat was meant for your backpack, not Jasmine's. Yeah, I read about your abductor's pet rat and how he taunted you with it. Even Rambo tried to scare you off, but you were too stupid to take a hint." Spit flew out of her mouth from her vehemence. "But dumbass Dante was obsessed with you once he found out who your father was from all those articles in the paper. Once he found the gold, he was gonna swindle money out of your rich-ass daddy." She rubbed her shoulder beneath her neck. "He hit me when he found out I was trying to scare you off."

For the countless time that day, shock slammed through my torso. Martina planned all that? Not Dante?

"What about Marco?" I wanted her to spill the goods while I waited for an opportunity.

"Marco went home, dumb cow."

"No he didn't."

Thoughtful, she froze and tipped her head to the side. "What do you mean?"

I hated saying it aloud for the kids to hear, but I needed to disarm her. "He's dead, Martina," I said under my breath. "Dante killed him."

The gun drooped. "No. He wouldn't do that. Not to Marco."

"Are you so sure?" I kept my voice lowered. "He killed Carla and she was his aunt."

She shook her head vigorously. The gun dipped farther as my words registered.

"Let me have the gun. You walk. Dante takes the blame."

Face ravaged in confusion, movements jerky, she paced the stage, muttering to herself. The gun faltered in her hand, but she was far enough away to give me an advantage. I hopped onto the stage, skirting Rambo lying in a moaning heap.

"Dante hurt you." I rubbed my collarbone area. "I saw the bruises."

She wheeled toward me, the gun pointed at me again. I kept my arms out, showing my open palms and crept out from the rear of the stage, steering her with me. Out of the corner of my eye, I saw Logan enter the room, ducked low below the top of the stage deck. Nick and Jesse slipped closer to the front of the stage.

"Quit moving," she yelled.

"Take me hostage until you get away."

Sirens blared in the distance, the piercing noise growing louder. Martina's gun-toting arm dragged down as reality registered. I lunged at her, kicking my leg out like Logan taught me, my foot landing on her hand. Hauling my leg back, I rocked on the floor to catch my balance. The weapon slid across the stage and clanged against the far wall. Unable to break her fall, Martina face-planted on the stage.

In a flurry of motion, Logan rushed the stage. I leaped on top of Martina, butting heads with Logan as we tackled her down. She screamed, thrashing beneath us. Knowing the futility in fighting us, she quieted, silent sobs shaking her shoulders against my chest.

Jesse and Nick rushed to help. Nick tied Martina's ankles with duct tape, while Logan tied her wrists, and then they flipped her into a sitting position. No longer a threat, Rambo had passed out, blood seeping out of his leg wound, congealing on the scarred hardwood floor. Logan tied a rope around Rambo's thigh to slow the bleeding. For the second time that day, he'd saved another gunshot victim from biting the bullet.

The cries and screams of the kids added to the din. Laurel and the other Cabin Leaders tried to quiet them. I caught Laurel's eye, and she gave me a thumbs up, her fist to her heart. Tears cascaded down her cheeks when she locked eyes with Logan.

Amid the melee, Martina babbled, "I didn't mean to kill Carla. She tried to burn the map. I was simply trying to stop her." She clasped her neck, her fingers brushing over the fading bruises dipping beneath her polo. "It was an accident. An accident. I loved her like a mother." Sobbing, she rolled into a fetal position.

Whoa. Martina killed Mrs. Amadori? Logan and I traded stunned stares.

Unable to budge, I reached out my arms to him. In an eye blink, he was holding me, smoothing down my hair. Laurel joined us and we moved in for a group hug.

Sheriff deputies stormed the dining hall, boots stomping, guns waving. Shouts, kids screaming and crying created a mad cacophony in the large room.

A scary, bald-headed deputy approached us, gun trained on Logan. Logan stepped in front of me, held up a hand, and lowered his weapon, an act of good faith. "I'm not the bad guy here," Logan said. "I'm Logan Montgomery, the one who called the sheriff."

The deputy holstered his weapon and took the gun from Logan. I had a momentary lapse of sanity and almost fought the deputy for possession. But the moment they apprehended Martina, the nightmare finally ended. A profound relief zapped all my energy and I sagged onto the steps, hugging my knees to my chin. Laurel hung back as another deputy began talking to Nick, but I could tell she was being torn in two. I guess the sheriff's office thought the boys had staged this coup and weren't interested in talking to us lowly girls. Ha! Laugh's on them.

"Go to your boy." I waved her off. "I'm fine here. Logan's with me."

"Is he really *with you*, with you?" She gave me a tired wonky grin.

"I think so," I whispered for her ears only, my gaze feasting on the boy who held my heart in his hands, in his every touch and look. *I hope so.*

As Logan spoke to the deputy, he kept glancing over his shoulder at me, as if fighting between his need for me and serving justice.

"Miss Bailey, can you give us the location of Dante Amadori and the other camp workers?" Another deputy's voice filtered into my fried brain. He looked so young to be a cop. So like Dante with his dark layered hair and dark complexion. I almost hauled back my leg and planted my foot into his man junk.

"You're Allie Bailey, correct?" The deputy frowned, looked at his smartphone. Had my mugshot already hit the airwaves?

"Yes, sorry." I stretched out my legs and stood. "The other camp workers are locked in the kitchen storage room." He relayed the info into his radio. "As for Dante, can I draw you a map?" He whipped out a notepad and pencil, and I drew a detailed map to where I'd left Dante bleeding out.

When I handed the notepad and pencil back, the deputy gave me an appreciative look, handed the map to another deputy. "Nice map. Coordinates and all."

I shrugged. "Might be the last one I ever draw." Waiting my turn for the inevitable grilling, I gathered my waning strength and walked around the room to ensure the kids were unharmed. First checkpoint, Neal, Jeff, and Richie. My wingmen high-fived me. Bullies had some use after all. I hugged them all, suffering the stench of their B.O. I wrinkled my nose at the assault, breathing easier knowing the kids were all okay. At least okay on the outside. Inside was another story. I knew it. I'd lived it. I'd do it again to save even one soul. The Dragonfly Lily girls all hugged me tight. Bedraggled, I hugged them, saddened that our summer of fun and freedom froze at such a gruesome end.

Laurel waved me over where Nick was giving his statement about what'd happened while I was chasing down Dante. We hugged fiercely, wiping a few random tears on our shoulders.

"You saved the day," she said.

"No. The three musket-rats did." I bumped my hip into hers. "With a lot of minion help." I nodded my head at Nick.

Laurel's turn came, and I heard the story a second—more vibrant—time. "That Rambo freak returned to snag the love of his life, Martina. While Nick and I hid behind the serving counter, we overheard them making plans to escape. They'd threatened the boys guarding the storage room with bodily harm. The boys didn't buy it and stayed strong just like we trained them." She preened a little as if she were their leader. I hid a snort behind my hand. "Nick and I escaped unnoticed to see if Nick could get the freak's motorcycle started to get help, or to find a phone in his bags. We found this instead." Gloating, she handed a crumpled piece of paper to the deputy. "Whack-a-noodle's bike is registered to Richard Cardona. Ya know, a Cardona of *the* Cardona and Amadori gold legend. Anywho, we couldn't get the bike started. We brought the registration back to show Martina, hoping she'd dump the lying shyster. Rambo had already gotten her out of the storage room, and they'd confiscated the weapons from the guards. Once she saw the registration, she went batshit crazy, turned on Rambo, and took him *and* the campers hostage."

While Laurel recited her story, the EMT crews carried Dante down the hill on a stretcher, wrists, torso, and ankles strapped down. Pain and guilt etched his face in lines, bruises, and dirt. Not an ounce of hate existed in his expression, and it gave me a skosh of relief.

"Miss Bailey, we'd like you to take us to Mrs. Amadori's remains," the sheriff said behind me. "Then we'll need to take your statement."

One hand gripping my scarred wrist, I spun around. My heart beat triple-time, prepping to launch outside my chest.

Logan's arm snaked around my shoulders. "I'll take you. Can you wait to take her statement until I return? I don't want her alone."

The sheriff gave his grudging assent, probably not used to dealing with a bunch of minors with no parentals. Could they even question us without a parent present? I didn't know. Didn't care. I wanted the world to know my story sooner rather than later.

Logan pulled me against his lean body. I kissed him, drowning in the silkiness of his lips on mine, linking my fingers in his, unwilling to tear my hand away until the sheriff touched my shoulder.

News crews arrived, hogging the scene, and some of the nearby parents drove into the parking lot, freaking out until they held their scared and excited children. A major crime scene turned the campground into the Dragonfly Meadows Madhouse.

After leading the sheriff and a CSI crew to the ravine, Logan returned and it was my turn to give my formal statement. He held my hand in his strong comforting grip. Having found my inner strength, his presence bolstered me throughout the succinct telling of events leading to that moment. Wistfully, I handed the sheriff Mrs. Amadori's dragonfly necklace, and he stuck it in a small plastic evidence bag.

The sheriff left to talk to other kids, and I turned to Logan. "Thank you for believing in me, for being here. For putting up with me and my crazy paranoia."

"I wouldn't have it any other way. Say the word, and I'm there for you."

"Word." I angled my head and his lips landed on my mouth.

Another deputy interrupted our moment. He handed me a cell phone to call home.

Mom's cell rang two times. "Mom, it's Allie."

"Honey? What's wrong?"

"I'm okay. But you need to come get me."

"What happened?" she nearly screamed into the phone.

I smiled at Logan, his fingers laced tight within mine, not letting go for a second, not that I wanted him to. "You were wrong."

A long pregnant pause. "About?"

"I *am* strong enough to take care of myself now."

Finally, after rescue from the abduction, when age

and fear kept me paralyzed and unable to rescue myself, I experienced a sense of pride and confidence. This time, I didn't let the nightmare conquer me. I conquered it, and knew without a doubt that I could make my way in the outside world without melting into a puddle of fear every time someone blinked at me wrong. The Dragonfly Meadows nightmare had liberated the real Allie Bailey.

CHAPTER 32

Mom's paranoia was also spot on about me confronting hazards outside home. I'd never live it down until the day I died. For now, I'd shocked my parents silly with what I'd endured, accomplished, and overcame at camp. They encouraged me to enroll in a beginner's martial arts class for self-defense. Logan was over the moon since he was the assistant to the class instructor. Laurel disowned me for a day after hearing I planned to geek out with Logan. I forced her to join me, telling her it was for her own good to learn self-defense.

Upon learning about our quasi-hero status on the news, a local teacher contacted Logan and me and asked us to help create an awareness and self-defense program for the district from a kid's perspective. Logan and Laurel liked the idea of speaking at schools about bullying, crimes against kids, and teaching self-defense. More bonding time with the three musket-rats. Laurel liked the stipend they promised to pay us the best.

Dad and I made plans to bond at the local firing range, once we picked out guns. Mom hated the idea, but I told her it was better I knew how to handle a gun than pretend like I did. We were on new ground now. But it was a fearless ground dotted with smooth patches of confidence versus potholes of fear. I thought I might go to law school and help rid the street of the bad guys in a sane and safe manner.

I took off my black dress and slipped into shorts and a T-shirt. I'd attended Marco's funeral that day with Logan, Laurel, Nick, and some of the older local kids from camp. In a sense, it gave closure to the nightmare. Not an end, though, as we'd eventually have to testify in court.

Thank you cards teetered on my desk. Many of the parents and kids from the camp had sent them, thanking me for everything I did and wanting to keep in touch. We had a camper reunion picnic planned at Golden Gate Park in August.

The doorbell rang. I shouldered my hoodie and hopped down the stairs. "Got it," I yelled.

Mom's sandals click-clacked in the foyer. "Not too late, okay?"

I kissed her cheek. "Stop fretting. I have the bodyguard brigade with me. You know Logan's a black belt. He's a lethal weapon."

She wobbled her head. "That's what I'm afraid of. Stay out of trouble."

I opened the door to find Laurel, Logan, and Nick waiting on the doorstep.

"Sure, Mom. But you know how trouble has a way of finding me." I laughed at her stricken face. "Kidding."

After all I'd suffered, it was great to be home, great to have a new life with Logan, the ability to go out and have fun with friends. Summer camp had opened up my life in so many different ways.

Logan drove us to a local Mexican hole-in-the-wall cantina. Once the hostess seated us in a booth in the dim rear of the restaurant, Laurel pounced.

"Spill. What did Marco's mom say?"

Mrs. Lorenzo had given me an earful in her home office during the funeral reception. She was immensely grateful that I'd tried to help Marco. I'd barely made it out of her home before I bawled my eyes out.

"It's what we thought when we read those papers. Dante was up to his eyeballs in debt. Carla's father had cut her brother, and then Martina and Dante, out of the will. Since Carla had no kids, if she died, the property passed to Martina and Dante. Carla's father didn't want anyone destroying the property to find the gold he believed never existed. It was his dying wish to preserve it as a historical site. Carla was trying to keep Dante and Martina away from it, keep them from fighting the will, and had hired Marco's mom to help."

I took a slug of cola, letting the bubbles pop and tickle in my throat, loving my rapt audience. "Then Dante threatened Carla and caused her to fall and break her leg. She had a fake map to the gold and tried to burn it. That's when Martina pushed her away from the fireplace and beat her with the fireplace poker, killing her." I swigged more cola to get my emotions under control. "Dante buried her and covered up for Martina." I shivered and Logan slid his arm across my shoulders.

"So weird. All that time you thought Dante had killed her." Laurel flicked tortilla chip crumbs on the table, landing one on my lap.

"It's not like he was innocent." I flicked a chip at her, hitting her left boob, prepping for a war. "Once he received that offer to buy the property, he probably would've offed her himself. Martina just beat him to the punch."

"You're gruesome." Laurel tossed a chip at me, narrowly missing my ear.

"But you had an awesome time at summer camp with me."

Logan and Nick laughed so loud everyone in the restaurant stared at us.

"Yeah, I don't think I'm going back." Laurel smiled our crazy wonky smile. "Did Mrs. Lorenzo say what'll happen to the property? Did Rambo find all the gold?"

"The property will go to the historical society for state use. They're closing the summer camp, but they might rent it out for large groups. Rambo had all the gold in his saddlebags on his motorcycle. He and his family have claimed it. Who knows what will happen to it."

"So who sabotaged the vehicles and phones?"

"Dante did that to keep us from leaving or calling the authorities until he found the gold and escaped. He knew that offer to buy the property would never fly since his grandfather bequeathed the gold mine to the historical society in perpetuity."

Mrs. Lorenzo had gotten hold of the police documents for the answers burning holes in her brain too. Dante had confessed to certain things about cutting camp expenses to save a buck, but not to other crimes that'd make him Billy Bob's Prison Bitch for a good long time. Rambo and Martina had pled the fifth.

"The police are charging Dante with Marco's murder." I wiped a tear from my eye and pressed on my left wrist, on the healing scabs.

"Was he seriously planning to blackmail your father?" Nick caressed Laurel's hand on the tabletop, changing the subject that affected us all the most. "I mean, that's crazy times ten."

"The dude was whacked," Laurel said. "He could've sold you river rocks and had you believing they were gold nuggets."

"Not Allie." Logan knocked his head against mine. "Nothing slips past her."

"You got that right." I winked. "Anyway, he denies it, but the cops found tons of documents about my dad and my kidnapping on Dante's tablet and in that file. The DA may charge him with attempted fraud or something." I shrugged. "The cops nabbed his tablet and found nasty emails between him and Carla and saw how he'd hijacked her email account and was working to sell the property."

I dug into my pocket and produced the four nuggets I'd scavenged off the ground. I doled them out. "In case you need a memory of our summer."

"You're a loon." Laurel kicked me under the table.

"I tossed one onto Marco's coffin before they buried him. I'm cashing mine in and donating the money to the charity his mom picks out."

On cue, Logan, Laurel, and Nick slid their nuggets toward me.

We spent the rest of the evening not talking about Dragonfly Meadows Campground and our nightmare trip. By the time Logan dropped Nick and Laurel off, I was glad to be alone with him. We hadn't had much alone time since returning from camp four days ago. We sat in his Jeep in my driveway in the safe darkness I welcomed. Too many unspoken words thickened the air. We had a long future to speak them, but one thought needed voicing ASAP. Even though I wanted to sit there and embrace his strength and warmth, I forced the words up that had boiled in me for too long.

I stared at the double garage doors. The coach lights lent a faint glow inside the vehicle. "I forgive you, you know. I know you did what you thought was right for you...for me."

It grew so quiet in the car I thought Logan had

vanished into the night. I shifted to find him staring at me, his face crumpled. Underneath the embedded lines and pain, love and acceptance was on full display.

"I was an idiot. I'm so sorry."

I touched his cheek, cupped his chin in my hand, reveling in his bristly skin. He gloved my hand in his, drawing it to his lips. He kissed my palm, the gentle brush of his lips sending tingles to my toes.

If he'd stayed behind and confessed his guilt four years ago, I think we would've drifted apart. Every day I saw him would've reminded me of the abduction and the aftermath when I'd nearly died inside. I would've refused to see him or let him see me tangled up in an empty ball.

For four years, I'd had a weird lack of closure. Now, I understood why. How much I'd changed in a week's time. How much I'd learned about myself, about Logan.

"Suppose you want to go play video games?" I asked, wishing like mad to go inside and play *with* Logan.

"Girl, there's a lot you don't know about me anymore. I haven't played a video game since—" He reddened ten shades of scarlet.

"It's okay. You can say it now. Since the day I was kidnapped?"

"Yeah." He stroked his finger over the scars on my wrist. "Why'd you do this?"

My pulse quickened. "I guess for the same reason you drank."

Logan reached into the back seat and handed me a white gift box. "Didn't have time to wrap it."

"What's this?" A multi-colored ribbon secured the box lid.

"Open it."

I slid the ribbon and lid off. My heart clutched up. Nestled inside a bed of tissue paper was a snow globe. Reverently, I picked it up, shook it, and watched the ironic snow drift upon San Francisco and the Golden Gate Bridge. The words on the brass label on the base read, "A bridge to the lands of your dreams." Tears threatened. "Thank you. I love it so much." I hugged it to my chest, blinking back tears. "I won't hide this one away."

"I figured you'd want a new one to replace your old one." Logan had found the pieces of mine in the woods. We didn't know why it was taken or exactly who had taken it. Dante topped the suspect list.

I leaned over the gearshift and pressed my mouth to Logan's lips. I kissed him softly, his hands holding my face to his. I touched the tip of my tongue to the tiny dimple on his chin as I'd been dying to do for over a week. He grunted low in his throat, head knocking the headrest. I felt like it was our first kiss, my first breath of air, like I'd been remade, taking my first step of freedom. No longer just surviving my life, I was living it. Logan made me feel like the real me, not the post-kidnapping shell.

"I don't need it any more. I just need you. I want you to walk that bridge with me."

"You've had me forever." Logan's lips parted mine in a soul-reaching message.

I melted into his message of hope, the steering wheel pressed into my side, into the intrepid bruises I wore with pride.

DID YOU ENJOY *DRAGONFLY NIGHTMARE?*

Reviews are gold to authors! If you've enjoyed this book, would you consider rating and reviewing it at your favorite online retailer or review site? Your review is greatly appreciated!

To stay up to date on Erin Richards' latest happenings, including new releases, sales, special announcements, exclusive excerpts and giveaways, subscribe to her newsletter at: **www.erinrichards.com/connect.htm** or click the image below.

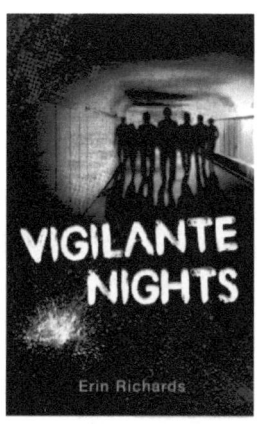

Praise for *Vigilante Nights*

"The premise of *Vigilante Nights* is absolutely fascinating. It's part contemporary urban street gang, part ghost story, part haunting journey from grief to hope. An action-packed second half should appeal to readers who enjoy urban thrillers with a hint of supernatural." ~*YA Books Central*

"Richards' keeps the paranormal aspect of the story subtle, adding to its mystery and tension." ~*Publishers Weekly*

"*Vigilante Nights* thrusts readers headlong into a powerful journey for redemption, revenge and, ultimately, peace. It's a classic whodunit tale, but the twists and turns threw me for a loop every time." ~*Melissa, I Swim for Oceans Blog*

The plot is fast paced... Red herrings throw suspicion on various characters until the action culminates in a page-turning climax. A multifaceted story of revenge, violence, romance–and a touch of the paranormal–that will appeal to a broad audience. ~*School Library Journal*

"*Vigilante Nights* started out not with a whimper, but with a bang. A book that clearly goes under the category of "unputdownable." Richards creates a story that anyone would love. While it is scary and it is heart-pounding, it's the theme of love, determination, grief, and letting go that really draws the reader in. This is a fantastic YA debut from Richards. I can't wait to see what story she has to tell next. ~*Christine @ The Bookish Daydream*

About the Author

After lamenting the lack of young adult books to read, Erin Richards wrote her first novel at the age of eighteen hoping to shift the tide. But the only tide she shifted was moving from high school to college. Then everyday life took its toll on her writerly dreams until 2003 when she couldn't ignore the writing bug any longer. By then, she had immersed herself in reading adult fantasy and romance novels. Writing paranormal & fantasy romance was a no brainer and she went on to publish two adult romance novels. But her muse wanted to give that YA writing gig another chance, and Erin finally realized her lifelong dream of publishing a YA novel with the debut of *VIGILANTE NIGHTS*.

Erin lives in Northern California. In her spare time, she enjoys reading and re-landscaping her backyard, even though she hates digging holes...unless she's burying fictional bodies! She also confesses to a fascination with American muscle cars and reality TV.

Please visit Erin Richards online at:
www.erinrichards.com